SATIE ON THE SEINE

GERALD VIZENOR

SATIE ON THE SEINE

Letters to the Heirs of the Fur Trade

Wesleyan University Press

MIDDLETOWN, CONNECTICUT

WESLEYAN UNIVERSITY PRESS
Middletown, CT 06459
www.wesleyan.edu/wespress
Manufactured in the United States of America
Typeset in Parkinson Electra Pro by Mindy Basinger Hill

Library of Congress Cataloging-in-Publication Data

Names: Vizenor, Gerald Robert, 1934– author.

Title: Satie on the Seine : letters to the heirs of the fur trade / Gerald Vizenor.

Description: Middletown, Connecticut : Wesleyan University Press, [2020] | Description based on print version record and CIP data provided by publisher; resource not viewed.

Identifiers: LCCN 2020025023 (print) | LCCN 2020025024 (ebook) | ISBN 9780819579355 (ebook) | ISBN 9780819579348 (trade paperback)

Subjects: LCSH: Indians of North America—Fiction. | GSAFD: Epistolary fiction. | Historical fiction.

Classification: LCC PS3572.I9 (ebook) | LCC PS3572.I9 S38 2020 (print) | DDC 813/.54—dc23

LC record available at https://lccn.loc.gov/2020025023

5   4   3   2   1

*Ignatius Vizenor was born 4 May 1894,
son of Michael Vizenor and Angeline Cogger,
on the White Earth Reservation in Minnesota. He was
a dapper dresser, wore a fedora, and fought for a nation that
once inspired natives in the fur trade. The surname Vizenor
was derived from Vezina in New France. Private Vizenor
was killed in action on 8 October 1918,
at Montbréhain, France.*

*Ignatius Vizenor was buried at
Saint Benedict Catholic Cemetery on the
White Earth Reservation. The military coffin was sealed,
and no one at the funeral could account for his entire remains.
Thousands of soldiers were harrowed in the soil that
early autumn at Alsace, Lorraine, Champagne,
Ardennes, and Picardy in France.*

CONTENTS

THE BEAULIEU
CHRONICLES OF LIBERTY

Basile Hudon Beaulieu wrote fifty letters to the heirs of the fur trade between October 1932 and January 1945. The messages were copied and circulated to family and friends on the White Earth Reservation. At the end of the war the letters were translated as native chronicles in a six-volume narrative sequence, *roman fleuve*, and published by Nathan Crémieux at the Galerie Ghost Dance in Paris, France.

The letters convey the mercy of *liberté*, the torment and solidarity of Le Front Populaire, the Popular Front, an alliance of political leftists, and the contest of ethos and governance in the French Third Republic. Basile relates the massacres of natives and the misery of federal policies on reservations to the savage strategies of royalists, fascists, communists, and antisemites during the eight years before war was declared against Germany, and to the end of the Nazi Occupation of Paris.

The letters to the heirs of the fur trade during the war reveal the cruelty and deprivations of the Nazi Occupation, the persecution of Jews, the devious collaboration of the Paris Préfecture de Police, and the eternal shame of the Vélodrome d'Hiver Roundup. Maréchal Philippe Pétain, clever cringers of the Vichy Regime, and the betrayal of résistance networks are condemned, and at the same time the insurrection and liberation by *Les Forces Françaises de l'Intérieur*, the French Forces of the Interior, and the *littérature engagée* and integrity of Romain Rolland are celebrated in the last emotive letters.

The final six letters to the heirs of the fur trade were written after the liberation of France and relate the massacre at Oradour-sur-Glane, the honor of *Sénégalais* soldiers in Sanary-sur-Mer, and the Galerie Ghost Dance in Paris; and the last letter includes a hand puppet parley between Romain Rolland and Adolf Hitler at Place de Panthéon.

Basile was born on the White Earth Reservation in Minnesota on 22 October 1895. Aloysius Hudon Beaulieu was delivered on the same day, and then abandoned with no name at Saint Benedict's Mission. Margaret and Honoré Hudon Beaulieu raised the boys as twins, native heirs of the fur trade, but one was a reservation stray.

The brothers attended the federal government school on the reservation and sold copies of *The Tomahawk* at the Ogema Station of the Soo Line Railroad. The newspaper was an independent weekly published by their uncle Augustus Hudon Beaulieu. The national and international news reports became an early passage to the cosmopolitan world outside the White Earth Reservation.

Aloysius was an untutored painter of natural motion and abstract blue ravens. Basile became a writer, and the brothers served with more than forty other natives from the White Earth Reservation in the American Expeditionary Forces in France during the First World War.

Basile and Aloysius returned to the liberty of art and literature in Paris after the war and lived in the back room of the Galerie Crémieux near the Cathédrale Notre Dame de Paris. Nathan Crémieux, owner of the gallery of native art, exhibited the blue raven series of paintings by Aloysius, *Corbeaux Bleus, Les Mutilés de Guerre, Nouvelles Peintures,* and at the same time published selected war stories about the First World War by Basile, *La Retour à la France, Histoires de Guerre,* on 25 October 1924.

The Indian Civilization Act was passed that year and provided for the first time that natives "born within the territorial limits of the United States" were "declared to be citizens." Basile and Aloysius returned to the reservation several years later, but could not find work or recognition for native art and literature during the Great Depression.

They were heartened by the Bonus Expeditionary Force and gathered with thousands of other combat war veterans at Capitol Hill in the summer of 1932. The veterans paraded, protested, and demanded a cash bonus for service in the First World War. The controversial bonus legislation passed in the House of Representatives on 15 June 1932, but was immediately defeated in the United States Senate.

The Bonus March ended with the rout of veterans from camps on the National Mall and Anacostia Flats. President Herbert Hoover decreed the expulsion, and General Douglas MacArthur commanded an armed military assault against the united combat veterans. MacArthur and his aide Major Dwight Eisenhower ordered uniformed soldiers to use tear gas and bayonets to remove the veterans and their families from the United States Capitol.

Basile and Aloysius boarded the *Île de France* in New York on Saturday, 30 July 1932, and returned to live in the Galerie Crémieux and court the liberty of Paris. Later they moved to a narrow barge christened *Le Corbeau Bleu*, The Blue Raven, moored on the Quai des Tuileries near Pont de la Concorde on the River Seine.

Aloysius continued to paint abstract blue ravens in a new style of totemic fauvism, and he carved marvelous hand puppets that were staged in fifteen lively conversations based on the actual quotations of Adolf Hitler and Gertrude Stein, Edith Cavell, Hermann Göring, Henri Bergson, Joseph Goebbels, Nathan Crémieux, Anaïs Nin, Apollinaire, and the novelist Romain Rolland. The distinctive literary parleys continued between other hand puppets, Victor Hugo and Sitting Bull, Voltaire and Chief Joseph, Émile Zola and Carlos Montezuma, and Charles de Gaulle and Maréchal Philippe Pétain.

Aloysius created some hand puppets from discarded objects, such as a rusty tin of *Pastilles Vichy État* fashioned as Adolf Hitler. By Now Rose Beaulieu and Prometheus Postma created two hand puppets from a purple eggplant and a black sock, Aubergine Violette and Rabbin Royale, for a special dinner party at Villa Penina in Sanary-sur-Mer.

Margaret responded to every letter, although there was no regular international mail service during most of the Nazi Occupation of Paris. She read between the lines of political events reported in newspapers about surveillance, betrayals, and antisemitism, and she worried about the miseries related in the letters and insisted on more stories about the security of the natives and friends who gathered at *Le Corbeau Bleu* and the Galerie Crémieux.

Margaret favored her niece By Now Rose Beaulieu, of course, because she had served as a nurse in the First World War and rode a horse named Treaty to the Bonus March in Washington. Margaret praised the extraordinary adventures of Nika Montezuma, who was born on a fur trade route near Gunflint Lake, and she was certain that no one could resist the blunt and witty bywords of Solomon Heap of Words.

Honoré celebrated the knowledge of Pierre Chaisson, the native Houma from Terrebonne Parish in Louisiana and a graduate student at Sorbonne University; the courage of André and Henri, *mutilés de guerre*, who wore masks to hide war wounds; and the pluck of honorable poseurs of native cultures, Olivier Black Elk and Coyote Standing Bear.

Most readers of the letters to the heirs of the fur trade admired the virtues of Léon Blum, the socialist and former Prime Minister of France; and everyone praised the irony, humor, and compassion of Prometheus Postma, an exiled raconteur from the Frisian Islands.

Basile declared in the last letter, "Romain Rolland was never swayed by political cues or delusions, the pretense of *liberté*, feigns of *egalité*, rescripts of *fraternité*, or the favors of fascism. His résistance was the ethos of literary engagement, and celebrated the stories that inspire the spirit."

Basile carried out the literary tradition of résistance and the *littérature engagée*, teased the ghosts of liberty in his letters to the heirs of the fur trade, and recounted the popular parleys and talk back puppet shows of résistance against the fascists and conspirators of the Vichy Regime and Nazi occupation of Paris.

Hand Puppet Parleys

LIBERTY TREES

Sunday, 2 October 1932

Paris is dewy this morning, and the liberty trees of the revolution are far-away memories. The wet cobblestones on the Quai des Tuileries shimmer in the early sunlight, and the autumn hues of plane and linden leaves brighten the quays, squares, and boulevards near the River Seine.

France was once a great empire of the fur trade, and the classy vogue of fur coats, *manteaux de fourrure*, almost ruined the ancient totemic unions and native dream songs of the natural world. The oriental fashions of silk, but not ethos or shame, saved the beaver and marten, and there are no furry coats, collars, or hats on the quay today, only the reek of wet wool, creased fedoras, and the native tease of totemic heart stories that we carry out in art and literature.

Natives betrayed the great totemic companions of the woodland, but the heirs of the fur trade have matured since then with imagistic dream songs and creative stories of totemic associations that have become the new literature of liberty.

This is my first letter to the heirs of the fur trade, poetic, ironic, and with grave episodes that reveal the fascism of the royalists, the antisemitism of nationalists, and confirmation of the moral duties of native stories to create a sense of presence and literary ethos for readers here and on the White Earth Reservation.

Aloysius Hudon Beaulieu, my brother, would rather paint blue ravens and tease the moody *bouquinistes* on the Quai du Louvre than worry about finding a heavy winter coat at the crowded street markets, but the city has never been as cold as a winter on the reservation.

Native stories of the seductive Ice Woman on a cold and snowy night would be superfluous at the Place Pigalle in Paris. Lusty outsiders were once teased with stories of an erotic death in the sensual splendor of winter snow, but not at the Moulin Rouge. Painters, poets, poseurs, and cultural strangers were favored at the famous brothels, Le Sphinx, and the opulent One Two Two, a private mansion near the Galeries Lafayette.

Many versions of the Ice Woman stories are told today in any season, and around the world, and surely provocative editions of the Parisian Ice Woman are heard once or twice a night at Le Monocle, a lesbian night-club, but sensual teases and a native outlook are never quite the same as stories on a wintery woodland reservation.

The most worrisome scenes are not carnal, or the want of snowy seductions, but rather the absolute misery of the economic depression and gray faces of poverty. Daily columns of weary and hungry women, children, and lonesome men in dark coats, caps, and fedoras, wait for a bowl of hot soup delivered from huge cauldrons mounted on bicycle wheels. There is nothing erotic in the stay of queues, and some men slowly turn away and vanish in narrow passageways.

Only the ritzy, showy young women and clowns wear big bold colors, a glossy handbag, bright blocky shoes, silky sleeves, and waves of red umbrellas. Churchy days in every season are much brighter on the boulevards, and the steady communists and socialists favor red banners, armbands, and foulards.

The River Seine was shamed overnight with human waste, and the murky backwash blackened the quays. The *bateau lavoir*, laundry boat, and three other barges were moored with no traces of visionary color or hues of grace near the Pont de la Concorde.

Camille Pissarro, Claude Monet, and other artists once painted the river in colors of fancy, the touch of reverie and brush turns of rosy light, but never the taint of dreary barges or intimate waste on the quay.

Aloysius saluted the dark barges on the river, and then imagined great waves of painted colors, rouge on the prows, blues on the tillers, and with hand gestures shouted out the names of artistic hues. My brother revered the ravens in the birch trees on the reservation with the same teases and painterly hues of natural motion.

We were enchanted by the wistful sound of a piano on the River Seine. One by one people slowly moved from the cold benches through the slants of light toward the source of the music. An upright piano was mounted on the back of a narrow barge moored at the Quai des Tuileries near the Pont de la Concorde.

The nostalgic melody wavered on the river, and gray faces leaned over the bridge parapets to watch a lovely young woman in a blue scarf play the piano. The grizzled man next to me was teary and told me the music was the *Gymnopédies*, composed by Erik Satie. The music was poetic, elusive heartfelt chords with tender pauses, and the name of the piano composition was unclear, dance or nudity on the River Seine.

The pianist moved her hands slowly over the keys, and the slight waves on the river seemed to move the barge in the same steady measure. The slight repetitions of melody created a sensation of motion and liberty, a buoyant tease and stay of passion for a moment, the sound and gestures of unity and endurance in the warm glances of morning light, and with no heavy traces of opera or triumphant crescendos out of the military past.

The man wiped tears from his face, and then raised his arms to praise the music. The melody was moody and haunting on this dewy morning. Not even the crack of wagons and wheeze of cars distracted the spirit of the music, and no one on the bridge turned away until the morning concert had ended. The woman covered the piano on the barge, and then walked alone down the quay. The music seemed to continue with the waves on the river, and the sway of her wide blue neck scarf was a concert of natural motion.

Paris is the melody of mercy.

Solace even with the rage of politics.

Paris is the summer in the spring.

Nathan Crémieux was very generous, as usual, and invited us to stay in the back room of his gallery of Native American art on Rue de la Bûcherie near the Cathédrale Notre Dame de Paris. He moved a heavy heirloom desk with inlaid mahogany and a bookcase to the room. The art books were for my brother, and for me, poetry and novels, including Marcel Proust, Guillaume Apollinaire, Émile Zola, James Joyce, Ezra Pound, Frank Harris, Gertrude Stein, and familiar plays, *Coriolanus*, *The Merchant of Venice*, *King John*, *Hamlet*, *Macbeth*, *King Lear*, and *The Tempest*. Nathan trusted and honored natives, and he remembered our stories about the unforgettable production of plays by Shakespeare at the Carlisle Indian School.

The Galerie Crémieux displayed native art in three rooms that faced the narrow Rue de la Bûcherie, and the high ceiling of the back room was painted the hue of the night sky, and *giiwedin anang*, North Star, was visible on the ceiling at night. The gallery became the center of our world, day and night, and the polestar reminded us of our native sense of place in art and literature.

Nathan inherited the original collection of native art from his father who was a respected trader with natives on pueblos and reservations in the American Southwest. We first celebrated the collection many years ago as veterans of the First World War, but this time the presence of traditional native objects of art, glorious pueblo pottery, clay figures, sashes, mantas, turquoise and silver jewelry, ledger art, and blankets created an aura in the gallery and the presence of native spirits.

Five Ghost Dance shirts and two hand drums were on display, secured from a dubious native art trader in Germany, and a ceremonial Ghost Dance doll, brightly decorated with beads and feathers, was purchased at auction from a reliable art dealer in New York City. Aloysius turned away, even though the sacred objects were mounted and enclosed in heavy glass cases.

Nathan described the acquisitions as rescued secrets and explained that he would never present sacred Ghost Dance shirts for sale or trade, and yet he was aware that many people visited the gallery only to view the faded ceremonial shirts and hear the stories about massacres and the Ghost Dance Religion. Naturally, we were relieved that the shirts were not marked with blood or gunshot holes. Sometimes late at night in the gallery we heard Ghost Dance songs and envisioned dancers in natural motion, the native ghosts of an ancient continental liberty.

The presence of native spirits in the gallery was not the same as the augury of flâneurs or the stories of ghosts on the narrow streets near the River Seine. Native ledger artists were at hand with blue horses and in visionary motion, the ancient blankets carried the scent of mesquite smoke, and the shadows of healers danced near the windows at night.

Ghosts of the River Seine forever haunt the quays and are related to the citizens who were tortured and beheaded in the name of the revolution, the spectacle of deadly justice at the Place de la Concorde. The ghosts carry on as the ironic spirits of liberty.

Nathan recently dedicated a gallery exhibition to the memory of Howling Wolf, the Cheyenne ledger artist who was once imprisoned at Fort

Marion, Florida. He painted visionary scenes of the Sand Creek Massacre. Naturally we were honored to stay at the Galerie Crémieux with the solace of the common polestar, the ceremonial spirits of the Ghost Dance, and the radiant blue horses of Howling Wolf. Otherwise we might have been stranded in a dark and dank hotel room with the specters of revolutions.

Wovoka, or Jack Wilson, his ranch name, envisioned that the enemies of peace and liberty, the cavalry soldiers and greedy settlers, would vanish, and at the same time he avowed the mysterious resurrection of the native dead in a world of starvation and the cruelty of reservation agents.

The Paiute prophet had a vision during a solar eclipse in his early thirties, and since then he had told visionary stories about the return of the dead if natives carry out the dance, common virtues, integrity, and precise traditions of the Ghost Dance.

The Seventh Cavalry Regiment murdered hundreds of Lakota natives, women and children and Ghost Dancers, at Wounded Knee Creek in South Dakota, about a year after the great vision of Wovoka.

The Ghost Dance was probably never experienced or observed in combat during the First World War in France, and yet every native soldier must have sensed the shadows of a sacred dance, a dream song, or visionary scenes that would restore liberty and remove forever the scent and grunt of the Imperial German Army.

Wovoka, the great visionary of native liberty, died last week in Yerington, Nevada, and was buried in a Paiute Cemetery. He worked as a rancher his entire life and never traveled more than a few hundred miles from home in Smith Valley. The visions and ecstatic stories of the Ghost Dance have been heard around the world since that solar eclipse more than forty years ago.

POETIC BRUISES

Sunday, 23 October 1932

Nathan closes the Galerie Crémieux two or three times a week in the morning, and we gather at the Café de Flore or Les Deux Magots on Boulevard Saint Germain to hear lively translations of the headlines and short selection from several newspapers.

"The French Third Republic is in decline," declared Nathan. The political and fiscal problems have worsened, but newspapers hardly mention the economic stagnation and depression, and yet the soup wagons, bearded vagrants with the scent of mold, and listless children reveal the daily headlines of the slump, poverty, and human misery.

L'Humanité reported the struggle against the war of the imperialists, the thieves of workers, and political unity, "La lutte contre la guerre impérialiste," "Les braconniers de l'unité ouvrière." *Le Matin*, the nationalist newspaper, reported "Les retraits," or the withdrawal by La Banque de France of gold in the United States, but "Captifs des bandits chinois," the heartfelt story of the release of two compatriots, was given twice as much space on the front page as the economic depression.

Le Figaro, a conservative newspaper, noted that the government created a committee to examine the economies of the various ministries, "Le gouvernement crée un comité des économies." The conservative newspaper *L'Écho de Paris* reported on the same economic committee and on the presidential election in the United States, "Une enquête en amérique: La physionomie de la bataille électorale," with a photograph of Franklin Roosevelt, Governor of New York.

The *Paris Herald Tribune*, the European edition of the *New York Herald Tribune*, was the most popular newspaper at the time, but the stories were braced mostly for Americans in Paris. The editors boasted about class and culture, and ministers of the government steadied any critical reports about political movements against the French Third Republic.

"Newsy stories for expatriates," said Nathan.

The Tomahawk was an independent newspaper and better by far than *Le Matin*, or *La Croix*, the haughty rightist newspapers of the French Roman Catholic Church. The weekly published on the White Earth Reservation was critical of federal agents and government policies, and loyal to the native community in the grand spirit of *L'Humanité*, the daily newspaper of the Communist Party.

August Hudon Beaulieu, our resolute uncle, published *The Progress*, and later *The Tomahawk*, and once accepted the sanctuary of Saint Benedict's Mission Church, some fifty years ago, when the federal agent ordered the removal of the editor and publisher from the reservation for distributing a newspaper without the specific permission of the fascist agent. The first independent newspaper on the reservation resumed publication about a year later, after a favorable decision in federal court, and continued with the critical reports of government policies.

American artists and literary expatriates are leaving Paris because of the expense, decline of the dollar, and at the same time hundreds of newcomers, émigrés and persecuted refugees arrive every day in Paris. Most of the émigrés are desperate, forever on the roads of chance, and some carry silver menorahs buried in dark bundles of clothes.

We are not weary émigrés, exiles, or showy gadabouts with trust money, but native artists and veterans, visionary flâneurs with a creative circle of stories about the fur trade, moody memories of the war, and our unique encounters with the heirs of the fur trade in Paris.

Food is more expensive, but we have learned how to turn a meat bone, wild rice, maize, white oak ash, and even tired vegetables into a delectable stew. Even so, we buy fresh farm vegetables early in the morning, *pommes de terre*, potatoes; *choux*, cabbage; *oignons*, onions; *poireaux*, leeks; *navets*, turnips; and *carottes* at the nearby markets at Les Halles. Aloysius saved the last pouch of native white corn and wild rice for a special dinner with Marie Vassilieff, our friend and favorite cubist painter, sculptor, and creator of marvelous cloth puppets.

Aloysius creates hand puppets, and continues to paint blue ravens, an abstract style of totemic fauvism with slight traces of rouge and minimal brush strokes to create the spirit and motion of birds and animals, similar to the *sumi-e* style in Japan. The totemic scenes are in natural motion, and not the mere evocative expressions, imitations, and decorations of Japonisme.

Nathan has already scheduled an exhibition of his watercolor scenes of totemic fauvism and, at the same time, the publication of my recent poems and stories for the event early next year at the Galerie Crémieux.

My concise poetic images are related to native dream songs, totemic stories, and the ancient haiku of the Japanese. Ezra Pound, the moody expatriate, was the most persuasive poet in the imagistic movement, and especially for younger poets in England and America.

Pound was a prominent literary artist, but even his particular images could easily be heightened with a native touch of color, a poetic bruise, or a translatable hue for any reader. I have told the story many times about the incisive moment when my brother suggested the obvious, that the single word "blue" would create a more lasting visionary scene and sense of natural motion in the imagistic poem, "In a Station of the Metro," by Ezra Pound.

> *The apparition of these faces in the crowd;*
> *Petals on a wet, black bough.*

> *The apparition of these faces in the crowd;*
> *Blue petals on a wet, black bough.*

Black is unearthly, a churchy burden, the absence of color, not only death, but a creepy manger of dead voices, and the stories of black only feign natural motion, ecstasies, melodies, and the poetic images of creation. Black, black, black never lasted in the totemic memories of the fur trade or native stories, and my brother painted great blue ravens to celebrate the obvious radiance of feathers in the sunlight.

Natural motion is blue, not black.

Missionaries shun radiance.

Fascists dread natural motion and liberty.

Ezra Pound was one of the many authors and artists we met at Shakespeare and Company in Paris. Sylvia Beach, the owner of the bookstore introduced me to Pound, but he was rather distant, maybe evasive, and by the time we were close enough to reveal the tease of blue petals on the black bough in the poem, he had already moved from Paris to Rapallo in Italy.

Pound was black, motion was blue, and he might not have appreciated our revision of the heavy black bough in his concise poem with the rapture of lively blue petals as an apparition, and with no experience of natives he would not have recognized our cultural tease, or the sense of natural motion in native art and literature. Pound was a face in the clouds, and deadly serious about images, mostly his own, of course, but surely the great poet would have praised one of my own imagistic poems of blue petals.

> *blue faces*
> *bounce in a thunderstorm*
> *morning glories*

Pierre Chaisson and seven other native veterans staged a surprise birthday party for Aloysius and me yesterday at the Square du Vert-Galant, a prominent point at the end of Île de la Cité near Pont Neuf. Pierre, a native Houma from Terrebonne Parish in Louisiana, was wounded in combat and remained after the war with many other native veterans to study philosophy and literature at Sorbonne University in Paris.

André and Henri, the *mutilés de guerre* who wear metal face masks to conceal gruesome war wounds, the veterans with lost faces, marked the stone stairs down to the square on the river with red steamers, and decorated the autumn trees with red and blue ribbons as a tease of the guardian blue ribbons my mother sewed on our shirts. Communists wear red for the same reasons, but not with any sense of natural motion or curative native spirits. The veterans remembered the stories we told about blue ribbons as escort colors in combat and in visionary stories after the war.

Our friends were eager to hear about the courageous veterans in the Bonus Expeditionary Force and the tragic outcome of the mighty Bonus March three months earlier at Capitol Hill in Washington.

Pierre Chaisson read about the death of William Hushka, the veteran who was shot in the heart by the police, and a few days later the reports about the siege against the peaceable union of veterans by soldiers with tear gas and bayonets under the direct command of Army Chief of Staff General Douglas MacArthur and his sidekick Major Dwight David Eisenhower. General MacArthur ordered the soldiers to chase the decorated veterans, including natives from reservations and the Harlem Hellfighters and their families, out of the capitol of democracy and liberty. The soldiers set fire to the shacks and shanties of the Bonus Expeditionary Force at Anacostia Flats and on the National Mall.

My descriptive scenes, images, and perceptions were recounted in a series of school exercise notebooks, the same sturdy notebooks used by Guillaume Apollinaire and Marcel Proust. My letters to the heirs of the fur trade, and my letter today on our birthday, were written and revised in a school notebook.

Aloysius is my only native brother, and we were born on the very same day, 22 October 1895, but he was a stray, abandoned at Saint Benedict's Mission with no note or trace of maternity. The sisters at the mission may have named the boy as an ironic gesture to Father Aloysius Hermanutz. My mother embraced the abandoned infant as her own son, and we became native brothers of the heart.

Nathan provided the baguette, cheese, and Bordeaux Blanc that afternoon, and we celebrated our birthday with old friends, thirty-seven years on the reservation road to war and back again with friends and favors in Paris. The stories, steady teases, and the great bond of war veterans continued into the night on the River Seine.

Paris became our tribute of liberty.

Solomon Heap of Words, a Pojoaque veteran and poet from Santa Fe, New Mexico, never missed a beat to create abstract scenes out of original bywords and tricky drop names, and our birthday inspired a steady bounce of pithy imagery.

"Autumn salon of native teases," said Aloysius.

Heap of Words was clever to enlist in the infantry as a code talker, but the talk back was obscure and could not be easily translated because he was never fluent in any native language. Tewa catchwords were no more than blather in his conversions, so he was removed as a telephone code talker and survived as a native messenger in risky combat areas.

Olivier Black Elk and Coyote Standing Bear, veterans and charismatic poseurs, were ready with their usual stance of obscure native traditions, a marvelous concoction of feathers, leathers, and dance circles to celebrate the birthday of two native veterans. Olivier and Coyote were not native, and their connections to native traditions were imaginary, no more than glints of an expatriate culture. Yet, these two extraordinary poseurs were loyal friends, more than blood and culture, and their native praise and creative poses were so believable that no one has ever thought to challenge their native authenticity.

Olivier and Coyote had actually earned our favor and respect because they truly appreciate the irony of native pride, and they eagerly answered those tedious public questions about traditions, romance and tragedy, the curiosity about native customs, and hearsay about the demise of General George Armstrong Custer at the Battle of Little Big Horn. They wore black hats, feathers, beaded vests, and eased into pretentious gestures as native warriors. Their poses were perfect, and they barely mentioned the elusive cultures of the woodland and plains.

Aloysius raised a wine glass, and together we saluted their loyal spirit and native manner. Poseurs were necessary in every community because airs and imitations were related to favors and mockery, and native veterans were always ready for the count of irony. Natives create ironic trickster stories to counter the boredom of the obvious and to tease the tedious notions of truth, absolute traditions, and death. Native veterans of the fur trade and war bear the cruel ironies of empires and the tease of honors and decorations.

We poked fun at the whimsical dance moves of steady hunches and heaves, shouted out our praise of the poseurs, and then teased them about the double prohibition of alcohol on reservations. Gray people gathered in the alcoves of the Pont Neuf to observe the wild dance beats, and they were moved by the decorations, contrived traditions, and by the heady birthday chants of the mighty *Indiens d'Amérique*.

"All the world's a stage," shouted a gray man.

"A world of native players," said Olivier.

"Natives play many parts," chanted Coyote.

"Shakespeare was Anishinaabe," said André.

"Indiens d'Amérique dans les masques," American Indians in masks, shouted Henri. The muted voices of the *mutilés de guerre*, veterans who wore metal masks, silenced the gray citizens on the Pont Neuf.

William Shakespeare was an Arapaho student at the Carlisle Indian School, we declared in a union of totemic truth after two glasses of wine, a natural outcome of our birthday celebration on the Square du Vert-Galant. Aloysius swore the name was true, proven authentic, and forever documented by the government.

Nathan was ready with a countertease, and that afternoon at the square he proclaimed that Moses was a fur trader at La Pointe on Madeline Island, and Sigmund Freud was a vested tiptoe timber cruiser in the white pine on the White Earth Reservations. The Ice Woman beguiled Freud with snowy sexual stories and the reveals of stumpage dreams.

The contest of ironic names continued with artists, authors, and politicians. James Joyce was a Matachine ritual dancer in blue ribbons with the miter of a bishop at Jemez Pueblo in New Mexico. Sinclair Lewis vanished in the scene dock of a comic opera staged by the Chippewa. Nathan almost convinced us that evening that Léon Blum, the great literary socialist, was related to the native medical doctor Carlos Montezuma.

Coyote and Olivier were hesitant to enter a name in the irony game because they were already esteemed as great poseurs. Nathan poured more wine, and we continued to tease each other with names. I shouted out that Shylock in *The Merchant of Venice* was a native shaman and voyageur from the Headwaters of the Mississippi River. More wine and we picked and placed other characters from the plays of Shakespeare. Black Elk named King Lear an Oglala Lakota fancy dancer from the Pine Ridge Reservation. Standing Bear presented Julius Caesar as a Chinook salmon trader who presided over the Lewis and Clark Expedition. No, no, no, we chanted and then turned the stories back to the actual Carlisle Indian School.

The *Carlisle Arrow* tabloid pictured Benedict Guyon as Shylock, Alta Pintup as Portia, and Mary Ann Cutler as Nerissa in *The Merchant of Venice*, Andrew Connor as Marcus Brutus and Donald Crown as Caesar in *Julius Caesar*, a marvelous cast of native actors, Anishinaabe, Tuscarora, Cayuga, Cherokee, and Lakota. The native actors never corrected their school names with traditional, sacred, or romantic nicknames.

Black Elk staggered and shouted out that William Shakespeare was a student at the Carlisle Indians School more than ten years before we were born, and the native Shakespeare became a rancher and great visionary in the American Indian Church in Wyoming.

Henri raised his metal mask, guzzled more wine, and then asked me how everyone could know so much about natives and Shakespeare at the Carlisle Indian School. The *mutilés de guerre* removed their masks only in the dark, and that night the wounded veterans were cockeyed with white wine.

"Shakespeare, really an Arapaho?" asked Henri.

"Great actor in his own culture," said Olivier.

"General Ferdinand Foch is my name, a wounded soldier and decorated warrior of the noble Nez Perce, and later Supreme Allied Commander in the First World War," said André.

Nathan saluted the veterans and praised the native actors. Shakespeare tragedies and comedies were everyday scenes on reservations, and natives were savvy actors in the presence of federal agents.

Coyote rushed in with a related cultural story about Chief Maungwudaus, the native minister who had visited Stratford-upon-Avon more than eighty years ago and wrote a poem to honor William Shakespeare. Coyote moved closer, gestured as an actor on stage, and shouted out two of the twelve lines from the poem:

> *the spirit is with manidoo*
> *who gave thee all thou didst do*

We were silent for a moment after the stagy delivery of "didst do," and then everyone burst into wild laughter. We danced and pretended to rehearse the ironic words of the spirit *manidoo*, didst do, didst do, didst do several times on the River Seine. Didst do was one of many weird words of godly conversion at native missions, an archaic trust in some other didst do culture.

Aloysius recounted other ironic stories and doubts about Chief Maungwudaus, or the everyday native named George Henry. The exhibition healer sold herbal medicines at his lectures, and promised the hocus pocus native herbs cured pains in the back, bleeding of the lungs, jaundice, bilious complaints, dysentery, costiveness, ulcers in the mouth, and more. As boys we were always amused by the sound of "bilious" and "costiveness."

Coyote said Henry posed for a studio photograph with a chain of heavy bear claws, decorated porcupine quills, the huge feather headdress of a warrior, and a shiny steel war axe.

Maungwudaus was not an easy name to pronounce or translate, and many nicknames overreached native teases, praise, and irony. The word for "big heart" is *mangidee*, but that was not the same as "great hero" or "courage" as some would say of the minister and the churchy translation of his native name. Chief was an avowed name with more mission credit for manners than any native stories of inheritance or fur trade royalty. His churchy turnaround name could have been *mangindibe*, or "big head." The Credit River Mission in Canada taught him how to dance as a new conversion healer and dealer on the colonial stage.

Aloysius gathered everyone around the crown street lamp that night on the square to present the native Niinag Trickster for the first time in Paris. The hand puppet wore leather chaps, a bisected breechclout, cocked fedora, and a black sash decorated with beaded flowers.

Dummy Trout, the mute native puppeteer, presented my brother with two hand puppets, the Niinag Trickster and the seductive Ice Woman, last summer at the Ogema Train Station on the White Earth Reservation when we departed for the Bonus Expeditionary Force in Washington.

Dummy braved desire and mockery as a mute for more than thirty years with the motion of hand puppets and loyal mongrels. She miraculously survived a firestorm on her eighteenth birthday, gestured to the clouds, and since then has never voiced another word, name, or song, and snickered forever in silence. Nookaa, her only lover, and hundreds of natives were burned to ashes and forgotten in the Great Hinckley Fire of 1894.

Dummy taught her mongrels how to smile and tease relations with slaver, ear cocks, thigh bumps, and aesthetic silence. She rightly sensed that my brother would delight the world and divert the enemy with hand puppets, and especially with the outrageous Niinag Trickster.

"Thou know'st that my fortunes and precious parts were not carved at the same time, and my pecker was created last, and waits to celebrate a separate birthday," said the Niinag Trickster, and then the puppet jerked his head from side to side. "So, gentlemen, pray thee honor my late born dick," and slowly the trickster raised his enormous wooden penis as the Niinag Hamlet, a new Shakespearean comedy of boasts and promises on the River Seine.

"Niinag Hamlet of Paris," shouted Heap of Words.

Nathan circled the trickster and raised his arms to favor the gesture of the huge wooden penis. Coyote turned and shouted, "Alleluia, Alleluia, Glory Be to the Father, the great wooden willy has arisen." The *mutilés de guerre* veterans doubled over with laughter, and then together they chanted *bon anniversaire, bon anniversaire* under the street lamp on the Square du Vert-Galant.

» 3 «

ENEMY WAY

Thursday, 20 April 1933

Nathan invited artists, authors, gallery owners, and gadabouts to an ironic Enemy Way ceremonial birthday party for Adolf Hitler at the Galerie Crémieux. The Nazi fascist is the enemy of culture, art, literature, humor, and ethos at forty-four, and only the masters of cut and run mockery would dare to deliver flowers, recite poetry, or croon to the clouds *bon anniversaire* to honor the Führer of the Third Reich.

The traditional native ceremony was carried out over several days in the summer, but this year the season of care and custom was not observed since the enemy was revealed as the despot of cruel strategies, antisemitism, and brutish author of *Mein Kampf*.

Nathan learned from his father, the trader, that the Navajo created the Enemy Way ceremony to counter evil and misery, and to restore the union of peace and natural motion in the world. Navajo irony was elusive and barely understood by outsiders who were invited to the traditional ceremonies.

Show me the way, the creative way of liberty to sway the enemy, chase away the churchy outback hem and haw of betrayal, and outplay the treachery of traditions. The last ceremony at the gallery was held almost twenty years ago with the start of the First World War.

The Enemy Way was curative mockery.

The Nazi Party dominated the German Reichstag, and then Hitler was named Chancellor. Rather, he maneuvered curses and deceptions to become dictator with the decline of the Weimar Republic. Nathan was sullen and depressed over the sudden rise of nationalism and the severe fascist persecution of Jews. Rabbis, teachers, musicians, doctors, bankers, and merchants were betrayed as loyal citizens, and burdened with the great traditions of education and liberty. Nathan shouted out the names of many scientists, artists, and authors who became exiles to escape the tyranny of the Nazi Party.

The Enemy Way never outplays vengeance.

Hitler was born in Austria, and he was stateless until last year, not a citizen of Germany or Austria. He could have been deported with no civil rights or election, but that ironic story would not carry the day. The observation teased the notion that the dictator might have become a backfire artist if his father had not sent him to a technical school, or *Realschule*, in Linz, Austria.

Just last month the deadly dictator blamed the fire at the Reichstag on the Communists. The Bolsheviks, red, right, or otherwise were fingered near and far for crimes against church and state, and sometimes for opposition to the very doctrines of democratic governance.

Even the pocket dictators and tradition fascists on the reservation kept an eye out for the communists, crossblood outsiders, and bedeviled those who dared to challenge or provoke the pathetic conventions of authority. Reservation autocrats, federal agents, native police, and missionaries cursed those natives who told ironic stories, a necessary tease of tradition, churchy conversions, and the absence of individual rights and liberty.

Augustus Hudon Beaulieu, our steadfast uncle, never hesitated to face down the tradition fascists, federal agents, and the hocus pocus of conversion shamans in critical editorials in *The Progress*, and later in a larger independent newspaper, *The Tomahawk*. Augustus surely would have denounced Adolf Hitler and his toadies in editorials on the front page, and declared the pouty despot as decadent or a "putrescence," as he had once described the reign of federal agents in a headline.

Nathan decorated three cedar boughs with bright ribbons, a tradition of the Enemy Way ceremony, and prepared food for the participants. Naturally, we insisted on blue ribbons on the boughs, shirts, and in the window of the gallery. Standing Bear and Black Elk carried the boughs and swished the presence of celebrants and native objects. We honored the ceremony but seldom participated in sacred gestures or traditional dances of other cultures because the spirit of imitation was much too close to the native favors of tease and mockery.

Aloysius made puppets for the Enemy Way.

Nathan mounted on an easel two images of the Enemy Way ceremony, and on an exhibition counter he displayed a Navajo Germantown Eye Dazzler blanket, woven more than fifty years ago, and baskets with creation designs, red, white, black, night, rain clouds and traces of lightning, the sacred mountains, and sun in morning. The Navajo Enemy Way ceremony was public, and the sentiments of that cultural practice were continued at the Galerie Crémieux.

Nathan introduced his wife, Françoise, lovely daughter, Hélène, and the stout family spaniel named Churchill. This was the first time we had met his family, and learned that his wife was an independent research anthropologist at the Musée d'Ethnographie du Trocadéro. Aloysius smiled, held back his usual sardonic demotion of *anthrovoyageurs* in the fur trade, and politely inquired, "What end of mortals do you investigate, foot, mouth, or disease?" She smiled, and whispered, "Mouthy mortals, my subject is linguistics."

"Double touché," said Nathan.

Françoise was great company, and later she explained that her actual research was ancient inscriptions on stone, but she could not resist a witty comeback to the insinuation about the fur trade and cultural studies. Aloysius overcame the evil eye of anthropology with the idea of natural motion present in the native images on stones in the canoe country of Minnesota and Canada. He drew outline images of handprints and magical shaman figures as a totemic sense of presence and native motion.

André and Henri, the *mutilés de guerre* veterans, were the first to arrive at the gallery, a strategy that enabled them to raise their metal face masks, eat and drink early, and avoid the gaze of strangers. Later, the veterans leaned against the back wall and watched others crowd around the vegetable stew, baguettes, cheese, and wine.

Benjamin Crémieux stood alone near the wounded veterans at the back of the gallery. His long and narrow nose was distinctive, and with dark lonesome eyes he seemed reserved or hesitant, but my impression was not accurate, because he smiled easily and responded to my praise of his full beard and moustache. He might have teased me in turn about the absence of any trace of a beard, but instead we talked about native art, literature, and curse of the fur trade in New France.

Benjamin said his knowledge of *littérature amérindienne*, American Indian literature, was introductory, and mostly derived from anthropological and sociological studies of native cultures published by Franz Boas, Joseph Deniker, Frances Densmore, Natalie Curtis, and Émile Durkheim and his nephew, Marcel Mauss, in French and English.

Frances Densmore was an easy cue for me to relate my stories about the curious voyageur of native cultures and dream songs, an ironic gesture of the new fur trade, but then, as now, my interests were modern native literature, the actual creation of new totemic visions, stories, and dream songs, not the mere imitation of traditions.

Benjamin understood that translations of native dream songs and stories were literature, as much as classical myths, the *Odyssey*, the Bible, or translations of any songs, stories, or ancient scriptures. He was concerned about the actual sources of native songs and stories, the revealed methods of translation and interpretation, the early conversion literature of any culture, and, of course, modern creative literature.

Densmore was praised because she transcribed the recordings and asked each singer to translate the words of the dream songs. Benjamin immediately understood my criticism of translations that imposed pronouns, causation, and a dominant grammar with no sense of a totemic presence, or associations or native visionary scenes of natural motion in dream songs.

My original critique was that native dream songs in cursory translations become distant rumors with no tease of chance or creation. Densmore was dedicated, smart, wore heavy dresses, and was courteous when she recorded some of my relatives more than thirty years ago on the White Earth Reservation.

Benjamin was a brilliant listener who understood the literary challenges of authors, and who seemed interested in my initial critical ideas about native literature and the necessary categories of native authors and literature in the past century, from the publication of *A Son of the Forest*, by William Apess, and *Wynema: A Child of the Forest*, by Alice Callahan, to *Deep Woods to Civilization*, by Charles Alexander Eastman; the popular *Wah'Kon-Tah: The Osage and the White Man's Road*, by John Joseph Mathews; and *My People the Sioux*, by Luther Standing Bear.

Benjamin mentioned *The Mind of Primitive Man*, by the anthropologist Franz Boas, and discussed several cultural conditions that might form the content of each of the novels, and the potential sway of colonial and mission experience of the authors. As several more people arrived at the gallery, he proposed an outline of two origins of native literature, the oral creation stories and dream songs, and the literary art of memory; and then he named at least three native literatures, but warned me they should never be compared to other cultures because of the originality of totems, colonial fur trade, résistance, religious conversions, and acculturation.

"Surely you read more than Frances Densmore and Franz Boas," was my response to his literary categories, a way to ease my doubts that anyone could so clearly create an instant outline of native literature.

Benjamin mentioned similar summaries about the two literatures of Italy and À la recherche du temps perdu, by Marcel Proust. The novel was published in translation a few years ago as Remembrance of Things Past. Benjamin would have favored In Search of Lost Time as the translation.

The first native literary genre was translation, and the many secular versions of native stories in research publications. The second genre was conversion, the personal narratives of natives educated in mission schools. The third native literary genre was modern, creative literature, including historical fiction and original literary styles that created visionary scenes and a sense of motion and native touch of memory.

"Totemic crease of memory," was my counter.

Benjamin said Marcel Proust "clears and illuminates the road to the novelist of tomorrow." Benjamin and Proust certainly cleared the road for me to continue critical studies of native stories in translation and creative literature, and that includes my own stories and letters to the heirs of the fur trade.

Nathan told me later that Benjamin was a respected scholar of French and Italian literature who had contributed essays to Nouvelle Revue Française, New French Review. One of his essays published in Le Ving-tième Siècle, a collection of thirteen essays, is about the spirited literary style, continuity of presence, and the mystical touch of memory in the prose of Marcel Proust.

Nathan and Benjamin are distantly related to Adolphe Crémieux, the liberal lawyer and former minister of justice who founded the Alliance Is-raélite Universelle, dedicated to international human rights and education. Adolphe was elected to serve in La Chambre des Députés, the Chamber of Deputies. He ended the death penalty, and slavery in the colonies of

France. Adolphe was born in Nîmes, France, died in Paris in 1880, and was buried in Montparnasse Cemetery.

Marie Vassilieff wore a wide black gaucho hat and a rough woven shawl for the ceremony. Aloysius invited her at once to the back room to show the three hand puppets he had carved out of discarded blocks of wood. Adolf Hitler, Guillaume Apollinaire, and Gertrude Stein were mounted in a row on the bookcase. He had partly carved several other puppets but would not reveal the names.

Marie is revered for her distinctive cubist paintings, including *Café de la Rotonde, Pieta,* and *In the Café,* but when we first met about fifteen years ago at her courtyard atelier in Chemin du Montparnasse, my brother was inspired by the marvelous masks and cloth puppet dolls that she created with huge evocative eyes, puffy lips, long cloth fingers, and enlarged cubist features, especially the puppet portrayals of Matisse and Picasso, and the marvelous cloth puppets of a married couple named Sigrid Hjertén and Isaac Grünewald, an expressionist painter. Sigrid wore a red rose on each shoulder, and Isaac wore a tuxedo with a silver bow tie.

Aloysius has been inspired many times by the artistry and spirit of hand puppets, and especially by the distinctive creations of Paul Klee, Marie Vassilieff, and the brilliant Dummy Trout of Spirit Lake on the White Earth Reservation.

The Hitler hand puppet was blocky with bloated rouge cheeks, a thick square moustache, and grimace. Dark hair draped over his left eye, and four clefts were carved between his eyebrows. He was dressed in a heavy black cape with a huge red swastika. The enormous right hand on a long and thick wooden arm was poised for the Nazi salute.

Marie shunned the swastika puppet and reached out to touch the oval head of Apollinaire. The carved head was pale, smooth, and shiny with curved eyebrows, an angular nose, puckered lips, and a chin cleft. Aloysius was clearly prompted to create the poet puppet based on portraits by the fauvist and cubist painter Jean Metzinger.

Apollinaire was decisive that afternoon with his first gestures as a hand puppet. He removed his fedora, cocked his head to one side, then the other, leaned forward, and reached out with his blunt wooden hand to Marie. The poet pushed her hat back and touched her cheek, and in turn she recited two lines from his poem, "Le Pont Mirabeau."

Sous le pont Mirabeau coule la Seine
The Seine runs under the Pont Mirabeau
Et nos amours
And our love

Daniel-Henry Kahnweiler, the art dealer; Sylvia Beach, owner of the literary bookstore Shakespeare and Company; Gertrude Stein; Michel Leiris, surrealist poet and novelist who had just returned from Africa; his wife, Louise Godon Leiris; Michel Laroux, a close friend and collector of Lakota Horse Dance Sticks who served at the Officers School of the Gendarmerie Nationale in Versailles; Pierre Chaisson; Nika Montezuma, a native from Gunflint Lake in Minnesota; new artists; authors; and many others from Sorbonne University crowded around the food and wine near the window of the gallery.

Nathan recited an honoring song that he learned from his father, and then started the ceremony with an obvious disparity, that the "Navajo Enemy Way ceremony is not the same as our observance, because the outcome of our stories and indictments on the birthday of a brute will at least restore an ironic sense of balance, humor, and state of mind for the afternoon, and a few overnights of memory."

Nathan honored Henri Crémieux, his father, the trader with natives in the American Southwest, and the native art in the gallery, sacred, obscure, totemic fauvism, and then solemnly announced his regrets to native cultures, "the modern world has never been in balance."

"Sieg Heil Germany," shouted André.

The celebrants turned away in silence, unsettled at first by the crude gesture, but when my brother raised the long arm and crude hand of Hitler the puppet in a Nazi salute, the sense of an unspoken ceremonial balance was realized in mockery and ironic gestures.

"Fools mock puppets," shouted Heap of Words.

I declared that bold salutes are never heartfelt, and hand puppets are the masters of taunt, tease, and ridicule, and only authors, artists, and their creations would dare to imitate and mock Adolf Hitler with a birthday party at the Galerie Crémieux in Paris.

"Double ironies," shouted Heap of Words.

"Puppets shame the fascists," said Nathan.

Nathan read a recent headline published in the *New York Times*, "Reich Gags Press, Ends Prussian Diet," and another headline earlier this month, "Hitler Proclaims War on Democracy at Huge Nazi Rally," but most of the stories about Hitler and the Nazi Party were buried on the inside of newspapers. The *Wall Street Journal* described Hitler in one news story as "the fiery little Austrian from Munich, foe of Jews and Communists and leading exponent of a belligerent German Nationalism." Nathan read one more selection about the communist arson of the Reichstag in Berlin that "provided the expected basis for measures of repression throughout the Reich unprecedented save in time of war or revolution. An emergency decree signed by President von Hindenburg . . . suspended all constitutional articles guaranteeing private property, personal liberty, freedom of the press, secrecy of postal communications and the right to hold meetings and form associations."

Nathan was rightly worried about his relatives and many close friends in Germany. He pleaded with them in letters, telegrams, and telephone calls to leave the country and endure as exiles in the French Third Republic.

I announced several ironic headlines this afternoon, as Enemy Way mockery, "Nazi Gang Gagged *Liberté*, Seized Decadent Native Art and Trickster Stories," and "Burned Birch Head of Adolf Saved a Nation." Marie could not resist the mockery and continued with other ironic headlines, "Blue Ravens Downed the Geezer of Shame," and "Hitler Counts Backwards to Nothing." Aloysius carried on with "Private Hitler Salutes the Prince of Darkness," and Nathan created the last ironic headline that teased his good friend Daniel-Henry Kahnweiler, "Cubist Art Dealer Exiled with Johann and Three Friedrichs."

"Adolf Cuckoo Clock," shouted Heap of Words.

Adolf Hitler the hand puppet was presented at the gallery for the first time and saluted the wine and cheese, and then turned to face each of the celebrants. The Führer was nose to nose with Gertrude Stein, and she stared back without a blink. Hitler jerked to the side, tapped the metal masks of the *mutilés de guerre*, and then shouted out, "It is not truth that matters, but victory."

"Puppets mock the masks," said Henri.

"Masks mock the puppets," said André.

Herr Hitler the hand puppet might have sidetracked the poseurs and outwitted the censors, but that concern was hardly necessary in a nation of *liberté, égalité, fraternité*, the obvious ethos and truisms of the French Third Republic.

Hitler saluted and returned to the bookcase.

Kahnweiler tolerated irony and praised the sense of balance in the Enemy Way, and until a few weeks ago he was convinced that the Nazi Party would fade away once the citizens became aware of the crude corruption of power. "Germany was a nation of great poetry, literature, music, philosophy," he said, and then praised the names of Johann Wolfgang von Goethe, Richard Wagner, and the three Friedrichs: Schiller, Hölderlin, and Nietzsche.

Germany in the care of the romantic memories of poets and philosophers was never comparable to the antisemite Joseph Goebbels, the vendor of violence who was named with unintended irony the Reich Minister of Public Enlightenment and Propaganda, or the brutish Hermann Göring, founder of the secret police and minister without portfolio, who boasted in a recent fascist speech at a Nazi demonstration in Frankfurt, "Fellow Germans, my measures will not be crippled by any judicial thinking. My measures will not be crippled by any bureaucracy. Here I don't have to give Justice, my mission is only to destroy and to exterminate, nothing more!"

Kahnweiler changed his benign views of nationalism when his brother Gustave and other relatives and friends escaped from the antisemitism and tyranny of Germany. This afternoon in the gallery he related the consequences of the "Law to Remedy the Distress of People and the Reich," the declared amendment to the constitution that granted Hitler absolute power, and ordinary civil liberties were terminated to serve only the despot of the Third Reich.

Kahnweiler was persecuted in France at the start of the First World War because he was German, and hundreds of cubist paintings by Pablo Picasso, George Braque, Juan Gris, and Maurice de Vlaminck were removed from his gallery by the Préfecture de Police, and later sold at auction. At the end of the war he returned to Paris, in spite of the state thievery and antisemitism, and opened a new art gallery to honor the great abstract painters.

The Enemy Way ceremony was renewed once more with more wine

and mockery. Kahnweiler converted the Enemy Way ceremony to gusty praise of Edouard Monet and the impressionist painters, who created the deliverance of light and the perception of natural motion rather than mere depictions of time and place. He paused, and turned toward the window to watch the gray faces on the square. No doubt some faces were exiles of the enlightenment and forever on the road, and then Kahnweiler gathered his thoughts and praised cubism, cubism, cubism.

Paris is our empire of art and the literature of liberty despite the contradictions of royalists, communism, and the rush of party favors and fascism. We stay under the polestar with blue ravens, hand puppets, and memories of the ledger artist Howling Wolf, and stories of native natural motion in a glorious gallery of irony for the start of another empire war of cravers and vengeance.

» 4 «

STOLEN SCRAPS

Friday, 12 May 1933

Native dream songs are forever in the clouds, and once more the empire wars are underway. The lilies and daffodils are in bloom, and at the same time we hark back to the stories of shamans that war never ends, since evil, envy, greed, and predatory vengeance never end. The last empire war started with a royal murder, and the next world war of resentments and revenge starts with the fiery purge of books and libraries.

Nathan ordered the usual *petit déjeuner*, croissant, confiture, and espresso at Café de Flore, and then read out loud the unbelievable headline from the *New York Times*, "Nazis Pile Books for Bonfires Today, 25,000 Volumes Gathered by Berlin Students—Other Cities to Follow Suit." The recent story on the front page described a "huge bonfire of books."

The Third Reich was undone by authors and books and worried that art, literature, and philosophy might beat back racial hatred. The liberal traces, drift of irony, and aesthetic stories of the world, the very plumb of every modern culture, were denounced as the fascists turned to students, libraries, and bonfires to resurrect the deadly nationalism of Germany.

"Pretenders of class and covenant," said Nathan.

German students burned thousands of library books, purged centuries of canons, and renounced the tease and booty of the enlightenment, but the words of James Joyce, Franz Kafka, Sigmund Freud, Thomas Mann, Stefan Zweig, Bertolt Brecht, Rosa Luxemburg, Lion Feuchtwanger, Joseph Conrad, André Gide, Ernest Hemingway, John Dos Passos, Jack London, Helen Keller, Aldous Huxley, Franz Boas, and hundreds of other authors who created the clever seasons and mighty scores of liberal cultures would last forever in the libraries of the French Third Republic.

"Bonfire of liberty," shouted Heap of Words.

The Berlin students feigned a coup count with enemy authors and books by Jews, and surely these recruits of fascism never noticed how slowly cultural ethos, irony, and the words of liberty burn to ashes, and never overnight.

The Nazis celebrated empire traditions, saluted the ruins of culture and literature, and Joseph Goebbels, the empire boy and creepy master of vengeance with low set ears, absurdly named the Reich Minister of Public Enlightenment and Propaganda, paid tribute to the bonfires of books as a "symbolic significance."

Kahnweiler, the gallery owner, told me at the Enemy Way ceremony last month that Germans set aside heavy cultural morals to celebrate the kings and knaves of state in popular plays by William Shakespeare. The Minister of Public Enlightenment and Propaganda and the fascist students of bonfires never noticed the literary irony in the character of Moth, the page of teases in the comedy *Love's Labour's Lost*, "They have been at a great feast of languages, and stolen the scraps."

The White Earth Reservation never had a library, not even a bracket of native books, but only the tradition fascists might have banned the first books written by natives who graduated from mission and federal boarding schools and the marvelous *Manabozho Curiosa*, that rare parchment book of the ancient erotic heart dance of monks and totemic animals. Rightly, the thousands of ethnographic studies and federal reports could provoke bonfires for a hundred years, but the federal blather and eyewash of government documents must be secured to provide forever an untold historical source of native stories, unintended irony, and cultural mockery.

The federal government built saw mills, dams, schools, fisheries, but not reservation libraries. The mission teachers delivered catechisms and were shied by shamans, native dream songs, the erotic trickster stories of creation, and even a wild book in hand. The native students in the government school would never burn a book for a priest, a federal agent, a propaganda poseur with low set ears, and never for the Great White Father.

Native stories of the fur trade and war were chancy on the page and stage, and scenes of totemic custody evolved with the turn of seasons, shame, duty, and irony, and with the worldly intrigues much the same as the sly strategies of William Shakespeare and Shylock, the Jewish moneylender in *The Merchant of Venice*.

La Pointe at Madeline Island was a great trade center in the late seventeenth century, the Venice of Lake Superior, and heady voyageurs in grand canoes with precious bundles of totemic beaver, marten, and mink carried out the risky and despicable ventures for the alien merchants of fashion and romance in the colonial fur trade of New France.

Shylock was a native in the empire fur trade.

Totems, beaver, and liberty were never secure.

Aloysius packed two hand puppets into a shoulder bag that brisk morning, and we rushed to several bookstores in search of the original two volume edition of *Mein Kampf* by Adolf Hitler. My brother bought the last copy, and he was determined to stage that book as a mockery of the fascist students in Germany. He tore pages from the confessions of a dummy state prisoner and started a tiny counterbonfire on the portico of the Place du Panthéon in Paris.

My duty was to roll the thick pages of *Mein Kampf* and hand them over to the people who had gathered around the slight fire. They understood the gesture and stoked the fire with care. Adolf Hitler was demoted to torn pages, and the treacheries of his words were burned for liberty.

Two officers of the Préfecture de Police pushed through the crowd to the source of the spectacle and examined a few pages of the bonfire book. The officers might have been tempted to set a few pages afire, but instead gestured with approval and continued their saunter toward Sorbonne University.

The hand puppets were out in public for the first time, ready to stage a sudden talk and gesture show near the ash pile of *Mein Kampf* on the portico of the mausoleum in the Latin Quarter of Paris. Aloysius raised Adolf Hitler on one hand, saluted twice, and bounced his heavy birch head, and then on the other hand my brother nurtured the stout, busty, and pouty Gertrude Stein.

Nika Montezuma was marvelous, a translator and voice actor at the same time, and she easily followed the fast pace of discussions and back talk between the puppets in French, and then mocked the pompous voice of Gertrude Stein in English.

Gertrude cursed, out of breath. She wore a cloche hat and slowly waved at the audience with huge wooden hands. Nika gladly staged the singsong voice of the austere author and modern art collector; my brother was the maestro of two hand puppets, and my unsteady falsetto voice was the Führer in English. Adolf and Gertrude avoided the sight of each other as they circled the fire that neighborly gray day at the Place du Panthéon.

Adolf Hitler jerked his huge polished head from side to side, and once more saluted as the bonfire was stoked with pages of *Mein Kampf*. Some people turned away in disgust, but others were charmed with the puppets and the gestures of mockery. Adolf Hitler was an original hand puppet but never close in character to the clever Guignol de Lyon.

ADOLF: Millions of copies of my book have been translated and sold around the world, so burn more pages to stay warm and make me richer.

GERTRUDE: What books would you pardon?

ADOLF: Books are the enemy of the Third Reich.

GERTRUDE: Surely not every published book.

ADOLF: Natty Bumppo in *Leatherstocking Tales*.

GERTRUDE: *This Side of Paradise* by F. Scott Fitzgerald?

ADOLF: The students burned his books.

GERTRUDE: *Mon corps et moi* by René Crevel?

ADOLF: The students burned his books.

GERTRUDE: A *Hilltop on the Marne* by Mildred Aldrich?

ADOLF: The students burned her books.

GERTRUDE: Do you read George Sand?

ADOLF: The students burned his books.

GERTRUDE: Amantine Lucile Aurore Dupin?

ADOLF: The students burned every last word.

GERTRUDE: Luther Standing Bear the Sioux Indian?

ADOLF: Reserve his books and heroic traditions.

GERTRUDE: Karl May and the Apache Winnetou?

ADOLF: Great heroes never need books.

GERTRUDE: *La Retour à la France*, by Basile Beaulieu?

ADOLF: The students burned the war stories.

GERTRUDE: *The Sun Also Rises*, by Ernest Hemingway?

ADOLF: The students burned his books.

GERTRUDE: The lost generation is not burnable.

ADOLF: Jews were never a lost generation.

GERTRUDE: *Mein Kampf* shouts out for an editor.

ADOLF: No one revises my prison story.

GERTRUDE: Too many buts and preposition starts.

ADOLF: Better than your adverbs and conjunctions.

GERTRUDE: But you were never there there.

ADOLF: That rose is a rose is a rose is decadent.

GERTRUDE: A Nazi is a nazi is a Nazi is depravity.

ADOLF: Third Reich for a thousand years.

GERTRUDE: Delusions of a Bavarian corporal.

ADOLF: Revenge for Treaty of Versailles.

GERTRUDE: *Mein Kampf* is a wordy wet dream.

Gertrude turned slowly to the side, raised her stout head with a slight shimmy, and chanted, "Nazis are dead, dead, dead with the burned books in Baden-Baden and Berlin." The crowd around the hand puppets roared with laughter and shouted out, "Dead, dead, dead a thousand years," as Hitler jerked his head, saluted three times, and then backed away.

Gertrude was demure as she moved slowly around the circle of the bonfire, and then she reached down, caressed the cheek of a shy girl and said, "Puppets are the great spirit of dreams." The girl blushed, and then touched the wooden hands of the puppet.

Nika tore out random pages of *Mein Kampf* and slowly read out loud several sections in three languages, German, French, and English, and whenever she hesitated or repeated a word someone in the crowd would shout out the correct translation. People moaned and groaned over every word, the fascist tone and jingoism of the feigned struggles of a fascist. More and more people gathered as she read, and cheered when she tossed each crumpled page into the fire.

Herr Hitler moved closer to Nika and jerked his head with the translation. He jerked to one side, and then the other, saluted a few words, and twice pitched his head back with laughter. He raised his head high with the original German, turned a cold shoulder to the translation in French, and leaned closer to hear the English.

*Sicher war zunächst nur mein ersichtlicher Misserfolg in der
Schule. Was mich freute, lernte ich, vor allem auch alles, was ich
meiner Meinung nach später als Maler brauchen würde.*

*Mon échec scolaire était d'emblée évident. J'apprenais ce qui me
plaisait, et surtout ce qui à mon avis me servirait plus tard en tant
que peintre.*

*Surely my progress was evident as failure in school. This made
me feel happy above all everything learned would be needed as a
painter.*

*The charges against Judaism were grave when I discovered the
Jewish activities in the Press, in art, in literature and the theatre.
All unctuous insincere protests were futile. One could look at the
posters that announced the hideous productions in movies and
theatre, and study the names of authors praised to resolve the
Jewish questions. Here was a pestilence, a moral pestilence, and the
public was being infected. Worse than the Black Plague. And what
doses of this poison was made and circulated. The lower the moral
and intellectual level an author of artistic work the more unlimited
in new growth. Sometimes one of these fellows, acting like a sewage
pump, would shoot his filth directly in the face of other members of
the human race.*

*Germany waged war for existence. The purpose of war propaganda
should have been to strengthen the fighting spirit in that struggle
and help it to victory.*

Herr Hitler bowed his head, and then with the last translation about
strength and victory, he stared at each face around the fire and saluted in
the defiant manner of a Nazi. The last few pages of *Mein Kampf* were torn
out by two huffy men and thrown into the fire.

The French were angry about the notion of a fascist victory and shouted
names at the Führer puppet in several languages, *despote, imposteur, be-
trüger, sauvage, grande folle*, monkey painter, monster, predator, suicide
bait, and sewer antisemite.

Gertrude Stein raised her huge wooden hands, patted Adolf on the head, and loudly enunciated in singsong, "A knock is a knock is a knock is a knock is hollow." Then she muttered, "My singsong says, curse subdued sex and cock a snook shows with barren faces and paper clowns at fascist bonfires." The sound of the cheers over the bonfire that late spring morning reached to Sorbonne University and the Jardin du Luxembourg.

CRI DE COEUR

Tuesday, 6 February 1934

Place de la Concorde is haunted with cris de coeur and the rage of revolutions, and the bloody guillotine baskets of royal heads in the First French Republic. The callous shouts of the crowd, pathetic gasps, and shivers of horror continued after the heavy guillotine blades severed the heads of Citizen Louis Capet, Marie Antoinette, Georges Danton, Charlotte Corday, Maximilien Robespierre, and many others. Rowdy shouts and bloody wheezes last forever in the savage clouds of terror, and echo over the tarnished statues and fountains in the Jardin des Tuileries.

"Headless history," shouted Heap of Words.

"Ghosts of Wounded Knee," said Aloysius.

Today the cobblestones were stained once more with the blood of fascist demonstrators, more than twenty men were shot dead by the Garde Républicaine, Horse Guards, and thousands more were wounded, some gravely, in the push to cross the Pont de la Concorde to the Chambre des Députés of the Third French Republic.

"Heads to spare," shouted Heap of Words.

"Bloody gutters," said Aloysius.

Anishinaabe natives praised prominent totemic entities in the ancient past, and later were counted out as primitives by explorers and colonial emissaries. The woodland natives of the fur trade were never republics with royal parks, statues, cold stone palaces, curly wigs, or bloody guillotines.

Natives have endured the reigns of terror, discoveries, the ravages of colonial diseases, churchy collusions, and savage empires with totemic stories, entities, and primeval trade routes.

The First Anishinaabe Entity evolved with the native diplomacy of continental liberty and the virtue of natural motion and trade routes, and that era of ethos and liberty was cursed and misused in the royal course of con-

cocted discoveries, slavery, and the crude commerce of at least five predatory empires, the French, British, Spanish, Dutch, and the Americans.

"Russians dickered," shouted Heap of Words.

The Second Entity was the wicked contest of the empire fur trade and
the decimation of totemic animals, a treachery of fashion that has never
been relieved in native memories or put right in visionary stories.

"Wounded totems," shouted Heap of Words.

The Third Entity was La Grande Paix de Montréal, the Great Peace of
Montréal, a native mainstay and singular treaty signed forever by our native
ancestors and never forsaken in the diplomatic trade of the voyageurs and
royal bigwigs of New France.

The Anishinaabe Fourth Entity was a charter of default that was first
put to name almost seventy years ago with a federal promissory treaty that
separated native families and established a metes and bounds reservation.

The White Earth Reservation was started with a tricky treaty in 1867, a
crude separatism, and a year later slavery and separatism were not put right
with the ratification of the Fourteenth Amendment to the Constitution
of the United States. The amendment clearly stated that persons born
in the country were citizens, but that did not include natives, who were
restricted by federal agents and were not recognized as citizens until ten
years ago, after generations of political deceit and timber barons. Natives
were drafted as aliens to serve in the First World War in France. Now we
live as native exiles with heirs of the fur trade in a nation of great artistic
visions and liberty.

Nathan Crémieux warned us to be elusive and wary of the *manifestants*
or fascist demonstrators as we set out in the cold wind to view the marvelous *Nymphéas*, or Water Lilies, by Claude Monet, and a new exhibition
of realistic art at the Musée de l'Orangerie.

France had declared five governments in the past two years, and there
had been more than a dozen political protests in the past month, so the
easygoing notice that afternoon was surreal and situational, the constant
ferment of nationalists, communists, royalist, and fascists over political
chicanery and economic depression, and even with great impressionist
flowers in mind we could not avoid the public outcry of the fascists at
Place de la Concorde.

Barges were docked in perfect rows on the quay, new diesel trucks fouled the air, a man pushed a cart of miniature sailboats, and pedestrians moseyed on the bridge. The loyal pigeons circled a woman on a bench, and there were moody crowds of anxious gray men on the square near the Fontaine des Fleuves, Luxor Obelisk, and the Hôtel de Crillon.

The Water Lilies and *Les Peintres de la Réalité*, a new exhibition of seventeenth century painters of reality at the Musée de l'Orangerie, were sidetracked that cold afternoon in a civil war with the party fever of *anciens combattants*, or war veterans, the Solidarité Française, Croix de Feu, Camelots du Roi, and other fascist leagues that unnerved the moody Cartels des Gauches, the leftist democratic coalition of socialists and others. The fascists goaded the police and Gendarmerie Nationale, and browbeat Édouard Daladier to resign after only a few days as the prime minister.

There were no bright flower carts painted by Louis Marie de Schryver, no children tasting grapes on a park bench, no elegant schoolboys at a market by Victor Gabriel Gilbert, and no fashionable women on the square in wispy black with thin waists and tight shoes portrayed by Jean Béraud. There were only the gray, gray, gray fascist faces under caps and fedoras on Avenue des Champs-Élysées.

"Fascists bloody gray," shouted Heap of Words.

"The *anciens combattants* are renegade war veterans in fedoras," said Aloysius. "We fought with some of those veterans in the cause of liberty, and now they march with the blue shirts to knock down democracy."

My brother circled the fountain twice and then moved slowly through the gray crowds with slight salutes, the ironic gestures of neutrality, but the fascists hardly noticed our presence in the hue and cry of the uncertain outcome of a coup d'état. We secured a park bench on a gravel path at the very edge of the crowds and lost count of the posters and shouts and bywords of revolution near the Hôtel de Crillon and United States Embassy.

We watched a woman in a giant brown hat, bright red lips, and a black cape care for the birds in the park. A century earlier she might have worn a fur hat, and with no totemic memory of the beaver. The rock pigeons cooed and waited on the back rail of the bench for the trusted feather doctor to treat minor wounds with a touch of olive oil. The steady healer of the birds never seemed to notice the columns of gray fascists that gathered on the square and from every direction, Avenue Gabriel, Rue Boissy d'Anglas, Rue Royale, and Rue de Rivoli. The sublime woman and eternal pigeons of the royal fountains and gardens were at home with the daily crowds, riots, and demonstrations.

"Pigeons of mercy," shouted Heap of Words.

Moneyed Americans and colonial expatriates were shunned at times as sexual and literary tourists, the cause of moral corruption, and the fascists, strange royalists, and the knotty religious right berated the exiles and émigrés as the cause of cultural setbacks, debauchery, and decline of the economy. The Solidarité Française and other fascist leagues of the overnight revolution were nothing more than a crusade of political envy, fishy religious morals, and revenge to ruin a democracy only to reign with nostalgia over the miserable remains of an extravagant empire.

The Anishinaabe were once fugitives of the colonial fur trade and outlasted native traditions and totemic ethos. Yet some natives were favored, considered exceptional warriors in romance stories of the noble savage, and praised for the grasp of primitive decency.

Aloysius demonstrated his courage as a noble savage that afternoon by carving the head of Léon Blum from a rough block of birch at the fitful start of a coup d'état. The nearby fascists were curious but did not recognize the likeness of the enemy, the socialist editor of the newspaper *L'Humanité* and prominent Parisian Jew. Blum, we learned later, was one of only a few deputies who did not desert the Assemblée Nationale in the face of fascist violence. He marched with factory workers and maintained a humane distinction of political power, the "conquest of state power," and the "exercise of state power."

Aloysius repeated the great distinctions of state power the first time he raised the puppet politician, and carried out the strong political pitch of liberty in every contest with other humans and hand puppets. Léon Blum, the latest hand puppet, scolded several wounded fascists that night at the Café Weber on Rue Royale.

Paris was our refuge of art and liberty, a stranger but never our enemy, and the great democracy was not some overdue cause of vengeance to right the legacy of colonial rule or indict the heirs of lusty voyageurs who decimated totemic animals in the fur trade.

"Fascists furriers," shouted Heap of Words.

Soldiers arrived with horsedrawn field kitchens and parked the carts near Le Grand Palais. The huge kettles steamed, and the stench of pig fat and cabbage wafted over the park and down the River Seine. The street lamps were out and later the demonstrators built barricades with park benches, wagons, ladders, and vehicles on the circle, and shouted the comeback name Chiappe, Chiappe, the return of Chiappe.

Jean Chiappe had been sacked three days earlier as the premier conservative and patriotic Préfet de Police in Paris. He was pictured in a car on the front page of *La Croix*, and the fascists who surrounded the car were roused with the mere notice of his name. The newspaper picture revealed a crowd of men with fedoras raised, a salute to the severe nationalist.

Chiappe was the monarch of *érupation*, the royal agent of purity, and the dutiful rightist banned carpet beating, sexy postcards, goats in the city, pederasty, and erotic books sold by the *bouquinistes* along the River Seine. Paris became a cold stranger that night, and the gray fascists brushed us aside as foreigners in a scene of hatred and violence at the ancient theatre of vengeance on the Place de la Concorde.

"Mirage of empires," shouted Heap of Words.

"Adolf Hitler and the Nazi Party are the only real enemies of democracy and the French Third Republic," shouted Aloysius.

The gray fascists were crazed and never heard a word of our counter-protests, and later they carried away the last park benches to build more barricades and set fire to a bus near the Luxor Obelisk. We were distraught about the brutal rage of the fascists and waited too long to escape from the riot and violence. Slowly we pushed our way across Avenue Gabriel to the main entrance of the Hôtel de Crillon.

The floral scent of a modern perfume overcame the acrid traces of gunpowder and bloody body odors of the wounded in the lobby of the Hôtel de Crillon. A stylish young woman with a furry collar was frightened by the sound of gunfire and had dropped a bottle of perfume as she hurried into the hotel, and the heavy scent was immediately recognized as L'Aimant, the magnet, one of the most recent perfumes concocted by François Coty, the very cozy fascist millionaire who had funded the Solidarité Française and other rightist enterprises of the contrived patriotic coup d'état.

"Fragrance fascists," shouted Heap of Words.

A picture of horse drawn wagons with a detachment of *mitrailleuses*, or military machine guns, was published on the front page of *L'Écho de Paris*. The headline in the late edition declared "Les anciens combattants entrent en scene," or the war veterans entered the scene, apparently with machine guns for the demonstration. The report was false, a rightist ruse, but the Préfecture de Police, Garde Républicaine, and the Gendarmerie Nationale were rightly worried about the report of machine guns and a deadly outcome, and that alone might have been the provocation to charge and shoot the gray fascists of the Solidarité Française and other fanatics and fascists on the Pont de la Concorde.

"Chiappe purged the pigeons," said Aloysius.

The familiar crack and stamp of gunshots that night revived our memories of the war. My combat nightmares were held back only by creating countervisionary stories. Aloysius raised his hands above his head, wagged his fingers, and told a story about magic flight over the ruins of a watery landscape. "My giant shadow reached across the desolation and changed the shapes and hues of the country. My songs were in the clouds, my great shadow became a blue raven."

"Heirs of the fur trade," said Heap of Words. "I am the wordy heir, the tease of words, the chance of drift, and my words are totemic, never set, the original totems of tease and motion. My words are not worries on a stage or in a story, and my words are more than sound, more than whispers, more than an overnight gist or pitch of a coup d'état."

Words, words, words are never steady sounds, but words create images and memories, the touch of a healer on a park bench, impressionistic art, flowers, riots, gunfire, and the stink of cabbage are the theatres, the catwalks, and the bandstands of words in my letters. My words are forever in totemic motion, and always ready to mock the poseurs of revolutions and national banners.

Doctor Charles Bove, the surgeon at the American Hospital of Paris, walked out of the Hôtel de Crillon, ducked for cover, and then hurried past the fascist retreat and police gunfire on his way to care for the wounded at the nearby Café Weber on Rue Royale.

We tracked the doctor on the street and boasted that we were combat veterans and steady under fire. He stared at me, and then in silence pointed at the surreal scene of bloody fascists plonked outside on cane café chairs between the round tables at the Café Weber.

"Yes, *Indiens d'Amérique* artist, writer, and veterans," my brother told the nervous waiters. "Monsieur Thomas Wolfe, vous savez," said a waiter.

Thomas Wolfe, the author of *Look Homeward Angel*, and the Café Weber was his favorite when he attended the theatre. Wolfe would have torn a shirtsleeve to stop the bleeding of a fascist at his favorite restaurant.

Doctor Bove treated the gunshot wounds, and the waiters tore table-cloths for tourniquets and bandages as the frantic fascists rushed past the terrace toward La Madeleine. Their breathy chatter of vengeance was a disguise of retreat from the furious try of a coup d'état to end the French Third Republic. Only a few hours earlier the very same fascists joined a crowd of headstrong street singers of "La Marseillaise" on the Rue Royale.

"Conquest teasers," shouted Heap of Words.

The fascists were the delivery boys of a moral crusade, a crude nationalism that crashed in the blood of envy and vengeance about midnight, and with no humor, no art or poetry of destiny, and revealed no sense of tease or mercy. The fascist riots never were a revolution, and the bloody gray men that stained the cobblestones were lost overnight by chance and the curse of vengeance, the deadend politics of nostalgia, and distorted royal memories.

The Solidarité Française deserted most of the wounded on the bloody cobblestones, and at first light only two names of the dead lasted overnight on the square. Gali Meziane fought with the North African Brigade and was mortally wounded in the rush over the Pont de la Concorde to the Chambre des Députés at the Palais Bourbon. Raymond Rossignol, a member of the Jeunesses Patriotes, or Patriotic Youth, died in the same assault, and he was honored as a fascist martyr because his father was one of the founders of the Union of National Combatants.

Claude Monet, Louis Marie de Schryver, Victor Gabriel Gilbert, Jean Béraud, and other painters were celebrated in museums, and their portrayals last forever in the memory of the Place de la Concorde. Yet the secure scenes of water lilies, wispy women in black, soldiers in red trousers, grand bouquets, rosy children, healthy market scenes, and the bright hues of royalty never revealed the bloody revolution or the steadfast grudges of fascism and vengeance.

» 6 «

COMIC LADDER

Thursday, 2 August 1934

Nika Montezuma could easily charm a mongrel and dodge our steady
teases of the prominent names she raves about at every camp and party.
She leaned closer to me at the table, raised her goosey neck, touched my
hand, and with wavy gestures told marvelous stories in the masterly way
of natives and early fur traders, the pace of overnight character coups,
surprise take backs, and rightly overplayed with hearsay that gentle night
at Les Deux Magots.

Nika first observed the death today of a distant relative, Paul von Hindenburg, the President of Germany, and then she set in motion fantastic
stories about Henri Bergson, the steadfast philosopher of evolution, memory, and liberty; Sigmund Freud, the dream master; Carlos Montezuma,
the native activist and medical doctor; Francis Picabia, the hasty cubist
of clowns and comic contrivances; and Amedeo Modigliani, the earthy
painter of high necks, thin faces, and unworldly eyes. The trade stories
were entwined, elusive at just the right moments, and we waited on every
word and gesture to catch sight of the seductive motions of her lovely
elevated neck.

"This is my native presence, and nothing more of the past than this
instance, a single moment of memory," she declared that balmy night over
white wine and a buttery herb omelet. "I create the *élan vital* of family
and friends, an intuitive experience, and the names in my stories are more
spirited than any federal policy, bloody baptismal records, or cemetery
markers. You must agree that my truth stories are always timely, that a
distant relative of empire nobility died today, Paul von Hindenburg."

Solomon Heap of Words countered with a rundown story that he was
the mighty heir of the big chief of France, Napoleon Bonaparte. "My empire is the conspiracy of war and the *élan vital* of nobility."

"Big chief of dead metaphors," said Nika.

Nika wore a loose creamy blouse and the nape of her neck was bare and moist in the shadows. Truly she must have been one of the high neck models, dashed with rouge, who posed for the lusty Modigliani. She was silent, demure about her time with the artist a year before he died, and then explained that her nickname was the only word for the great Canada goose in the language of the Anishinaabe.

"Migratory with a long neck," said Aloysius.

Nika stretched her high neck as a tease and calmly continued the boasts of prominent relations with trade stories about her father, who had escaped from Germany to France, and then in the late eighteen hundreds was a fur trade exile at Grand Portage on Lake Superior.

"My father was related to Luise Schwickart, mother of the military officer and president, and that was our only connection to the stern and noble descent of the Prussian Paul von Hindenburg."

"Prussian poachers," shouted Heap of Words.

"Furry trade stories," said Olivier.

"Beaver pelt royalty," said Coyote.

"Barrique, my native Métis mother, portaged with Jacob Jude Weil and a mongrel named Highbrow from Grand Portage to Gunflint Lake," said Nika. "My parents stayed together in a remote cabin and conceived me forty years ago, and they never married. Jacob told me that he read novels by James Fenimore Cooper in German and French, and that literary romance was the start of a portage that lasted forever." She turned away and was silent for a moment, and then portrayed her father as a "solitary trapper at the dead end of the fur trade, but he lives in native liberty with a Star of David."

Nika raised a thin gold necklace and displayed the Star of David. "My father gave me this for painting the ancestral star with six points on the bow of his canoe. Anang was his portage nickname, the word for star in Anishinaabe. He changed his name to Jacob Jude Anang at the start of the First World War to avoid persecution as a German. Yes, my mother was given the ironic nickname for an oak wine cask, a native tease of envy, because she was small, slender, and a strong voyageur."

Nika said Highbrow was "my loyal friend for nineteen years, and then one winter night she walked out of the cabin and never returned. Highbrow died alone with no trace in the heavy snow, and she taught me that memories must continue in the motion of stories, not in the stone markers of the dead." Names on gravestones were a double death, and with no sense of motion, no tease or season of stories.

"Motion of memory," shouted Heap of Words.

Les Deux Magots has always been a grapevine post, a culture of motion and stories, political, showy and ironic, and this was our night of native memories. The statues of Les Deux Magots traders, seated on ornate pedestals and dressed in oriental robes and blunt shoes, one decorated with a totemic crane, surely overheard every tease, promise, political setback, and republic turnaround stories for more than sixty years. The Magots statues heard the literary hearsay of James Joyce, Simone de Beauvoir, André Breton, Pablo Picasso, Jean-Paul Sartre, Ernest Hemingway, Man Ray, Harry Crosby, Djuna Barnes, and many, many others on the aesthetic turns of modern literature.

Black Elk imagined that the decorative metal bells on the corners of the two pedestals would ding, ding, ding over and over with "the take of fake healers, cheapjack words of praise and honor, the warmongers, ruse of tyrants, and rush of gobbledygook."

"Dings of deception," shouted Heap of Words.

Les Deux Magots would have heard the political rows over the death of Paul von Hindenburg and the end of nobility in the military. Chancellor Hitler terminated the laws and constitution and sacrificed political parties and the *Sturmtruppen*, storm troopers, otherwise named the savage Brownshirts, to reign with absolute power over Germany. The Magots heard the news that Herr Hitler ordered the execution of hundreds of veterans and Brownshirts, and the number of dead grew with each evolved story of the Nazi Party. The purge of conservatives, nationalists, and other enemies was named the Night of the Long Knives. Les Deux Magots and every person there must have heard the nightly double ding, ding, ding, ding of the many bells.

"Ernst Röhm a dead dong," said Olivier.

"Gestapo scary dongs," shouted Heap of Words.

Nathan praised *La peste brune*, or *The Brown Plague* by Daniel Guérin, a new book about the grave threat of fascism in Germany. Most of the chapters, published last year in the Socialist newspaper *Le Populaire*, warned the world of the radical dissent and backhanded conversion of detached young people to racism, nationalism, and the Nazi Party. Guérin described the dire politics of workers, socialists, peasants, and the homoerotic young campers that he encountered around the country, and declared that the rise of fascism was not a cause of courage, trust, or heroic liberty, but rather a desolate sense of defeat, decay, and atrophy, a fascism of failure and the absence of cultural irony.

"Waiting for a führer," shouted Heap of Words.

Les Deux Magots, the grandiose traders, listened to a short selection translated from *La peste brune*, and not a single ding, ding, ding, dong of bunk or blather was heard at the end of the reading by Nathan Crémieux.

> *Yes, we have been tardy in our visits with friends to see what life is like in the other Germany. The abyss is very wide, wider than a frontier, and a much deeper separation than an ocean.*
>
> *"The confederation or unification of the people," the fascists proclaim, but the people of Germany have never been more divided, two irreconcilable factions or camps.*
>
> *So, on this rainy day in the other Germany, along the highway from Cologne to Düsseldorf, imagine two young men walking side by side, bare legs, worn boots, curly hair, and black whiskers on their scraggy chins.*
>
> *Not possible, you are French, they observed. Finally we can talk with no fear of informers. When two young men recognize my sentiments they revealed the insignia, hidden in the lining of their coats, of the Communist Party.*

Nika told trade and heart stories in the spirit of natural motion. We teased native storiers, as every story must be teased to stay in natural motion and to scare the pretenders, shamans, and tradition fascists out of bully time and despotism, but we never cheated or dared to betray heart stories.

"No churchy peals," shouted Heap of Words.

Nika and several other students climbed a ladder to a theatre window to hear lectures by Henri Bergson at the Collège de France. The afternoon orations were crowded with the rush of fashionable women, echelons of the leisure class and habitués of original thoughts from the poet of presence. The classy women arrived much earlier than the students and occupied most of the seats in the theatre hours before the scheduled lectures.

"I perched at the open window once a week and never wrote a single note," boasted Nika. "Bergson created a sense of motion in his lectures, not liturgy, poses, or a daily diary, and seminar notes were never expected by the philosopher and poet of praise, intuition, memory, and duration."

Nika recounted several times that Bergson pointed at her in the window, and said, "She climbs a comic ladder, *échelle comique*, to listen, and never with a note or précis of my lectures. Some students laughed because they thought the comment was critical, maybe ironic, but he was amused by my response, that his lectures were the comic steps of the present, not the count, count, count of minutes, but the bout of the past in memory, and radical change in every moment of duration." Bergson smiled and surely noticed the gold necklace with the Star of David.

"Précis of trade stories," shouted Heap of Words.

"Sigmund Freud carried me away in dreams," chanted Nika. "My heart floated in his stories about dreams, and his touch of motion escaped with me in the morning light." She closed her eyes and ended the story with a dreamy whisper of his name.

"Carlos Montezuma truly inspired my mother with his progressive native ideas, of course, not to overturn her great love for my father, but rather for me to discover a new fur trade presence in the world," said Nika. "Paris became my post of promises at the end of the First World War."

"We were here in the twenties," declared Aloysius.

"I was a student at the Sorbonne," said Nika.

"We should have met you then," said Olivier.

"Modigliani died at the end of the war, not by gas or cannons, but of tuberculosis after weeks of high fever and headaches," said Nika. "I was one of the many women who cared for him at night, even though he hardly remembered our names."

"Anonymous portraits," shouted Heap of Words.

"Montezuma died three years later of the same disease, tuberculosis, and my mother wrote to assure me that the motion of his spirit touched my heart, and sometimes the sway of his words seem to quiver in my body," she said and then raised her hands, as if to balance his ideas of native résistance and liberty. "He wrote in the first issue of *Wassaja* that without discrimination there would be no Indian Bureau, and the name Indian would be obsolete."

"Native liberty," shouted Heap of Words.

"Everything must always be in motion, seasons, names, identities, histories, you know about that, and the trade stories of this very moment is in motion," said Nika.

Carlos Montezuma, she murmured, "lives forever in my heart and memories, he is my sense of duration, and my mother encouraged me to meet him for the first at the Eighth Annual Conference of the Society of American Indians in Minneapolis in early October 1919."

Nika traveled by wagon from Gunflint Lake to Grand Marais, and then boarded the Northern Pacific Skally Line to Minneapolis. She waited in the lobby of the old Saint James Hotel on Washington and Helen to meet the great activist and native doctor. Charles Alexander Eastman, one of the other great native doctors, smiled as he walked through the lobby, and a parade of other famous native progressives made their way to the conference.

"I was at a loss for words when Doctor Montezuma walked slowly through the lobby, a strong man with a wide smile and melancholy eyes," said Nika. "Never been in the city, never traveled on a train, never visited a hotel or waited in a lobby, and my excitement that morning was expressed only with silence, but he seemed to understand my situation, and gestured that we walk together into the conference room of natives from around the country. That moment was the start of my heart stories, a short walk that granted me the right to bear his esteemed name."

Nika was teased at the conference, of course, because of her name, and mostly in the presence of the doctor. She had already learned that teases in good company were hardly wounds, rather the best native teases were poetic bruises that mostly become memorable scenes and stories.

"That was the only encounter with the doctor and spirit of my name, a meander from the lobby to the conference, and a few precious words of praise," said Nika. "Carlos Montezuma died four years later, and my heart was never the same. Paris could not heal my loneliness, my namesake was in the clouds, and after several weeks of despair Henri Bergson mentioned in a lecture the notion of *élan vital*, the creative spirit and mood of experi-

ence, or the intuitive sense of motion and liberty. Montezuma never met
my parents, you know, but his spirit was always with me in stories about my
father, and my mother forever boasted that his name was mine by nature."

"Montezuma heart story," said Coyote.

"Montezuma tease," shouted Heap of Words.

Theodore Hudon Beaulieu, our uncle, was elected vice president of
the Society of American Indians, but we had returned from the war two
months earlier and were not in a state of mind to muster the progressive
politics of native rights and citizenship at a conference.

The Tomahawk, a weekly newspaper published by our favorite uncle,
Augustus Hudon Beaulieu, reported on the front page, 9 October 1919,
that a "college bred man, the professional man, the business man, the
Carlisle and Hampton graduate and a large number from the lower walks
of life, but all bent and absorbed in the one great fundamental principle
of American citizenship for Indians." I read that much out loud with disgust and never forgot parts of the story in the very paper that we had once
sold at the Ogema Station. *The Tomahawk* reported the turnout of the
"college bred man" and others "from the lower walks of life," but never
once mentioned the native veterans who had served and died with honor
in the First World War.

"Bent over natives," shouted Heap of Words.

Nika never forgot the words of Carlos Montezuma at the conference,
"What is good for the goose is good for the gander. What is good for my
son is good for the father, mother and the rest of the children."

"Nika goose neck," shouted Heap of Words.

Montezuma was right about the goose, gander, rights, and liberty, and
we had already refused to accept the federal invitation and conditions as
veterans to become citizens of the United States. The federal government
had ignored the Fourteenth Amendment that defined a citizen as a person
born in the United States. Natives were betrayed by the nation, separated
on federal reservations, and denied equal protection, liberty, and the ordinary rights of citizens in a constitutional democracy. We actually evaded
the political controversy of citizenship and became native émigrés in a
culture of liberty in Paris.

Charles Alexander Eastman was the principal speaker at the convention of the Society of American Indians. Nika recited selected sections of

his lecture that night, fifteen years later, at Les Deux Magots. "We Indians laid the foundation of freedom and equality and democracy long before any white people, and this country was absolutely free to every race. I want to say that we have contributed to this country, but they have not given us the credit. We developed the principles of democracy, and our people have never gone back on their diplomacy, their word once given always remained."

Aloysius had not painted for several months when we returned to the reservation, and the scenes in my stories were downcast by memories of combat. We barely survived the honors, praise, and glory stories of our service in the war, and moved to the solitude of a remote cabin on the shoreline of Bad Boy Lake to escape the night terrors and sounds of the war.

Bad Boy Lake has been on my mind for the past fifteen years, the brush of bright colors, maple, birch, and sumac that autumn of our return from France. The shimmer of golden birch on the water, and the sway of leaves were abstract scenes with the slightest breeze. My brother was moved every day by the motion of natural colors, and after hours of silent meditation on the shoreline, he painted blue ravens on the surge of waves.

Misaabe and his incredible mongrel healers lived in a shack nearby. The old healer watched us at a distance for several days and then waved his arms, an invitation to eat supper at his cabin. He was small, never wore shirts, ate in silence, and later told stories about the fur trade, the royal war against animals. The fur butchery was directly connected to his question, "How did the animals and birds survive the war in France?"

Native stories should create shadows and the sense of colors in motion, but every sound in the cabin at night, the mere crack of a beam, and the last insects on the lantern, became a menace of shadows and sounds, the curse of war memories.

Misaabe teased me with hand shadows on the ceiling, monsters in the beams, and without a pause encouraged me to continue with stories about the most miserable scenes of the war. I told the healer about the soldiers and horses that exploded in an artillery attack, shards of bone, bloody horse hair in the trees, scraps of unshaved cheeks, morsels of tongues, toes, ears, and organs covered the tents, and the faces of other soldiers. I could not erase from my mind the hordes of blue bottle flies that swarmed on the chunks of bloody flesh, and later the maggots created the ecstasy of motion in the putrid mush, bone and muscle of horses and humans.

Mona Lisa, one of the mongrel healers, moved closer and leaned against my thigh. Nosey, the second mongrel healer bumped my waist and noisy belly. Ghost Moth licked my hands and rested at my side. Misaabe encouraged me to imagine the actual motion of the maggots that devoured the bloody scene and then create new stories that fly away with the nightmare. The bloody scenes shimmered with maggots and then vanished in flight, and mostly the deadly memories of war ended that night with the touch of the mongrel healers, and with stories of bloody soldiers, greedy maggots, and thousands of flies in natural motion.

"Les Deux Maggots," chanted Heap of Words.

"Fur trade maggots," said Aloysius.

Nika was delighted by the native teases and stories, and ordered two more bottles of Clos St Jérome, Vin Blanc, and a selection of regional cheeses. She dedicated the first salute to her father, Jacob Jude Anang, a solitary man who worried more about fascism and war than the end of totemic animals in the fur trade. "My father carried out the tradition of the trade in every season, but beaver, marten, and other animals were decimated, and there were too many lonesome hunters and trappers in search of furry animals, an eternal search of the romantic voyageurs."

Nika was a new student at Sorbonne University at about the same time that Aloysius was exhibiting his watercolors of blue ravens and my poems and stories were published at the Galerie Crémieux. She had met other war veterans, and might have noticed the *mutilés de guerre* at one of our spirited encampments ten years earlier on the River Seine.

Carlos Montezuma, Charles Alexander Eastman, and the Society of American Indians had not considered the art of totemic fauvism or cubism, but abstract scenes of the fur trade, floppy beaver felt hats, broken natives, wild rice and liberty, and the count of white pine might have reached a more dynamic audience, more than the bent of college breeds or the lower native walkers at annual conferences. Native stories were the sway of liberty in every abstract scene of creation, by trade, by tease, and obstructed the absence of cultural irony.

"Nickname irony," shouted Heap of Words.

Nika had arrived as a student in Paris several years before we returned

to the White Earth Reservation with the passage of the Indian Civilization Act in 1924. Fortunately, she had never been removed to a federal
reservation and was never counted in the treaty remains of a constitutional
democracy. She was born a natural citizen at Gunflint Lake, close to the
border with Canada.

Nika was a serious reader, educated at home by her parents, and later
attended a nearby country school; but not many natives ever studied at
colleges. Her father read out loud daily selections from *Le Dernier des
Mohicans*, by James Fenimore Cooper, and she repeated every sentence
first in French and then translated every scene into English. She was highly
recommended by educated natives, and that was evidence enough to be
accepted at Sorbonne University.

"French was never easy, of course, and my fur trade patois was at times
more of a handicap than an advantage," said Nika. "I studied hard for
three months and was ready to attend public events, lectures, movies, and
theatres to hear the actual performance in French." She served the last
bottle of wine and told more display stories about Paris.

"Shadow dancer," shouted Heap of Words.

"The *Relâche* ballet by Francis Picabia was advertised in the *Journal
de l'Instantanéisme* in November 1924," she said, and then leaned closer.
Heap of Words reached out to touch her high neck, but she smiled and
turned away. "The word *instantanéisme*," she explained, "means perpetual
movement, or action, in translation, and that same sense of motion is at
the heart of native stories."

Francis Picabia, the cubist artist of pretensions and ironic scenes,
mocked the ghosts of certainty, teased the masters of portrait poses, and
fractured the tidy ships of mores and fortunes. The theatre sway of outright
liberty outlasted cultures of dead reason and war, and much later the feral
scenes of surrealism, the absurd, and tricky shadows of Dadaists became
the wild and sardonic season of the *Relâche* ballet, and with music composed by Erik Satie.

Nika forgot the actual night of the *Relâche* ballet at the Théâtre des
Champs-Élysées on Avenue Montaigne, and arrived a day late, only to
learn that the ballet had been canceled. The word *relâche* was still posted
on the door, an interval, rest, or slacken. The translation of the word
relâche was doubled with the delayed event, a sick dancer, and the name

of the ballet. Later, she was told that the actual name *Relâche* ballet was a literary tease of André Breton and surrealism, and a mockery of Dadaism and Tristan Tzara.

"The advertisement for the ballet clearly revealed the irony, *et la queue du chien*, and the tail of the dog, by Francis Picabia. The next line was directed at the surrealists, *apportez des lunettes noires et de quoi vous boucher les oreilles*, bring black glasses and whatever you use to stop your ears."

"Hear nothing, see nothing," said Coyote.

Maybe the native sense of chance can be compared to the absurd staged as a ballet, but the outcome is never the same. Native stories of chance are creative, and in visionary motion, not just the staged performance of a script, score, or surreal liturgy.

Nika described the *Relâche* ballet as "absurd, a wild riff of style, a counterballet, and in that sense the dance moves were similar to the native trickster and fur trader stories on a winter night at Gunflint Lake." Most trickster and fur trade stories start with action, *instantanéisme*, continuous motion, and the characters are never certain, an absurd and ironic reversal of the real, sometimes animals and birds, totemic characters, and the fantastic motion pauses but never ends. Some lusty trickster stories reveal the contradictions of nature and reason, such as the giant penis that topples over unusable when erect and ready.

Nika told similar stories about native motion, chance, and trickster erections at a seminar discussion on memory and duration, but the other students were hesitant to enter the conversation, "because they overlooked the obvious, the irony of staged erections, or the satire of an absurd ballet, and, of course, the absurdity of true stories."

The *Relâche* ballet was staged with a backdrop of more than three hundred bright lights on reflective cones. Erik Satie composed the music, and the dancers were on stage with *Entr'acte*, between the acts, a short satirical movie with a cast of avantgarde cubist and surrealist artists, Picabia, Satie, George Auric, Man Ray, Marcel Duchamp, Jean Börlin, and the filmmaker René Clair.

Nika said the "dancers were distorted by the bright lights, an avalanche of lights, and that was hardly ironic surrealism night or day. The ballet was precise, obscure, and absurd, and maybe that was the surreal achievement when Francis Picabia and Erik Satie drove around stage at the end of the production in a small Citroën Trèfle."

"Citroën surrealism," said Aloysius.

Henri Bergson, the great professor, was present in the spirit of every story that night at Les Deux Magots. Nika learned about the ideas of evolution, existence, and memory from *L'évolution créatrice*, and she recited an excerpt from the book, "My memory is there, which conveys something of the past into the present. My mental state, as it advanced on the road of time, is continually swelling with the duration which it accumulates."

"Chance and tease," shouted Heap of Words.

Nika paused to salute the philosopher, and then she continued the recitation on evolution, "The truth is that we change without ceasing, and that the state itself is nothing but change. The more we study the nature of time, the more we shall comprehend that duration means invention, the creation of forms, the continual elaboration of the absolutely new."

"Ditto, ditto, ditto," shouted Heap of Words.

"Mock my duration," said Coyote.

The subject of creation, presence, duration, and native memory received many salutes that night, and not once did anyone hear the telltale ding, ding, ding, ding of Les Deux Magots.

CULTURAL MERCY

Tuesday, 25 June 1935

André Gide, Henri Barbusse, Aldous Huxley, Bertolt Brecht, Lion Feucht-wanger, André Malraux, Robert Musil, Heinrich Mann, Isaac Babel, Boris Pasternak, and many other prominent authors were saluted over four humid days at Le Congrés International des Écrivains pour la Défense de la Culture, the first International Congress of Writers for the Defense of Culture, and in the face of many enemies, the Soviet Union, and the Nazi Party.

"Culture on the run," shouted Heap of Words.

Aloysius created abstract images of the great authors, a stream of literary envoys with pen and paper but no horses, canes, or pistols. The nightly canons of writerly talk, slant of literary politics, and cultural codes of realism were broadcast on several loudspeakers outside the Palais de la Mutualité on Rue Saint Victor.

André Gide, the novelist and elder communist, started the literary conference with a tribute to books. "Literature has never been more alive," he declared with a strong voice. "Never has so much been written and printed in France and in all civilized countries. Why then do we keep hearing that our culture is in danger?" The danger is in nationalism, not the clouds, and in the stories of veterans who endured the evil and barbarity of the First World War.

The art deco auditorium was overcrowded with more than three thousand sweaty authors and spectators. The champions of the novel were neatly seated, and others were crammed in the aisles, ready to stand forever with literature and communists over the fascists and royalists, and with the shifty Soviets over the Germans.

Aloysius portrayed Gide with a huge head slanted over a willowy body, tapered arms, and an elongated nose with round smoky spectacles. The enormous hands and bony fingers were folded over stacks of books, books, books, and the shadow of the author was a wash of faint ravens.

"Grace of shadows," shouted Heap of Words.

Gide was moody, sometimes stagy, but the temper of his commitment to literature, *littérature engagée*, was precise and steady, and the elegant author was celebrated in many newspaper stories the next day. Sylvia Beach, the founder of Shakespeare and Company, praised *Les Faux-Monnayeurs*, *The Counterfeiters*, and loaned me a copy to read.

One narrator in the novel was vexed with the "question of sincerity," and a lost sense of continuity. "Nothing could be more different from me than myself," and at times, "I felt that my life is slowing down, stopping, and I am on the very verge of ceasing to exist." Yes, the narrator endures only in a literary scene, an estranged heir of the revolution with no memory or stories of totemic unions.

Gide wrote, "Edouard dozes; insensibly his thoughts take another direction. He wonders whether he would have guessed merely by reading Laura's letter that her hair was black. He says to himself that novelists, by a too exact description of their characters, hinder the reader's imagination rather than help it, and that they ought to allow each individual to picture their personages to himself according to his own fancy. He thinks of the novel which he is planning and which is to be like nothing else he has ever written. He is not sure that *The Counterfeiters* is a good title."

The novel was an uneasy tease of omniscience, a quirky autobiography of homosexuality, heavy social dialogue, mostly the residue of class cues, and the labor of morality. The characters were tangled in tricky memories on every page, more cubist than estate manners, and with only a trace of natural motion.

"Novelist are revered fakers," said Coyote.

"Fake omniscience," shouted Heap of Words.

Nathan translated in whispers sections of the breathy lecture by Bertolt Brecht, an intense literary artist. "Let us not talk about culture. Let us have only mercy on culture, but let us first have mercy on mankind." Brecht paused, and with a timid smile touched his head, and then continued with his lecture on fascist cruelties and property ownership. "Culture will be saved when mankind is saved. Let us not be carried away and claim man is there for culture, and not culture for man."

"Totemic mercy," shouted Heap of Words.

Henri Barbusse leaned forward at the head table on stage, tightened his narrow, ancient face, touched his thick mustache, and seemed to write steady notes about the lectures of the other authors. I was moved by his presence as a war veteran, and recited a scene from his First World War novel *Le feu, Under Fire*, to my brother, Heap of Words, Pierre, and Nika. War, war, war, and some of the "invalids break the silence, and say the word again under their breath, reflecting that this is the greatest happening of the age, and perhaps of all ages."

"War is not an era," shouted Heap of Words.

"Yes, and here we are in a theatre of great authors at the start of another war," said Pierre. His voice was intense, and several people nearby frowned and waved a finger of silence. Wars have never been sidetracked with shushes, or the recitation of a great poem, and not even with the publication of a novel that breaks the silence.

"Breaks the soldiers," shouted Heap of Words.

"Natives imagined revolutions, and the speedy death of the enemy, but wars were not necessary," said Aloysius. "So, we are the veterans in a war that was never imagined as a revolution, only as a cruel war of vengeance."

Léon Blum, the steady politician and literary critic, reached out to shake hands with the poet Louis Aragon, the renegade surrealist and dandy communist, who wrote the murky poem "Le Front Rouge" with the deadly antisemitic phrase, "Feu sur Léon Blum," in translation, "fire or shoot Léon Blum." Nathan told us the pose of unity was expected, and no less between a socialist statesman and advocate of democracy and a tetchy surreal poet turned Stalinist.

Romain Rolland, the critical novelist and essayist who received the Nobel Prize in Literature twenty years ago for his original literary work, mainly *Jean-Christophe*, a visionary story of music, art, peace, and cultural renaissance that was first published in ten parts as a *roman fleuve*, or river novel, should have been one of the principal speakers at the Congress of Writers for the Defense of Culture; but we were told he was on a literary tour in the Soviet Union.

"Seduced by Stalin," shouted Heap of Words.

Waldo Frank, a novelist, one of the few authors from the United States, was listed as a member of the League of American Writers. Pierre overheard the author praise the assembly of writers who would change the world, and then conceded that Paris was no longer the city of escapists.

"Frank was wordy, and only visionaries and shamans can change the world without fascist traitors, tanks, and conspiracies," said Pierre. "One more getaway communist, a lackluster escape artist of socialist realism."

"We are exiles, not escapists," shouted Nika.

"Stories are in motion, not escapes," said Aloysius.

"Faker Frank," shouted Heap of Words.

"No Stefan Zweig," was my shout.

"No Henry Miller," said Nika.

"Zweig never serves the deceptions of literature," said Nathan. "He praises the mysteries of creation, but not the politics of literature."

The surrealists were taunted, and some were shouted down by the agents of socialist realism, the Stalinists. More than two hundred literary delegates traveled from some thirty countries to warn, cajole, enchant, and chitchat over the politics of literature, and rows of spectators and factions seemed more secure with communist maneuvers than the rapture and ironies of creative literature. The dreary hours of testimony wafted with the heavy stink of beer, garlic, and sweat of bodies out of the auditorium that humid night.

The monotony of socialist realism disabled natural motion and the tease of literature, and ruined native dream songs, irony, and totemic unions in stories. No analogies, poetic visions, or surreal fractures of salon aesthetics were heard by the third day of lectures because the temper of the stony socialist realists drove every creative storier and novelist into silence and literary exile.

"Soviet *wiindigoo*," said Aloysius.

Some of the spectators were beguiled by the sway of socialist realism and authors aligned with the totalitarian and communist chronicles promoted by the Stalinists. My brother was right to name the literary creed of socialist realism a *wiindigoo*, an evil spirit, greedy monster, a cannibal in native stories. Federal agents delivered similar deceits of socialist realism as assimilation policies on the reservation, and declared the false promises of a new cultural realism over the natural motion of native dream songs and fur trade stories.

"Realism is the death of irony," said Coyote.

"Realism is a Soviet Gulag," said Nika.

"Realism of the dead," shouted Heap of Words.

Nathan was very pleased when the German and Jewish novelist Lion
Feuchtwanger was introduced that night. He told me the author was one of
the first to warn the world about the evils of the Nazi Party. They had met
at a dinner party of exiled writers in Sanary-sur-Mer where Feuchtwanger
and many other Jewish authors had escaped the terror of the Brownshirts
and Nazi Party. Nathan owned a vacation house in the same fishing village
between Toulon and Bandol on the Mediterranean Sea.

Nathan gestured to Feuchtwanger when he started his lecture, and
then whispered selected translations to me as we stood at the rail near the
stage. Feuchtwanger talked about the critical practice of historical novels
as a weapon against the violence of the fascists. His smile was confident,
his voice was steady, and his original ideas were moral invitations to the
liberty of literature.

Nathan touched my shoulder when the lecture started, a personal touch
that was meant for me and for the author of *The Oppermanns*. Then he
translated in whispers, "For me, since my start as a writer, I have tried
to write historical novels based on reason, against stupidity and violence.
Perhaps there are some weapons in literature that are more effective, but
my best use of this weapon is the historical novel."

"Liberty is a historical novel," said Pierre.

"Mockery is a weapon," shouted Heap of Words.

"Dream songs beat socialist realism," said Nika.

Aloysius used sweat as a wash on the distorted line drawings of Aldous
Huxley, who was lanky and wore a comic hat, and in the same way he used
sweat as a wash for Lion Feuchtwanger; Anna Seghers, the émigré novelist; Tristan Tzara, the Romanian poet who pranced on the surrealist high
road of antifascism; and Bertolt Brecht, the great poet and playwright of
revolutionary theatre who had escaped the fury of fascists and the bonfires
of books in Germany.

Feuchtwanger was portrayed with a reserved smile stretched over the
entire paper, and Tzara was depicted with thin creases around his eyes,
and contorted behind an enormous monocle. The round pudgy face of
Brecht was a composite of seven unbroken contours. My brother used our
sweat, one by one, to create a shadow wash of ravens around the images
of the great authors.

The determined protestors in the crowd outside raised critical banners and posters. "Stalin Déteste des Juifs," Stalin Hates Jews, was waved back and forth at the entrance, and the authors had to duck under the huge signs to enter the auditorium. An enormous banner on two sticks, "Meurtriers Soviétiques," Soviet Murderers, was carried slowly through the crowd of spectators, and the couriers shouted messages in French and English.

The Committee to Liberate American Captives in the Soviet Union, Le Comité pour Libérer les Captifs Américains dans l'Union Soviétique, was launched last year by the friends and relatives of Americans who had migrated to the Soviet Union at the start of the Great Depression. Hundreds of unemployed farmers, autoworkers, engineers, steel workers, pipe fitters, machinists, barbers, and distraught dreamers with their families were swayed by the crafty propaganda of communist adventures and salaries, and they were persuaded to boot by the enthusiasm of cosmopolitan entertainers and political tourists in the Soviet Union.

George Bernard Shaw broadcast on radio four years ago a "few travelling tips" for skilled machine workers of "good character" who would be hired at new factories in the Soviet Union. The prominent playwright was deceptive, and should have shouted out about the famine, an obvious socialist realism, and the secret police.

Walter Duranty, reporter for the *New York Times* in Moscow, wrote about the great migration of foreigners who were employed and with "plenty to eat." Regrettably the most eager, desperate, and idealistic migrants inspired by the favors of communist propaganda would turn over their passports to work in a totalitarian state as captives.

Nika recognized two protesters as former students from Sorbonne University. She united with the protest and passed out printed leaflets about the captives at factories in the Soviet Union. Pierre raised his right fist and read out loud one side of the leaflet.

Henry Ford is a Criminal and Jew Hater
Named in Mein Kampf

"Ford River Rouge Complex in Dearborn, Michigan, polluted the river, exploited labor, cut wages, rushed the assembly line of the Model T, and then laid off workers in the Great Depression.

"Henry Ford created the greedy bust, ran away with the money, and left the workers and their families in the dust of poverty. The workers protested for support to feed their families, and the police hosed them with cold water and tear gas.

"Henry Ford signed an agreement that same year with Joseph Stalin to build a plant at Gorky on the Volga River east of Moscow to manufacture trucks and Model A cars for a payment of forty million dollars in gold. The gold was mined from the teeth of prisoners and slave laborers in the Soviet Gulags. American migrants were hired to assemble the Model A for the Soviet Union."

The reverse side of the leaflet listed the names of some of the migrants who had worked at the automobile plant, played baseball, learned a new language, and were reported missing, probably captives at a slave labor Soviet Gulag.

Americans Captives in Soviet Gulags
Arthur Abolin
Carl Abolin
Arnold Preedin
Albert Lonn
Joseph Sgovio
Sam Herman
Victor Herman
Robert Robinson
Joe Grondon
Walter Duranty

The last name on the list of migrant captives, Walter Duranty, was an ironic gesture to remind the world that the reporter for the *New York Times* was aware of the secret police, torture, and labor camps, but never wrote about the hundreds of captive Americans.

Gabrielle, one of the protesters, carried a tattered photograph of the Hammer and Sickle, and the Red Stars, two American baseball teams that played at Gorky Park in Moscow. The young factory workers played baseball, a game that must have reminded them of their families in the United States. Stalin exploited the popular image and built several baseball stadiums as Potemkin villages with bats, balls, bases, and communist team

shirts. Three years later the games ended and some of the confident players were arrested by the secret police for espionage. They were tortured
and murdered, and some must have survived as captives in Soviet Gulags.

"Murder at third base," shouted Heap of Words.

"Ford turned to torture," said Pierre.

"Model A Massacre," said Coyote.

"Socialist realism baseball," said Nika.

Nathan was silent as we walked away that night from the auditorium.
The comments of the authors and urgency of the protesters caused him to
worry even more about the persecution of his relatives and friends in Nazi
Germany. Later, over white wine at Les Deux Magots, he told fantastic
ironic stories about literary émigrés.

Nathan started with stories about the nearby Café Mephisto, one of
the popular basement haunts of famous literary émigrés. Bertolt Brecht,
Lion Feuchtwanger, Josef Roth, Heinrich Mann, Alfred Döblin, Walter
Mehring, and others favored the culture of the Deutscher Klub.

Nathan met André Malraux and his wife, Clara, during a book event at
Shakespeare and Company, and remembered Clara saying that Le Front
Populaire was created in ourselves, a natural union, and what remained
was the creation of the movement outside of the heart. Nathan smiled,
and said, "Clara was born a progressive, maybe a communist of the heart,
and she was not yet burdened with the radical politics of Leon Trotsky or
Joseph Stalin."

"Trotsky a chitchat revolutionary," said Coyote.

Native dream songs and totemic stories never turn cursory to serve political fronts, deceptive manners, or the pretenders of omniscience. My
poetic bruises, images, and stories were closer to the conscience of natural
motion than any critical discussions that night, a predictable outcome of
the heavy, deadly beat of socialist realism at the Congress of Writers. My
dreams created me, and my dream songs were forever in the clouds, and
the images were natural motion, never the inside or outside of the tragic
feigns of realism.

"Jesus waits in desperate hearts," said Pierre.

"Fronts are not unions," said Nika.

"Stations of the Cross," shouted Heap of Words.

"Yes, socialist realism stories are the Way of the Cross," said Nathan, and then he burst into laughter. He was never shy to declare his views on politics, but seldom entered our easy mockery of religion and missionaries.

I write to the heart and natural motion, and tease native ethos, relations, and empathy, but not to the socialist realism of federal reservations. My letters are written to the heirs of the fur trade with a sense of natural motion, moral liberty, *littérature engagée*, and then copied and given away on the White Earth Reservation and in Paris.

Natives are hardly passive about the images of totemic unions, dream songs, the deadly tease of shamans, overnight stories of the fur trade, and are downright antagonistic about any pose of absolutes or wiggle words that run closer to the dead end of politics and romance than liberty.

Nika smiled because she learned from her father how to poke holes in poses of the obvious, and a feisty mother bestowed the native tease and sense of natural motion. That much, the tease and how to debunk pretensions with humor and mockery, inspired her to meet great native thinkers, and especially her namesake, Carlos Montezuma.

My letters start with a calendar date, a time of native motion, memories, and chance stories, and more than mere benchmarks or the gravestones of history. My letters to the heirs of the fur trade are stories written to the heart, and forever tease the burdens of time, the counterfeit realism of history, and counter the poses of high culture, reason with no sense of irony or natural motion. My letters reveal the betrayal of native liberty.

Dates and time have no scent, no touch, and no native sense of motion or memory. The chance curves of seasons and ironic stories of creation are never the course of time or political history. The literature of liberty is the creation of ironic deviations, the elusive tease of dream songs, and heart stories of the fur trade forever in motion. The totems of nature and the seasons are never deadend treaties with nations or the sovereign proclamations of empires.

» 8 «

BASTILLE DAY

Sunday, 14 July 1935

Nathan Crémieux arrived early this morning at the gallery with a copy of *L'Humanité* and read out loud the banner headline, "Le peuple de france se lève," The People of France Wake Up. We were awake and ready to march with Le Front Populaire, a coalition of leftists and factory workers to deride and defeat the fascists on Bastille Day.

Aloysius rushed out of the gallery to gather together veterans and our friends, Nika Montezuma, Solomon Heap of Words, Pierre Chaisson, André, Henri, Olivier Black Elk, Coyote Standing Bear, and promised heavyweight politics, revolutionary poseurs, and countercuts with communists, socialists, and union radicals of Le Front Populaire from the venerable Place de la Bastille to Place de la Nation.

"Mock the fascists," shouted Heap of Words.

"Tease the commies," said Coyote.

"Dance with the socialists," said Olivier.

"Honor the *mutilés de guerre*," said André.

Nathan surprised everyone, as we set out to join the demonstration, with a plan to publish *Le Journal Indien*, an original monthly journal dedicated to native literature, art, and culture in Paris. The journal would feature original stories, reviews, and related events at museums in Paris.

"Radicals of *Le Front Indien*," said Aloysius.

"Literary favors," shouted Heap of Words.

"Manifesto between the wars," said Pierre.

"Tributes to liberty," said Nika.

Nathan announced *Le Journal Indien* as we crossed the Pont de l'Archevêché near the Cathédrale Notre Dame. He was feisty, intense, more insistent than usual, and we wondered what had prompted the rush to protest and publish; but we saluted the church, shouted out our praise of the new journal, and somehow, come what may, declared our proposed contributions as we headed to the massive march at Place de la Bastille.

Pierre Chaisson proposed a prose poem to honor the memory of Alfred Dreyfus, the artillery officer who was betrayed by the military and wrongly accused of espionage, and Howling Wolf, the Cheyenne ledger artist who was unjustly incarcerated as a political prisoner with seventy other native leaders and warriors at Fort Marion in Saint Augustine, Florida.

Howling Wolf was fifteen years old at the time of the Sand Creek Massacre on Tuesday morning, 29 November 1864. Colonel John Chivington and the First Regiment of Colorado Volunteers carried out the massacre. Howling Wolf was removed with his father, Eagle Head, ten years later to Fort Marion.

Captain Alfred Dreyfus was a respected officer and a French Jew. He was falsely charged with treason, convicted with forged military evidence and concocted testimony, and unjustly imprisoned for three years at Île du Diable, or Devil's Island, in French Guiana. Ten years later the artillery officer was exonerated by a military commission and returned to service.

Nathan covered the mirrors in the gallery two days ago to mourn the death of Alfred Dreyfus, and today we saluted his memory as the funeral cortège passed nearby on the way to the Cimetière du Montparnasse.

Nika said she would write a creative essay about native dream songs and the motion of *élan vital* in fur trade stories for the new journal. Coyote proposed outsider stories of the many sleight of hand healers, handshake medicine men, and sham shamans in the name of native traditions.

I was ready to publish my new poems and stories, and my brother had already created line drawings and abstract scenes at the fascist riots last year, many more images at the march of leftist workers a few days later, and then late last month he created images of sweaty authors at the Congress of Writers. His images were not easy to determine or define by name, favor, or salon connections, but his abstract scenes always reversed the romantic expectations of museum curators. The images in my stories for the journal were related to totemic unions, and at the same time countered with mockery the crude strategies of fascists, royalists, and the creepy cult of Stalinists.

"Agents of fascism," shouted Heap of Words.

"Royalists and thieves," said Nika.

"Communist favors," chanted Pierre.

"White pine speculators," said Aloysius.

I shouted that natives easily outlive the romance and envy of royalists, capitalists, and communists with totemic unions and ironic trickster stories. Native tricksters mock the envies of tradition, but not with vengeance, separatism, or violence. Rather, trickster stories tease pride, power, shame, and resentments with caricatures, and ridicule nostalgia and heavyhanded conventions.

Our chants and pithy shouts became a casual street choir as we marched together. Our tone of voice changed from one shout and comment to another, and those who overheard our native teases and road show could hardly sing along in unity.

A huge picture of the July Column, Colonne de Juillet, at the Place de la Bastille was printed at the center of the front page of *L'Humanité* and enclosed by news stories about the demonstration of workers in the country. The Spirit of Liberty, *Génie de la Liberté*, the golden winged figure at the top of the column, holds a torch in one hand and broken chains in the other, and stands in the center of the headline "Le fascisme ne passera pas!" Fascism Will Not Be Allowed.

"Great spirit of liberty," shouted Nika.

Aloysius created an abstract blue raven on the top of the column with the caption, "Corbeau de la liberté," the Raven of Liberty. The beak and huge wings of the raven were a wash of blue hues. Nathan embraced my brother, and then declared that the abstract blue raven would be the image on the cover of *Le Journal Indien*.

Our column of natives and wounded veterans merged that historic afternoon with hundreds of other marchers on Rue de Rivoli to the Place de la Bastille. The Soviet Union had sanctioned for the first time a coalition of the socialists, radicals, and communist factions to oust the scary fascists.

"Soviet Wild West," shouted Heap of Words.

The fascists and royalists turned savage last year at the fake coup d'état when they cut the tendons of horses and bombarded the police, and with cobblestones raised near the fountains at Place de la Concorde. The fascist fray was reported around the world, and the patriotic hatred awakened factory workers to declare a general nationwide strike. The strikers shouted the cause of unity, a proletarian unity, and by the end of the day mourned the death of six workers. Thousands of factory workers demonstrated to defend democracy and the liberty of the republic from the curse of royalists and fascists, and yet the communists and socialists never shouted about the rise of Adolf Hitler and the Nazi Party five hundred miles to the east in Nuremberg, Germany.

"Fair weather liberty," shouted Heap of Words.

"Hitler and Stalin are the fascist enemies of the heart," shouted Nathan. He clenched his hands and cursed the tyrants of the Soviet Union and Nazi Germany. His shouts were hardly noticed over the passion and clamor of factory workers on Rue du Faubourg Saint Antoine. Nathan was enraged by the accounts of pogroms and purges, the racial removal of Jews in the Soviet Union, and the calculated starvation of millions of peasants in the Ukraine.

Communists everywhere were divided over the stories of slave labor, purges, torture, and the Soviet Gulags. The devious politics of denial was revealed at every turnout and comment at the Congress of Writers. The Soviet decrees to unite the radicals, socialists, and labor were carried out with some mistrust, but irony over communist propaganda was shouted down on the march to the Place de la Nation.

"Cavalry purges," shouted Heap of Words.

"Wounded Knee was a pogrom," declared Nika.

"Stalin is a universal fascist, along with many other missionaries of fascism, who carried out the mass murder of natives and at the same time courted churchy warriors to preach in favor of conversions," was my first rant on the union march.

The first coalition of communists and socialists was not our cause or demonstration, but we marched with the union against the demise of liberty, and against the pogroms, state executions, starvation, and the atrocities of nationalism in a world that was much too similar to the stories told on most native reservations.

The Front Populaire would march forever against the fascist overthrow of the French Third Republic. The heave and touch of the crowds, and the spirit of the workers enchanted me. The passion of "La Marseillaise," "Allons enfants de la patrie," Let's go children of the father land, "Le jour de gloire est arrivé," The day of glory has arrived, was a song of the heart, and then the crowd sang the leftist anthem "The Internationale," Stand up all victims of oppression, For the tyrants fear your might. The tender voices of the children moved me to tears. I lost my sense of distance, my sense of native presence, and moved with the crowd, and with no outlook that set me apart in time, place, songs, or stories.

That sense of partisan motion and ecstasy has captured me only three or four times in forty years. The first ecstatic scene was with a shaman who chanted dream songs with a vision of bears and ravens, and created magical sounds with a rattle and hand drum. The sound of his voice and the drum carried me to a moment of rapture, my body floated in some other consciousness, an incredible sense of native motion and transcendence.

I was enchanted a second time as a combat infantry soldier in the First World War. The sergeant ordered my brother and me to creep undercover to the enemy lines at night and capture Germans. We slithered through the heavy undergrowth in a rainstorm, revealed only in flashes of lightening, and waited in absolute silence near the enemy machinegun emplacement. The German soldiers reeked of trench culture, but the sweet scent of tobacco, porridge, and sausage touched my memories of wild rice and maple sugar camps on the reservation. My sense of presence as a native scout that stormy night was transmuted into a party of soldiers at a feast, even during the breaks of lightning and echoes of thunder, and truly there was never a perception of the enemy camp.

The scent of red pine in the summer, and a bald eagle over the face of ancient granite, was a totemic memory on the shoreline of Lake Namakan. The natural motion of an eagle was in the heart, not the eye, and envisioned later as fur trade stories over a campfire. The native totems, eagle, crane, bear, fox, muskrat, and many others, were visionary associations and imagined in ceremonies and stories. The native scenes of motion and totemic unions were not the same as the touch of a hand or steady brace of shoulders in a parade with communist and socialist on Bastille Day.

The solace of soldiers, union of veterans in white shirts and fedoras, and the close touch of shoulders that summer of the Bonus Expeditionary Force outside the United States Congress were revealed in the heart, not the eye. The songs, stories, and sense of partisan presence came to mind on the march to the Place de la Nation.

9

RELAY OF LIBERTY

Wednesday, 30 October 1935

Paris once courted empires, communes, and conversions, and weathered revolutions, royalists, fascists, communists, honored émigrés, and expatriates in a culture of mercy and mockery, and at the same time conveyed the curves, creases, and creative genres of irony that strained the salon traditions of music, literature, theatre, and art in a relay of liberty.

The art galleries were stacked with cubist dares and fancies, abstract and modern impressions, and new journals published ingenious and aesthetic escapades, surreal, erotic, and comic, the concise tease of imagistic poetry and emotive literary mappery. No matter the weather or the economic depression, the swing of guitars and violins, we gathered to hear the sensuous piano music of Erik Satie at least twice a week on the River Seine.

"Moods of liberty," shouted Heap of Words.

"Chords of mercy," said Nika.

The First World War started slowly with cultural deceit and the sounds of horns, drums, fearsome crescendos, the prance of horses, and heavy beat of soldiers in dress parades. The demons of vengeance silenced any meditation of the seasons, poetic reveries, or traces of natural motion. No war general ever engaged the enemy with soft hammers and the strings of a piano, the moody and spirited sounds of liberty.

I would much rather bend with thunderstorms that ravage the white pine, maple, and birch, erode the mighty stones, and leave by first light, than endure the trench misery and the remorse of cannons and crusades. Natives call to mind the turn of seasons and stories of natural furies that create an elusive sense of presence.

The empire fur trade war on animals and totems has never been forgiven, and yet there was mercy in the sunrise turn of garden flowers, the migration of booted eagles and sandhill cranes, the close meander of

royal pigeons on the cobblestones, and the original piano chords of Erik
Satie. His lonesome melodies were not composed for the beau monde or
mannerly salons of traditional music and art. Satie must have created the
moody music for those who steady the waves on barges and mosey on a
balmy morning near the Pont de la Concorde.

"Satie creates natural motion," said Nika.

"Nazis never mosey," shouted Heap of Words.

"Satie composed hues of blue," said Aloysius.

The German Reichstag, at the same time that we were enchanted by
the sound of piano music on the River Seine, had established the Nazi
menace of the Wehrmacht and Luftwaffe, denounced the Treaty of Versailles, and enacted the Nuremberg Laws, the decrees of unreserved cultural vengeance, hatred, and antisemitism for the Protection of German
Blood and German Honor.

Jews were marked, calibrated by ancestry, separated as a race for removal, and then reduced overnight to the status of aliens in a culture created by their genius and honorable labor, trade, music, philosophy, and
literature. Jews were denied civil rights, could no longer own property or
serve the government. Doctors, lawyers, and professors were removed
from their positions, and personal unions with Jews were forbidden by
order of the Nazi Party.

"Nazis cut kith and kin," cried Heap of Words.

"Hitler, Stalin, Mussolini," shouted Pierre.

"Three connivers of fascism," said Aloysius.

Pierre announced that "Henri Barbusse, the veteran of peace and lib-
erty, died of pneumonia in Moscow." He was buried with honors at the
Père Lachaise Cemetery, and we heard the great novelist of *Le feu, Under
Fire*, recently at the Congress of Writers.

"Stalin was his only fault," said Nathan.

"Stalin at Bad Medicine Lake," said Aloysius.

"Stalin the *wiindigoo*," said Nika.

The *wiindigoo*, the monster of winter who devoured lonesome natives,
roamed with shamans and tricksters in stories of fear and separation since
the colonial fur trade and decimation of totemic animals. Some natives
were forever burdened with nightmares of the *wiindigoo*, and the monster
was not easily distracted with chance or ceremonies. Shouts into panic

holes chased away ordinary monsters, but not the most deadly demons of envy, vengeance, and the horror of war.

Misaabe, the native healer at Bad Boy Lake, told stories about a reservation missionary possessed by the *wiindigoo*, and cured only when he lived alone in the remains of the white pine and created fourteen stump stations near Bad Medicine Lake, similar to Stations of the Cross. Jesus in the new cure was converted to a distinct totemic animal, and the stations of the beaver, marten, bear, otter, and more, more, more, were returned to the forest at each stump, a reversal of the scenes of condemnation, sacrifice, and the crucifixion of Jesus of Nazareth. The only slight comparison of the stumps to churchy stations is the resurrection of totemic animals of the fur trade.

Bad Medicine Lake, once an ancestral native outlook of shamans and elusive spirits, red and white pine stands, and continental liberty, was devastated in a scriptural civil war and treaty partition of federal stumpage on the survey metes and bounds of the White Earth Reservation.

Paris has become our story and relay of liberty, two centuries since the fur trade wars and the Great Peace of Montreal, and now our country of exile after we served as combat infantry soldiers fifteen years ago in the Battle of the Argonne. My native stories are in the clouds, and at the same time the warmongers and machines of vengeance are once again on the roads to misery.

Nathan announced that afternoon that he had rented a barge for my brother and me on the River Seine. The back room of the gallery had been our sanctuary, and it would now become a home for refugees from Germany. Aloysius shouldered his pouch of hand puppets, and we moved our books and clothes to a barge moored at Quai des Tuileries near the Pont de la Concorde.

Angelika Kauffmann and two children, Renata and Samuel, arrived that afternoon with no passports or travel visas from Berlin. They had actually escaped on a night train with only handbags, the name of Nathan, and a single address, Galerie Crémieux, Rue de la Bûcherie, close to the Cathédrale Notre Dame de Paris.

Moses Kauffmann, Clément Henri Crémieux, named Henri the Trader by natives, Jefferson Young and his son Odysseus, Julius Meyer, and many others were trusted traders with natives on pueblos and reservations in the

Southwest, and the traders gathered several times a year in Santa Fe, New Mexico, and in good weather at the Hubbell Trading Post in Ganado, Arizona.

Nathan related that his father, Clément, and Moses Kauffmann were very close friends, and their sons continued that honorable trade of native blankets, pottery, traditional objets d'art, and modern art in private galleries. Friedrich Kauffmann, son of Moses the Trader, opened the Galerie der Indianischen Kunst in Berlin, and Nathan, son of Henri the Trader, opened the Galerie Crémieux in Paris. The Jewish traders, fathers and sons, promised to protect each other and their families, and now was the time to honor that bond of traders and protect Angelika, Renata, and Samuel. Friedrich stayed behind to transfer the native art and ownership of the gallery to a close friend in Berlin, out of reach of the thieves in the Nazi Party.

Samuel was ten years old and rather shy, but smiled as he pointed at *giiwedin anang*, the North Star, painted on the ceiling of the back room in the gallery. The bond of traders continued with my brother and me, other natives, veterans, and the *mutilés de guerre* who taught the children how to catch fish in the River Seine. The children were allowed to stay overnight on weekends at *Le Corbeau Bleu*. Samuel was obsessed with astronomy, and every clear night he would tour by name many of the constellations. Renata, who was eleven years old, was a natural puppeteer, and amazed her mother with the hand puppet gestures of Léon Blum.

Angelika, Renata, and Samuel could read, write, and easily speak three languages. German was natural by birth and culture, and at the same time the family learned French and English. The solace of their homeland language turned to menace overnight, and ended with a national curse of race, blood, and religion.

France has always been a country of survival and the language of liberty in the face of fascists, and a sanctuary from the Nazi Nuremberg Laws. The children had studied English with a French teacher, and the tone and accent revealed a Rive Gauche Parisian. How would anyone notice by accent that the children had learned to recite many stories in Yiddish? Moses Kauffmann, their grandfather the trader, told his grandchildren that he taught the very same stories to native children in Arizona and New Mexico.

Nathan worried that the children would not be accepted to attend school without official documents, passports or birth certificates. The recent restriction on immigrants was a cruel response to the refugees and children who escaped from the vengeance of fascism, in search of a sanctuary. Natives have endured treaty separation, racial cuts and conventions, and the wanton authority of federal agents. The policies of exclusion never protected natives, and would never protect the children of France.

Fakery and artifice were necessary strategies to outlive fascism and the Nazis. Nathan contacted his close friend Michel Laroux, who served in the Gendarmerie Nationale nearby in Versailles, and asked for advice on how to obtain counterfeit birth certificates and passports from the criminal underworld. Forged passports and other documents were common, and the cost had increased every few days because of the recent demand for counterfeit credentials.

The Unione Corse, the Corsican Mafia, the heart of criminal societies, ruled the world of forgery, we were told, and any direct contact was rather obscure, only through an older woman who sold flowers near Place Pigalle. We bought flowers, and she smiled, but never said a word as she walked away. She must have raised a finger or gestured in some way to others because a few minutes later a nervous man escorted us to a nearby café, waved his enormous hands at the waiter, and at first he only talked about local politics and the weather. Nathan was silent, suspicious at first that the man was a faker, a police informer, or a petty criminal of Le Milieu, the underworld of prostitution and drugs in cities.

Marcel, probably a criminal trade name, rested his heavy hands on the table, turned and ordered me to write down exactly what documents we wanted. Marcel slowly looked over the list, asked about names and dates, but we refused to provide any specific information until we were certain about the reliability of the criminal trader and the cost of forged documents.

Nathan negotiated the price much lower, from seven thousand to five thousand francs, which amounted to about two hundred dollars for one pricey passport and three birth certificates. The agent recommended the documents show a country other than France. Marcel explained that the police inspected more closely local documents because there were so many forged passports.

Nathan provided the necessary information for the counterfeit documents to show birth dates in Santa Fe, New Mexico. We were told that the counterfeit passport, stolen from a citizen, would be forged in Marseille. Angelika was concerned at the time that the passport might have been stolen from the desperate volunteers who work at factories in the Soviet Union. Nathan heard stories that hundreds of passports were seized by the secret police and either sold to criminals or converted to new passports for spies on their way to the United States.

The United States passport was very impressive, gold type on a hard red cover. Angelika Kauffmann was pictured over the proper seal of the Department of State, Washington, and with the date and place of birth,15 March 1898, Ogema, Minnesota. Renata and Samuel were listed on the passport as minor children. "In Case of Death or Accident Notify," Angelika printed the name of Nathan Crémeiux, Rue de la Bûcherie,

The names and dates on the birth certificates were hand written and on document paper with the seal of the State of New Mexico, and the strange motto, *Crescit Eundo*, "It grows as it goes." Renata was born in Santa Fe County on 25 October 1923, only eleven years after New Mexico became a state of the United States, and Samuel was born on 12 August 1925. Forgers signed the name Aloysius Hudon Beaulieu as the attending physician at birth, and in the space for the father, Friedrich Kauffmann, born in Ganado, Arizona, and his occupation was entered as "Indian Trader." Angelika Berger was listed as an artist and teacher, born in Ogema, Minnesota. The forged place suggested she was a native from the White Earth Reservation.

Aloysius was inspired to create a passport of the White Earth Nation of the United States of America. He designed an impressive four page folded document printed on heavy parchment paper, almost the same size as a conventional passport. A blue raven was the seal on the cover, and inside was a concise reference to the totemic nation of fur traders and an official tribute to New France and the Great Peace of Montréal.

Aloysius ordered a hundred copies of the White Earth Nation passports, and issued the first eighteen documents of native identity to Nathan Crémeiux, Friedrich Kauffmann, Angelika, Renata, Samuel, Marie Vassilieff, Gertrude Stein, Sylvia Beach, Michel Laroux, Daniel-Henry

Kahnweiler, Michel Leiris, Pierre Chaisson, Nika Montezuma, Solomon Heap of Words, André, Henri, and the loyal native poseurs Olivier Black Elk and Coyote Standing Bear.

Renata broke into tears at a surprise birthday party that afternoon, Friday, 25 October 1935. Nathan planned the party and we were ordered to casually escort the children to the Square du Vert-Galant on the River Seine. The party was actually a surprise celebration of three birthdays: Renata's, a delayed party for Samuel who had missed his father more than his birthday two months earlier, and three days after, our birthday on the White Earth Reservation.

Nika decorated the trees with abstract blue ravens, the names of artists on white banners, Picasso, Picabia, Matisse, Chagall, and her favorite, Modigliani, and reserved a bench to honor Moses and Friederich Kauffmann.

Aloysius carved a hand puppet in the fashion of the French Guignol, and Angelika arranged piano lessons for Renata with the woman in the blue scarf who played the music of Erik Satie on a barge near Pont de la Concorde.

Nathan served Neufchâtel, Cantal, Livarot, and Port Salut cheeses with baguette, white wine, and for a birthday party dessert, Berliner Pfannkuchen, the favorite pastry of the children. Many more friends arrived later that afternoon with birthday wishes: Marie Vassilieff; Gertrude Stein, who was on her way to the market; the gallery owner Daniel-Henry Kahnweiler; his wife, Lucie Godon; and Silvia Beach, who presented Renata with a book about Guignol, the most famous puppet of France.

10

Panic Holes

Sunday, 9 August 1936

By Now Rose Beaulieu, our favorite cousin and veteran nurse, warned me with only nine words on a badly worn Saint Anthony Falls postcard that she was on her way to Paris. "By Now Be There soon with two great surprises," but no date of arrival was noted. She was always a teaser of time, place, and presence.

By Now arrived last week from Le Havre with a great burst of native spirit and many holdover stories about labor unions, communists, fascists, mobsters, and then she eased back against the blue tiller of *Le Corbeau Bleu* and turned an ear to the feathery chords of Erik Satie that wafted from the piano on the barge near Pont de la Concorde.

"Rapture on the River Seine," said By Now.

She was fast asleep on the deck before the river concert ended that afternoon. We stood near our cousin, watched her steady breath, catnap smile, and related how close we had become as veterans three years ago at the Bonus March in Washington. She was asleep for several hours, and later told heart stories about labor unions and communists, the Truckers' Strike in Minneapolis, the terrible murder of two cousins, and strategically delayed the great surprises that she carried in a pouch from the White Earth Reservation.

By Now boarded the *Île de France* on 23 July 1936, the same art deco steamship that we had sailed on four years earlier. John Leecy, the generous reservation hotelier who loved opera music and honored native veterans, paid our travel and did the same for By Now, a special Pullman train car and cruise no less classy or spectacular than ours.

Aloysius lighted the oil lantern on *Le Corbeau Bleu*, and the ancient cast iron stove reminded our cousin of the cold winters on the reservation. The sway of the barge was mostly steady, almost natural motion, and only heaved with the waves from large cargo barges.

By Now arrived on the first day of the Olympic games in Berlin, and we were invited later in the week to listen to the daily radio summary of events at the Galerie Crémieux. The quay was dimly lighted, and we sat on the deck early that evening, listened to our cousin, teased the stray mongrels, and waved at the clochards, or vagrants, who camped under the bridges.

Nathan came by earlier to meet By Now, but she was sound asleep on the deck. So we sat around the native nurse and started an easy kindred tease and creative heart stories to reach her dreams. Aloysius told about her early tour of the reservation on a horse, and her service as a nurse during the war. My stories were about her journey to the Bonus March on a horse named Treaty. She was the only veteran to arrive on horseback. Nathan listened to our stories over wine and cheese and expected our cousin to awaken at any moment.

By Now toured the entire White Earth Reservation on a chestnut wagon horse named Stomp, and with the company of two loyal mongrels, Torment and Whipple, named after an Episcopal Priest. She was twelve years old at the time and slowly trotted through the white pine stumps from Bad Boy Lake, White Earth Lake, Naytahwaush, and the headwaters of the Mississippi River at Lake Itasca, to Bad Medicine Lake and Pine Point, and then returned by way of Callaway.

By Now was born late, more than a month late on the conception calendar, so late that her father boasted that she could speak three languages by the time she was delivered one warm spring morning. "That child should be here by now," her father shouted several times, and she was born a few hours later. By Now was her nickname at delivery, of course, and later the catchy byname was entered as a given name on the federal birth certificate, By Now Rose Beaulieu.

She was born in a tiny house on Beaulieu Street in Ogema, and lived there most of her life, but she decided to name Bad Boy Lake, a few miles away, as home when she was an army nurse because the soldiers were curious about the place name, and that was always an invitation to create stories about the lake. She once associated the sudden turn of the seasons to the mysterious healer named Misaabe and his mongrels at Bad Boy Lake. Later, she declared that the old healer inspired her to become a nurse.

By Now was a veteran of the Army Nurse Corps and had treated hundreds of soldiers with combat wounds, and at the same time she had treated and shoed a few military packhorses in the First World War in France. She road Black Jack many times into combat near the Hindenburg Line, and in violation of direct military orders she treated soldiers with severe wounds from the heavy enemy artillery.

Black Jack, named in honor of General John Pershing, was her favorite mount between the combat areas and the medical aide stations, and she rescued many horses with combat fatigue and trained them to carry the wounded soldiers. The soldiers reported that the steady sway of a horse was the calm after a storm, and much more curative than the noisy and bouncy ambulances overloaded with bloody bodies.

By Now should have been decorated for her courage, but the distant commanders avoided any official mention of the native nurse, the name of the horse, and unauthorized combat duty. The French Army commanders, however, honored the unique medical services by a native nurse on horseback and awarded her the French Croix de Guerre.

Treaty, the name of the horse she rode to Washington, was a direct descendant of the original federal treaty horses, and was given to her as a native tease. Treaty was once a wagon horse, the last of the breed to serve overnight guests at the Hotel Leecy on the White Earth Reservation. Treaty was sidelined and favored in the hotel stable with the arrival of motorcars.

By Now was the first veteran to leave the reservation for the Bonus March. She read about the move of veterans from around the country and could not wait to depart, but the tour by horse was much slower than jumping boxcars.

Treaty raised her head and cantered over the Potomac River on the Arlington Memorial Bridge, and then trotted through the campsites on the National Mall toward Capitol Hill. By Now dismounted and talked with three veterans smoking rolled cigarettes near a shanty named the Dug Out. They told her about the schedules of the bonus marches, and warned her several times to watch out for the communist troublemakers in the veteran camps. Treaty neighed at the communists, and whinnied at the senators.

Aloysius carried on with a great story about a devoted veteran who could not live without the true love of a native nurse. Le Caporal Pierre Dumont, a smitten French infantry soldier, followed her home to the White Earth Reservation. Nurse By Now had hoisted the wounded soldier onto a horse, and that singular touch became a fantastic romance for the lonely soldier, and many months after the war he arrived healed and lusty on the reservation. Pierre was enchanted with the romance stories about natives, and especially by the desperate and sentimental novel *René* by François René de Chateaubriand. Louisiana and Minnesota were utterly distinctive, of course, and only connected by the Mississippi River, but that was close enough for the corporal to complete his wild romance with a real native woman.

By Now would never marry, but never hesitated to carry out the lusty motions of the ancient fur trade with the French. Pierre was never at ease with the native tease and returned to his family fish counter at Les Halles in Paris six months later, after the second wicked snowstorm and the scary native stories about the Ice Woman. By Now raised her head, looked around the deck, and said she had "strange dreams about Pierre Dumont."

"I waited to meet you, By Now," said Nathan.

"Nathan, your good name is part of our family on the reservation, and my mother wanted me to invite you to visit anytime, but not much in the winter," said By Now. "Father Valerian sends his steady blessings, and everyone from Rice Lake to White Earth knows your name from the letters to the heirs of the fur trade."

"We told stories about your adventures with horses, and waited for you to wake up so we could hear your story about William Hushka," said Aloysius.

"The motion of the barge became a horse in one dream and then a cradleboard in another, a perfect motion of peace with my mother in the warm sun at the maple syrup camp, and six months later at the wild rice camp," said By Now. "The barge has already become my dreamy mount and family cradleboard in Paris."

"So, now is the time for surprises," said Aloysius.

By Now untied the canvas bundle and pulled out two hand puppets, one a woman with a long nose, wide toothy smile, golden ringlets, and black feathery wings, and the second hand puppet a piebald mongrel with a wide mouth, a floppy black beret, and a coat with blue quilted sleeves. The two puppets were carved out of blocks of fallen birch, heads polished and painted by the native maestro of hand puppets, Dummy Trout.

Dummy wrote a letter about the puppets, and By Now read the rules of practice as Aloysius mounted the woman puppet on his right hand, and the magnificent mongrel on the other. Dummy surprised my brother and me four years ago in the same way, with the present of two hand puppets, Mikwan Ekwe, the wispy Ice Woman, and the lusty Niinag Trickster, as we got ready to depart by train to join veterans from around the country in the Bonus Expeditionary Force in Washington.

Papa Pius, Snatch, Makwa, Miinan, and Queena, five loyal mongrels, lived with the puppeteer in the Manidoo Mansion, a messy shack covered with cracked tarpaper at Spirit Lake on the White Earth Reservation. Papa Pius, an ironic nickname that honored the popes, died last year and was buried next to three other mongrels behind the shack. Queena, a rangy collie, was so named to honor the famous coloratura soprano at the Metropolitan Opera.

Dummy had carved two diva hand puppets, Geraldine Farrar and Alma Gluck, world famous sopranos, and carried out the motion of sopranos at an opera. Miinan, a blue mongrel, and Queena the collie were great singers, and moaned, groaned, and bayed with the recorded voices of the sopranos, and were well known on the reservation for their memorable version of "Life Is Just a Bowl of Cherries" and a crude rendition of "Old Black Joe," the popular song written by Stephen Foster.

By Now raised her hand, cleared her throat, and read the puppet letter written by Dummy Trout. "Nurse By Now carries two new hand puppets for you to charm people way over there, and win over the fur traders with sopranos. At least once a week my Queena and Miinan mongrels howl and bay along with the great Norwegian soprano Kirsten Flagstad in the *Die Walküre*, Ride of the Valkyries, by Richard Wagner. You know the loyal mongrels in my mansion, so you must have a mongrel on hand to sing on that barge your mother told me about.

"Aloysius, Basile, By Now, you need my puppets and a few mongrel singers to haunt those Nazis. You know what a good haunt means, not just a *wiindigoo* monster, but besides that the wicked nag and torment of a woodsy hand puppet on the River Seine. Aloysius, you tease old wordy Basile, put his nose right about stories and make sure he writes about the new hand puppets, the haunts, and the new mongrel singers.

"Panic, the name of my new mongrel, a black and white spaniel with great floppy ears, is a natural opera singer, one of the best, a smooth high tone and bay waver, and she barks high the battle cry of Brünnhilde, *ho, jo, to, ho,* the Wagnerian Bark in the Ride of the Valkyries. Panic practices every day to sing, bay, and bark with a steady tone, and she imitates some of your relatives who shouted into panic holes on that blue meadow near Bad Medicine Lake. Panic is my best mongrel diva, and she continues two native traditions, the curse and bellow over panic holes that ease the trouble of reservation time, and the spaniel mongrel sings along with those marvelous sopranos of the world.

"I turned to silence, as everyone knows, and decided to live with the spirit of mongrels, divas, and hand puppets, but if panic holes had been around at the time of the great fire, maybe my heart and bone deep sorrow would have been healed with a great and lasting shout into a panic hole, and then, who knows, traveled with my loyal mongrels and stayed at your barge house and listened to more great divas in the night air at the Bayreuth Festival and the Metropolitan Opera.

"I was deeply moved by the incredible soprano voice of Kristen Flagstad, and John Leecy once again kindly invited me and other opera devotees to the old reservation hotel to hear the radio broadcast of *Die Walküre* at the Metropolitan Opera on 2 February 1935. I will carry forever that great soprano performance close to my heart, and loyal mongrels will always be my bay chorus for the spirited hand puppets and Wagnerian Bark of Panic.

"Aloysius, you create spectacle and beguile the Nazis with the hand puppet Flagstad, and with Wagner on the other hand, and find a few stray mongrels there to bay and learn the Wagnerian Bark. I want to know every panic word you write about the Nazis.

"Basile, you come back home soon, we need your good words about the reservation. I send my teases evermore to you wild boys on the River Seine in Paris." She signed the letter, "Dummy and the Diva Mongrels."

By Now was a dedicated storier and remembered that my brother and I once worked as occasional stagehands for the Orpheum Theatre in Minneapolis. Better paying jobs were hard to find at the end of the war. Most employers spurned the unions and would not hire anyone without some official endorsement to prove the job hunter was ready for an enterprise culture, and not a communist or a member of a union and against an open shop.

Yes, we were native rebels and veterans of war with ironic stories of totemic unions and enterprise liberty, and some managers would surely be suspicious that we came from a closed shop on a federal reservation and, no doubt, reviewed as defective workers because one cold winter day we were desperate and hired out to carry union picket signs with other hungry veterans who menaced the private owner of the Wonderland Theatre.

"Native veterans a double union," said Nika.

"Closed shop communists," said Aloysius.

By Now told heart stories and created scenes that were prompted by memories and conversations, more than mere recitations, and that mostly accounts for my mention of theatres and trade union pickets. She started with serious trade union stories that balmy evening on the deck of *Le Corbeau Bleu*, the tragic murders of William Hushka, Harry Ness, and two of our cousins, Truman Vizenor and Clement Vizenor.

"William Hushka was my only true lover," she said and then paused. By Now slowly covered her heart with both hands, and whispered, "William was shot in the heart by the police and died slowly in the debris near the Old Armory in Washington." She had been blocks away and not there to hear "his last tender breath," and she pleaded on the deck of the barge that only the shamans could explain why he was murdered as an honorable bonus veteran. William was always ready to march with other veterans for the cause of the cash bonus, and never was a threat to the police or to anyone.

General Douglas MacArthur carried a crop, wore high leather empire boots, railed about the communists and red menace, and ordered the rout of peaceable war veterans. Masked soldiers used tear gas, tanks, and fixed bayonets to chase the hungry warriors and their families out of the city.

By Now said her "lover was a migrant who served in the Forty-First Infantry Division in France and died as a war veteran in the Bonus Expeditionary Force on 28 July 1932." Private William Hushka was buried with military honors at the Arlington National Cemetery. "I created dreams songs in his memory that night at the grave, and at dawn mounted Treaty and rode back to the lonesome lakes and white pine stumps of the White Earth Reservation."

Henry Ness was a local union member, and the police murdered him on

Bloody Friday, 20 July 1934, at a general strike in Minneapolis. The union strikers were not armed, but the police were issued shotguns and ordered to carry out their duty and to shoot to keep the delivery trucks of produce on the road. When union strikers blocked the first truck, the police started to shoot. Henry Ness and John Belor were murdered without cause, and once more the Citizens Alliance, that nasty gang of starched conspirators, fascist bankers, class breeders, and high collar business owners, railed with the military officers that the unions and hungry veterans were communists.

"Nazis are red bogeymen," said Aloysius.

"Trotsky was a faith healer," said Nika.

"Léon Blum a socialist dreamer," said Nathan.

"Bloody days near and far," said Aloysius.

By Now continued with her stories on the deck of the barge. More than sixty strikers were wounded, and some of them were brought to the union hospital in a warehouse on Chicago Avenue, not far from Elliot Park and the Band Box Diner, familiar places to natives who moved from the deadly rule of poverty on the reservation to that dreary and decrepit neighborhood just south of downtown Minneapolis.

"I was a nurse at the union hospital at the time, but not at first because the union men consigned me to an auxiliary of women, the wives of union strikers who served meals and carried out other womanly duties," she said. "That manly union way was never acceptable to me, but after strong protests as a veteran army nurse, and with combat medical experience, the union and war veterans recognized my service and teased me with new names, Nurse Nearly, Nurse Pretty Soon, Almost Beaulieu, and Nurse Two Boot. You know, I wear heavy boots, and that became one of my nicknames." Four days later, on a hot and humid Tuesday, more than a hundred thousand citizens waited in silence to salute the funeral procession and honor the memory of Henry Ness.

The coal strike had started the prevous February, and the general union strike lasted three months. The governor declared martial law and ordered National Guard soldiers to protect some of the truck deliveries. The strike was finally resolved six months later.

Happy Holstein, a good friend from the reservation, and other natives, Joe Belanger, Doc Tilotson, Bill Rogers, Ray Rainbolt, and Bill Bolt, were active in the union and took part in the duties as drivers and strikers. Clement and Truman Vizenor, our cousins, were employed as house painters, and at the same time worked for the union in a building downtown on Eighth Street.

By Now said that Alice Beaulieu Vizenor, our favorite aunt and feisty teaser, left the reservation a few years earlier to live in a rooming house on Nicollet Island in Minneapolis when her cocky husband, Henry Vizenor, the White Earth Reservation police chief at the time, ran away with a younger woman to Chicago. Alice moved a few months later to a dilapidated flat in the Curtis Apartments on Tenth Street downtown with her five sons and two daughters, Ruby, Lorraine, Lawrence, Clement, Truman, Joseph, and Everett. The four older boys were hired as painters by a contractor named John Henry Hartung.

Two years later Clement and Truman were murdered in the same month, June 1936. The police never investigated the gangland crimes, and there were many other murders in the city that were ordered by Isadore Blumenfeld, otherwise known as the notorious mobster Kid Cann. William Liggett, a journalist, was shot dead near his apartment because of his articles critical about organized crime and political corruption. Three eyewitnesses identified the shooter as Kid Cann; even so the mobster was acquitted in court.

"Clement and Truman were active in the union, and they were forever teased about the furry trade unions on the reservation, and the closed shop of federal agents," said By Now. The Citizens Alliance was sinister and secretly paid thugs and mobsters to menace active union members, and "most of our relatives were convinced that the boys had talked to federal agents about the time they refused to carry alcohol for the mobster Kid Cann from Canada through the White Earth Reservation to moonshine farmers in Stearns County during the Prohibition."

Clement Vizenor was murdered a few months before his son was three years old, and everyone worried about the rest of the family. The White Earth native was buried in an unmarked grave at Saint Mary's Cemetery in Minneapolis, and a few days later Alice Beaulieu moved back to the ironic sanctuary of poverty on the White Earth Reservation with her two daughters, Ruby and Lorraine, and first grandson, Gerald Vizenor.

"I returned to the reservation that same week in early July 1936, and then decided to sail away from the mobsters of the city and the nasty politics of the reservation," said By Now. "I was ready to live with my favorite veterans and cousins Basile and Aloysius on the River Seine. So, now you heard my stories of the past few years since we were last together at the Bonus March."

Aloysius waved to the clochards on the quay and three mongrels raised their noses in our direction, but waited at an escape distance. The natives of *Le Corbeau Bleu* were new to the quay, and the stray mongrels were hungry but wise and always cautious.

By Now poured a glass of white wine and turned from the heart stories of unions and murder to native mongrels, and coaxed each of us to name the three stray mongrels on the quay. She pointed at the dirty white mongrel with long hair and named him The Vicar.

"The Vicar is a stray Pyrenean Shepherd," said Nathan. "The two other strays are distinctive, a Papillon, a surprise stray, smart and spirited, and the black mongrel with traces of white is a Picardy Spaniel."

"Pig Ears, the Papillon," said Aloysius.

"High Road, the Picardy Spaniel," was my name play for the mongrel because of his high head and bounce on his front paws, but human and mongrel nicknames can change with experience.

By Now shouted out the mongrel names, The Vicar, Pig Ears, and High Road, clucked her tongue several times, as she once did with horses, and the strays moved closer to the barge. Slowly she reached out and handed each mongrel a double break of baguette, and then whispered eye to eye the three names once more.

A short and classy woman dressed in a shiny black shawl and a bright feathery hat reined back her curious Petit Basset Griffon Vendéen on the cobblestone quay near the Pont de la Concorde.

11

STRAY MONGRELS

Thursday, 22 October 1936

My letters to the heirs of the fur trade are heart stories of native memory, and clearly not in the manner or distance of history. Bear in mind that federal agents concocted cutout cultures and bloodline fakery on reservations as documents of history, but they never noticed our dream songs of natural motion, or even mentioned the native tease, the great ironic trickster stories of earthdivers, hand puppets, or mongrel divas and healers.

Historians favored the same heavy tread of discovery, destiny, diseases, deserted landscapes, the tragic fade away of mounted warriors and great buffalo herds, and disavowed the fascist removal of natives and the constitutional trouble of liberty for natives. Historians dishonored the totemic rendezvous of bears and wolves, beaver and marten, and cast aside the native trade routes, original names of mountains, canyons, rivers, lakes, and visionary totemic stories in the ruins of the enlightenment and civilization.

Totemic unions on the native margins of history are more secure than the devious deals of timber barons, or evasive recitations of deadly agents, or missionary conversion stories of salvation. The narratives of cultural ascendancy were measured in fast time as native oak and white pine were cut for barns, boats, barrels, houses in the cities, and thousands of migrant homesteaders cleared and cut the earth, brewed beer, and hardly noticed natives as doctors, nurses, painters, and writers, or as combat soldiers in the First World War.

My stories never turn back native reason or chance, never enact nostalgia, play out jealousies, or wavers of shame. Native heart stories and dream songs tease regret and nostalgia, and create a sense of presence with natural motion and liberty.

These letters to the heirs of the fur trade start with dates, more than mere chronicles, and then tease time and motion with heart stories. At the same time my letters bring to light the teardown crusades of fascism, the risky politics of appeasement, crimes of cross and royalty, and the racial violence of the Nazi Party.

Anaïs Nin, the lovely erotic storier, moved into a rental houseboat, *La Belle Aurore*, Beautiful Dawn, late last month nearby on the Quai des Tuileries. She became my fantasy at first sight, and always worth the wait to watch her write in a journal on deck in early morning light. The houseboat barge with a high studio and windows was nearly across from the Gare d'Orsay.

Aloysius noticed on the first day she moved to the barge that Henry Miller, the novelist and hearty lover by hearsay, was out and a new man with long black hair was at the tiller of *La Belle Aurore*. Miller was already endorsed as the author of sinewy and sexual backstreet fiction, and the lovely Anaïs Nin praised and promoted the *Tropic of Cancer*, his first person "fuck everything" novel published last year by Obelisk Press.

Anaïs Nin could easily sidetrack the native *wiindigoo*, federal agents, and other monsters of war and peace with poetic gestures, shy poses, aesthetic smiles, or even the slight show of a hand or finger in the air. Her flyaway moves on the deck were gracious and erotic.

"Calm before the storm," shouted Heap of Words.

The Vicar, High Road, and Pig Ears slowly circled and sniffed the two stray mongrels, *chiens bâtards*, on the quay that morning, a blotchy, woolly Barbet water mongrel, and a stately Basset Hound with a mellow baritone bay. We could not resist the stray mongrels on a tour of barges that landed with trust at *Le Corbeau Bleu*. By Now named the Barbet, Black Jack, the ironic nickname of General John Pershing, commander of the American Expeditionary Forces in France during the First World War, and had used the same nickname to honor her favorite military mount as a combat nurse. The Bassett Hound bayed twice on the deck and earned the name Panzéra, in honor of the famous French concert baritone Charles Panzéra.

Today, our birthday party was partly a ruse to invite our friends to visit *Le Corbeau Bleu*, the White Earth Embassy on the River Seine. We were beguiled with two lovely and mysterious women, and we needed the deception of a party to meet them. I was charmed by Anaïs Nin, our houseboat neighbor on the quay, but could not get past cordial waves and smiles.

Aloysius used the party to pursue the pianist in the blue scarf. He delivered the party invitation in person and with gentle praise of the barge concerts, but she never turned to reply, and as usual hurried away in silence down the quay. The pianist missed the incredible hand puppet performances of Kirsten Flagstad, Wagner, Gertrude Stein, Anaïs Nin, and Apollinaire.

I pretended to be a mongrel with a baritone bay when Renata created a poetic song and staged the first show with Wagner, one of the new mongrel hand puppets made by Dummy Trout. My hearty bay in turn roused the other barge mongrels, and the first spontaneous chorus of party mongrels got underway that afternoon of our forty-first birthday.

Paris was melodramatic and burlesque but never the right theatre for another war; the moods were showy and the rehearsals were badly staged. The play of politics was stormy last summer, badly directed street operas with the race of character, fascist resentments, coalition wavers, and at last a united government of radicals, communists, and socialists of Le Front Populaire, the Popular Front.

Léon Blum was elected as the prime minister of the French Third Republic on 10 May 1936. Three months earlier he was assaulted and beaten by the Camelots du Roi, a mob of young fascists and royalists on the busy intersection of Rue de l'Université and Boulevard Saint Germain. The police and others rushed the politician to cover at the nearby La Ligue Catholique, League of Catholics, surely an ironic sanctuary for a socialist and literary Jew. His wounds were treated at the Hôtel Dieu de Paris, and Blum said at the time that he "now knew what lynching means."

Natives and others marched, saluted, and shouted last year with Blum and Le Front Populaire, and the great turnout of workers must have scared the fascists and weary royalists into radical coup d'état operas. Only twitchy boneheads of tragedy would trade liberty for the royal return of powdered wigs, queer boots, cracked grins, the guillotine, and moldy totemic fur from an empire colony.

Bad Boy Lake comes to mind, the rouge of maple and sumac, the scent of motion, and the bright golden birch of autumn memories were interwoven with the tender hues of plane and linden trees on the Quai des Tuileries. The tiller on the barge was painted blue, and paper cutouts of blue ravens decorated the rough deck. The hand puppets were polished and ready to perform at our birthday party.

Nathan, Daniel-Henry Kahnweiler, Gertrude Stein, who was always the last to arrive, Marie Vassilieff, André, Henri, Angelika, Renata, and Samuel Kauffmann, Pierre Chaisson, Nika Montezuma, Solomon Heap of Words, Coyote Standing Bear, Olivier Black Elk, Anaïs Nin, Violette Morris, and many others were crowded on the quay and narrow deck of *Le Corbeau Bleu* for a first performance of the new hand puppets.

Nathan first met Violette, a newcomer to our parties, at an auto parts store several years ago, but that was a strange story because he never owned a car. She was a famous athlete who was educated at a convent; she was short, strong, fast, and daring, and had won two gold medals in the shot put and discus throw at the international Jeux Olympiques Féminins, the first Women's World Games in Paris in 1922. She lived on a houseboat named *La Mouette*, The Seagull, moored around the great curve of the river at Neuilly-sur-Seine.

Violette was recently denied permission to participate in the Fédération Française Sportive Féminine because she was a lesbian, a boxer with short hair, dressed like a man, wore polished brogues, drove race cars, smoked cigarettes, and cursed in public.

"Stray mongrel," shouted Heap of Words.

"Le Monocle habitué," said Anaïs Nin.

"But can she rein a horse?" asked By Now.

Nathan had invited the usual collection of friends to hear the radio broadcast, two months ago, of the final events at the Nazi Summer Olympics in Berlin, and we came away with the reserves of race, chase, and fascist salute stories. Jews were not allowed to participate in the games, but Helene Mayer won a silver medal in fencing and saluted the Third Reich. Albert Wolff, a French Jew and fencer refused to participate because of the antisemitism in Nazi Germany. Jesse Owens easily won four gold medals and trounced the fascist notion of the racial superiority of Aryans. The mighty sound of our shouts and roars of great respect and racial irony reached to the Cathédrale Notre Dame de Paris and the River Seine.

"Adolf Hitler invited the stray mongrel and convent lesbian to the Summer Olympics," declared Nathan. "Yes, she was discreet and must have been honored for more than a womanly shot put and the manly pose at the wheel of a race car."

"Maybe not so strange," said Pierre. "That prissy fascist with a moustache courts a lesbian because she has become a spy for the Nazis."

"Heil Violette," shouted Heap of Words.

Aloysius raised Kirsten Flagstad the soprano on one hand and Gertrude Stein on the other, and the two puppets waved in silence at the barge audience. Gertrude clapped her white wooden hands, slowly bowed on the deck of *Le Corbeau Bleu*, and announced the start of a new puppet show.

Renata practiced the gestures of the mongrel Wagner, and the hand puppet shivered and cued me with a go away paw to bay and bark as a baritone. The mongrel puppet warmed the audience. Panzéra, the baritone basset, raised his head and mocked the tone of my hearty bay. Pig Ears, the Papillon, leaned closer with a cocked ear, and then she sneezed three times in harmony.

Wagner charmed the audience with a short operetta, a poetic song about a magical blue medicine that was created by Renata. Samuel carried a tray of blue bottles labeled *Médecine Bleue*, and my bay was accompanied by the great baritone bay and bark of Panzéra.

> *Come closer to the mongrel bay*
> *buy a big blue bottle*
> *Médecine Bleue*
> *only a franc*
> *one drop a day*
> *lasts forever*
> *and with a wild bay*
> *scares the monsters*
> *moustache and sieg heil*
> *Adolf Hitler*
> *turns blue and stays away*

Renata repeated the last three lines of the poetic song with my baritone bay. Wagner bowed and everyone on deck shouted, brava, brava, brava. Renata was a natural with the mongrel hand puppet at the first show, and the wild gestures would have pleased Dummy Trout.

The first puppet show on the barge might have ended with the rise of the trickster dick, and more bawdy mockery of Adolf Hitler, but my brother thought about the children and decided not to elevate the wooden willy of the Niinag Trickster. Anaïs Nin surely would have applauded the raunchy talk and the mighty rise of the birch dick, but that performance was reserved for another puppet show.

Anaïs Nin posed on the deck of *La Belle Aurore* several times a day, and my brother watched her moves, smile and hand gestures, morning shivers, and in the past few weeks, carved her lovely head out of a block of birch with a heart shaped face, high forehead and puffy cheeks polished white, a slight cleft on the nose and chin, dimples, and bright red angelic lips.

Aloysius mounted Anaïs Nin on his right hand, and the puppet slowly turned to glance at me, and then touched her heart with a wooden hand. I turned slowly in the same manner as the hand puppet, and touched my heart with both hands.

"Touch and tease," shouted Heap of Words.

"Heap of tease," shouted Aloysius.

Anaïs was bouncy at her first performance and turned to one side and then the other. Guillaume Apollinaire was mounted on the other hand, and the great poet raised his bandaged head and pointed downriver in the direction of Le Pont Mirabeau. He cocked his head and stared first at the hand puppet, and then jerked to stare at the real Anaïs Nin on the deck of *Le Corbeau Bleu*.

APOLLINAIRE: Your red lippy smile enchants me.

ANAÏS NIN: Only the elusive start of a poem.

APOLLINAIRE: Your polished head entices me to tease.

ANAÏS NIN: Le Pont Mirabeau was a tease of lost love.

APOLLINAIRE: Joy comes after pain.

ANAÏS NIN: Love flows away with the river.

APOLLINAIRE: You imagined me more than once.

ANAÏS NIN: Twice ashore at Le Pont Mirabeau.

APOLLINAIRE: More beautiful than the Mona Lisa.

ANAÏS NIN: Stolen art is your obsession.

APOLLINAIRE: Prison time was my surreal time.

ANAÏS NIN: Mona Lisa was a prisoner of your heart.

APOLLINAIRE: Sly smile and alone forever.

ANAÏS NIN: She travels in a million erotic memories.

APOLLINAIRE: Travel with me tonight.

ANAÏS NIN: Overnight favors on a barge of liberty.

Anaïs Nin was truly moved by the creative play of the hand puppets. She leaned over, kissed the namesake puppet on the forehead, touched my brother on the cheek, touched me on the chest, and bought two bottles of *Médecine Bleue* to chase away Adolf Hitler. She raised her arms and praised the puppet show created by Renata and Samuel.

Anaïs told me that the easy wave motion of the barge created a sense of departure, and now the marvelous motion of the hand puppets created a sense of presence. We walked together that night on the Quai des Tuileries, over the Pont de la Concorde, then along the Quai Anatole France to the Gare d'Orsay, and sat on a bench to talk and watch the rush of travelers. The motion of strangers, migrants, tourists, and the steady stream of beggars gave rise to our stories at the train station. The manners and gestures of the travelers and migrants touched memories, and several times we turned to each other and teased a hunch, an idea, cultural marks, but mostly an image or fancy about a stranger.

"Travelers never seem jealous," said Anaïs.

"Mostly excited, let down, lost, or lonesome," was my response, and then the conversation turned to natives, how the missionaries and settlers were jealous of natives who lived and traveled on the land and told stories of totemic custody, but not as a possession or merchant colony.

"Everyone is jealous," she declared. "It is a perversity to be jealous of the past," because the past is made of ashes, but with the artist, "the past survives in another form."

"Natives are artists in natural motion, not the ashes of politics or portrayals," was my reply. "Natives are storiers of the heart, dream singers, tease talkers, markers on stone, wood carvers, puppeteers, and now a writer and painter in motion on a barge on the River Seine."

"I can understand those who are jealous of the past of an artist," said Anaïs, because art "becomes a monument."

Most people are ashes in "a neat cemetery. But examine the past of an artist and you find monuments to its perpetuity, a book, a statue, a painting, a poem, a symphony."

Native art was discovered and diminished as cultural artifacts by the crude agents of realism, deadly realism that was more churchy and utilitarian than the creative scenes of natural motion in a dream song

"The monster I have to kill every day is realism," said Anaïs, and then she pointed at a man who wore a blue cape, black and white wingtip shoes, surely dancing shoes; he carried a fine leather suitcase. The svelte man had arrived on the electric train at the Gare d'Orsay, and we speculated about his destination in Paris.

"He is a woman on her way to Le Monocle, the lesbian nightclub," was my observation. Anaïs agreed and noted the perfectly cut short hair, and she can dance the night way and later wear only the wingtips and a cape.

"So, how is realism a monster?"

"I have to turn destruction into creation over and over again," she explained, because the "monster who attacks me every day is destruction."

I related how the native *wiindigoo* is an evil monster that devours the human spirit, and the best way to outwit the demon is to tease the obvious and create original and ironic stories about the natural world.

Anaïs was persuaded that ironic stories could distract even the portrayals of highbrow devils in a salon, but not just portraits or the native tease. Adolf Hitler was teased about his art, and now we see what he has become. She thought he should have been encouraged as an artist, not spurned or shamed. The outcome of his humiliation was hatred and vengeance.

"Germans were never generous teasers," was my rather hazy response to monsters of the Sieg Heil. The best native teasers practiced the art of tough compassion, not the politics of throwaway cultures. Natives were never very good at the tease of federal agents because these men were selected as sycophants with a dense sense of loyalty to authority and a dedication to the absence of irony.

Natives told marvelous stories of natural motion in a world of shamans, voyageurs of the fur trade, and mocked the absurdity of federal policies and concocted realism, but now natives are persuasive teasers in creative art, puppetry, and literature.

Anaïs was sidetracked by a weary man in a shabby suit and oversized shoes as he walked slowly into the train station. He was stooped with a slightly twisted back, and we first thought he could have been a teacher or a jeweler who lost his business in the economic depression. Sullen and jerky the man avoided eye contact.

Maurice was his first name, but he never revealed his surname. Slowly, and with practiced pauses, he told us that he once owned a haberdashery, *le tailleur des hommes*, and then fabrics became scarce, styles changed, most men were out of work, and three years ago he tailored the last suit for a rich cubist artist. Then after a long pause, he revealed that at the same time the business failed his young wife ran away with an *apache* dancer and gangster. The man said he lived only for the ideas of fashion, and now he tours train stations for a meal and to overcome suicide and the news of another war. Anaïs gave him money for a good meal. He bowed, turned in silence, and hobbled out of the station.

"Men think they live and die for ideas. What a divine joke," said Anaïs. "They live and die for emotional and personal errors, just as women do."

The lights on the quay shimmered on the slight waves of the river, and we walked slowly with that natural motion to the Square du Vert Galant at Pont Neuf. At that moment a heavy, dark cargo barge raised the waves and shattered the sway and reflection of gentle lights. We sat close to each other on the cold stones, and touched hands and thighs that autumn night of teases and stories.

"One must know how to float as words," said Anaïs as the waves broke higher on the black stones. "When words and feelings have learned to float, they reach the poetic *mouvement perpétuel*. To float means to be joined to some universal rhythm."

Yes, native motion is *mouvement perpétuel*, the natural motion of stories and the seasons, rage of thunderstorms, overnight crack of river ice, and a moccasin flower in the shadows turns with the slightest breeze. The seasons were totems, and storms were the stories of natural motion. Anaïs pointed to the late night waves, there too was the very heart of natural motion.

"The absolute means the pulsing moment of rhythm," she declared, and then held me closer. "It is while floating, abandoning myself to experience, that I became tied to the whole world."

"My heart is natural motion."

"I let myself be pushed by everything that was stronger than myself, love, pity, creation, I floated thus into unity," she murmured and moved back and forth in my arms with the waves of the River Seine.

12

LEBENSRAUM

Friday, 5 November 1937

The native heirs of the fur trade tease care, custom, and salvation, envision dream songs in the clouds and create stories of natural motion in every trace of seasons, the reveal of moccasin flowers, blue ravens in the autumn birch, the court of cedar waxwings in the sumac, the steady count of cicadas, the totemic care of bears, martens, the lament of loons at dusk, and the great dance of sandhill cranes.

Creation stories are necessary teases of tradition, and rumors of native tricksters in every stone and story once healed the uneasy sway of shamans and poseurs, even as the rage of war and racial vengeance wounds the heart of dream songs and chase the summer in the spring.

"Shamans chase the lonely," said Aloysius.

"Nazis shame liberty," shouted Heap of Words.

Misaabe and the great healer mongrels of Bad Boy Lake provoked me to recognize the native tease as totemic and observe as natural motion the dance of black flies, intricate webs of spiders, the whoosh of nighthawks, and the mimicry of birds, butterflies, mosquitos, bats, and bears. The creatures with eyespots and background colors displayed survival disguises, and the cache of tricky ravens, click of bats, roundabout of black bears, and the wounded wing dance of plovers were elusive teases and vital deceptions. Natives carried out in stories that totemic tease to denature and deceive with irony the mission of race and predatory politics that wounded the spirit with deadend words and promises of salvation in the churchy comedown of civilization.

"Bears masturbate," shouted Heap of Words.

"Totemic onanism," said Nika.

The Anishinaabe heart stories of *aki*, the earth, created the breath of seasons, and *awasaakwaa*, the other side of the forest, envisioned natural motion that was never the same in creation stories, and our dream songs since the war have continued that native wit and perception on the other side of the clouds, the forests, and the ocean.

Continental liberty was at the heart of native stories, and the earth was never a political estate before the fur trade and treaty reservations of separatism. The constant state ridicule of native cultures, and the colonial possession of land was a mean prologue to the autocratic policies of lebensraum, the cocky nationalist rush for living space advanced with savage vengeance by Adolf Hitler and the Third Reich.

"Nazis copied reservations," said Aloysius.

Heap of Words was ready to tease me about the notion of colonial estates and totemic ravens and mongrel bays in the wispy clouds, but instead he shouted out several times the word *awasaakwaa*, the vision of time with distance, and waved away federal reservations with a dream song, "Summer in the spring is the season of our liberty in Paris."

The Third Reich obstructed natural motion, denounced dream songs, cut stories, burned books, berated literary irony, sidelined creative diversions, and converted the nostalgia of a wimpy empire into fascist vengeance and the rage of nationalism. The Nazis had no creative sense of motion or cultural tease.

"Third Reich savages," said Heap of Words.

"Empires of revenge," said Aloysius.

"Nostalgia with no literary irony," said Pierre.

The Anishinaabe and other native cultures negotiated La Grande Paix de Montréal, The Great Peace of Montréal, in 1701 with the governor of the royal province of New France, and for sixty years honored the ethos and chance of native governance; and then the stories of peace were cast aside in the empire wars, the wicked fur trade, faraway fashions, and the lebensraum of Manifest Destiny in the United States.

The Anishinaabe barely endured the greedy fate of fur fashions, and outlived the missionary finger wags of shame with the word *miikindizi*, the creative tease, and mockery of priests of the fur trade. Even so the devious missionaries and federal agents maligned native nicknames, and some churchy natives were bothered by the totemic tease that overturned the hearsay of salvation. The backdrop catechists never grasped the native choice of *miikindizi*, the tease, diversion, and irony of trickster creation stories.

"Ethos of irony," shouted Heap of Words.

Natives were removed to reservations in the bloody lunge for land, and new dream songs evolved with the manifest manners of fate and fortune. Once the totemic creatures were decimated in the fur trade, the stories were told with new totems on the road with heavy memories. The native mountains, forests, prairies, and rivers were given away to railroad companies and homesteaders, the new nationalist "living space" of a constitutional democracy. The Indian Removal Act of 1830 was an act of lebensraum more than a century before the Nazi Third Reich.

Native creation stories were mutable, an uneasy union of natural motion and totemic character. The creation stories were never liturgy, or comparable to biblical fury, and with mockery survived the cause of monotheism and the possessive pronouns of nationalism. The memorable creations were a totemic tease, and trickster stories carried out the natural motion of the seasons. As exiles from a federal reservation and the lebensraum of Manifest Destiny our ironic stories on *Le Corbeau Bleu* have set in motion a new native creation of liberty on the River Seine.

"Barge of liberty," shouted Heap of Words.

"Fur Trade Treaty of Versailles," said By Now.

"*Blut und Boden*," said Nathan.

"Third Reich blood and beer," said Pierre.

Nathan now buys three or four daily newspapers, the conservative *Le Figaro*, occasionally the chauvinistic and nationalist tabloid *Le Matin*, and he always reads *L'Humanité*, the communist newspaper, and the socialist *Le Populaire*. We tease him several times a week about *Le Matin*, and each time he creates the ironic conversions of headlines, "Léon Blum, Jews, and Le Front Populaire Saved the Third Republic." Then he declares that everyone must overturn with ironic stories the devious captions of the enemy way and stand with the liberty of France.

"Besieged with unintended irony," said Nika.

Joseph Stalin was pictured in the left corner near the masthead of *L'Humanité*, and with a long potted message from the executive committee of international communists. The Nazi menace was not newsworthy, but the dictator of slave labor camps was prominent. The cures and *médicaments* advertised on the back pages were similar to the promotion of patent medicine cures for a wide range of aches and atmospheres in *The Tomahawk* on the White Earth Reservation.

Nathan pointed to an ironic picture of Maryse Bastié on the front page of *L'Humanité* who had presented the Legion of Honor to Madeleine Charnaux. Bastié, the famous aerobatic aviator, had actually received the Chevalier de la Légion d'Honneur earlier and staged the ironic esprit de corps event to honor another woman aviator at a grand café on the Champs-Élysées.

Nathan saluted the aviators and then read out loud a bold headline on the front page of *Le Figaro* about Joseph Goebbels. "Le Dr Goebbels fera ce soir une communication officielle sur les revendications colonials de l'Allemagne," Doctor Goebbels, This Evening, Will Make an Official Communication on the Colonial Claims of Germany. The statement had already been delivered by the time the paper was published. Nathan shouted with disgust that Joseph Goebbels, Reich Minister of Propaganda, would first attack the foreign press, as usual, and then declare the "Versailles Treaty is dead, and French opinion is favorable to abrogate the treaty."

Goebbels proclaimed that the pathological criminal madness to destroy civilized people was invented by the Jews. The Third Reich erected an imaginary wall to block the rush of the communists and Bolshevism, and warned that communists were Jews. Adolf Hitler raised the banner of vengeance and fascism in the name of a superior culture, and then with his crooked gray hand saluted the menace.

"Minister of Menace," shouted Heap of Words.

"Nazis are irony deficient," said Pierre.

Aloysius could not resist the ironic comparison of the Treaty of Versailles to the treaty of 1867 that established the White Earth Reservation, and pointed out that the federal treaty promised care, services, education, houses, and farm horses for two million acres of land with valuable timber. The white pine was cut to build houses elsewhere, lakes and rivers were diverted forever, and natives were scorned and turned over to missionaries and mercenary agents.

"Versailles was vengeance," said Pierre.

"White Earth treaty of greed," said Nika.

"Abrogate Goebbels," said Nathan.

"White Earth revocation," shouted Aloysius.

"Legion of Honor for survival," said Nika.

Every serious moment trailed into ironic stories and testy humor, teases of the barge mongrels, *chiens bâtards*, or lusty memories of the woman in the blue scarf and wistful piano music of Erik Satie on the River Seine, and the favor of jazz musicians in Paris.

Nathan was buoyed by the native tease talk and ironic stories about crackpot missionaries, revolutionaries, newsy fascists, and loony peacemongers, and he was always ready for a native tease, the same pose or pitch of irony that his father had learned from native storiers at trading posts in New Mexico and Arizona Territory. He revealed in casual stories about the fiddlers of melancholy that the ordinary tease of mongrels, trickster creations, and heart healers were never directly mentioned in synagogues or traditional stories of the Rabbis.

"Fiddlers of jazz," shouted Heap of Words.

"Shtetl swing," said By Now.

"Cubist harmony," said Aloysius.

"Yiddish cranks of intimacy," said Nika.

"Jewish fiddlers were always in motion in market squares, and with the tease of music and an original swing of traditions, a salute to melody, but never promises," said Nathan.

"Jazz is liberty not a promise," said Aloysius.

Radio Cité broadcasts swing music and the Manouche or Gypsy Jazz of Django Reinhardt, and a few months ago with Stéphane Grappelly, the innovative violinist, relayed a live performance of the *Quintette du Hot Club de France* on "Saturday Night Swing Club" produced by the Columbia Broadcast Company. The performance was broadcast to several countries from The Big Apple in Paris, or the Chez Bricktop on Rue Pigalle, a cabaret owned by the great jazz singer Ada Smith. The broadcast was early in the morning, and the shortwave transmission wavered and created a strange tremor of swing.

Samuel listened to the *Quintette* several times on the radio at the Galerie Crémieux. Nathan had a large radio at home but not a record player, and he replaced the small radio at the gallery with the purchase of a new Ducretet Thomson from the *mont-de-piété*, the municipal pawnshop. The deep sound of the big radio roused the spirits. Samuel would stand in front of the radio cabinet, swing his arms, and move with the sound of the re-corded music. He heard the swing guitar and violin renditions of *Dinah* and the likeable melody of *Minor Swing* several times on radio. His first moves were with the rush and wonder of the guitar by Django, and then a few months later he was enchanted with the rich, marvelous, and moody melodies of Stéphane Grappelly.

"Samuel pretends to play," said Nathan.

"Music is his play," shouted Heap of Words.

"Satie on the Seine is our radio," said Aloysius. "The woman in the blue scarf plays the piano for me because she must know there are no electrical connections for a radio on *Le Corbeau Bleu*."

Panzéra raised his head high and bayed that afternoon at the sight of Anaïs Nin on the deck of *La Belle Aurore*. Pig Ears, the mongrel of the barge tiller, danced on her tiny back legs around the deck and then pushed the tiller to the side. The deck dance was a comic opera scene, and the motion of her ears was wacky, but she never barked, aware, no doubt, that the sound of her bark was screechy, and not related to the marvelous songs of coyotes or timber wolves.

Anaïs Nin and her lover Gonzalo Moré, a native exile from Peru, joined us on *Le Corbeau Bleu* that night after our critical and ironic tour of news stories and the daily mongrel bay and tiller dance. Gonzalo was a painter with black hair and bare arms, and he seemed hazy from some tonic or opiate. He was the main barge successor to the novelist Henry Miller.

"Barge of paradise," said Heap of Words.

Pierre and Nika prepared a casual dinner of potato salad with olive oil, basil, scallions, and parsley. Nathan provided the wine and cheese, as usual, and we saluted our relatives, the heirs of the fur trade, and every artist who came to mind over the wine, especially the memory of new-comers with great artistic visions, Marc Chagall, Chaïm Soutine, Moïse Kisling, the lovely Marie Vassilieff, and the memory of the steamy Amedeo Modigliani.

"High necks rouged," shouted Heap of Words.

Later, at exactly ten, the exposition music and light show started at the Palais de Chaillot and the Eiffel Tower. The *Fête de la Dance* was com-posed by Marcel Delannoy for the second to last night of scheduled music broadcasts on more than forty loudspeakers wired to the trees, barges, and buildings close to the River Seine.

The International Exposition of Art and Technology in Modern Life, *Exposition Internationale des Arts et Techniques dans la Vie Moderne*, commissioned eighteen composers to create and record music for more than forty nights between June and November 1937.

Panzéra bayed with every melody.

Last month at this time was the conclusion of three wistful and melancholy broadcasts of *Fête des Belles Eaux*, or Festival of Beautiful Waters, composed by Olivier Messiaen. *Fête de la Lumière*, the timely display of fountains and lights, was magical with the recorded music, and the smart motion of shine and shadows decorated the Palais de Chaillot, the new museums, Musée de l'Homme, Musée de la Marine, Jardin du Trocadéro, and the majestic five arches of the Pont d'Iena and the many national exposition pavilions on the banks of the River Seine.

Messiaen composed the haunting melodies for six ondes Martenot, a new electronic instrument, for broadcast on three nights that summer. The dreamy melodies and captivating harmonies of *Fête des Belles Eaux*, a romantic waver of tender moods, was heard on *Le Corbeau Bleu* and resonated from every side of the river. The piano tones, timbre, vibrant pulse, and vibrato of a cello remained in the night air and seemed to slowly fade away with waves on the River Seine. Pig Ears cocked her head to the side, raised a grand ear, and strained to locate the actual sources of the music.

The Vicar moaned with the echoes.

Aloysius imagined the secretive pianist with the blue scarf, and we waited in silence on *Le Corbeau Bleu* for the last two broadcasts of *Fête des Belles Eaux*, by Olivier Messiaen. The entire city was enchanted every night by the recorded broadcasts, the romantic motion and vibrant nature of the melodies.

"The music of liberty," said Nathan.

The Spanish Civil War continued in the abstract art, ethos, rights of conscience, and the mighty reign of pavilion architecture at the *Exposition Internationale*. Adolf Hitler saluted the savagery of the monarchist Francisco Franco and the fascist Nationalists. Stalin posed at a great distance with the communists and anarchists on the side of the Spanish Republic. These two political poseurs of peace and progress were revealed in the construction of the pavilion empires at the end of Pont d'Iena on the River Seine.

The Nazi Pavilion, enclosed in massive rectangular pillars of rose granite, and with no sense of motion, faced downriver. An enormous predatory eagle, wings cocked, was perched on the crown of a swastika. Nathan reported that the floor on the inside of the pavilion was coated with red rubber, but we refused to set foot in the fascist empire of vengeance and book burners.

The Soviet Pavilion was constructed of marble and tiered rectangles, and was futuristic with a sense of light, motion, and the irony of peace. A gigantic sculpture was mounted on the marble prow of the pavilion. Nathan announced in a loud voice as we entered that the modern design was by the architect Boris Iofan, a Soviet Jew from Odessa.

The enormous sculpture, *Worker and Kolkhoz Woman*, by Vera Mukhina, depicted a factory worker, muscular and heroic, with a hammer raised overhead, slanted to the wind, the lunge of social realism with a peasant woman, nipples erect, dress billowed, thick streams of hair, and one arm raised with a sickle. No trace of terror in the hefty sculpture, and no mention of socialist realism or the thousands of factory slaves and peasants who vanished in labor camps. The ironic sculpture, almost eighty feet high, faced the flow of the river and the stone pavilion of the Third Reich.

Thousands of visitors sauntered every day over the widened Pont d'Iena between the two pavilions of crafty communism and the brute force of fascist vengeance, and never cursed the Soviet or Nazi presence as the reveals of another world war.

The splendid museums and outlook of the Palais de Chaillot at one end of the vast exposition easily eclipsed any glance of terror or war, and at the other end stood the mighty monument of the Eiffel Tower. The French government, we learned later, had subsidized some of the construction costs of both extreme national pavilions.

"Favors of sycophants," said Heap of Words.

The Nazi Luftwaffe had bombed and destroyed Guernica, a town in Basque Country, on market day, Monday, 26 April 1937, and only a few weeks before the grand opening and public celebration of the *Exposition Intenationale* in Paris.

"Nazi thugs of war," shouted Heap of Words in front of the stone entrance to the Nazi Pavilion, but no one seemed to notice the résistance and commotion, or the shouts about the thugs of war was so obvious that no public response was necessary.

Aloysius was our platoon leader that afternoon and we marched past the stone monuments of vengeance, massive sculptures of fascism and communism to the nearby modernist pavilion of the Second Spanish Republic. My brother entered the gallery and caught his breath at the first sight of *Guernica* painted by Pablo Picasso. Nearby the great sorrow of the scene was eased by the *Mercury Fountain*, a marvelous mobile sculpture created by Alexander Calder.

"More than twice my height," said Black Elk.

Nika and Pierre walked slowly toward the huge canvas and were moved to tears. The black, gray, and white cubist scenes of panic, terror, and misery covered the entire back wall of the gallery. Fractured body parts, heads, arms, and feet, humans and animals, a horse and horned bull in space, a broken sword and flower, mouths opened wide with rage and horror, an everlasting lamentation, and we imagined more intensely the torrent of blood in the absence of any trace of the color red. The gallery was heavy, humid, and unbearably silent.

Nathan raised his arms in sorrow.

Nika opened her mouth and gasped.

Heap of Words turned away and moaned.

By Now closed her eyes and wept.

Black Elk reached out to embrace the scenes.

Standing Bear covered his ears.

Pierre kneeled close to the canvas.

Nathan backed away from the totemic horrors with me and turned toward the *Mercury Fountain* at the center of the gallery. Calder created the monumental sculpture to honor the memory of slaves and laborers in the mercury mines of Almadén. The modernist mobile was painted red, and in magical motion with real mercury. Curious visitors tossed coins on the mirror of heavy metal. The gallery attendant said as much as three hundred francs a day was gathered from the mercury and donated to the children of the Spanish Civil War.

The Spanish Pavilion was completed a month late, and was hardly noticed or reviewed after the grand opening of the *Exposition Internatio-*

nale. The Nazi, Soviet, and many other national pavilions promoted the modern advances of technology, aeronautics, automobiles, and machines of war. The Spanish Republic presented the ethos and conscience of the modern world in art, sculpture, literature, and the horror of war. The photographs of soldiers and dead children were mounted at the entrance to the pavilion, an emotive memoir of the Spanish Civil War.

Picasso was commissioned to create a painting for the pavilion. He was probably working on many other projects when he learned about the bombing raid and destruction of Guernica. Anaïs Nin told me that Picasso was haunted by the massacre, painted furiously for about a month, and completed *Guernica* in time for the opening of the pavilion on 4 June 1937.

The painting was eleven feet high and more than twenty feet wide, and mounted in the main gallery with the *Mercury Fountain* mobile sculpture. We returned to the pavilion and cubist lamentation many times to view the everlasting torment of market day in Guernica.

"Lakota Pavilion and Wounded Knee," Standing Bear shouted over and over at the Jardin du Trocadéro. That afternoon we wandered around the gardens and asked hundreds of visitors if they could direct us to the Lakota Pavilion, the Sand Creek Pavilion, the Maria River Pavilion, and the Bear Island Pavilion. Only one person paused to respond to our inquiries, and she was a schoolteacher, a Cherokee who lived in California.

Aloysius proposed that we pitch a tent and name it the Bear Island Pavilion. Standing Bear would pitch another tent named the Lakota Nation Pavilion. Heap of Words shouted out that we should rename *Le Corbeau Bleu* the *Pavillon des Massacres des Indiens d'Amerique*, Pavilion of American Indian Massacres, and dock the barge on the quay near the Nazi and Soviet Pavilions.

"Nazi red rubber, steel, and war machines attract more people than cultural ethos, a native conscience, or the shame of Guernica," said Pierre. "So, better to play irony and carry placards that promote and celebrate the power of native shamans and the tease of dream songs."

"Modern fur trade warriors," said Nika.

We traveled five times by river ferry to the exposition, and dedicated an entire day to the flighty adventures of the *Parc de la Gâité*, the park of gaiety and delights. Black Elk mounted a camel for a ride in the park. Heap of Words and Nika parachuted from the Eiffel Tower. Pierre and

Aloysius flew in circles in simulated airplanes. By Now sat with a palm reader, and was sternly warned to be prepared to care for a wounded horse and a handsome Frenchman.

Posters and notices celebrated the *exposition coloniale*, but we avoided the empire servants on display with curious attire and crafts, and fantastic cultural practices invented for the occasion in the names of Africa, the Middle East, and the Orient.

By Now convinced me and my brother not to visit the pavilion of the United States of America because of the way veterans of the Bonus Expeditionary Force were treated by elected senators and the United States Army, and we never forgot that the police murdered her lover William Hushka.

13

KRISTALLNACHT

Thursday, 10 November 1938

Romain Rolland, the novelist and pacifist, appealed about six months ago to the union of French authors, artists, and scientists on the front page of *L'Humanité*, 31 March 1938. *O mes collègues de la pensée française—écrivains, artistes, hommes de science—permettez à un de vos doyens d'âge, en cette heure grave pour la France, de faire sa confession et la vôtre!* Nathan was heartened by the urgent appeal, and translated part of the literary petition that morning at Les Deux Magots. "My colleagues, writers, artists, men of science, allow one of your most senior members, at this critical hour for France, to make his confession and yours."

Rolland continued his appeal, "France has the formidable honor of becoming, in the eyes of the world, the last bastion of liberty on the continent, a liberty in all its most vital forms, the most essential for all human order, for all progress, political and social liberty, intellectual liberty, even religious liberty, since at this moment the stampede of barbarism threatens to bring disorder to free thought and the ideal of social justice, to mutual respect, equality of men and races."

The Cherokee Nation and other natives made similar petitions to the federal government for more than a century, and continued with their formal appeals to reverse the Indian Removal Act of 1830. President Andrew Jackson prevailed and the heartless removal of natives in southeastern states became the Trail of Tears, the deadly forced march of entire cultures to Indian Territory west of the Mississippi River.

"Fugitives of god, gold, and greed," said Aloysius.

"Les Marais liberty," shouted Heap of Words.

Samuel Kauffmann was swayed by the bright sounds of violins, and mimicked the manner of street musicians in Les Marais and on the busy boulevards near the River Seine. He waved a pretend bow in the air, canted his head, pressed strings on the neck of an imaginary fingerboard, and pretended to create the motion of violin music.

"Heart music," said By Now.

Nathan declared that Samuel was obviously inspired by the great tradition of Jewish fiddlers, and he praised the melancholy turns of cultural memory, traces of whimsy and exile, mellow tones of motion and light, and, of course, the magical abstract image of a green violinist by Marc Chagall.

"Mock the muse of motion," said Aloysius.

"Music is always mockery," said By Now.

Samuel continued to imitate the gestures of the violinists for the barge mongrels that sunny autumn afternoon on *Le Corbeau Bleu*. Pig Ears cocked an ear and pretended to bark as she pushed the tiller to the port. The Vicar turned his head from side to side and practiced his best bay with Panzéra.

Nathan arrived later with a mysterious bale tucked under his arm. He untied the strings, slowly removed the blanket of newspapers, and presented a French Mirecourt violin and a horsehair bow to Samuel. The beautifully crafted instrument was gently worn and radiant in the late glance of sunlight.

Nathan had inherited three violins from his late father, Clément Henri Crémieux, and recounted that the first violin was a German Cremona. The Germans mimicked the violins of Antonio Stradivari, and when war and colonial politics ended the glorious creation of violins in Cremona, Italy, the market favored the master makers of violins in Saxony.

Clément bought the German Cremona violin, made of spruce and maple, almost thirty years ago from the maker Ludwig Gläsel. The second was a Huichol cedar violin that he obtained in trade, and it was for sale at Galerie Crémieux. The third violin was made by one of the many famous luthiers in Mirecourt, and was the gift from a socialist writer for *L'Humanité*. Clément had supported the writer and many other exiles from the Pale of Settlement in the Russian Empire. Many of the Jews that he encouraged became professionals and merchants, some in leather and clothing, and others owned restaurants in Les Marias.

"The French Mirecourt is a perfect violin for the music and politics of the time," declared Nathan. "The French and Nazi fascists might suspect the source or worth and actually fancy a German Cremona."

Nathan had learned to play the violin, but his interests in music were modern, more innovative than traditional, and he would rather listen than pretend to play the great waves of new music, the jazz and innovative swing melodies of Django Reinhardt, Stéphane Grappelly, Louis Armstrong, and Sidney Bechet.

Nathan sidestepped passive music and never hesitated to scorn the waltz as the deadly chords of royalty, the *walzen* of limp lace and mercenary empires. "Jazz might rush the waltz with an original beat, and the untamed accents rightly ridicule the rehearsed dance moves of every boot-licker in the monarchy."

"Natives never waltz," shouted Heap of Words.

"Not a natural motion," said Aloysius.

"Rather canter than waltz," said By Now.

Samuel stayed on deck that warm night, three days after the whole moon, and watched the buoyant shadows, *couloir de l'automne*, the autumn corridors of sycamore, linden, chestnut, and plane trees move slowly over the cold statues and stone monuments in the Jardin des Tuileries. The mongrels were at his side, and the first plunks, strums, and shy shivers of his new violin wavered on the River Seine.

The music of fiddlers and native stories stay forever in the clouds, the dream songs of liberty, and these generous moments of cultural memory were recounted on the very same night that fascist Brownshirts persecuted thousands of Jews, raided their stores, schools, homes, and destroyed synagogues in Berlin, Nuremberg, Munich, Cologne, Leipzig, Hamburg, and hundreds of other cities in Germany.

"The night of broken crystal," said Nathan.

"Nazi nights of vengeance," said Aloysius.

"Rage of envy," shouted Heap of Words.

Nathan related the fear and heart stories he heard from many friends late last night about the pogrom, and the next day the Paris *Herald Tribune*, *L'Humanité*, *Le Figaro*, and other newspapers reported that Jews were forbidden to practice medicine or law, to own automobiles or telephones, and were ordered to leave Germany. Jewish newspapers, the chronicles of culture, were closed, and children were not allowed to attend state schools. Jews were arrested, beaten, removed, and personal property confiscated by criminals of the Third Reich.

The *Édition Parisienne* of *L'Humanité* reported on the front page, in three headlines, that "Von Rath a succombé." "L'empressement de la Gestapo à exploiter sa mort souligne encore le caractère trouble de l'attentat." "Nouvelle vague de terreur raciste en allemagne." Nathan slowly translated the headlines that night with restrained rage, "Ernst von Rath succumbed, and the Gestapo eager to exploit his death underlines the murky character of the attack, and the new wave of racist terror in Germany." The headlines, he declared, "should have used the words massacre and pogrom."

Ernst von Rath, an attaché at the German Embassy in Paris, was shot three days ago and died yesterday. Herschel Grynszpan, a teenage refugee, was the assassin who grieved for the fate of his family and other Jews. The Nazis named him a devious conspirator in political propaganda. Adolf Hitler blamed the Jews for the attack, and used the death of a minor diplomat to carry out the savagery against Jews.

Nathan had already heard stories that the assassination was more sexual than political, but he was hesitant to repeat the baggy rumors that the Nazi diplomat was a homosexual who frequently visited Le Boeuf sur le Toit, one of the popular avantgarde cabarets in Paris. The Nazi diplomat mingled with artists, writers, jazz musicians, and fancied teenage refugees. Von Rath was secretly teased in discrete corners of fascist lechery with several nicknames, including the ironic "Madame Ambassador."

"Heil Schwuler," shouted Heap of Words.

"Deadly disclosure," said Nathan.

Jews were blamed everywhere for the turmoil of the economic depression, but that treacherous excuse for the persecution would never stand as a reason to turn away exiles and refugees. The First World War fractured cultures, economies, and families in France, Germany, Britain, and many other countries. The breach of empire cultures was obvious in the wild turn to cubist art and surrealist literature, and once again courage was crucial to confront the tyranny and murder of citizens, the savage attack against an ancient culture, and the wanton destruction of thousands of synagogues.

"Fascists of envy," shouted Heap of Words.

"Fascists of envy and vengeance," said Aloysius, "and the very same civilization of racial supremacy that carried out the mass murder of natives, death marches and theft of land, militia bounty hunters, starvation, and the removal of natives to separatist federal reservations in a constitutional democracy."

"Envoys of death," shouted Heap of Words.

"Delegates of a pogrom," said Aloysius.

"Eugenics on the Fourth of July," said By Now.

The Évian Conference was convened last summer, a woeful gathering of evasive toady back talkers to parse and decide in back rooms the number of Jewish refugees each country would accept. The Nazis had already declared a pogrom and drove more than a hundred thousand Jewish citizens out of the country, and yet promised to pay the break out fare of the others, the fascist kickback after the plunder of money and property, but only the honorable delegates from the Dominican Republic agreed to accept the Jews as refugees. The delegates from thirty other countries devised diplomatic schemes that evaded the moral duty to rescue refugees from a fascist pogrom.

The United States, United Kingdom, France, Australia, Canada, Ireland, New Zealand, Argentina, Brazil, Chile, and twenty more countries turned their backs on the persecution of Jews in the Third Reich.

Olivier Black Elk and Coyote Standing Bear proposed that the United States Bureau of Indian Affairs sponsor the relocation of every Jewish refugee, individuals and families, on federal reservations and other enclaves as an honorable expansion of the progressive policies and programs of the New Deal.

Jews and the conscience of the world were deserted at the conference in Évian-les-Bains, France. The delegates no doubt cured their bloated bodies in the natural spring water, and were served *haute cuisine*, cognac aged in oak barrels, cigars hand rolled in the colonies, and always with elegance and a grand view of Lac Léman.

"Curse of Évian," shouted Heap of Words

"Taking the waters of infamy," said Aloysius.

Jews were held in custody, and then forsaken by fascists, political deceit, the evasive dictates of secure governments, and the ruthless turn away

clauses of nationalism that revealed the ruse and impotence of the enlightenment and civilization.

Nathan was outraged that *L'Humanité*, his favorite daily newspaper,
had not published a story on the front page about the Évian Conference,
not a word of concern during the ten days of delegate maneuvers. He
shook the newspaper every day, but the news stories on the front page
remained the same, no mention of antisemitism, the torment of refugees,
or the pogrom, and he shouted that the communist newspaper was no
longer a reliable source of international news.

Nathan reasoned at the time that the dreadful economic and political negotiations between the Third Reich and the Soviet Union probably
suppressed any news that was not favorable to the Communist Party and
the Nazis. At the same time he was reassured by at least one newspaper;
the conservative *Le Figaro* published a jump story on the front page, 7
July 1938, the second day of the international conference, with the bold
headline, "La Conférence réunie à Evian pour l'examen du problem des
réfugiés politiques, s'est ouverte hier sous la présidence de M. Henry
Bérenger." Nathan read out loud a translation of the headline story, "The
Conference came together in Évian for the examination of the problems
of the political refugees, and the conference opened yesterday with comments by the principal delegate Henry Bérenger."

"Delegates of naught," said Aloysius.

"Réunion de rien," shouted Heap of Words.

Olivier Black Elk and Coyote Standing Bear, native poseurs and loyal
friends in the best tradition, arrived fit and ready to renounce the political
apathy of the delegates from thirty nations, and, with no feigns or mockery
of moral duties, proposed to rescue the refugees, end the pogrom, and
hold Adolf Hitler to his word that he would pay for the cost to transport
Jews out of Germany.

The White Earth Trace, a proposed native sanctuary of refugees, and
Le Corbeau Bleu of Paris solemnly resolved to liberate the Jews of Germany, and to establish communities on hundreds of native reservations and
enclaves with initial services provided by federal policies and programs,
relief, recovery, reform, and work projects enacted as the New Deal in
the United States.

Black Elk declared that President Franklin Roosevelt promised a New

Deal for the country, and declared six years ago that the men and women who were "forgotten in the political philosophy of the government, look to us here for guidance and for more equitable opportunity to share in the distribution of national wealth."

Standing Bear revealed that the Native New Deal, or Indian Reorganization Act, established two years later, reversed two federal policies, the removal and then the assimilation of natives, and encouraged native traditions and cultures. New constitutions of native governance were provided, and natives were allowed to manage the land and resources on more than three hundred treaty reservations.

The New Deal of the White Earth Trace proposed that at least a hundred to three hundred refugees, individuals and families, based on the extent of the reservations, would be relocated to each of the three hundred reservations in the country, a native moral duty that would provide a secure community for more than thirty to ninety thousand Jews.

Olivier Black Elk and Coyote Standing Bear were honored as envoys of the White Earth Trace, and at the end of the conference signed the formal rescue proposal on Monday, 18 July 1938. The dauntless declaration was delivered to every newspaper in Paris, including the Paris *Herald Tribune*, *Le Figaro*, and *L'Humanité*, but the editors were evasive and never reported a single word about the resolution of liberty and the Native New Deal.

Nathan printed a broadside of the Native New Deal rescue proposal and distributed hundreds of copies at Paris Metro stations, municipal offices, and at every familiar café and public place in Paris. For several weeks he told stories about his father and the honor of natives in the trade, the trust and tease of barter, debts and deals, personal associations, and shopkeepers. Jews and natives shared the everlasting moral conscience and liberty of the trade in stories.

Nathan created stories that summer about the integrity, courtesy, and decency that would emerge from the cultural union of natives and Jews, and he compared the rescue proposal to the vital associations of natives and traders more than fifty years ago. "Moral duties are never registers of dues and debts," he declared. "Moral duties are a necessary union of conscience and liberty, and no culture has ever endured without the enactment of moral duties in extreme circumstances."

14

EMPIRE PRIMATES

Monday, 4 September 1939

By Now, Aloysius, Samuel, and the barge mongrels were on deck to hear the music of Erik Satie. That lovely woman in the blue scarf started to play the piano at dawn, much earlier than on any other morning in the past. The moody melody was barely heard over the unearthly rush of people with handcarts, and thunder of trucks and automobiles on the Pont de la Concorde.

"Newsy war of panic," said By Now.

Aloysius was enchanted with the pianist and every note and original chord that wavered on the River Seine, however faint, but whenever he gestured to the woman in the blue scarf with a hand wave, cocked his head with a wide smile, or beckoned the tribute brava, brava, brava, she was cautious, turned away, shy and sensuous, and never responded to my brother or to any other stranger.

"I am captivated by that woman," Aloysius declared from the tiller of *Le Corbeau Bleu*. A gust of wind raised the blue scarf, and the pianist paused for a moment, distracted by the congestion on the bridge, and then continued to play in a rosy glance of sunlight.

Samuel raised the violin bow and with only slight pressure on the strings he created an original version of the melody, a bright, slightly hesitant tone that roused Pig Ears and the other mongrels. The sound of the violin wavered with the mellow piano tones on the Quai des Tuileries.

The music was a crucial gesture of liberty because newspapers and radio broadcasts around the world reported the dreadful news of another war. France, Great Britain, Australia, and New Zealand declared war against Germany late yesterday, and *Le Figaro* published the declaration today with banner headlines. Samuel and the pianist in the blue scarf played together at a distance for more than an hour as the sun moved slowly over the dark water of the River Seine.

LA FRANCE ET L'ANGLETERRE
sont en état de guerre avec l'Allemagne

The two banner headlines were direct, and much too easy to translate, "France and England are in a state of war with Germany." Other headlines continued with precise schedules and conditions:

DEUX SUPREMES DEMARCHES AVAIENT ETE FAITES

LES DELAIS ONT EXPIRE

"Two supreme steps had been made," and the formal deadlines expire, *à 11 heures pour l'Angleterre*, at eleven hundred hours for England, and, *à 17 heures pour la France*, at seventeen hundred hours for France.

The precise communiqués of the declaration of war were ironic gestures of reason and culture, a ceremony of curious diplomacy, and carried out by obedient editors of newspapers; but the course of manners was never the convention of fascist warmongers. The German Wehrmacht had invaded Poland three days earlier, and the expiration of merciful statecraft was now measured in hours to withdraw military forces and avoid war.

"Countdown to another war," said Pierre.

"English air of manners," declared Aloysius.

"French air of eminence," said Nika.

"Hazy maneuvers," shouted Heap of Words.

The Préfecture de Police prepared a map of automobile escape routes from Paris. *Le Figaro* published a map of the eleven routes on the front page yesterday, and caused more panic than the actual calculations of war with the Third Reich. Children were evacuated on trains, and thousands of worried citizens packed mattresses, furniture, buckets and baskets of worldly goods on automobiles, horse wagons, and handcarts, others carried bundles on bicycles and rickety baby carriages, and the reluctant fugitives of war rushed to every passable exit route from La Ville Lumière, the City of Light.

The first escape route was Porte de la Chapelle north to Beauvais, Abbeville, Chantilly, and Amiens. The sixth route was Porte d'Italie south to Nemours and Malesherbes. The ninth escape route by car was from Porte Dauphine to Nantes. The tenth route in the circle of escapes routes was west from Porte de Champerret to Meulan.

Nathan never owned an automobile, so we were not tempted to break away from Paris. There were no smart or easy getaways from the start of the war because the roads were crowded with thousands of citizens, and surely the rural communes would not be pleased to court the escapees with overloaded carts, and distraught motorists. Demands for gasoline and food alone would create night terrors on escape roads of doubt, fear, and second thoughts.

"Roads to nowhere," shouted Heap of Words.

"Children lost," said Nika.

"Mongrels stranded," said By Now.

Some escape routes were reversed when thousands of escapees, rural citizens, farm families, and cutaway soldiers from the north and east were on the road with the dreadful memories of the First World War, and even more desperate refugees from other countries were on the risky roads with faith in chance and lucky escapes from the absolute menace of the Wehrmacht.

American automobiles, many with bullet holes in the doors and fenders, were parked near luxury hotels in Paris, the destination of ritzy citizens from the east, Holland and Belgium, who had escaped the savage armored advance of the Nazis.

"Cashed out liberty," shouted Heap of Words.

Nathan was determined never to leave Paris, and declared that he would continue as usual to manage the Galerie Crémieux, and would transfer ownership of the gallery to my brother and me when the fascists started to seize property. Only then would he escape the terror with his family to a vacation house in Sanary-sur-Mer on the Mediterranean Sea.

Frederich Kauffmann transferred the ownership of his gallery and apartment in Berlin several years ago to avoid the confiscation of property by the Nazis. Angelika had not heard from her husband since then, and now after the formal declaration of war she was determined to escape in silence with her children. Samuel continued to practice the violin every day on the deck of *Le Corbeau Bleu*, and Renata created puppet scenes with Aloysius.

"Horses, mongrels, forsaken with only the declaration of war," said By Now. "Children sent to the country, and some lost in crowds at train stations, and the destinations were never reservations or government schools." She was angry, and with no cause or obvious duty sat on deck every morning, watched the unnatural scurry of citizens on the quay and bridges, and listened to sweet violin music by Samuel.

The empire primates were overdressed once again in heavy military costumes decorated with bogus medals, the new masters of war machines. The empire mercenaries were once admired natives in romantic literature and the horse dance shows, but never matured as discrete warriors.

The colonial swashbucklers and voyageurs of the fur trade never practiced the stealth and bravery of native coup counts. The pretenders could have emulated the warriors who teased and taunted the enemy with a touch of a hand or coup stick and escaped with stature, and later told nightly stories about the shadow wars. Yet, the risks of contact were always great, and the native warriors were honored in stories of their coup counts.

"Headline coup counts today," said Aloysius.

"Deadly bylines," said By Now.

"Escape route mockery," said Nathan.

"Nazi tank coups," shouted Heap of Words.

Native warriors were once responsible for everything, and that included the motion of stories, but were not answerable to the politics of corruption, deception, or depravity. The peacock feather despots of rage and war, and the beaver hat mercenaries of church and state, concocted a civilization of debauched nobility and engines, the politics of coal and oil, and the savage clank of war machines, distant cannons, poison gas, and a cultural vengeance that ruined the natural motion of the earth.

By Now practiced the old native virtues of communal responsibility, and, at the same time, she carried out a crazy sense of chance and independence, a quirky manner, more surprise than nicety. She revealed courage in critical and ordinary situations, and a strong sense of cultural duty. She learned these virtues on a federal reservation of cultural separatism, and was honored for her service as a nurse in the First World War. Now, at the start of another war, that sense of duty was necessary with good grace to secure a supply of food. Surely everything would be more severely rationed during the war, leeks, coal, coffee, cigarettes, and she reached out to connect with an old lover as a communal duty.

Corporel Pierre Dumont came to mind, the combat soldier with the fantasy of a native princess and nurse on horseback. Our plucky cousin teased and healed the wounded soldier, and several months later when the war ended, he followed her to the White Earth Reservation. The French lust, leave, and crusade stories about *Les Indiens de Natchez* in the French colony *La Louisiane* recounted in the airy romance novel *René* by François-René Chateaubriand were his only preparation. Pierre probably never knew that the author was in America for only about five months and apparently never visited the native places that he described in the novel.

> *En arrivant chez les Natchez, René avait été obligé de prendre une épouse, pour se conformer aux moeurs des Indiens, mais il ne vivait point avec elle. Un penchant mélancolique l'entraînait au fond des bois; il y passait seul des journées entières, et semblait sauvage parmi les sauvages.*

> *Arriving amongst the Natchez René was obliged to take a wife to conform to the customs of the Indians; but he never lived with her. A melancholy person connected to the depths of the woods, he spent the days in solitude, a savage among the savages.*

Pierre had actually landed near the serene source not the sultry mouth of the Mississippi River, and stayed with his princess two months longer than Chateaubriand, but he was not ready for the steady winter teases and native stories about the erotic enticements of the Ice Woman. Bone cold and weary the veteran trudged out of the deep snow a few months later and returned to the family fish counter at Les Halles in Paris. Aloysius was convinced that even twenty years later the romancer of an exotic *Princesse Indienne* was just the same besotted with lusty memories of the lovely bare-faced native horsewoman and nurse named By Now Rose Beaulieu.

"Wrinkles to boot," shouted Heap of Words.

Nathan was named the platoon leader, and very early the next morning we set out with By Now, Aloysius, Samuel, Nika, and Renata for the huge food and fish markets at Les Halles near the Gothic Parish of Saint-Eustache. Seafood, fish, fruit, cheese, vegetables, flowers, and stout merchants were on display in the eight massive cast iron pavilions connected by covered aisles, and outside, crowded on both sides of the streets, Rue Pont-Neuf, Rue Montmartre, and Rue Rambuteau, hundreds of merchants mounted glorious bright carrots, leeks, celery, cabbages, artichokes, onions, beans, and other vegetables on wooden crates.

Émile Zola described Les Halles as a bourgeois market of decadence, and mocked the huge mounds of food as the belly of gluttony in his novel *Le Ventre de Paris*, translated as *The Belly of Paris*.

Nathan admired Zola and had read most of his novels in French, and as we approached the pavilions that early morning he recited from memory the first poetic sentence from *Le Ventre de Paris*, published in 1873.

Au milieu du grand silence, et dans le désert de l'avenue, les voitures de maraîchers montaient vers Paris, avec les cahots rythmés de leurs roues, dont les échos battaient les façades des maisons, endormies aux deux bords, derrière les lignes confuses des ormes.

Through the deep silence of the deserted avenue, the market carts moved towards Paris, the rhythmic beat of the wheels echoing against the front of the houses on both sides of the road, behind the vague shapes of the elms.

The merchants of rosy and golden fish, tender flowers, carrots, cabbages, mauve aubergine, and other bright and seductive vegetables were in the natural motion of color that morning, every morning, and evoked the memory of our visits to the market pavilions in the past few years. Aloysius said the touch of colors was a natural abstract show of art, and brought to mind *Le Marché aux Halles*, *Le Pont Neuf* and the spectacular hues of blues in *Le Marché de Pontoise* painted by the humane impressionist Camille Pissarro.

The thick neck porters or huskies wore hard hats with narrow brims to balance the fish crates carried from the drays to the wet stone auction counters. The easy scent of seaweed lingered as we searched every face in the pavilion, but surely the lusty corporal would have changed, stouter, cheeky, more decadent in the twenty years since he chased down our cousin on the White Earth Reservation.

By Now could not actually describe his face, but with more teases about the reservation chase she was able to recount his hands and naked body, muscular thighs, white chest, bright smooth scars, tender, skinny fingers, and then concentrated on his face. Deep blue eyes, but that connected with almost everyone at the market. We moved through the pavilions in search of a personal memory, a romance story, and lastly she remembered his high cheekbones, an aquiline nose, and the plump earlobes that were more discoverable than sexy blue eyes.

"Scottish earlobes," said Nathan.

"Catch the earlobes, not the eyes," said Aloysius.

Nathan remembered the food riots that summer at the end of the First World War. "Food prices increased and the riots were spontaneous and mostly women against the local shopkeepers and merchants" in the seafood pavilion at Les Halles. Then the *petits commerçants*, or small shopkeepers, "carried out a separate riot and overturned crates, and later attacked the egg and butter merchants."

Aloysius reminded me that we had visited Paris for the first time about two months after the Armistice on 11 November 1918. The war was over, millions of soldiers were dead and disfigured, and widows outnumbered the men. The forests, farms, and communes were in ruins, and we were savvy native soldiers on furlough from the First Pioneer Infantry of the Army of Occupation in Germany. We had arrived on a slow train at Gare de l'Est from Koblenz, and wandered down Boulevard de Sébastopol to Les Halles. Later we walked along the River Seine, and finally circled around and landed at Rue de la Bûcherie in the grace of Nathan and the Galerie Crémieux.

"Paris was a blue raven," said Aloysius.

Samuel was enchanted with the street violinists on Rue Pont-Neuf and closer to the market on Rue Rambuteau near the Paroisse Saint-Eustache. He sat for more than an hour with a street fiddler and mimicked the rapid finger moves of two contracted and creative compositions, a violin concerto by Pyotr Illich Tchaikovsky, and the second was a haunting alteration of a violin concerto by Felix Mendelssohn.

Renata was curious about the dark eyes and distinctive rosy undersides of fish neatly stacked in wicker baskets, the perfect rows of eyes, hundreds of eyes that stared down the queues of customers at the auction counter. The gaze of the fish was diverted by the monotonous chant and count of the auctioneer. Renata was a spectator, not a fish eye customer, and turned away from the counter. She was more interested in the two children hiding in huge baskets of bird feathers.

Twice we meandered through the pavilion of seafood and fish, past the spiny red gurnard, flatfish flounder, cod, conger eels, plaice, haddock, carp and crayfish, and sacks of black mussels in search of a corporal with sexy blue eyes and plump earlobes. Not one market porter or merchant caught our eye as a conceivable romancer. Most of the market men in the fish pavilion were portly, thick necked, and dominant, and bore no resemblance to the lusty veteran of memory.

Aloysius created a story that the corporal might have been promoted from the fish market to the cheese pavilion, Cantal, Neufchâtel, Port Salut, Roquefort, hard, creamy, mild, or tangy blue, or maybe he was advanced to the tripe and calves head market, but surely no other markets were conceivable, so we meandered through every pavilion once again, and paused over the pathetic motion of dying fish.

Nathan told a story about Roquefort as we moved though the distinctive aromas of regional cheeses, *arome de moisi de fromage*, musty cheese, *rustique*, rustic, floral, fruity, grassy, and yeasty in translation. Roquefort was discovered when a boy abandoned his lunch of cheese and bread in a cave and chased after a lovely girl in the distance. When he returned from the amorous adventure the cheese and bread had turned moldy. The outcome of the chase was a famous blue cheese aged in the natural caves of Mont Combalou in Southern France.

"Moldy romance," shouted Heap of Words.

By Now was our platoon leader in the other pavilions, and within an hour she discovered the corporal in a thick gray apron behind crates of carrots, cabbages, and onions. Yes, she caught his eye, and that concluded the search, but not the tease of memory.

Pierre could barely continue serving a customer, as his plump earlobes turned red, cheeks puffed, and long fingers trembled. He was strong, solitary, and not ready by chance of memory, or surprise union, to embrace his lovely princess By Now Rose. Naturally, we were very pleased, and my brother was the first to honor the good corporal with an original story about the Ice Woman who seduced a fur trader named the Marquis de Sade from New France. Pierre blushed even more, and then turned away.

Nika moved closer and handed the brave corporal of carrots and cabbages a new passport in his name, Pierre Dumont, Citizen of the White

Earth Nation. "A photograph, official seal, and you can travel to any native reservation and around the world," said By Now. He smiled, studied the passport, and then explained that he could not leave France. "I must serve my country in the war, not as a soldier but in some other way." By Now quickly corrected the idea that he was expected to leave for another try on the reservation, "the passport is a gesture of respect, an honor, and the memory of our time on the White Earth Reservation."

The Dumont family relocated from the *poisson* pavilion to the legume market when his father died about ten years ago. Pierre and his mother moved back to the nearby family farm and planted vegetables for the market at Les Halles.

By Now slowly untied the apron, and held his hand. Pierre burst into laughter, and then embraced our cousin and whispered either secret sexual messages or a romantic poem in her ear. She refused to reveal what he said, except that he was not married and had never forgotten her touch and spirit.

15

DREAM DOCTOR

Sunday, 24 September 1939

Nika Montezuma is a memorable storier, come what may, and standing at the tiller of *Le Corbeau Bleu* she related a haunting dream scene with Sigmund Freud, the pensive mind doctor and fantasy trader, who died from cancer of the mouth early yesterday in London.

Freud was at the window of a musty, smoky library, and she was on the outside caught in a dream of his death, by an actual overdose of morphine. Nika tapped several times at the window, and then broke through the glass in the dream scene and climbed inside. "I heard heavy wheezes and last breaths, shy whispers, and hesitations," she related from the dream, and then he turned in circles and cursed the sexual tyranny of Prince Hamlet. "Freud was cold, gray, fishy eyed, empty, almost dead, and when he reached to touch my face his fingers broke into pieces."

"Gruesome dream parts," said Aloysius.

"Handful of joints," shouted Heap of Words.

Sigmund Freud studied with the famous neurologist Jean Charcot for a year in Paris, but he probably never met Henri Bergson. Nika, just the same, continued with strange dream stories about the psychoanalyst and philosopher of *élan vital* that started in the Jardin du Luxembourg. Freud was dressed in a gray suit, fedora, and shrouded in plumes of cigar smoke. He was taking notes about the children and laughter, mostly the excitement of schoolboys who sailed miniature boats on the Bassin Rond. Bergson was seated on a bench on the other side of the basin taking pictures with a Voigtländer Bessa. Freud smiled and slowly faded away with each click of the camera. Nika clearly remembered the name of the camera because she reached out to cover the lens and crushed the bellows, but not soon enough to save the dream scenes of Freud.

"Fade away Freud," shouted Heap of Words.

"Bergson told me in the dream that Sigmund Freud was a comic spectacle, as he pretended to study the humor of boys with sail boats," said Nika. "I asked what was comic about the scene and the philosopher smiled and faded away on the bench, and when the boys waved at me and laughed the sail boats faded away."

"Freud always fades away," said Nathan.

"Save the boats, save the boys," said Aloysius.

The dream scenes she revealed on the barge were a collage of strange images, and yet the scenes faded away. Freud might have wrongly interpreted her park basin dreams as a reaction formation, or the need for recognition by important people. Nika admired the dream doctor, and was rather worried about his reputation as a psychoanalyst because he refused to consider that native dream scenes were real, and not a mere fantasy or duality.

"Dream junk," said Aloysius.

"Goaty Freud," shouted Heap of Words.

"Freud misused women with crafty dream gossip and the highbrow hooey of psychoanalysis," said Nathan. He firmly denounced the dream game practices because the doctor misinterpreted the anxieties of Jews, mainly women who were diagnosed with sexual neuroses and bourgeois hysteria in *The Interpretation of Dreams*. "The only real frenzy was in the head of the dream merchant, and he pretended to measure the real worries of women and Jews."

"Dream doctor blues," shouted Heap of Words.

"Nika actually revealed scenes of the dream theories," declared Aloysius. "Freud faded away with the mere click of a camera, a mortal flight, and surely his teeth must have crumbled at the same time his fingers broke into pieces."

Nika wrote a poem about the dream scenes, and with no punctuation, service to grammar, or crease of history. She read the poem to Henri Bergson, and "he laughed over the famous fades in the dream, and told me that the pale of psychoanalysis was nothing more than tease talkers in a cultural comedy."

"Freud the poseur," shouted Heap of Words.

"My dreams are on the crest of waves, in the clouds with dream songs, and natives dream the turn of seasons, and my dreams shimmer on the river at night," chanted Nika.

Anishinaabe dream scenes, songs, and visionary stories are waves of creation, the virtue of natural motion, but some scenes fade away with the strained translations of empire promises. Native dream scenes and stories create the real, not the other way around with tedious interpretation, and dreams are heartfelt, the actual creation of native motion and cultural reason.

"Freud got it backwards," said Aloysius. "Dreams are real, not the theories, not mere repressions, or interpretations by dream doctors and charlatans of culture."

"Cigar smoke quackery," shouted Nathan.

Nika told us a few years ago that Carlos Montezuma, her namesake, was always in her dreams, and the native medical doctor engaged in a seminar lecture with Henri Bergson about how the turn of native chance subverts the course of evolution in creation stories. Carlos declared in the dream that the sense of native presence was totemic and visionary, solely perceived with the chance and natural motion of creation, and then he slowly walk to the window and flew into the clouds over the Collège de France.

"Several students rushed to rescue the native doctor, but he had already vanished," said Nika over wine one late night at Les Deux Magots. "Henri Bergson was poised at the window and ready to fly in a dream with Montezuma, but the students shouted no, no, not now, not before the end of the seminar."

"Dream games of chance," said Nathan.

"Dream doctor envy," shouted Heap of Words.

Montezuma, or Wassaja, was against war, the savage close of dream scenes, and more than twenty years ago he argued that natives should not be obligated to serve in the First World War. His editorials were published on the front page of *The Tomahawk* on the White Earth Reservation and in many newspapers around the country. The declaration of another war was only a strategy of vengeance, the grudge of empires, not the tease of dream songs. We trusted the wise declarations of a native doctor, but despite his moral credo we served during the war as infantry soldiers and returned to the reservation with combat nightmares.

Nika moved the tiller from side to side and started another dream story to counter the tease of dream, demon, and doctor envy. "I was a *Pays d'en*

Haut voyageur in a fur trade dream with Carlos Montezuma and Sigmund Freud, and at the back of the canoe carried out the native box stroke in silence on Gunflint Lake to a campsite at the rocky north bay of Magnetic Lake in Canada."

"Magnetic Freud," shouted Heap of Words.

"Compass of dreams," said Aloysius.

"Carlos dragged the canoe ashore," said Nika.

Freud was dressed for analyses, as usual, in a gray suit, vest, loose cravat, sturdy, shiny shoes, and watch chain, she revealed, and his regal pose on a rounded outcrop of granite with one hand on his hip and the other hand raised with a cigar was a stately anomaly in the Boundary Waters of the Superior Nation Forest.

"He puffed on a cigar and the blue smoke fouled the sweet scent of red pine," said Nika. "Carlos undressed and together we slipped into the calm, clear water. We swam close to each other, touching shoulders and thighs at times, and then turned to float on our backs and watch the great storm clouds gather in the west."

Freud stood erect on the rocky shoreline, and at first he refused to even soak his boney white feet in the lake, but later, "when we teased him about motherly inhibitions, sex, and paternal tyranny, he very slowly removed his clothes, down to the union suit underwear, and stacked his shirt, shoes, coat and cravat neatly folded on the granite." Nika continued to tease the dream doctor with honorary names and then shame, and finally the bearded dreamer slowly submerged his body in Magnetic Lake.

"Carlos emerged from the lake, and his body glowed and black hair shimmered in the low blaze of sunlight," said Nika. Aloysius pretended to flesh out the image of his nude body, the slight pout of his belly, strong thighs, and asked if the native doctor was "erect in the water."

"Niinag Trickster," shouted Heap of Words.

"The mouthy northern pike might have aroused you, but this is my dream and the state of his *niinag* as he swam on his back is not your story," said Nika. "Freud was on his back in the water, and his stubby white *niinag* jumped right out of his underwear and bobbed with the gentle waves, a natural bait."

"Freud dream bait," shouted Heap of Words.

Nika described the sunset dash of rouge and blues, a glorious dream scene over the distant thunderclouds, the haunting sounds of loons, and "the most memorable native dreams come with the whole moon, *miziweyaabikizi*, so there were no worries in the dream about paddling in the dark back to the boat dock at Gunflint Lake."

Freud never understood natural motion, or perceived the heart of colors, and surely he would have excused the native sense of presence in dreams and creation stories. He was distant by descent, style, touch, and quite hesitant, but decisive as a minder of dreams, and a stranger in the natural world. The tidy beard, tight vest, and heritable gold watch and chain confirmed his stature as a master of measured wit and professional manners.

"My dreams are creative," declared Nathan. "Freud might consent to that much, but dreams are not histories, and certainly not some secret structure that would advance the quackery of psychoanalysis."

"Dead end dreamers," shouted Heap of Words.

"Freud came ashore at sunset in the dream, lighted a cigar, and sat on a granite mound," related Nika. "The fierce mosquitoes were weakened in the blue cigar smoke, so we sat close to the shiny body of the doctor, two nude natives and a bare white dream catcher in soggy drop seat underwear. "

Carlos pushed the canoe back from the rocky shoreline and waited for the strange dream doctor to board the cruise of liberty. "Freud shouted at the face of granite stones and cursed the huge shadows of red pine, and was determined then and there to swim nude back to the boat dock," said Nika. "We gathered his neat pile of clothes, heavy wet underwear, and paddled toward Gunflint Lake."

"Freud swam slowly at the side of the canoe, a klutzy crawl, and then in my dream he turned over on his back to recite theories of dreams, Oedipus and Prince Hamlet," said Nika. The old dream poacher restated a dream scene from one of his many lady patients, ridiculed his own concepts and interpretations of the dream as he crawled though the dark water, and with each episode of automockery he swam underwater for short distances.

"I was worried at first that he might have drowned when only a few faint bubbles came to the surface, a grave interpretation," said Nika. "Freud slowly emerged, out of breath and ready to mock another one of his dreary dream interpretations."

Freud continued his steady strokes underwater, and after the fourth mockery of his own analyses of cravat and neckties as dream symbols of a *niinag*, he smiled, waved, and then plunged under the bow of the canoe.

"The tiny bubbles burst and the nude doctor vanished in a dream on Gunflint Lake," said Nika. Carlos steadied the canoe and Nika dove into the dark water to search for the psychoanalyst, and only twice saw a pale flash of a fish or Sigmund Freud.

"Wet dreams," shouted Heap of Words.

"Freud drowned, dead and gone in my dream, and then in a later dream his fingers fell to pieces," said Nika. She was emotional and unsteady at the tiller of the barge, and declared the last of the dream scene stories with Freud and Montezuma.

By Now pretended to be attentive to the dream stories on the deck of *Le Corbeau Bleu*, but not about the deep dive death of Sigmund Freud. Rather, she listened to the natural sounds of the uneasy barge mongrels as they closely watched the other deserted mongrels in search of food and comfort on the Quai des Tuileries.

Thousands of mongrels, fancy sleeve and leash breeds, birds, and horses were forsaken as citizens rushed out of the city to the countryside when war was declared three weeks ago against the Germans. Many mongrels, birds, and horses were abandoned outright, and some loyal mongrels tried to board trains with the children, and other mongrels trotted behind wagons, cars, carts, and bicycles on the endorsed escape routes, and some wandered back to the city.

High Road raised his head, bounced on his front paws, and barked twice at another Picardy Spaniel on the quay. Pig Ears raised her ears and wheezed in the presence of a scruffy Petit Basset Griffon Vendéen. Nika was certain that the bearded stray was familiar, once leashed to a woman in a bright feathery hat. The barge mongrels bayed and barked with favor several times a day when the strays gathered nearby.

By Now listened only to parts of the dream stories on *Le Corbeau Bleu*, but not the smoky fade away of Sigmund Freud. Naturally she might have recited every word about a nude psychoanalyst on a horse, but not the boney bits and clouds of cigar smoke. She was engaged in a daydream that started with only a murmur in her ear a few weeks earlier at Les Halles.

Pierre Chaisson arrived at the same time with several bottles of wine, ready to celebrate the ironic stories of the *drôle de guerre*, the Phoney War. "Declare war every other day, at least twice a week," he teased, "and the empire primates might turn back their deadly declarations for one more day of parties in London and Paris."

Nathan reasoned, as he opened a bottle of red wine, "three weeks of runaway citizens, lost children, abandoned animals, gas masks, sandbags, food rations, and designated bomb shelters would be enough preparation to declare an armistice of the Phoney War." The Nazis were named the enemy three weeks ago, after the invasion of Poland, but the actual war was disguised by discrete actions of torpedo boats and fighter planes.

"Dogs out in shelters," shouted Heap of Words.

Aloysius raised his wine glass for the third salute that afternoon on the barge and proposed new and distinctive nicknames for the native Pierre of the Sorbonne and the Pierre of Les Halles.

"Louisiane and Les Halles," said Nika.

The By Now Rose and Pierre Les Halles romance of war wounds reminded Pierre Louisiane of a cultural and racial reverse of the love story in *The Surrounded*, a novel published a few years ago by D'Arcy McNickle. The book revealed a savage change of heart and cultural treason from the original manuscript that was entitled "The Hungry Generations."

Louisiane learned that the native author had created romantic scenes in the original uncut novel of daring and courage by Archilde Leon, a native violinist on the high road to literary presence with a courteous and cultured woman named Claudia in Paris.

"By Now is no Archilde," said Aloysius.

"Claudia no Les Halles," shouted Heap of Words.

McNickle sacrificed the creative trace of native liberty when the New York editors shamefully persuaded him to convert the great passion and cosmopolitan adventure of love in the original manuscript to the popular western sway of fatalism and vengeance in *The Surrounded*, a cruel novel that might have been more than just another story of native separatism and reservation casualties.

"Archilde and his lover Claudia are with us tonight on *Le Corbeau Bleu*, rescued from the revised novel, and with no shame, turnabouts of race, or editors laughing up their dirty sleeves," said Aloysius.

"Archilde and Claudia were created only once in a lost generation of

tease and native liberty," said Louisiane. The second round story became
an editorial deceit that inspired a book reviewer for the *New York Times* to
write that Archilde, "A Half-Breed Hamlet," was caught in that timeworn
notion of "two worlds," the inside and outside of native separatism, the
partitions and racial slights on federal reservations and boarding schools,
and the swing of music in the liberty of cities.

"Halfwit reviewer," shouted Heap of Words.

"Many native worlds," said Nika.

"Count the breeds to market," said Nathan.

"Archilde was a violinist, played with an orchestra, and never a scape-
goat or reservation specter of fatality conceived by the enemy camp of
book editors and publishers," said Louisiane.

A more learned book reviewer might have read in the *Carlisle Arrow*
about a native Shylock, or a native Marcus Brutus in productions of the
Merchant of Venice and *Julius Ceasar* at the Carlisle Indian Industrial
School. The natives were serious character actors, not the parts or fraction
breed visitations of Hamlet, King Lear, Macbeth, Romeo, or Juliet, or
Cleopatra, and certainly not comparable as breeds of partition characters
in a native novel.

Archilde was an aesthetic character, skeptical at times, but not crazy or
a royalist, and he never lived in a castle. He studied music and learned to
play the violin with a native sense of whimsy in a federal school dormitory,
in a cabin on the reservation, and during solitary time in jail. Hamlet ends
in silence, "Go, bid the soldiers shoot," and the native novel ends with a
dream song, "I have seen my dream of power walking the clouds of water!"

The reviewer of *The Surrounded* might have likened the loyal character
Archilde to Ishmael, the steadfast whaler on the *Pequod* in *Moby-Dick*,
the mighty novel of natural motion by Herman Melville, rather than cast a
contender, the tragic royal character of Prince Hamlet by William Shakespeare. Hamlet was crazed, immature, obsessed with nasty ghosts, spirits,
weird and erotic flights of fancy for his mother, and clearly more comparable to Captain Ahab and the revenge of Moby Dick.

"Hamlet was tragic," shouted Heap of Words.

"Archilde was romantic," said Nika.

"Hamlet was detestable," said Nathan.

"Archilde was a lover," said Louisiane.

"Hamlet was an assassin," said Aloysius.

"Archilde protected his mother," said By Now.

"The reviewer for the *New York Times* was mistaken about *The Surrounded* partly because the publisher tailored the manuscript of 'The Hungry Generations' into an empty melancholy tragedy," said Louisiane. "The reviewer might have teased or even imagined Archilde playing a violin on a whaler, and in the great company of the magical native harpooner Tashtego."

"Not to be," shouted Heap of Words.

D'Arcy McNickle and Herman Melville together on the Pequod was a much better literary story of natural motion than the splendid miseries of Prince Hamlet and the death of the treacherous King Claudius. The editorial trickery of race and fatalism could hardly conceive of the great characters Ishmael and Archilde, the literary whaler and a loyal native violinist, in the tragic adventure of Captain Ahab and the revenge of the white whale named Moby Dick.

16

SECULAR BARRICADES

Saturday, 2 March 1940

This letter to the heirs of the fur trade celebrates the first wood violets, primroses, lily of the valley, daffodils, tulips, and bright cherry blossom, only two days after emergency surgery in the American Hospital of Paris. My appendix was removed on a leap year day with no medical complications.

By Now was at my side and actually worked with the nurses in the operating room. Pénélope, a senior nurse, asked me if there was anything the doctor should know before surgery, but the general anesthetic had already put me under. My cousin told the surgeon as he started the incision, "Basile is writing a book of historical letters to the heirs of the fur trade, and he is determined to live long enough to write about the end of the war in Paris."

I was not in the hospital with war wounds, and my unease over a mere appendectomy was obvious to everyone. The private hospital rooms were converted with more beds to prepare for the arrival of wounded soldiers, the ironic wait for the end of the Phoney War. Some of the hospital volunteers lived in tents near the beautiful gardens behind the hospital, and my nurse refused to move me outside to recover in a tent near the spring flowers.

Doctor Thierry de Martel, the surgeon, examined the sutured gridiron incision yesterday, and told me that the pouch at the end of my intestine was swollen, but had not burst. He assured me, as he looked out the window, that the hospital stay should not be more than a week, and complete recovery in a month or two.

De Martel is French, and several other doctors at the hospital, counting Charles Bove and Sumner Jackson, are Americans. Doctor Bove remembered my brother and me from the fascist and royalist civil war six years ago. Bove had treated Randolph Hearst at the Hôtel Crillon, and came under police gunfire when he left the hotel. We ducked the random shots and escaped with the doctor on Rue Royale to the nearby Café Weber, and served with the waiters as an emergency medical corps. We prepared bandages for the wounded fascists on cane chairs.

Aloysius marveled at the blue windows, *fenêtres bleues*, painted and sealed, and the blue light bulbs in the hospital. "Marvelous, truly marvelous," and the next day he painted four blue ravens near the window and enormous faint blue raven wings on a privacy screen. The hospital doctors had decided on the very day that war was declared to paint the lights with blue as a precaution during the war.

Adolf Hitler and his fascist minions broadcast to the world that the English and French had started the war, and now his soldiers were obliged to defend Germany. The Nazis never revealed the brutal invasion of Poland, and lied about the purge of outcasts, the destruction of markets and synagogues, and the persecution of Jews.

The American Hospital of Paris was turned over to the military about five months ago with the official declaration of the war, and at the same time the directors changed the name to L'Hôpital Américain Bénévole de Guerre, the Voluntary American Hospital of War. Many American women, some the wives of soldiers, volunteered to serve as drivers in the American Hospital Ambulance Corps. The women were trained to treat wounded soldiers, and to deliver the most critical cases to the hospital for emergency surgery.

Paris was transformed with barricades of sandbags, the mirage of a military defense around buildings, statues, and national monument; but in the face of enemy bombers and tank cannons, the sandy sacks were never comparable to the noble concrete ramparts, casemates, and armored cloches of the Ligne Maginot, the Maginot Line.

By Now easily persuaded Nika, Heap of Words, the two Pierres, Aloysius, and me to volunteer as packers and stackers of sandbags to protect the Cathédrale Notre Dame. Pierre Les Halles climbed on a scaffold to the first level of the barricade and stacked the secular sandbags we hoisted over our heads. The mighty heaves, teases, and mockery of salvation and reservation labor were steady for about an hour, and then suddenly my laughter turned to an unbearable stroke of pain in my stomach. I doubled over and could not stand or walk, the pain was so severe.

Paris at the start of another world war was worse than a medical emergency on the White Earth Reservation. The reservation hospital was nearby, with native nurses in uniforms, starched and ready. The American Hospital of Paris was five miles away. No ambulances were available to deliver me to the western suburb of Neuilly-sur-Seine.

By Now shouted out for a bicycle taxi, and held me in the back for almost an hour. Every crack and stone was a rush of pain in my stomach as we crossed the Pont d'Arcole to the busy Rue de Rivoli, Avenue des Champs-Élysées, and Boulevard Victor Hugo to the hospital. My face was ashen, cheeks droopy, cold eyes and hands, and my heartbeat was heavy. Doctor de Martel was chief surgeon, and the nurses rushed me into the operating room.

De Martel was a maestro of surgery, not a teaser, and he was rather slow to appreciate chance and natural motion in native stories, but he was at my bedside several times on that first day of recovery. He asked questions about federal reservations, and he was curious about natives in combat during the First World War.

Aloysius was there and ducked the questions with an original hospital story about the Ice Woman, but that only elicited a perfect medical smile. The ironic stories about the twiggy federal agent earned a wide smile, and the good doctor broke into laughter over the story about our cousin John Clement Beaulieu who tried to outwit the mission priest with doses of moonshine, and then the drunken priest was lowered into a ready grave at the cemetery on the White Earth Reservation. Clement and his boozy friends waited behind the headstones, and at dawn the priest raised his head out of the grave, looked around, and declared, "Bejesus, this is the resurrection and a reservation priest is the first to rise."

Doctor de Martel was particularly interested in native stories about hand puppets and Dummy Trout. As a child he was enchanted, even captivated, he said, with the antics of the puppet named Guignol. The puppet was created by an out of work silk weaver who decided to become a tooth extractor more than a century ago in Lyon.

By Now told us that the nurses were worried about Doctor de Martel because he had never recovered from the death of his son in the last war, and he was downcast by two wars in a generation. The doctor was sixty-five years old, a famous brain surgeon, devoted to his patients, and never hesitated to declare that he was raised in a family of royalists and nationalists in the French Third Republic. De Martel had served as a surgeon at the American Hospital of Paris for more than twenty years, and we were convinced that the good doctor had never been teased with native stories or the mockery of hand puppets.

Aloysius outlined the face and noted precise gestures of the surgeon, and overnight my brother carved a resemblance of Doctor de Martel from a block of birch, a high and mighty forehead, huge polished head, curved eyebrows, dark feral eyes, sharp nose, and a coy smile with two deep dimples on each side of his mouth. The hand puppet wore a white coat with a stethoscope made of wire and a button, and the name Docteur Appendice printed on a round badge.

I pledged not to lift more than a spoon of soup, a glass of wine, or a hand puppet if the doctor would release me early from the hospital. De Martel declared with a smile that he wanted to hear more native stories, and that would take another few days. By Now encouraged the nurses to tease me several times a day as a curative practice, and one nurse, a mighty woman from Normandy, almost convinced me that the doctor was very concerned that there were bloated blue platelets in my blood, a possible indication of acute fur trade condition of royalty.

Doctor de Martel continued the tease by confirming the diagnosis of heavy platelets, *cicatrice bleue sanglant*, a bloody blue scar, and agreed to sign a release from the hospital at the end of four days, but only to return to *Le Corbeau Bleu* on the River Seine.

By Now, Nathan, Corporel Pierre, Aloysius, Nika, Heap of Words, Olivier Black Elk, Coyote Standing Bear, and Samuel entered the room with several nurses and volunteers when the doctor read out the conditions of a release in two days, "No horse or bicycle rides, no leaps of faith, no sacred sandbag duty, no sex, and no war games for several weeks."

The doctor and nurses were taken by surprise as my brother raised two hand puppets from a shoulder pouch, Docteur Appendice on the right hand, a royal gesture, and on the other hand, Adolf Hitler with three arms. De Martel frowned and then turned away, obviously not pleased with the ironic likeness of the puppet. He easily misconstrued the generous tease and native mockery of a hand puppet as bad manners and disrespect.

Heap of Words rightly rescued the native tease of the original puppet show with more than his usual pithy shouts, "Docteur Appendice defeats the enemy with a new surgical procedure that turned a war monster into a halfwit painter with a cubist three armed salute."

Aloysius had attached a third arm to the chest of the fascist puppet. He practiced overnight the difficult three finger arm gestures and salutes, and mimicked the steady voice of Docteur Appendice. Coyote feigned the whiney pitch and drone of Adolf Hitler. Samuel simulated scene music for the fascist hand puppet, a clever and melancholy violin version of the Magic Fire Music from *Die Walküre*, by Richard Wagner.

DOCTEUR: Three arms and fifteen dirty fingers.
ADOLF: Paint from my great creations.
DOCTEUR: Third Reich criminals, spurned at home.
ADOLF: Nothing but communist superstitions.
DOCTEUR: Communists dance in your head.
ADOLF: Communists created the Treaty of Versailles.
DOCTEUR: Political sleight of hand.
ADOLF: Polish Jews were out of hand.
DOCTEUR: You are out of hand with three arms.
ADOLF: Führers needs three arm parades.
DOCTEUR: First arm from a communist in Paris.
ADOLF: France wrongly salutes the communists.
DOCTEUR: Second arm from a Jew in Paris.
ADOLF: Paris became a cubist one armed Jew.
DOCTEUR: Third arm from an Apache dancer in Paris.
ADOLF: La Danse Apache debauchery.
DOCTEUR: Nazis need three arms to masturbate.
ADOLF: Surgeons need three hands to operate.
DOCTEUR: Nazis salute the street shadows.
ADOLF: *Mein Kampf* is my truth and glory.
DOCTEUR: Bad grammar and dimwitted readers.
ADOLF: Third Reich is my vision of liberty.
DOCTEUR: Nothing more than a nightmare.
ADOLF: My vision has changed the world.
DOCTEUR: Putsch and prison boasts are not a vision.
ADOLF: Paris and your hospital will be mine.

DOCTEUR: Not with three armed salutes.

ADOLF: Stand aside surgeon of the past.

DOCTEUR: Delusions of a halfwit fascist painter.

ADOLF: Swastikas will wave on the Eiffel Tower.

DOCTEUR: Nothing waves over your dead body.

ADOLF: Swastikas will wave everywhere.

DOCTEUR: Only communists salute with three arms.

Doctor de Martel smiled, nodded his approval, and then formally asked Docteur Appendice to join him one day when he visits other patients in the hospital. The nurses applauded the gesture, certain that a hand puppet show would raise the spirits of the patients.

Nathan sat at the back of the room in silence during the entire hand puppet show, and later, when Doctor de Martel and the nurses left the hospital room he explained that the doctor was a "royalist, aristocrat, antisemite, once a member of Le Faisceau of Georges Valois, a fascist political party, and he endorsed the false evidence, conviction for treason, and the imprisonment of Captain Alfred Dreyfus."

"Fascist with no mercy," shouted Heap of Words.

"Doctor de Martel is a brilliant surgeon, and you were lucky he was at the hospital to remove your appendix," said Nathan. "The doctor was a fascist and antisemite, but not as a maestro of surgery."

17

Rabbi of Gordes

Friday, 4 October 1940

Nathan Crémieux easily traced his ancestors back three generations as honorable and worthy citizens of France. Yet, he now worried for the first time as a citizen that his stature and *liberté* would no longer be respected or secure.

The Vichy Regime revoked the citizenship of Jews who were naturalized after 1927. The Jews who had earned the rights of citizens in the past thirteen years of the French Third Republic were now turned away as unwanted exiles in the nation that once promised state *liberté* in the heartfelt refrain of "La Marseillaise," *Le jour de gloire est arrivé*, The day of glory has arrived, and *liberté, égalité, fraternité* in the ethos of the revolution, democratic governance, and constitutional justice. Overnight tens of thousands of Jewish citizens of France were forsaken as undesirable, abandoned, and vulnerable to deportation by the Nazis.

Nathan has been distracted since yesterday when the first *Statut des Juifs* of the Vichy Regime commenced with the registration and outright exclusion of Jews from customary civil duties, commerce, travel, public service, occupations and professions. Only certain medical doctors were allowed to practice medicine. At the same time the fascist statute sanctioned the internment of alien Jews.

Daniel-Henry Kahnweiler and Lion Feuchtwanger were both exiled first as Germans and then as Jews. Kahnweiler owned an art gallery that was seized at the start of the First World War, and the Préfecture de Police sold at public auction his collection of cubist paintings by Pablo Picasso, George Braque, and many other artists. Kahnweiler returned at the end of the war and opened a new art gallery, but not in his name. The Galerie Simon was located at 29 Rue d'Astorg, not far from the prominent Paul Rosenberg gallery on Rue La Boétie, and jointly owned with André Simon. Then with the declaration of war, the name was changed to the Galerie

Louise Leiris. Louise Godon Leiris was the wife of Michel Leiris, and
sister-in-law of Kahnweiler. The roundabout hearsay reveals, however,
that Louise Godon is the daughter of Léontine Lucie Godon, the wife of
Kahnweiler. That clever disguise of gallery ownership convinced Nathan
to immediately transfer the title of the Galerie Crémieux to Aloysius and
Basile Hudon Beaulieu.

William Christian Bullitt, the flamboyant United States Ambassador
to France, posted a notice in *Le Matin* that any American citizens could
escape from the war and sail from Bordeaux on the steam ship *Washington*
of the United States Lines. No warning from the embassy or passage on a
luxury liner to escape the fascists could ever change our loyalty to remain
with Nathan Crémieux.

The Paris of revolution, *liberté*, literature, music, and the art of exiles
that once swayed the world had ended, and the citizens who stayed at
home with history were doubly deceived when the pathetic national government ran away with the advance of the Wehrmacht.

The flowers were in bloom in the Jardin des Tuileries, and royal park
pigeons preened as usual on 14 June 1940, the day of heartbreak that will
never be forgiven in hearsay or history. Nazi soldiers marched in wide columns down the Avenue des Champs-Élysées and with contempt through
the Arc de Triomphe.

Paris was occupied, desecrated, and the citizens were menaced by soldiers in noisy boots, an unpardonable crease in the memories of *liberté*.
The soldiers captured the best cafés, secured the luxury hotels, censored
every newspaper, ruined the witty banter at the bird market, silenced the
book gossip of testy *bouquinistes*, and plundered every museum and art
gallery in Paris.

Our close friends, André and Henri, *mutilés de guerre*, were rightly
worried about the Nazi purge of imperfections, and decided to move back
to an ancestral mountain farm in Marchamp, east of Lyon. The Nazis
sacrificed abnormal and disabled children, and that was enough reason
to escape the occupation, but the enemy would poison the fish and the
mutilés de guerre lived on the River Seine.

"Plague, purge, plunder," shouted Heap of Words.

"Exiles in a literary underworld," said Nika.

Nathan was uneasy that the Nazis might plunder the art in the Galerie

Crémieux, but not the actual gallery, so he moved the Ghost Shirts and entire collection of traditional and ceremonial native art to a secure storage space at Villa Penina in Sanary-sur-Mer. The native art was packed in eight huge wooden crates, and stowed in a borrowed Citroën van. The sealed crates of art were disguised as "Domestic Property" and "The American Puppet Show." The van was rightly named Déménagements Michel Laroux, Michel Laroux Removals or Movers.

Nathan counted on Michel, a close family friend who had recently retired from the Gendarmarie Nationale, to help him secure the necessary identity cards and permits to travel across the demarcation line of the *Zone Occupée* to the *Zone Libre*, or the phoney free zone south and east of the occupied territory that included Paris.

Michel attended Wild West Shows as a boy and had been fascinated with natives ever since, especially warriors on horseback. He was older than most soldiers, and served in a combat unit with natives in the Battle of the Somme during the First World War. At the end of the war he traveled to the Pine Ridge Reservation in South Dakota, lived with the Lakota or Teton Sioux for about a year, and learned the native language, or at least the necessary words and phrases about food, sex, medicine, horses, thunder, and the names of stars in the summer sky over the Great Plains.

Michel had returned home and served more than twenty years in the Gendarmarie Nationale, and since his retirement early this year he always carried a traditional Lakota Horse Dance Stick decorated with ribbons as a remembrance of the native reveals of duty and liberty. Naturally he revered the sense of native solace in the Galerie Crémieux.

"By Now honored Black Jack, a medical war horse, and she favored a reservation horse named Treaty," said Nika. "The mounts were healers, not warriors, and the memories of horses were recounted with names, teases, and stories, but not with traditional dance sticks."

"War horses prance," said Aloysius.

"Hardly dance," shouted Heap of Words.

Angelika, Renata, and Samuel continued to live in the backroom of the empty Galerie Crémieux. Aloysius painted over any interior evidence of native art, and as a safeguard removed the outside gallery sign. The space appeared to be empty, but the Polestar painted on the blue backroom ceiling remained as a native place of memory.

Michel Laroux installed four seats in the back of the spacious van near the crates, and drove south that third week of September through the Porte d'Italie toward Lyon and Avignon. The sun moved slowly through thin banners of clouds and created waves of light and shadows that turned the gray soldiers into ghosts.

Nathan had tentatively scheduled our departure for Sanary-sur-Mer in the third week of June, but the Nazi soldiers occupied Paris a week earlier, and travel was not feasible, not even with permits, because of the second rush of worried citizens to the south of France. Then he considered our departure, but only as an ironic gesture, on the very day that Adolf Hitler visited for the first time the Eiffel Tower and the Palais Garnier, the magnificent opera house in Paris.

"Fascists on holiday," shouted Heap of Words.

"Fascists in heavy leather coats," said Nathan.

Michel handed over the necessary travel documents at two security barriers, and we presented our passports of the White Earth Nation. Nathan told the Vichy police, and then the Nazi soldiers at Chalon-sur-Saône, the first checkpoint at the demarcation line south of Dijon on the River Saône, that we were *Indiens d'Amerique* on tour with a traditional puppet show, *The Niinag Native Tricksters*, and scheduled for several public performances in Avignon and Marseilles.

Aloysius surprised the soldiers at the second barrier when he raised two hand puppets, Guillaume Apollinaire and Gertrude Stein, near the open van window as evidence of native puppetry. Herr Hitler, Hermann Göring, and other hand puppets were disguised at the bottom of his shoulder pouch. Apollinaire and Stein jerked their heads from side to side and waved. The soldiers forced a smile, but they were obviously not interested or even curious about how the *Indiens d'Amerique* were related to hand puppets.

APOLLINAIRE: Winnetou taught me how to be a puppet.
GERTRUDE: General Custer was my hand puppet.
APOLLINAIRE: Puppets never worry about war or disease.
GERTRUDE: Hand puppets have never been exiles.
APOLLINAIRE: You write with many echoes, echoes.
GERTRUDE: The River Saône is my script of liberty.

APOLLINAIRE: *Sous le Pont Mirabeau coule la Seine.*
GERTRUDE: The Seine flows under the Pont Mirabeau.

Michel told the police and soldiers at the demarcation line, as a friendly gesture, that there was no word for peace in the language of the Lakota or Teton Sioux. "Ma Lakota," said Michel, "I am Lakota." The gray soldiers were nervous, pasty, not ready for combat, and barely capable as guards on the demarcation line of fascism and the Third Reich.

Nathan was easily persuaded that we should slightly modify our route to visit Marc Chagall and Bella in Gordes, near Avignon, on our way to Sanary-sur-Mer. The artist and his wife had recently moved from a farmhouse located in the Loire Valley to the quaint stony village in the lovely foothills of Monts de Vaucluse in Provence.

"Chagall painted crucifixions," said Aloysius.

"*Camp des Milles* is an hour away," said Nika.

"Oblivious Chagall," shouted Heap of Words.

"Visionary of Gordes," said Nathan.

"Jews are exiles, no matter the art," said Nika.

"Exiles with the Torah," said Nathan.

"Totemic exiles," shouted Heap of Words.

Michel purchased precious gasoline with a special medical permit, and he had been driving for more than ten hours, so we decided to park and camp overnight on the bank of the river Rhône outside of Avignon. Nathan had packed cheese and stale bread so there was no need to signal our presence with a campfire. Overhead we heard the cry of a stray nighthawk, and nearby the motion of the dark river was hushed, only the faint sound of ripples as the water touched the shoreline.

"Camp Laroux," shouted Heap of Words.

"Overnight sanctuary," said Nika.

Michel told us that he had been a popular singer as a young man, and that night of liberty on the bank of the Rhône he sang by heart the melody of "J'ai Deux Amours" that he had heard live four years earlier by the beautiful Josephine Baker at *Folies Bergère* in Paris.

J'ai deux amours
Mon pays et Paris
Par eux toujours
Mon Coeur est ravi

I have two loves
My country and Paris
By them always
Is my heart ravished

Nathan and Nika sang again the phrases of two loves and a ravaged heart as a chorus, and that late summer night on the Rhône was as memorable as any on *Le Corbeau Bleu* and the River Seine in Paris. Michel was touched by the chorus, and told stories about the spectacular performances of the erotic, toothy, and nearly naked Josephine Baker.

"Paris and Pine Ridge, my two loves," said Michel.

Gordes was a village of abandoned stone houses and alleyways. Michel parked the van at the bottom of the hill, and we walked slowly up the narrow, curved road. The citizens were elusive about the residence of the artist, and surely everyone who lived there would have shared some gossip about the newcomers to the village. Finally a young angular woman who wore a black coat and bright green scarf recognized the name Chagall, and pointed to a huge stone building on the next curve in the road.

"We could easily hide here," said Nika.

Nathan, at that very moment, turned and pointed at two military trucks on the main road, but moving in the opposite direction. Michel teased me that the only place to hide was with the puppets on the Pont de la Concorde, or in the Jardin des Tuileries. Aloysius, who could not resist the obvious response of an artist and puppeteer, jerked his head from side to side, and shouted, "Marionnette en plein air."

"Dissimulation en plein air," said Nika.

"Mort en plein air," shouted Heap of Words.

Chagall was about to enter his studio when we arrived out of breath from the steady climb up the road. He paused, cocked his head to the side, a cautious bird on the shoreline, and with a shy smile waited for an introduction. Nathan rushed forward and explained that we shared many mutual friends among artists and gallery owners and decided to visit on our way to Sanary-sur-Mer.

Chagall was apologetic that he had not recognized the owner of the Galerie Crémieux. The artist was dressed in loose blue trousers marked with paint, and with dark eyes and bushy hair he might have been mistaken that morning for a great blue heron, or the benevolent Rabbi of Gordes. Aloysius reminded the shy artist that we had first met about fifteen years ago at his studio on Avenue d'Orleans in Paris.

Nathan translated my memory stories of Chagall, Bella, and daughter, Ida, at the small studio in Paris. "Chagall, you were curious about my brother, a native artist who painted blue ravens with a sense of natural motion, and you were very generous to show us the paintings in your studio."

Aloysius had honored his art with silent gestures, not with the oohs or ahs of museum fancy, and celebrated the genius of his visionary paintings at the time, *I and the Village* and the marvelous *The Birthday*, which was mounted on the back wall of the studio. Chagall and Bella were obviously pleased to remember the visionary paintings he created in that small studio in Paris.

I related that painters and writers must remember the studio mise en scène, the places of their creations, and with more details than the actual content of the paintings or the manuscripts. Chagall seemed to concur that the memory of places, *lieux de memoire*, lasted forever, and the stories of a creative place were much better than the counts of brush strokes or manifest sentences and revisions of a novel.

Aloysius mentioned that we viewed *The Praying Jew* in an exhibition eight years ago at the Museum of Modern Art in New York. The Jew was painted in prayer clothes, a shawl, leather phylacteries, and the image was mostly black and white with a slight hue of rouge on the angular face and hands of the figure. Chagall was rightly elusive about the museum hearsay that the actual model of *The Praying Jew* was an old man, a town beggar in Vitebsk, dressed in the prayer clothes of his father, and painted with a cubist tease of modernism.

"Paris is cubist," shouted Heap of Words.

"Paris is abstract motion," said Aloysius.

Chagall invited us to his studio and presented a new painting underway, *Still Life Gordes*, a bowl of fruit on a yellow table with a woman in blue, and the continuation of *The Madonna of the Village*, a magical scene of the beautiful Madonna in a white flowing gown with a child, blue angels in flight, and a buoyant animal and violin.

Bella served *navette provençale* cookies and precious café in the studio that late morning, and the conversation over art easily turned to the vulnerability of Jews in France. Nathan could not avoid direct references to Lion Feuchtwanger, the novelist, and Camp des Milles near Aix-en-Provence. Chagall declared that he was a naturalized citizen, but we cautioned him that the documents of citizenship of many Jews in the French Third Republic were not secure under the Vichy Regime.

Chagall smiled without comment, looked away, and then pretended to paint the streams of bright light through the huge windows. Obviously the artist would rather paint, paint, paint the visionary scenes of the moment, and forever *The Madonna of the Village*, than be obligated to bear the latest hearsay notes and cautionary stories about fascist enemies of art and liberty.

18

CREATE FATE

Sunday, 6 October 1940

Marc Chagall smiled, turned away in silence, and pointed toward the windows. The wind soughed in the loose frames, the rustle of distant conversation overheard from the past. The sounds of every season gathered in the studio that afternoon with the moods, torments, humor, and whispers of many generations of residents, and our easy voices were now embodied in the same way.

Chagall must hear the past in every moment and motion of the brush, and the sway of creation must overlook the menace of the enemy. The imagination of motion and color en plein air or envisioned in a studio is no sanctuary from the envy and vengeance of antisemites. The artist hears only the visionary voices, and the natural sighs of blue angels in *The Madonna of the Village*.

Nathan told an obscure road story as we departed from Gordes. The Jews of Algeria were granted citizenship in France, but the Muslims were never mentioned in the Crémieux Decree of 1870. "Adolphe Crémieux, a distant relative, was Minister of Justice at the time the decree was signed in his name," said Nathan. "The *Décret qui déclare citoyens francais les Israélites indigènes de l'Algéria* separated the trust of two devout religious communities, a political maneuver that created only dissent and hatred in the French colony of Algeria, and that decree was revoked by the Vichy Regime." Nathan mistrusted the reasons for the termination of the citizen decree and declared, "It was nothing more than fascist antisemitic politics." Yes, of course, the Vichy Regime would revoke anything related to the citizenship of Jews.

Michel drove south that early afternoon to the hilly village of Bonnieux, the cedar forests, and slowly through the Luberon Massif to Lourmarin and Aix-en-Provence to Sanary-sur-Mer. Aloysius sat in the front of the van and sketched with pencils an abstract scene of a hilly village with waves of wispy clouds in natural motion that resembled the eternal grace and visionary favor of a slender Madonna over Gordes.

The curvy road from Bandol to Sanary-sur-Mer was magical that night with the faint lights of houses in the distance, the great shadows of parasol pines and olive trees, and the spectacular late summer shimmer of the whole moon over the Baie de Bandol. Nathan was always precise about the pleasures of company, and he obviously planned our risky journey with great care to depart safely after the occupation, and to arrive on the night of the whole moon in the third week of September.

"Sanary is a place to hide," said Nika.

"Olives at hand," shouted Heap of Words.

"Parasol pine stories forever," said Nathan.

Nathan was our inspired leader the next morning as we marched down the narrow roads to Le Nautique for café and conversation, and to honor the great philosophers, novelists, and poets who recently lived in Sanary. The Port de Sanary was calm, and the steadfast fishermen had already returned with their catch, and moored the bright wooden *pointus*, or sailboats, but no one on the dock waited for the return of the émigrés of literature.

The lively café exiles, Lion and Marta Feuchtwanger, Franz Werfel and Alma Mahler, Walter Hasenclever, and many other stateless authors and artists had been removed as the secular heirs of an ancient religion, cursed for the ethos of civil laws and conscience, and then imprisoned as criminals of the state at Camp des Milles.

Hasenclever, the expressionist poet and playwright, had once gathered with other literary exiles at Le Nautique and Café le Marine, and at the same time the crude fascists denounced his poetry as decadent. The Nazis banned and burned his books, once the touchstones of emotive literature in the world. The poet and playwright had been imprisoned twice as an enemy of France. He was falsely confined, first as a spy from Germany, and then as a Jew. Hasenclever was exiled forever in the ruins of his haunting poetic scenes, and committed suicide four months ago at Camp des Milles.

Not to suffer one's fate, but to *create* fate,
Attempting alone and free, if it's possible;
Because we men are greater than we imagine,
Greater, than many of us understand.

Sanary was a pleasant scene with a sense of security, a natural lure for a stateless person, *apatride*, and for literary exiles. We were enchanted in the same way with the harbor cafés, abundant fresh food and fish, and the many painted *pointus* sailboats on the bay. Sanary was a perfect port to dock a barge or houseboat, but there was no piano or violin music. The parasol pines and sailboats would never outdo the memories of music on *Le Corbeau Bleu* and the River Seine. That narrow barge with bench bunks was crowded, and the best place to eat, drink, tease the mongrels, and stage our stories in every season was on the open stern near the tiller.

The Pont de la Concorde, cobblestone quays, the constant sway of the River Seine, and the Jardin des Tuileries were not comparable to the great parasol pines, the peace of Sanary, or the mighty storms and heavy waves of the Mediterranean Sea.

"The Sanary of literary artists and prominent exiles no longer exists, only slight traces of their presence, the villas and cafés were secure in memory in the same way that the places of painters and literary artists were remembered, but not the actual palettes, brush marks, colors, rush of words, or mighty textual dares," said Nathan. "Feuchtwanger wrangled with every scene in his novels, and was twice imprisoned, Hasenclever created the temper and mood of worthy poetry and clever plays, and then took a lethal dose of poison at Camp des Milles." Our stories of their presence continue to counter the weakness of nostalgia.

"Manifest nostalgia," shouted Heap of Words.

Anishinaabe has no direct word for the abstract notions of nostalgia, comedy, or irony, but there are many variations of words for a story: *dibaa-jimowin*, a sacred story; *aadizooke*, or *wiinaajimo*, a dirty story. The clever sense of native irony, intended or not, was more than deception or the tones of speech, *wayezhim*, or *giiwanim*, to deceive; and yet the native trickster, *naanabozho*, or *wenabozho*, that subversive character created in stories, overturns time and traditions as a comic or ironic healer of heavy dreams and shamanic delusions.

"Native irony in motion," said Aloysius.

"Magical flight," shouted Heap of Words.

"Native irony is a hand puppet," said Aloysius.

Trickster stories reveal the marvelous scenes of double meaning, of transformation, sexual fantasies, perversity, and native irony; but critical definitions of irony and native mockery obscure the elusive play of time, and the fascists rule nostalgia.

Aloysius revealed the concepts of native mockery, such as mockery of a priest in a story, *naabinootaw,* to repeat what the priest said, or *baapinodaw,* to ridicule or show disrespect as mockery. The comic gestures of native hand puppets display mockery, and ironic stories heal with wonder and ridicule. Puppets create a sense of presence, a spirit, and tease traditions and the absolute, and forever mock the sentiments of regret and nostalgia.

"Mock the Resurrection," shouted Heap of Words.

Politicians and monotheists invented the notion of nostalgia, and the manner of mawkish regrets, to conceal the letdown of reason, liberty, and enlightenment; but nostalgia was never more than a personal weakness that was easily manipulated by royalists, fascists, racists, and now the Vichy Regime.

19

LITERARY HAVEN

Wednesday, 30 October 1940

Maréchal Philippe Pétain met with Adolf Hitler last week in a railway car at Montoire-sur-le-Loir to discuss an armistice with Nazi Germany, and today Pétain declared on radio, *J'entre aujourd'hui dans la voie de la collaboration*, I enter today in the way of collaboration. The notion of a way, path, road, or any course of collaboration with the enemy of art, literature, and *liberté* was a contemptuous retreat of cultural memory, courage, and a pathetic vow of capitulation.

Paris was overrun with enemy soldiers, and the creepy courtship of an old warrior on the way of collaboration was treasonous. Vichy collusion would not reverse the cultural desecration or the wicked plunder of treasure, art, manner, daily bread, and resources. That declaration of collaboration betrayed the loyal citizens of the French Third Republic, and rightly emboldened the résistance movement.

"Collaboration of antisemites," shouted Nathan.

"Pétain chicanery," shouted Heap of Words.

The Vichy Regime reigned from the ancient thermal baths with unintended irony, mocked the revolution of *liberté, égalité, fraternité*, and enacted antisemitic statutes of persecution and separatism. At the same time the novelist Lion Feuchtwanger, exiled as a dissident, was interned as the literary enemy of fascism, escaped from a prison camp with the support of several envoys, and safely arrived in Jersey City early this month on the *Excalibur*, a cargo and passenger liner of the American Export Lines. Lion and Marta departed from Lisbon, Portugal, with an extraordinary visa authorized by President Franklin Delano Roosevelt.

Nathan learned later that Varian Fry, the envoy of the American Emergency Rescue Committee, had arranged the final escape of Lion and Marta Feuchtwanger to Spain and Portugal, and once secure on a dock in New York Harbor, the cocksure author revealed to newspaper reporters his escape from prison and the actual secret routes of exiles and refugees over the mountains to liberty.

"Highfalutin visa," shouted Heap of Words.

"Lion was arrogant, and his revelation exposed the Rescue Committee and the many good citizens who risked their lives to rescue exiled artists and authors from Nazis and the Vichy Regime," said Nathan. The *New York Times* published the sensational rescue story on the front page, "Flight Described by Feuchtwanger," and then continued, "American 'Kidnapped' Him, Gave Him Women's Clothes to Escape Nazis."

"Foolhardy tales," shouted Heap of Words.

"Haughty historical fiction," said Nika.

Nathan had introduced Lion Feuchtwanger to Nika, Pierre Chaisson, Aloysius, and me five years ago at the International Congress of Writers for the Defense of Culture. Nathan was acquainted with many of the authors at the literary gathering, and he readily endorsed *The Oppermanns*, a recently published novel by Feuchtwanger. Nathan told everyone that the author was exiled because he warned the world about the savagery of the Nazi Party.

Feuchtwanger, André Malraux, Bertolt Brecht, André Gide, Henri Barbusse, who died later that year, and many other authors who delivered literary and political lectures had either countered or appeased the communists at the conference in Paris.

Lion was original and precise, and his lecture was directed to writers, and obviously that included me. Nathan stood next to me and whispered selected translations of the speech about historical novels as weapons against fascists and agents of brute force. "Perhaps there are some weapons in literature that are more effective, but my best use of this weapon is the historical novel."

Feuchtwanger was cursed and exiled from his native country, *apatride*, a stateless person, and twice endured the injustice of internment, first as a German, and then as a Jew. Last year he was imprisoned as an enemy alien at Camp des Milles, close to Aix-en-Provence, when France and Britain declared war against Germany. He was released in a few weeks when the government realized that he was not a spy for the Germans. Lion returned to Sanary-sur-Mer, reported to the police as ordered, and nine months later he was imprisoned as a Jew, once again at Camp des

Milles, and then mysteriously the prisoners were moved to Camp Saint
Nicolas, near Nîmes.

The Vichy Regime had dissolved the French Third Republic with no
warrant or constitutional authority, and signed an armistice with Nazi
Germany. The truce was a cruel irony and betrayal of national honor and
liberté, and very personal because we had served as combat soldiers to
defeat the same enemy in the First World War. France was turned over
to fascists, wimpy collaborators, and the gray hordes of jackboot Nazis.

"Jews out, fascists reign," said Nathan.

"Malicious mandates," shouted Heap of Words.

"Cavalry soldiers, newspaper editors, militia terrorists, renegade ranch-
ers, and collaborators carried out the same fascist maneuvers to remove
natives in California, Colorado, South Dakota, Oregon, Oklahoma, Florida, everywhere," said Aloysius.

"Myles Standish, the vice consul of the United States in Marseilles,
rescued Lion from Camp Saint Nicolas," said Nathan. "Lion and others
were bathing in the shallows of the Gardon River, a common practice of
the prisoners in the makeshift prison camp of tents, and Standish waited
nearby in a car to chauffer the exiled author through police security to
Marseilles disguised as an old woman in the back seat."

Feuchtwanger was exiled for writing about the menace of Adolf Hitler
and the brutes of the Nazi Party. His home in Berlin was plundered, students burned his books, and he was listed as a "traitor of the people." Lion
and his wife, Marta, emigrated about seven years ago to Sanary-sur-Mer.

Sanary was a literary haven for authors, philosophers, and artists, and
most of them were exiled as enemies of the Third Reich. Thomas Mann
lived with his wife, Katia, in a grand house, Villa La Tranquille, on Chemin de la Colline, not far from Villa Valmer at 164 Boulevard Beausoleil,
the residence of Lion and Marta Feuchtwanger.

"Five good years in Sanary," said Nika.

"Villa Valmer was a picturesque yellow house, three floors, wide terrace
views of La Baie de Portissol, and with fig trees and a garden of roses," said
Nathan. "Lion and Marta invited and sometimes summoned many literary
artists for philosophical discussions in that house."

Nathan owned Villa Penina, named in honor of his grandmother, a
cozy house on Allée Thérèse with a partial view of La Baie de Bandol,

and only a short distance from the residence of the novelist Aldous Huxley. Feuchtwanger, Thomas Mann, Franz Werfel, Alma Mahler, Bertolt Brecht, Ludwig Marcuse, Walter Hasenclever, and more than thirty other exiled writers from Germany and Austria gave rise to a nominal place name, "Weimar on the Sea."

Nathan met Feuchtwanger, Werfel, Hasenclever, the poet, and most of the other exiled authors who gathered regularly at Le Nautique and Café le Marine to argue about art, literature, fascism, and the ravages of European cultures by the Third Reich.

Nathan invited Nika, Heap of Words, my brother, and me to stay at Villa Penina in Sanary. We were tempted to stay, of course, but *Le Corbeau Bleu* was our place of heart stories, résistance, and sense of presence.

Aloysius was inspired with the harbor culture and characters, and some of the residents reminded him of the marvelous people painted by Chaïm Soutine. My brother created abstract fisherman with contorted bodies, angular faces, great blue ears, and huge rouge hands; and he painted abstract scenes of traditional wooden sailboats, *pointus* tapered at both ends, with bright hues and red and green spars, that were moored in perfect rows on the dock near the Hôtel de la Tour.

"White Earth on the Sea," said Aloysius.

Nika had met Soutine and other painters many times when she posed for Amedeo Modigliani the year before he died twenty years ago. Soutine had lived in La Ruche, a circular ramshackle building of art studios, at the time with several artists and poets, Marc Chagall, Moïse Kisling, Guillaume Apollinaire, Robert Delaunay, and Modigliani.

Aloysius had studied the brush strokes of *Portrait of a Boy*, the only painting by Chaïm Soutine that was included in an exhibition at the Museum of Modern Art in New York. We toured the exhibition of modern art a few days before we departed that summer eight years ago on the *Île de France* for Le Havre. The memory of *Portrait of a Boy*, and stories that Nika told about the intense manner, painterly play, and secrecy of Soutine moved my brother to use more colors in his paintings, and to simulate aesthetic brush strokes with a wide watercolor brush, curiously similar to the magnificent images of wood block prints, *The Great Wave off Kanagawa*, the mounds of willowy clouds, and feathery rouge reflection on Mount Fuji in *Fine Wind, Clear Morning*, prints created by Katsushika Hokusai.

Anaïs Nin bestowed another favor of chance with her stories about Henry Miller and Chaïm Soutine. Anaïs told me that she had lived with the novelist in the same row of modern apartments as Soutine, 18 Villa Seurat, near Parc Montsouris. Soutine was secretive, and seldom allowed anyone to view his paintings, and especially not his lover Gerda Michaelis Groth.

20

CELEBRITY OF NOTHING

Tuesday, 12 November 1940

Nathan shuttered the windows of Villa Penina, and early the next morning we set out for Hôtel Splendide in Marseilles to meet with Varian Fry, once a journalist and now the esteemed director of the American Emergency Rescue Committee.

Michel painted a new enterprise name on the sides of the van, Les Marionnettes Bleues, The Blue Puppets, and with a blue silhouette of Guignol, the most popular puppet in France.

"Blue Puppet road show," said Aloysius.

"Puppets out of hand," shouted Heap of Words.

Michel drove close to the bay in the grace of morning light, along the borders of parasol pines, past the ancient Viaduc de Bandol, the monumental vaulted bridge, slowly through the shrouds of ancient monarchies, the shadows of timeworn empires, trace of soldiers at every turn and corner, and the fascist collaborators of the Vichy Regime.

Bandol shimmered on the calm bay as we turned onto Place de la Liberté. The women and children presented their daily wicker baskets filled with vegetables on the square under the plane trees, and with no gestures of harm, worry, or cultural shame.

A thin lofty man with a magical smile was standing near a lamppost on the corner of Rue de la République. He wore raffia espadrilles, purple trousers, a rouge waistcoat, long gray overcoat, and white gloves. Michel was cautious about flamboyant strangers, and especially so early in the morning. The lanky dresser must have been inspired by the wild fashions of Oscar Wilde or Benjamin Disraeli, but we were much more curious about the pithy watchwords printed on the side of a shiny metal suitcase, *Célébrité de Rien*, Celebrity of Nothing, and, *Le Raconteur de la Liberté*, The Raconteur of Liberty.

"Spies are never that exotic," said Michel.

"Never that bright or literary," said Nathan.

Nika insisted that we stop to talk with the fantastic character. He was almost as high as the lamppost, seven feet or more, and declared his name, Prometheus Postma, as he leaned close to the van window. He told us with the poise and timbre of a stage actor that he was a raconteur from the Frisian Islands in the North Sea.

Prometheus was stateless, *apatride*, at least a triple exile on his way to secure an exit visa from the legendary Varian Fry, and escape forever to the state of California. That much of his story at the side of the van was more than enough to invite him to travel with our posse of puppeteers.

Prometheus was actually a raconteur of futurity and celebrity of nothing, as his stories of exile created a sense of motion rather than destiny. He assumed from the name on the side of the van, our faces, and gestures, that we were natives, and with that assurance he slowly climbed into the back of the van, and at once related an elusive story about a native named Ishi. The Yahi Indian was arrested and then rescued by Alfred Kroeber, the anthropologist, and named forever the last of his tribe in California.

"Rescued from bounty hunters," said Aloysius.

"Anthropology hearsay," shouted Heap of Words.

Prometheus carried a bundle of newspaper articles published in the *San Francisco Call* about the native named Ishi. He raised one finger and read the headlines for October 1911, "Ishi, The Wildman, to 'Tread Boards,'" and "Curator Decides Untamed One Must Be Exhibited Each Sunday" at the University of California Museum in San Francisco.

"Ishi was a native exile," said Aloysius.

"Alfred Kroeber was the émigré," said Nathan.

"Ishi was the storier, not Kroeber," said Nika.

"Only native exiles of the world are the storiers of chance and futurity," was my comment. "Choose the time, any date in history, and there were always native exiles in motion, forever on the course of futurity."

"Ishi became my exile," said Prometheus.

"Puppets are the exiles," shouted Aloysius.

Prometheus sat on his metal suitcase of watchwords, extended his long legs across the back of the van, and started his stories with a masterly sense of time, tone, and gestures. The raconteur created scenes with a few precise words, a raised brow, slight turns and tweaks of his head, and with one, two, three or more elevated fingers, a count related to the motion and revelations of the story. He turned his head to the side, got underway with the precise delivery of five declarations, and then described the magical presence of his father.

Postma was my best tease of futurity.
Mister Ishi was a barefoot visionary.
Frisian boys were barefoot on the sandbanks.
Ishi created the stories of native fires.
Prometheus carried the flame of the exiles.

Prometheus described his father as an unashamed sandbank artist, the second to the last of his tribe named Postma, Frisians of the Netherlands, and exiled with his wife and daughter to the sandbanks because he derided the sexuality of Queen Wilhelmina. He boldly denied the monarchy and religious doctrines, carved giant erotic scenes of royalty in the sand, and created origin stories of the barefoot prince of futurity, a more generous savior of mockery who mingled only with the celebrities of nothing.

Postma was a fisher carried away with his sand art on the mighty tide six months before the birth of Prometheus, the sandbank child of magical tides, sandy mounds, curvy silhouettes, and surrounded with natural motion and visionary stories of the future. The magnificent trees of a mighty forest were his only chance of liberty.

Postma breathed with the rush of waves, and returned with every high tide, a sandbank exile with clever stories of futurity. Prometheus inherited these paternal stories, the creative scenes of natural tidal motions, the sway of mighty trees in a vision of liberty, and the elusive shoreline curves of memory on the Frisian Islands.

Prometheus declared he was born on a sandbank, and was exiled from the Netherlands and Germany as a communist and subversive raconteur who ridiculed the rapt monarchy and mimicked the prissy poses, pouts, whiny shouts, and jerky hand and arm gestures of Adolf Hitler.

"Bandol became my sanctuary, but then the literary exiles of nearby Sanary were imprisoned at Camp des Milles, and it was time to leave for California," said Prometheus.

"Frisian raconteur of the redwoods," said Nathan.

"Ishi tended to the fires," said Prometheus.

"Fire and smoke," shouted Heap of Words.

"Celebrities of nothing," said Nika.

"Nothing is a perfect time," said Prometheus.

Michel parked the van near the Gare Saint-Charles in Marseilles. We walked abreast through the main train station and slowly down the wide stone stairs to the Hôtel Splendide on Boulevard d'Athènes. The wide street was crowded with people in every direction, and because of the restrictions and shortage of gasoline there were very few trucks or automobiles.

Nathan had warned us that the hotel would probably be crowded with desperate refugees waiting to secure exit visas and escape the fascists. The grand lobby was lively but not congested, and the receptionist informed us that Varian Fry was indeed registered as a hotel guest, but the American Relief Center, Centre Américain de Secours, had moved last month to 60 Rue Grignan near the Vieux Port.

Nathan was our chief of the exiles that afternoon, and we marched down Boulevard d'Athènes to La Canebière and the Old Port. Prometheus proposed lunch, but we were worried about police surveillance and decided not to delay our visit with Varian Fry, so we walked directly south to the narrow Rue Grignan.

The Centre Américain de Secours was situated by chance and unintended irony between the Église Saint Charles and the Palais de Justice. Jews and exiles were persecuted by the fascists and forsaken by the church and state justice. The last chance of survival and liberty was the relief center. There were double lines outside, and more than thirty refugees were crowded in the office. Nathan insisted that we meet with Fry, not his assistants, but Fry was away for the day, and an appointment was scheduled in the morning.

Aloysius noticed the scent of leather, and the security aide at the entrance explained that the building was once a leather company. The scent reminded me of the desperate time more than twenty years ago when we were hired to work for only a few days a week for a leather company in Minneapolis.

Nathan said he would cover the cost of four rooms, but only three tiny rooms were available at the Hôtel Moderne nearby on Rue Breteuil. Nika decided to share a room with Nathan, Michel and Prometheus shared the second room, and my brother would obviously room with Heap of Words and me.

Nathan decided we should inquire about exit visas at the Consulat des Etats-Unis d'Amérique a few blocks away on Place Félix Baret. He wanted to be prepared in the morning to discuss with Varian Fry the necessary visas for Angelika, Renata, and Samuel to leave France and travel without fear through Spain to Lisbon, Portugal.

Prometheus saluted and waved as we walked slowly down the long double rows of weary refugees, but no one returned the gesture. The refugees turned away to avoid any visual contact for fear that we were agents of the Vichy Regime. Jews and other exiles were not secure anywhere in the country, and they were even more vulnerable in a visa queue at the American Consulate.

"Last queues of liberty," said Prometheus.

Nathan had been given the name of a vice consul and told us to wait outside on a park bench. This was the first time we had been excluded from a contact or conversation, but we never doubted his reasons for secrecy. Michel and Nika sat on the bench, and the lines of refugees behind them never seemed to move. Prometheus bowed to some people who were walking nearby, saluted others, cocked his head, and spread his fingers in white gloves. A few people smiled, waved in return, and then hurried past the bench. He might have danced and told a story about gentle giants, but the children on the street that afternoon were lonesome, hungry, and mostly frightened refugees.

Nathan returned about an hour later, and pointed to the blue awnings of the nearby Café Pelikan. We moved two tables together on the terrace, and sat under the plane trees, a delightful place in a dangerous, crowded, worried, and deadend city on an ancient port.

"*Tragédie de Marseilles,*" said Prometheus.

"Prometheus, the trickster of fire and tragedy, is the same name in any language," said Nika. "Yes, your name is a perfect disguise, much more secure than the trade, place, and nicknames of natives and Jews."

"Lion Feuchtwanger escaped with an emergency visa in the name of James Wetcheek," declared Nathan. "The actual translation of his surname, *feucht*, damp or wet, and *wange*, cheek, in German."

Vice Consul Harry Bingham told Nathan the escape story, and that
he had secretly protected Mister Wetcheek and his wife Marta at his villa
for a month before they were escorted over the Pyrenees and into Spain.

Nathan was worried and angry when he heard the rumor that Assistant
Secretary of State Breckinridge Long had directed American embassies
and consulates to curtail emergency visas. Obviously the directive was antisemitic and intended to terminate the exit visas for exiles, refugees, and
particularly Jews. The thousands of exiles and refugees continued to wait
in lines because they could only believe that the last nation of mercy and
liberation was the United States of America.

"Jews and natives wait forever," said Aloysius.

"The godly visas are deliverance," said Nika. "The last airy moments
of chance, liberty, and futurity are precious emergency visas from the last
democratic emissaries of truth and honor."

"Despite the State Department," said Nathan.

Breckinridge Long discontinued the emergency visas for Jews, and the
Vichy Regime terminated exit visas for any exiles to leave France. The political collusion of fascists and antisemites was an obvious death sentence
for Jews. The lines of desperate exiles grew longer at the relief centers and
consulates, and with every hour of delay and denial the chance of escape
diminished, and dignity and liberty became more elusive for the Jews.

Nathan was in a state of rage over the conspiracy of nations to deliver
Jews and other exiles to the Nazis. "We show our rage in stories, and then
we must join a résistance movement," he declared. That was the first time
we heard him use the word résistance with such conviction, and we knew
he meant more than the forged documents and the honorable gestures of
escorts over the mountains.

We arrived at the Centre Américain de Secours early in the morning
to meet with Varian Fry. Yes, at sunrise, and there were refugees already
standing in line to hear a mere chance of equity, or to secure any document
or counsel of survival to leave France.

Fry wore a tailored suit, vest, cuff links, and polished brogue shoes, and
yet his generous manner easily defied the steady appearance of a banker,
broker, or political envoy with a heartfelt sense of moral duty to rescue
stateless exiles from fascists and the Third Reich.

Fry was a fancy dresser, and probably not ready for a native tease, even so he might have been pleased with our tricky gestures and mockery, but the purpose of our meeting was only to secure exit visas for Angelika, Renata, and Samuel. The risky route over the mountain, we were told, was probably the only way to escape.

Prometheus named the decked out director of escapes the Brogue of Liberty, and my brother was tempted to scuff one of his bright shoes for the native league of chance and contradictions.

The rumors about exit visas were correct, and even with a passport there were no emergency exit visas from France. Fry told several stories that morning about the surveillance on ships scheduled to sail from Marseille to Morocco and Gibraltar, and the risky journeys over the Pyrenees near the Mediterranean Sea. The Vichy police patrolled the foothills and mountain towns, and the Spanish border guards were bored and capricious, but most exiles were allowed to enter the country with honor or casual bribes. Fry provided the exiles with several packages of Camel cigarettes.

"Saved by a pack of Camels," said Prometheus.

Fry was desolate over the tragic death of the German and Jewish exiled philosopher Walter Benjamin. He had obtained a travel visa and struggled over the mountain, only to be denied entry into Spain. Fry said he committed suicide with an overdose of morphine on 26 September 1940 at the Fonda de Francia in Port Bou, Catalonia.

"Final exit visa," shouted Heap of Words.

"Every passion borders on the chaotic," said Nathan. He explained that the quotation was a translation from the essay "Unpacking My Library" by Walter Benjamin.

"The connoisseur of arcades," said Nika.

"Borders of fate and futility," said Nathan.

Varian Fry provided the necessary connections, escorts, and reliable routes over the mountains to Spain, but he was not convinced that border agents would acknowledge the passport of the White Earth Nation. United States passports were the most secure for travel through Spain and Portugal.

Fry never mention Lion Feuchtwanger or the reckless boasts about his escape, but the stories published in several newspapers endangered the lives of the rescue parties and thousands of exiles and refugees, and altered the routes and methods of escape. Lion surely never intended to cause so much fear, but his echelon of arrogance and sense of fate as a celebrated author overcame any sense of caution or honor for the desperate refugees waiting for a chance to escape as he had done from the Third Reich and the Vichy Regime.

"Célébrité de Rien," said Prometheus.

"Nothing but chance and celebrity," said Nathan.

Fry proposed that we dine at Le Restaurant Basso on Quai des Belges, one of the oldest restaurants in Marseilles. He suggested that we reserve a table on the outside terrace with a view of the Vieux Port. Food was rationed, of course, but for those with money or political or criminal connections, there was always a covert menu. He told us that the view of the busy port was marvelous, truly a spectacle of suspects, and the display of regular patrons was worth the cost of a meal, and he was right.

The bouillabaisse was reasonable, compared to other entrées, but mostly we were present for the view and to survey the spies, surveillance police, empire criminals, envoys of several nations, disguised fascists, and agents of the Gestapo and Vichy Regime. Fry warned us that direct stares were perilous, however casual or curious, but discreet or slight glances were more in line with political intrigue and espionage.

Nathan insisted that we depart before dawn and drive through Aix-en-Provence and Avignon to Paris. Michel was persuaded to take the back roads past Camp des Milles, the internment camp where Lion Feuchtwanger, Walter Hasenclever, the poet, and thousands of exiled novelists, artists, and scientists were detained as spies when the French and British declared war against Germany. Later the makeshift camp became one of the deadly transit centers for the deportation of Jews. Michel drove slowly past the camp. Our rage was obvious, and we were silent.

The roads were familiar from Avignon to Paris, but returns were never the same as the excitement of a new or dangerous destination. Nostalgia has always been a popular sentiment of discovery and returns, no longer the surprise of an arrival or entry, and that weakness of melancholy and regret was easily overcome with our good stories about the Rabbi of Gordes, Sanary-sur-Mer, and Marseilles.

Varian Fry was favored in dream songs for his courage and integrity, and we should have taken more time to tease him about his proper pose, calm gestures, the cut of his shirt, and moral certainty in the company of artists, authors, and untold exiles and refugees in Marseilles. He and others created an obvious sense of trust and comity at the Centre Américain de Secours.

Harry Bingham carried out that sense of democratic ethos and respect for exiles and refugees at the American Consulate. No manner or pose of sincerity was ever secure in the ancient port city of confidence gamers, conspirators, poseurs, miscreants, gangsters, and the devious traitors who betrayed Jews.

"Varian Fry is a secular saint," said Aloysius.

"Harry Bingham is righteous," said Nathan.

"Breckinridge Long a betrayer," shouted Nika.

By Now had rehearsed the chorus of mighty barge mongrels for a marvelous return celebration of bays, muffled barks, and tender moans, and Samuel played on his violin the heartfelt melody of the *Gymnopédies*, by Erik Satie, when we arrived at *Le Corbeau Bleu* on the River Seine.

"By Now is my Eleutheria," said Prometheus.

"By Now, Never Now," said By Now.

"Smitten in an ancient myth," said Nathan.

Nathan was teased last year for his purchase of several hundred packages of Columbian *Pielroja* cigarettes from an international merchant at the Port of Le Havre. The packs were decorated with the portrayal of an Indian warrior in a colorful yellow, blue, white, and red feather headdress. The four bands of color could represent two national flags, the strategic romance of a tobacco company. Columbia banners were yellow, blue, and red, and the French *Tricolore* was blue, white, and red, but that did not explain the reason for the cigarettes.

Nathan was not a smoker, and only Pierre Chaisson and Olivier Black Elk were smokers in our circle of gallery and barge storiers, so we could not understand why he bought so many packs of cigarettes at a time when tobacco was not yet rationed. Since the occupation some smokers rolled cigarettes with dried herbs and crushed weeds.

Many of the authors, artists, and gallery owners were smokers, but mostly they fouled the air with cigars, or the favored blue packs of Gauloises Caporal. The virtue of the cigarette cache was revealed on 11 November 1940, the commemoration of Armistice Day. Nathan had bartered two packs of cigarettes, worth about two dollars a pack, ten times the price a year ago, for several fine bottles of Vin de Bourgogne.

The wind was cold that late morning as we walked through the Place de la Concorde past enemy soldiers at command posts near the Hôtel de Crillon, past the Embassy of the United States, and onward to Place de l'Étoile and the mighty Arc de Triomphe.

The Nazis prohibited displays or demonstrations to commemorate Armistice Day, 11 November 1918, when the First World War ended with the signature of Germany at Compiègne. That humiliation of defeat and punitive treaties roused the vengeance of fascists and nationalists, and the rise of the Nazi Party and the Third Reich.

We turned a blind eye to the prohibition and marched as war veterans with hundreds of students from *lycées* and universities to honor the dead soldiers and civilians of the war, and the Tomb of the Unknown Soldier at the Arc de Triomphe.

The students circled the monument and ridiculed the soldiers by chanting the name of General Charles de Gaulle, the exiled leader of France Libre, Free France, and we chanted over and over the names of William Hole in the Day, Charles Beaupré, Fred Casebeer, and our cousins Ignatius Vizenor and Ellanora Beaulieu, natives from the White Earth Reservation who fought and died for France in the First World War.

The students placed a miniature French *Tricolore* and a crayon colored Union Jack of the United Kingdom on the Tomb of the Unknown Soldier. Police removed the students with force, and pushed them into waiting trucks where they were beaten for nothing more than their reverence for the soldiers who had died in combat more than twenty years ago, and, of course, for their courage to resist the fascist order not to celebrate Armistice Day.

Nazi soldiers pushed me and the other natives aside and attacked the students, hundreds were badly wounded, and hundreds of others were arrested and hauled away to prisons. The students, not the teachers or parents, were the first to demonstrate against the Nazi Occupation, and at the same time they honored *liberté, égalité, fraternité* and the memory of dead soldiers on Armistice Day in France.

21

ROCKY UNIONS

Friday, 13 December 1940

Paris has become a prison these past six months since the start of the Nazi Occupation. Just the same we gather every morning on the deck of *Le Corbeau Bleu* and praise the moral guardians of art and *littérature engagée*, the résistance literature of commitment, and stories of chancy irony.

Samuel plays the violin in the morning, cautious and bright, as the sun glances on the cobblestones. The magical tones and tender reveals of a sonata by Claude Debussy linger in the cold air, with tributes to the grace of the piano music Erik Satie.

Renata convenes the lost children at a train station to create marvelous hand puppets from debris found on the street, and then stages the costumes and comic gestures of hand puppet characters at Gare d'Orsay.

Nika mooches droopy vegetables on the gray market, *marché gris*, and a mush concocted with the scant leavings on restaurant dinner plates, *hasard de la fourchette*, the chance of a fork, gathered by *plongeurs*, the dishwashers, to feed the stateless children and refugees. The favor of food leavings from fork or finger has become a tournament of scavengers for scarce rations.

George Orwell was a *plongeur* during the economic depression, and wrote in *Down and Out in Paris and London* about his work in a murky hotel cellar in Paris. "A *plongeur* is a slave, and a wasted slave, doing stupid and largely unnecessary work. He is kept at work, ultimately, because of a vague feeling that he would be dangerous if he had leisure."

"Free the cellar slaves," shouted Heap of Words.

"Name the murky hotels," said Nika.

Aloysius continues to paint en plein air, abstract blue ravens that soar in visionary scenes, and at times the minimal wash of a blue wing in the style of totemic fauvism with muted traces of rouge. Nathan recently named my brother the native envoy of blue ravens and partisan hand puppets in the deadly world of nationalists, collaborators, and wily cringers of the Vichy Regime.

Companies of enemy soldiers invaded the solace of the Jardin des Tuileries, and we no longer hear the piano music of Erik Satie. The royal pigeons march around the benches as usual, the liberty trees have already flaunted their bright leaves to honor the memory of the revolution, and now the silent rows of bare branches stand as solemn reminders of the weary season of the Nazi Occupation.

Doctor Thierry de Martel, the surgeon who removed my appendix earlier this year at the American Hospital of Paris, injected a suicide dose of strychnine on a bright sunny day, 14 June 1940, and died as Nazi soldiers commandeered the Hôtel de Crillon, raised huge swastika banners, marched to the Arc de Triomphe, and occupied Paris.

Aloysius staged Docteur Appendice at several hand puppet shows for wounded soldiers at the hospital. The death of Doctor de Martel was the demise of the popular hand puppet Docteur Appendice. Coyote led a cortège and planted four prayer sticks to honor the doctor and the hand puppet. Olivier chanted a native tribute, and Samuel played phrases of a sonata by Claude Debussy. Docteur Appendice was buried with native honors near the Grand Bassin Rond in the Jardin des Tuileries.

Aloysius reminded me this morning that more than twenty years ago we were combat infantry soldiers, and in that course of political irony we discovered more about art, literature, and liberty than any banal missions, government schools, or federal agents could ever provide on the White Earth Reservation.

"Ghosts of liberty," shouted Heap of Words.

"Liberty trees stand forever," said Aloysius.

My letters to the heirs of the fur trade started eight years ago, and a year later President Paul von Hindenburg named Adolf Hitler the Chancellor of Germany. Since then the fury of fascists and nationalists, the depression politics of socialists, communists, and royalists bring to mind the name of Léon Blum, the judicious political leader. The generous and resolute socialist was elected Prime Minister three years ago, but could not overcome the intractable machinations of Le Front Populaire, a rocky union of party radicals, socialists, communists, and factory workers that dissolved overnight.

Blum never abandoned the ethos of governance, or the necessary political compromises of the Assemblée Nationale. The Jewish progressive
and torchbearer of *liberté* spurned the traitors and would never obey the
occupation pawns or pursue any favors from the patriotic cronies and criminal comrades of the Vichy Regime.

Nathan was enraged when he learned that the toady consorts of the
Third Reich terminated the French Third Republic, and the revolutionary
spirit of this great nation, *literté, égalité, fraternité,* was perverted with the
reactionary notions of *travail, famille, partie,* and endorsed by the hoary
collaborator with delusions of grandeur, *folie de grandeur,* Maréchal
Philippe Pétain, Chief of the Vichy French State.

"La mort de Vichy," shouted Nathan.

"Betrayal of liberty," said Pierre Chaisson.

"Pierre Laval was the worst of demon collaborators," said Nathan.
"He was a rogue lawyer, heavy smoker with bad breath, and earned the
nickname *Pierre Loin du Front,* Far from the Front, and for good reasons
because he was a poseur socialist and fatuous pacifist at large during the
First World War."

"Lackey of vanities," shouted Heap of Words.

"Fascist coward," said Pierre.

"Good news today, Pierre Laval was arrested and dismissed from the
Vichy Regime because he had secretly conspired with the Nazis," said
Nathan. "Laval was the fascist advocate of the statutes against the Jews."

The Vichy government enacted the first *Statut des Juifs* about two
months ago, and that was a clear declaration of war against the Jews of
France. The racial statute was a farcical decree that surmised the nature
and character of Jews by nose, hair, manner, blood, and descent, and
banned the most loyal and creative citizens of the country from public
service.

"Laval and Blum, evil and ethos," said Nika.

Léon Blum was arrested about two months ago and imprisoned with
other leaders of the French Third Republic in a medieval castle, the Château de Chazeron in Loubeyrat. Nathan was ready at first to enlist in our
hasty strategy to rescue the great leaders from prison by native stealth and
the play of puppets, but he wisely redirected our rescue gesture to other
schemes of résistance in Paris.

The Nazi and Vichy expulsion of Jews can easily be compared to the federal policies of native removal, treaties of separatism, military atrocities, and the militia murder of natives in America. The colonial elimination of natives, and later the denial of cultural liberty in the new constitutional democracy were similar to the pogroms, the fascist warp of reason and scientific smears of race, the termination of rights and vicious removal of ancestral blood and ancient religions by the nationalists and fascist heirs of greedy empires and the Third Reich.

The occupation, persecution, and sorry measures to remove selected citizens would deny Jewish poets, novelists, painters, bankers, professors, restaurateurs, furriers, owners of art galleries, war veterans, desperate refugee families, and loyal visionary exiles of the great revolutionary history of France.

"Basile, not exactly, but never wrong," my uncle, the clever publisher of *The Progress* and *The Tomahawk*, might have said, "much too extreme." Yet, surely my uncle never forgot the brutality of discovery, the heartless banishment of the Cherokee Nation, the Muscogee, Choctaw, Chickasaw, and other natives on the Trail of Tears, and the massacre of natives at Acoma, Zia, Sacramento River, Sand Creek, Marias River, Wounded Knee, and hundreds of other camps and communes; entire families and native cultures were terminated with no shame or censure in history.

Augustus Beaulieu never forgot that the first issue of his independent newspaper, critical of land allotment and many other venal government policies, was seized by federal agents and the native police, and my relatives were ordered to leave forever the White Earth Reservation.

"Vichy banishment," shouted Heap of Words.

"Vichy agents far and wide," said Aloysius.

Coyote Standing Bear chanted the names of Pontiac, Geronimo, Cochise, Crazy Horse, Sitting Bull, Chief Joseph, and Morning Star, and there were thousands of other unsung warriors in the native opposition to the colonial invasions, occupation, and denials of continental liberty. Coyote named Chief Joseph and Léon Blum the warriors of *liberté*, and then he continued with the honorable names of other native leaders, White Cloud, Hole in the Day, Plenty Coups, Little Bear, Black Kettle, and Conquering Bear, the great visionary diplomats who fought against the

colonial marauders of the depraved empires of discovery, racial entitlements, and contentious enlightenment.

"Popé of San Juan," shouted Heap of Words. "The Pueblo Revolt of
1680 was the first revolution of native liberty on the continent."

"Long live native résistance," said Pierre.

"Then and now," shouted Heap of Words.

"Popé ousts the Nazis," said Olivier Black Elk.

"Crazy Horse routs the Vichy," said Aloysius.

The crew of *Le Corbeau Bleu* carried on with the great names of visionary leaders and the analogies of résistance in America and France. The
heirs of the fur trade bear the right of conscience to declare the horrors of
colonial violence and racial separation in the world.

22

KARL MAY COUPS

Wednesday, 18 December 1940

Nathan Crémieux broadcast to the plane trees that the ethos of *liberté, égalité, fraternité* of the French Third Republic would never end with the craven capitulation of household traitors, *traître de ménage*, or fascist bootlickers, and a few days later he printed and widely posted the first résistance decrees against the Nazi Occupation.

The *Statut des Allemands* denied the right of enemy soldiers to wear the swastika, to enter restaurants, or ride a bus, and they were forbidden to own or listen to a radio, to drive, ride horses, dance an empire waltz, touch a hand puppet, enter a bookstore, eat sauerkraut, weisswurst, or stollen; and soldiers were never allowed to wear hobnailed boots, *les bottes allemande*, or raise their gray arms to salute anyone at cafés on the boulevards of Paris.

"Statut des Collaborateurs Vichy," said Nika.

"Statut des fascistes," shouted Heap of Words.

Nathan revealed the irony that he was at last a native because he no longer had a secure voice of art or literature in his own country, and, he warned, even with two passports, *Passeport Français* and White Earth Nation, the Nazis would no doubt attempt to commandeer his apartment, personal property, and the Galerie Crémieux.

Nathan anticipated the *Statut des Juifs* and transferred the entire ownership of the Galerie Crémieux to Basile and Aloysius Hudon Beaulieu, native citizens of the White Earth Nation. Our loyal friend reminded us several times in the past year that he would consign the gallery to avoid its seizure by the police and antisemitic pirates of the Third Reich.

Aloysius had secretly carved a handsome hand puppet named Nathan Crémieux, and at the end of the last hearty salutes to art and *liberté*, my brother emerged from the back room of the gallery with Nathan Crémieux on one hand and on the other Adolf Hitler.

"Crémieux coups," shouted Heap of Words.

"Puppet coup counts of *liberté*," said Nathan.

I refused several times to mock the the voice of Herr Hitler for obvious reasons, but my brother was persuasive, and together we staged the strange chitchat of two hand puppets as ironic diversions, if only for an hour of mockery on that cold and windy afternoon of the Nazi Occupation of Paris.

NATHAN: Galerie Crémieux will never be yours.
ADOLF: Everything is mine by conquest.
NATHAN: The gallery is now owned by natives.
ADOLF: Indian warriors never own art galleries.
NATHAN: Karl May dreamed your demise.
ADOLF: When did he dream that about me?
NATHAN: When he wore a mask at a Wild West Show.
ADOLF: Karl May was my Wild West Show.
NATHAN: Heil Hitler is a mere burlesque salute.
ADOLF: Winnetou forever rouses my soldiers.
NATHAN: Nazis are forbidden to climb the Eiffel Tower.
ADOLF: The elevator was out of service.
NATHAN: Even the elevator resisted the soldiers.
ADOLF: France is decadent and mine forever.
NATHAN: Old Shatterhand cursed you as a traitor.
ADOLF: Winnetou is my *edel Mensch* warrior.
NATHAN: The *Statut des Allemands* forbids babble.
ADOLF: Jerky hand puppets are demons.
NATHAN: Nazis are the puppets of catastrophe.

Jewish professors were cursed and hounded out of the universities, and four distinguished scholars were removed from the Collège de France. The Nazis overturned the favor of education, demeaned the academic stature of seminars and freedom of thought, and banned books created by Jews. The craven Syndicat des Éditeurs, an association of publishers, had agreed several months ago to deny the publication of books written by Jews. The chokehold on critical essays and studies in history, philosophy, literature, and medicine was carried out with the vengeance of the Third Reich.

"Henri Bergson stands alone," said Nika.

"Purged publishers," shouted Heap of Words.

Nathan related that Calmann Lévy, the prominent publishing house of great authors, Victor Hugo, Alexandre Dumas, Gustave Flaubert, René Bazin, Charles Baudelaire, George Sand, and Honoré de Balzac, was coerced by the fascists to change the obvious risky trace of the company name to Éditions Balzac.

"Éditions Dead Reich," shouted Heap of Words.

The Liste Otto is a record of banned books, an ironic honorary reference to Otto Abetz, the German Ambassador to Paris. The list included more than a thousand books that were banished from libraries and bookstores. Bertolt Brecht, Léon Blum, Franz Boas, Sigmund Freud, Gustav Jung, Stefan Zweig, Walter Benjamin, John Dos Passos, André Malraux, James Joyce, Lion Feuchtwanger, André Gide, Franz Kafka, Franz Werfel, Ernest Hemingway, Rosa Luxemburg, Marcel Proust, Joseph Roth, and thousands of other great books by celebrated authors were cursed and removed from libraries and bookstores, but not one native author was named on the list of banned books.

The Nazi book censors were no doubt romantic about native authors, and surely the fascist censors had never read George Copway, Charles Alexander Eastman, or the novel *Sundown*, by John Joseph Mathews; *The Surrounded*, by D'Arcy McNickle; *Cogewea*, by Morning Dove; *Wild Harvest*, by John Oskison; or *Land of the Spotted Eagle*, by Luther Standing Bear. Not even *Le Journal Indien*, the journal of original native essays, and *La Liberté Indienne*, the edited collection of journal essays, were listed as decadent. No doubt the most secure books at the time of the occupation were the romance novels about the proud and horsey warrior of concocted native cultures named *Winnetou*, by Karl May.

Nazi soldiers, censors, and Préfecture de Police searched libraries and bookstores and seized the books of menace on the master list, but American properties with an embassy red certificate of ownership were exempt from search and seizure. The Galerie Crémieux was secure because the actual title was in the name of Basile and Aloysius Beaulieu. No surprise that most of the banned books and risqué magazines were sold cautiously under the counter by the *bouquinistes*, the used booksellers near Pont Neuf on the River Seine.

Nathan created the ironic *La Liste de la Terre Blanche*, The List of White Earth, of absolutely banned philosophers, theologians, spiritualists, industrialists, and pundits, the risky agents and mediums of nationalism and fascism favored by the Third Reich. The most prominent masters of race on the banned list were Alfred Rosenberg, the fanatical antisemite and interpreter, censor, and bold connoisseur of decadent art; Martin Luther the pious and preachy antisemite; Martin Heidegger, the feral philosopher and antisemite; Madame Blavatsky, the creepy antisemite and founder of the surreal Theosophical Society; Arthur de Gobineau, the antisemitic racial theorist of skin color and superiority; Henry Ford, the haughty and greedy assembly line antisemite; and Friedrich Nietzsche, the moody creator of the concept of *Übermensch*, the overlord and superman of the Nazi Party.

23

PLACE DE GRÈVE

Wednesday, 25 December 1940

Christmas morning, the enemy occupation has ruined the season of music, cold and shivery, and yet the sly ghosts of winter danced over the deck of *Le Corbeau Bleu*. By nature my thoughts turn back to scenes of a crèche and celebrations at Saint Benedict's Mission on the White Earth Reservation. The priest and nuns were always serious, never a hesitation over liturgy, tease of creation, or native earthdivers, or sense of irony when the mongrels arrived with my brother for Midnight Mass.

Nika crowds around the cast iron stove, warms her hands, and creates fantastic original barge stories about the Ice Woman who enticed enemy soldiers on Christmas Eve to remove their heavy, dreary uniforms, national emblems of eagles and swastikas, and swim forever with a lusty native fantasy in the River Seine.

"Seduction of the Third Reich," said Aloysius.

"Karl May sacrifice," shouted Heap of Words.

Nathan declared the absolute end of the Enemy Way Ceremonies on the very day that columns of Nazi soldiers marched down Avenue des Champs-Élysées and Rue de Rivoli and invaded the Hôtel de Crillon on 14 June 1940, that loathsome date of the Brown Plague.

The Nazis landed directly next door to the Embassy of the United States, and that was no consolation to Americans in Paris. The Swastika was unfurled and flapped at the entrance to every monument and hotel. Twitchy soldiers enforced nightly curfews, travel was restricted, automobiles were confiscated, food and fuel was rationed, and fascists censored newspapers and other publications.

The United States remained neutral in the declarations of war and maintained diplomats at the embassy, and we were not constrained by the same occupation restrictions as the citizens, stateless exiles, refugees, and Jews of Paris.

"Red seal exiles," shouted Heap of Words.

Nathan had anticipated the conquest prohibitions, and during the Phoney War he published an edited selection of the critical essays and cultural stories from four years of the journal. *La Liberté Indienne* was published last spring with the original cover art of abstract blue ravens, and celebrated at Shakespeare and Company. Hundreds of writers, artists, gallery owners, and students attended the autograph party, only seventeen days before the noisy tanks, trucks, and the cadence of hobnails boots of the Third Reich.

Aloysius continued with stories about the occupation soldiers caught in webs of revulsion and silence, entire seasons of evasion, deadly doubts, and terror. The woman in the blue scarf no longer played the mellow notes of Erik Satie. She covered the piano and vanished. Several days later a young German officer uncovered the piano on the barge, and with great gestures played the *Grande Sonata Pathétique* by Ludwig Beethoven. The chords were pushy, sensitive, and beautiful, and the breathy tones of the melody were slightly out of tune.

The Nazi pianist would never find an audience for Beethoven, or any other German composer, on the first week of the Nazi Occupation. That spectacular sonata was played at the wrong time and place, absolutely out of tune in every sense of cultural memory, and no love of music composition and performance could overcome the roar and shouts of derision that came from the enraged citizens gathered on the parapets of the Pont de la Concorde.

The Nazis published propaganda posters at the start of the occupation that pictured respect for the citizens, and the soldiers were ordered to show strategic courtesy, especially to the children. One poster conveyed the charity and broad smile of a soldier with three children. The poster declared *Populations abandonnées* at the top, and at the bottom of the poster, *faites confiance, Au Soldat Allemand!* Nathan smiled and translated the notice with a tone of mockery, "The lost, abandoned people are invited to have confidence in the German soldiers."

Any lingering sentiments of the Phoney War or the strategies of trust and courtesy of the occupation soldiers ended two days ago when Jacques Bonsergent, a young engineer, was executed at Château de Vincennes, a prison east of Paris. Jacques was walking with several friends on Rue du

Havre near Gare Saint-Lazare and, as rumors and heartfelt stories revealed
in the past two weeks, the polite engineer, or one of his friends, accidently
bumped into an enemy soldier on the street, a trivial matter, eased with
a sincere *excusez-moi*, or excuse me. Jacques was arrested, a notice of an
absolute totalitarian occupation, as his friends ran away from the scene.

The Nazis posted notices of the death sentence, and good citizens secretly removed the posters, and that slight résistance was considered an act
of sabotage. The posters declared in bold letters, *L'Ingénieur Jacques Bonsergent de Paris, a été condamné à mort par le tribunal militaire allemande
pour acte de violence*, The engineer Jacques Bonsergent was condemned
to death by the German military tribunal for an act of violence. The crude
posters around the city were decorated overnight with rare flowers in winter, and some blooms were cut from colored paper.

Renata meets with lost children once or twice a week at nearby Gare
d'Orsay. The railway station could not provide the platforms for longer
trains, but the local suburban trains continue service at the station, a perfect place to meet the stray and wary sons and daughters of families that
escaped from the city when war was declared. Lists of names have been
posted everywhere since the occupation, and day by day a few children
were reunited with their parents.

More than a dozen children between the ages of seven and thirteen
gather at the station to create hand puppets with metal scraps, buttons,
remnants, shards, and discarded objects found at selected places in the
city, hotels, museums, and classy restaurants. Precious empty tins of cigarettes, the sleeve of a coat, a broken umbrella, and large black buttons
were used to make several new hand puppets last month. The children
created, practiced, and presented hand puppet plays at least once a week
near the vaulted entrance to the Gare d'Orsay.

By Now and Pierre Les Halles deliver vital bundles of vegetables once a
week, Jerusalem artichokes, beetroots, cabbages, potatoes, carrots, beans,
and stored onions from the Dumont family farm located near Paris. By
Now visits the farm to help gather vegetables, and to ride the wagon horse
on the back roads.

Meat, cheese, bread, wine, honey, and more were scarce. Market rations started many months ago with the declaration of war, and the por-
tions have become even more severe with the occupation. Ration cards,

cartes d'alimentation, were provided at the *mairie d'arrondissement*, the municipal town hall, near the Place du Panthéon. Our past parties and celebrations with selected wines, cheeses, baguette, and patisseries are no longer conceivable without corruption, or connections with the black market, so our salutes with wine are diluted, and we never grouse about scraps of stale bread. The rations for an adult are reduced to a starvation diet, and we are very lucky to share two or three eggs a week.

Many citizens have courted their country relatives, and endure the war rations with family favors of vegetables and scarce meat. Some of the trains from nearby communes are named after various vegetables, *train des haricots*, *train des pommes de terre*, bean, potato, carrot, and cabbage trains, because so many people return to the city with bundles of mercy rations. The exiles, refugees, and many others with no connections to relatives on farms wait in long lines for food, downcast in the cold weather.

"Jews at the end of the day," said Nathan.

Nathan saluted the pluck of the hungry citizens and then, with no explanation that night, he suddenly told me to read out loud a section of a moral story about a man about to be executed by guillotine in *The Last Day of a Condemned Man*, by Victor Hugo.

"Guillotine night," shouted Heap of Words.

"Reconciled with irony," said Aloysius.

I stood near the stove and read, "Now I must harden myself, and think with firmness upon the hangman, the wagon, the gendarmes, the crowd on the bridge, on the wharf, at the window, and that which is waiting expressly for me on that gloomy Place de Grève, which might well be paved with the heads it has seen fall. I believe that I still have an hour in which to grow accustomed to all this."

24

FINNEGANS WAKE

Tuesday, 14 January 1941

The heavy overnight snow decorated the benches, iron gates, parapets, statues, and great columns of trees on the Quai des Tuileries. The solemn fishermen, some with two poles in hand, stood as great blue herons on the bank of the River Seine. The mounds of snow brightened the mood of the gray city, softened the beat of soldiers, and disguised the misery of the occupation with poetic images.

mounds of snow
shroud the statues
stone parapets
pont de la concorde
crown the gates
ordinary memories
last overnight
liberty on the seine

James Joyce was tormented with sorry eyes, priestly curves, twitchy families, and a tricky stomach; even so the rawboned author converted customary literary modes to tease and brilliant irony, and created by clever maneuvers of classical allusions, comic diversions and marvelous nonce words, esoteric reveries, elusive metaphors, plucky visions, and mutable scenes in *Finnegans Wake*.

The tease and torment of native storiers were the same, the unconquerable recounts of creation, mockery of woe and remorse, totemic sway of visions, escapades of the fur trade, churchy delusions of shame and salvation, the ironic pitch of customs, and the countless treasons carried out every day on treaty reservations.

"Dublin at White Earth," said Aloysius.

Natives create catchy stories from the seasons, dream songs, envoys at the wake of cranes, bears, otters, and other totems, tease talkers and taunts, and the constant grievances over cockeyed accounts of devious colonial empires, and the charitable concessions of enlightenment.

Grievances over the massacre of native totems and separatist reservations are clearly heard in native stories and in these letters to the heirs of the fur at the start of another war of vengeance and envy. Bungled empires, and the jealousy, malice, and revenge of nationalists were the dry runs of antisemitism and fascism. The outcome was another generation of outliers and louts that favored martial music, uniforms over liberty, neighs of the cavalry, hobnail boot parades, and salutes to Adolf Hitler.

Pierre Chaisson shouted a salute to honor the memory of James Joyce, "*Finnegans Wake* is the first great unreadable book about nothing, and here comes everybody to read the ironic biblical sketchbook of portages on ancient rivers that never flow in the same direction twice."

"Here comes everybody," shouted Heap of Words.

"Tiptoptippy canoodle," said Nika.

Sylvia Beach enticed Nathan, Nika, Pierre, Aloysius, Heap of Words, Coyote, Olivier, Prometheus, and me to read *Finnegans Wake* when it was first published last year, and she invited authors and university students to join the Lending Library of Shakespeare and Company as *bunnies*, the nickname for *abonné*, or bookstore subscribers, and almost every native in the city became one of her *bunnies*, an inexpensive way to read new books published in English.

Heap of Words was more than enticed to read, he was truly besotted with the skinny bookseller, and lingered two or three times a week at the display window of Shakespeare and Company until Sylvia invited him inside for tea. Mostly he listened to the lively lilt of book talk, and was entranced by her graceful gestures. Later that night on the barge he described her narrow black shoes, frizzy hair, the slight pout when she pointed at a book, and the erotic tease of ordinary motion between a bookshelf and a chair.

"Stratford upon Odéon tease," shouted Nika.

"By the book enchantment," shouted Aloysius.

"Joyce was her ecstasy," shouted Pierre.

"Hemingway in the wings," shouted Nathan.

Nika saluted the memory of Henri Bergson, the eminent philosopher at the Collège de France who was disabled with muscular rheumatism. Bergson tottered in the streets and shouted out the truth of his mortality, that he was a Nobel Prize winner, a philosopher, and a Jew. He died last week and forgot to shout about another honor in his name, the Grand Croix de la Légion d'Honneur.

"Bergson was my mentor and a celebrant of intuition, natural motion, time and duration in creative stories," said Nika. She adored his wit and gentle manner as a teacher, and recited a familiar selection from *Creative Evolution*, "The more we study the nature of time, the more we shall comprehend that duration means invention, the creation of forms, the continual elaboration of the absolutely new."

"Not the duration of antisemitism," said Nathan.

Pierre and Nika started the first independent student seminar when so many prominent Jewish professors were removed from Sorbonne University and Collège de France. The ironic name of the seminar, Here Comes Everybody, was derived from the nickname of Humphrey Chimpden Earwicker, the "big cleanminded giant" in *Finnegans Wake*. The French students were uncertain about the appropriate translation, *voici venir tout le monde*, here comes everyone, or *voilà tout le monde arrive*, here everyone arrives, the name or the destination. The seminar met once a week for several hours to talk about the transition of chance and meaning in native creation stories, the curse of nationalism, the duration of memories, and the catch of cultural conversions in two books, *Creative Evolution* by Henri Bergson, published more than thirty years ago, and *Finnegans Wake* by James Joyce, published just last year.

Nika was haunted by an occupation dream early this morning with Henri Bergson and James Joyce. Bergson was her mentor, and she had met Joyce only once, at Shakespeare and Company about ten years ago at a poetry reading. She related that the dream started at a session of the seminar, and became the urgency of two scholars to find several more copies of *Creative Evolution* and *Finnegans Wake*.

Shakespeare and Company sold dozens of copies in the first week the novel was published, but since the Nazi Occupation and the Liste Otto of banned authors, the shipment of books from London to Paris was not possible.

"Henri Bergson was a *bouquiniste* in my dream, and with one arm disabled by rheumatism he readily sold books at a stall on Quai du Louvre near Pont Neuf. I was surprised that only copies of *Creative Evolution*, *L'Évolution Créatrice*, translated into several languages were stacked neatly, along with a few copies of *Laughter: An Essay on the Meaning of the Comic*, on two tables, and the withered author sat erect on a high wooden chair between his books. Bergson chuckled over the natural irony of the two words in the title and gave me two copies of *Creative Evolution* for the seminar, one copy in English and the other in French," said Nika.

"Bergson teased me about my comic ladder, *échelle comique*, to reach the window of his popular lectures at the Collège de France, and then he smiled and touched my necklace with the Star of David. I was weepy, of course, in the dream, and he wiped the tears from my cheeks with the sleeve of his shaggy coat.

"James Joyce shouted the title *Finnegans Wake* to the *bouquinistes* on Quai du Louvre, and bought two copies from a secondhand bookseller who was tense and jittery, the obvious gestures of an insecure under the counter dealer," said Nika. "I was the most nervous in the dream, and covered the books with a blue scarf, and as we walked slowly on the Pont Neuf we were stopped by soldiers and ordered to show our identity cards. I tucked the books under my coat and presented my passport of the White Earth Nation, and the severe soldiers, fascist flâneurs, shouted my name Nika, Nika, Nika Montezuma, and teased me, *La fille perdue de Winnetou*, lost daughter of Winnetou."

Joyce wore a blue eye patch, and when the soldiers pulled the patch aside, the author raised his right hand and shouted in German, "Guter Bürger von Zürich, die Schweiz," a good citizen of Zurich, Switzerland. The soldiers examined his sorry eye and passport and then shouted, "Earwicker, is that a German or Jewish name?" Joyce smiled and replied in the dream, "No sir, Earwickers are cleanminded masters of mockery from Dublin, Ireland."

The soldier stared, and then "touched the big bulge in my coat. I was angry and scared when he pulled my coat open, and interrogated me about the copies of *Creative Evolution* and *Finnegans Wake*." The soldiers noted

the authors and turned to search the Liste Otto for books by James Joyce
and Henri Bergson, and at that moment "Mister Earwicker of Zurich
turned, smiled at me, and hand in hand we jumped over the parapet of
the bridge," said Nika.

"I was floating in the cold air with a sense of liberty as torn pages of the
books floated around me down to the dark river. This was another me that
never landed in the water, but luckily was saved from the savage soldiers
in my dream just before three this morning," and at about the same time,
four hundred miles to the east, only a nurse heard the last breath of our
seminar author James Joyce.

"Nightmare on the River Seine," said Aloysius.

"Portmanteau words downriver," said Pierre.

"Several sindays after whatsintime," said Nathan.

"Bond of banned books," shouted Heap of Words.

James Joyce died yesterday in Zurich, Switzerland, after surgery for a
perforated ulcer, and now we run with the great visions of Henri Bergson
and James Joyce in our nightly stories on *Le Corbeau Bleu*. Joyce was
weak only by eye sight, but never by the original turns and tucks of irony;
rather he was an eminent heir of the fur trade on a grand native portage of
chance, natural motion, and comic scenes in a creation story.

"Fur trade fantasies," shouted Heap of Words.

"Bootifull totemic liberty," said Nika.

"Basile writes to the furry heirs," said Aloysius.

"Readable portage," said Pierre Chaisson.

Nathan could not escape the image of dream pages from two books,
Creative Evolution and *Finnegans Wake*, floating together in the cold air
down to the river. Several days later he was prepared to read the interrelated dream scenes from the actual pages of two banned books afloat in a
dream on the River Seine.

BERGSON: These memories, messengers from the unconscious, remind us of what we are dragging behind us unawares. But, even
though we may have no distinct idea of it, we feel vaguely that our
past remains present to us.

JOYCE: How bootifull and how truetowife of her, when strengly fore-
bidden, to steal our historic presents from the past postprophet-

icals so as to will make us all lordy heirs and ladymaidesses of a
pretty nice kettle of fruit.

BERGSON: The evolution of the living being, like that of the embryo,
implies a continual recording of duration, a persistence of the past
in the present, and so an appearance, at least, of organic memory.

JOYCE: When they set fire then she's got to glow so we may stand
some chances of warming to what every soorkabatcha tum or hum,
would like to know.

BERGSON: Can we go further and say that life, like conscious activity,
is invention, is unceasing creation?

JOYCE: For peers and gints, quaysirs and galleyliers, fresk letties rom
the say and stale headygabblers, gaingangers and dudder wagoners,
pullars off societies and pushers on rothmere's homes.

BERGSON: We perceive duration as a stream against which we cannot
go. It is the foundation of our being, and, as we feel, the very sub-
stance of the world in which we live.

JOYCE: Where cold is dearth. Yet see, my blanching kissabelle, in the
under close she is allso gay, her kirtles green, her curtsies white,
her peony pears, her nistlingsloes.

BERGSON: Matter of mind, reality has appeared to us as a perpetual
becoming. It makes itself or it unmakes itself, but it is never something made.

JOYCE: But vicereversing thereout from those palms of perfection to
anger arbour, treerack monatan, scroucely out of scout of ocean,
virid with woad, what tornaments of complementary rages rocked
the divlun from his punchpoll to his tummy's shentre as he dis-
plaid all the oathword science of his visible disgrade.

BERGSON: The finished portrait is explained by the features of the
model, by the nature of the artist, by the colors spread out on the
palette; but, even with the knowledge of what explains it, no one,
not even the artist, could have foreseen exactly what the portrait
would be, or predict it would have been to produce it before it was
produced—an absurd hypothesis which is its own refutation.

JOYCE: Retire to rest without first misturbing your neighbor, mankind
of baffling descriptions. Others are as tired of themselves as you
are. Let such one learn to bore himself. It is strictly requested that

no cobsmoking, spitting, pubchat, wrastle rounds, coarse courting, smut, etc, will take place amongst these hours so devoted to repose. Look before behind before you strip you.

Nika was teary over the puppet play of literature and philosophy, "persistence of the past in the present" and the "oathword science of his visible disgrade" ended on that snowy day in the dream songs of Henri Bergson and James Joyce on the River Seine.

25

FASCIST STAINS

Monday, 31 March 1941

The liberty trees were radiant, and daffodils and tulips were in glorious bloom after a severe winter with no coal or wood at hand. The River Seine was frozen over for the first time in more than a decade, a risky boulevard of ice, and *Le Corbeau Bleu* groaned against the quay in the cold wind.

Samuel walked on the magical ice from the Pont Neuf to the barge and tried to play the violin, but his fingers were too cold. Scared citizens shivered together in movie theatres and churches, and the splendor of heavy snow reminded us of long winters on the White Earth Reservation.

Nika and Samuel tamped out the poem "Courage," by Paul Éluard, in the snow near the Musée de l'Orangerie in the Jardin des Tuileries.

> *Paris is cold*
> *Paris is hungry*
> *Paris no longer eats chestnuts in the streets*
> *Paris trembles like a star*

Maréchal Philippe Pétain appointed Xavier Vallat the first Commissariat Général aux Questions Juives, General for Jewish Affairs in France. Vallat was favored for his crude manner and menace; a monarchist and antisemite, he was active in the Action Française, the extreme fascist league. He wore an eye patch and peg leg, wounds received in the First World War, and could have been cast as Captain Ahab of the whaler *Pequod* in search of Jews and Moby Dick.

Jews have even more to fear this month with the return of another enemy of *liberté*, the fascist hack Xavier Vallat was ready to advocate the abuse and removal of citizens and stateless Jews. These separatist, royalist, and fascist cults have condemned liberal democracies, demonized the French Third Republic, and cursed Jews as the cause of economic setbacks, but never mocked or denounced the enemy occupation or the Third Reich.

Robert Brasillach, the fascist antisemite journalist, had returned from military service last month, and was named the editor of *Je Suis Partout*, I Am Everywhere, the extreme antisemitic newspaper published weekly, and with wide circulation.

These two frightful antisemites were traitors to the cause of *liberté*, *égalité*, *fraternité*, and advanced to significant positions with fascist sway and authority. Vallat carried out the antisemitic statutes enacted by the Vichy Regime, and Brasillach wrote antisemitic editorials that undermined the liberal ethos and democracy of the French Third Republic.

"Wicked hearts of collaboration, but not the last beats of fascism," said Nathan. "Beastly Brasillach and Vile Vallat are two more reasons why Jews should serve in résistance movements."

"Messieurs Beastly and Vile," said Aloysius.

"Deadly mockery," shouted Heap of Words.

Pierre Chaisson had speculated several months ago that Nathan was active in résistance movements. Nathan was silent as he moved closer to the stove to warm his hands, and never revealed his secret duties. Heap of Words was always tempted to cut the silence or evasions with ironic catchwords, but smiled and held back as he had many times in the past year.

Panzéra leaned closer to Nathan, and the intuitive touch of the wise mongrel overcame the silence with a diversion story about the opera singer Charles Panzéra, the namesake of the Basset Hound baritone of *Le Corbeau Bleu*.

"Panzéra attended gallery openings, and the first time we met he mentioned Roland Barthes, a singer, and one of his students," said Nathan. "Barthes was a gadabout at the time of Le Front Populaire, creative and concise about the literary burdens of the novel, who never hesitated to honor the memory and nobility of Jean Jaurès, and then declared his 'hatred against the stench of the country,' an evasive denunciation of royalists and fascists." Barthes was always literary, a café cane chair philosopher, and he never dared to counter fascism with sabotage.

"Barthes probably never heard or read native stories," said Pierre Chaisson. "He might have appreciated the tease of creation and the visionary moments in trickster stories that reveal ironic scenes more than the cause and crease of words."

"Barthes was a place name," said Nika.

"Jaurès an inspiration," shouted Heap of Words.

Jean Jaurès was a social democrat, antimilitarist, a charismatic orator of social justice, and a popular leader of the French Socialists. Raoul Villain, an extreme nationalist and patriotic lackey, assassinated Jaurès on 31 July 1914 at the Café du Croissant on Rue Montmartre.

"The *wiindigoo* nationalist," said Nika.

Samuel announced the presence of enemy soldiers on the quay early last month with short breaks and repetitions of a sonata by Claude Debussy. He continued to play the entire sonata once we were on deck, and pretended not to notice the loud commands of officers and shouts of soldiers as they seized nearby barges.

The Nazis commandeered every barge moored on the river, except three narrow *péniche* canal barges. A squad of soldiers marched down the cold and snowy cobblestones to *Le Corbeau Bleu*. A puffy soldier with red cheeks and dirty hands pried open the engine hatch, turned and shouted, *nichts*, nothing, and then the squad marched to the next barge on the quay.

The piano barge of the mysterious woman who wore a blue scarf and played the music of Erik Satie, our ancient *péniche* barge, *Le Corbeau Bleu*, with the blue tiller, and the barge named *La Belle Aurore*, beautiful dawn, that Anaïs Nin, the exotic author, occupied about four years ago, were not seized, *nichts*, and were forever moored with no engines on the River Seine.

Nazi soldiers are fascist flâneurs, a perversion of fancy gestures and gray poseurs of fright in noisy boots, almost hollow without weapons. Stone by city stone the soldiers touch with envy and wound every memorable scene, an occupation of tawdry nightmares. The fascist flâneurs flout the café culture and leave their stains at markets and counters, window displays, on menus, wine glasses, and round tables at cafés, statues, doorknobs, trains, and park benches. Even a gentle morning breeze torments the peace of citizens with the noisy flaps of thousands of swastika banners and flags.

Paris was contaminated with the guttural pitch, sweat, and thick neck oils of the Third Reich. The only places to escape the fascist scent of the enemy were at obscure movie theaters, church pews, bookstores, musical productions, and at hand puppet shows.

The Aryan officers are more sinister than the gray drumbeat of pock-marked soldiers. The courteous officers, contenders of a perfect fascist empire, wear fur collars in winter, thin leather gloves, pricey polished boots, conduct gentile waltz music at brothel rendezvous, salute mopey images of the Führer with counterfeit grand cru wines, and at the same time the officers calmly order the internment and execution of the Jews.

For several years *Le Corbeau Bleu* has been our barge of solace and *liberté*, the literary embassy of a native nation on the River Seine. Last month the snowy peace of the river changed with the tread of soldiers as they inspected every barge moored on the river and ordered the removal of more than seventeen river residents. The soldiers seized every barge with an engine only to transport coal, oil, and other materials for the war. Jewish refugees banished from Poland and Germany were abruptly removed in the cold and snow from an abandoned laundry boat that had been moored for many years near the Pont du Carrousel and Musée du Louvre. Nathan and Nika escorted the family to the barge with the piano as temporary cover for the night.

The Nazi soldiers, traitors, entertainers, and double agents are nourished daily with meat, vegetables, fine wine, coffee, chocolate, and sugar confiscated or procured by black marketeers, but most citizens, exiles, and refugees are ashen with hunger and live with rotten teeth and bloody gums one day at a time on starvation rations.

The liberty trees are bright, almost luminous, and the children sail tiny boats on the Grand Bassin Rond and smile at puppet shows, and the slight curtsy of shy daffodils in the spring sunlight secure the memories of grace in the Jardin des Tuileries.

26

BOOTY CULTURE

Thursday, 25 December 1941

Samuel tuned his violin early this morning on the cold deck of *Le Corbeau Bleu*, and with the loyal mongrels at his side played a haunting, melancholy, and teary version of *J'attendrai*, the swing music first recorded two years ago by Stéphane Grappelly and Django Reinhardt.

"Fiddler on the Barge," shouted Heap of Words.

"Grappelly of the Seine," said Aloysius.

"Django Christmas," said Nathan.

Nazi Germany declared war against the United States of America two weeks ago, on 11 December 1941, and just four days after hundreds of Japanese warplanes carried out a deadly surprise attack on the naval base at Pearl Harbor in Hawaii.

The Enemy Way celebrations once carried out at the Galerie Crémieux have now been converted to active résistance against fascism and antisemitism. The clever moves and mockery of the enemy are now conveyed in literary irony, hand puppetry, and with courage at bookstores, museums, universities, and other public events.

The *Cirque d'Hiver* was permitted to continue regular performances during the Nazi Occupation. Joseph and Rosa Bouglione owned the circus and staged spectacular elephant, tiger, and lion shows, white horse dances, contortionists, and aerial acrobats of the flying trapeze in the coliseum on Rue Amelot near the Métro Filles du Calvaire.

Nathan bought eleven tickets for a performance last week in the second tier near the grand entrance to the circus ring. Samuel and Renata were ecstatic at the first tease of the clowns, and within minutes the entire audience seemed to forget that enemy soldiers were outside of the auditorium at every station and familiar place.

Joseph and Rosa, the lion trainer and dancer, were actually married in a lion cage thirteen years ago, and that sense of daring was no surprise to anyone. Nathan told me during the glorious horse show that Rosa Van Been was Roma, born in a circus caravan, and now with a distinctive Italian name, the couple carry out the spirit of partisans to protect the Jewish performers and deliver weapons to résistance groups.

American neutrality ended with one more declaration of world war. Overnight we became occupation denizens of the Nazis, and the distant enemy of the Japanese. The favors of official crests, seals, and certificates of property protection once provided by the United States Embassy were no longer honored by the Wehrmacht, but we were steadfast storiers and remained on *Le Corbeau Bleu* as native citizens with passports of the White Earth Nation.

"Native embassy adrift," shouted Heap of Words.

Samuel has played *J'attendrai* and selected phrases of a sonata by Claude Debussy almost every morning, mongrels at his side, no matter the weather, rain, sleet, or snow on the deck of *Le Corbeau Bleu* since the Vichy Regime terminated the rights and duties of Jews and carried out the fascist seizure of personal property.

The Institute for the Study of Jewish Questions, Institut d'Étude des Questions Juives, an ironic query and disguise of antisemitism, sponsored an exhibition, *Le Juif et la France*, the Jews of France, and several detrimental publications. Last year the fascist policy that required Jews to register with the police was a sinister system of residential identity, and the policy actually led to the removal of thousands of Jews a few months ago to the concentration camp at Drancy.

The Institut d'Étude des Questions Juives was stationed at 21 Rue La Boétie in the famous art gallery once owned by Paul Rosenberg, who represented Henri Matisse, Pablo Picasso, George Braque, Marie Laurencin, and many other modernist and cubist painters. "The generous memories of the gallery and celebration of great painters were shamed by the Institute for the Study of Jewish Questions, a fascist organization in the very property that had been seized by the Nazis," said Nathan.

"Booty culture," shouted Heap of Words.

"Nazi perversions," said Aloysius.

"The Vichy Regime carried out the treasonous demise of the French Third Republic, the connivance of an armistice between Maréchal Pétain and Adolf Hitler. The fascist agents of the *Statut des Juifs* trudge from the thermal baths to the Opera House in Vichy," shouted Nathan.

Every morning hundreds of people wandered along the Quai des Tuileries in search of relatives, friends, fuel, food, or the mingy shares of an edible royal pigeon, and the violin music was a tender distraction from hunger and the cruel constraints of the Nazi Occupation. Many people gathered near the barge in the morning and sang along with the violin rendition of *J'attendrai*, I Will Wait. The breath of the singers lingered in the cold air of the quay.

> *J'attendrai le jour et la nuit*
> *J'attendrai toujours ton retour*
> I will wait night and day
> I will always await your return

The singers were ashen with cracked skin, bad teeth, some were pockmarked and bent with diseases, and their best heartfelt voices were unsteady. The good citizens of labor and *liberté* barely survived on the food rations, an undeniable occupation strategy of starvation. The ritzy couturiers, collaborators, highbrow traders, and enemy soldiers were courted and served pâté de foie gras, oysters, game, and caviar at fine restaurants. Samuel played the music of reassurance on the cold and chancy morning of Christmas Day on the River Seine.

The Wehrmacht confiscated art, coal, honey, leather, soap, eggs, and more, but there was never a shortage for the beau monde and military. Yet, the occupation favors were never safe or sound, as the backstairs stories revealed today, the résistance had secretly infected hundreds of enemy soldiers with a serious disease at the Brasserie La Brune.

"Heil Malady," shouted Heap of Words.

"Salute the poison menus," said Nathan.

"Deadly sauerbraten," shouted Nika.

Samuel pleaded to remain on *Le Corbeau Bleu*, but his mother, Angelika, was determined to depart with her family for Marseilles and Lisbon, and then board a ship for New York. She has not heard from her husband, but she refused to stay as an American in Paris. The Wehrmacht soldiers were not obliged to honor the embassy certificates of protection and would surely attempt to seize the Galerie Crémieux.

"Brave the enemy way," shouted Heap of Words.

"The enemy denies my way," said Angelika.

Nathan arranged for Angelika, Renata, and Samuel to depart early in the morning, and contacted a network to escort them over the mountains to the border with Spain. Michel Laroux, retired office of the Gendarmerie Nationale, had obtained the necessary travel permits to leave the *Zone Occupée*, and would drive the family to Marseille.

"Mountain exiles," shouted Heap of Words.

"Galerie Crémieux exiles," said Aloysius.

"Jewish exiles the world over," said Nathan.

"Walter Benjamin, the creative archivist and mediator of art, literature, and culture, was on his way from exile to liberty through Lisbon," said Nika. "Adrienne Monnier, the bookstore owner, assisted the philosopher and many others to escape over the mountains."

Paris was risky, the police surveillance had increased since the declaration of war against the United States, and Angelika was convinced that her family would be more secure on the road than in the city with the constant fear of informers. She worried that the police could easily detect the forgery of their American passports and dispute their poses as citizens of the White Earth Nation.

Paris had become a wounded city of hunger, disease, separation, sorrow, and cold waits, waits, waits night and day for the return of a lost child, a parent, lonesome lovers, exiled neighbors, festivals, and mostly for the return of captured soldiers and the birthright of Jews.

Paris was similar in some ways to the separation and misery of reservations occupied by the cavalry, federal agents, and churchy saboteurs who denied totemic visions and stories of chance. The corrupt enemy agents diverted food and medicine, and abandoned natives on allotments in the stumps of white pine. Tuberculosis and other diseases were common on federal reservations and in cold and grim apartments on the back streets of occupied Paris.

"Paris Trail of Tears," said Aloysius.

"Sand Creek d'Hiver" shouted Heap of Words.

"Bosque Redondo Drancy," said Pierre.

"Wounded Knee France," said By Now.

"Blue lights of torment," shouted Nathan.

Sylvia Beach heard a rumor about rations of honey and waited in line for several hours for nothing, and two weeks ago the embassy certificate that protected Shakespeare and Company ended with the declaration of war. Naturally, she worried that at any moment soldiers would commandeer the bookstore and send her to prison as the enemy.

A Wehrmacht officer marched into Shakespeare and Company eager to buy a copy of *Finnegans Wake*, but brave Sylvia told him the book was not for sale. The officer was insistent, then furious, but his crude manner would never overcome her refusal to sell the last copy of the novel, no matter his cultural boasts, wrath, and military occupation threats.

"Sylvias Wake," shouted Heap of Words.

Aloysius might have changed the title of *Finnegans Wake* to *Chief Josephs Wake, Rosenbergs Wake, Geronimos Wake, Shylocks Wake,* or *Goebbels Wake,* but the novel was no longer in the display window, and the nasty officer was enraged when Sylvia declared that the last copy of the book was not available.

"Sylvia slowly turned away, and the officer declared that he would return later to confiscate the entire bookstore, and then he was chauffeured away in a military car," said Heap of Words.

The concierge of the building on Rue de l'Odéon had promised to provide an apartment for her on the fourth floor, and that afternoon Sylvia, the concierge, and her close friend Adrienne Monnier, who owned the French bookstore across the street, La Maison des Amis des Livres, packed the books in boxes, bags, and baskets, and in a few hours moved the entire bookstore, shelves, table, chairs, and five thousand books to the apartment.

Heap of Words heard about the threat, and when he rode a borrowed bicycle to Shakespeare and Company the "painter had just covered the last traces of a bookstore, and the outside sign had been removed." By the time the officer and soldiers arrived by car and truck to seize the bookstore and the last copy of *Finnegans Wake*, the famous Shakespeare and Company had vanished. The Wehrmacht officer in his shiny boots must have wondered if he had forgotten where the bookstore was located. He broke down the door in search of any trace of *Finnegans Wake* and Sylvia Beach.

"*Shakespeares Wake*," said Nika.

"Nazi horror story," said Nathan.

"Revenge of the bunnies," said Aloysius.

"Sylvia watched from the fourth floor as the officer looked across the street at La Maison des Amis des Livres, but the House of the Friends of Books was French, not American, so he marched back to the car and was chauffeured away," said Heap of Words. "The Nazis had no idea that Adrienne Monnier had sheltered and provided travel documents for exiled Jews, Arthur Koestler, Walter Benjamin, Siegfried Kracauer, and many other scholars and writers."

The Paris of cultural memory, *lieux de memoire*, creative literature, and avantgarde styles of art became the cultural booty of the Nazi Occupation. The common gray soldiers snatched perfume, leather, and silk, and the dressy officers stole original paintings from galleries and looted books, wine, furniture, dinnerware, gold jewelry, and antiques from the homes of Jews.

"The plague of monsters," said Pierre.

"Rottweiler looters," said Nika.

"Jackboot pirates," shouted Heap of Words.

"Third Reich savages," said Nathan.

Albert Rosenberg, the Minister of Occupied Eastern Territories and creepy master of racial theories, set up the Einsatzstab Reichsleiter Rosenberg last year, an official booty institute to systematically plunder art and other cultural property. Reichsmarschall Hermann Göring had absolute authority over the booty convention and ordered the seizure of art collections and precious personal property from the homes and galleries owned by Jews.

Nathan cursed the plunder of private art collections from the Rothschild, David-Weill, and Seligmann families, and from the Paul Rosenberg art gallery and many other galleries owned by Jews. The Nazis stole huge collections of art and treasure and moved the great paintings of Camille Pissarro, Paul Cézanne, Claude Monet, Edgar Degas, Pablo Picasso, Pierre-August Renoir, Henri Matisse, Vincent van Gogh to the Jeu de Paume for review by the fascist thieves of the Third Reich.

Hermann Göring was perched on the cold deck near the blue tiller of *Le Corbeau Bleu* earlier this month with his mouth wide open. His bright blue eyes were frozen fierce and freaky, an obese hand puppet carved from a block of grainy river wood. The Reichsmarschall puppet wore a soft fedora, a garish military uniform, two swastika armbands, and a heavy creamy cape for a risky hand puppet show of stolen art at the Jeu de Paume.

Nathan convinced my brother and me not to present the new hand puppet on the actual day, 2 December 1941, that Göring was scheduled to review the first collections of plundered art at the museum. Wisely the new puppet show was staged five days later on Sunday.

"Show of thieves," shouted Heap of Words.

"Morphine Göring," said Prometheus.

Aloysius named me as the despotic voice of Hermann Göring in the puppet production. Prometheus wore white gloves and mimed the gestures of the hand puppets, and with silent facial gestures mocked Göring. Samuel was eager to play the violin for the show; he practiced a few melancholy phrases of the *Liebesmelodie* from *Das Herz* by Hans Pfitzner, the wily romantic composer who was admired by Hermann Göring. Renata was moved by the breathy sounds of poetic words and the catchy cadence of *Living Room Music*, by John Cage, and was ready to create word wafts with the voice of the hand puppet Gertrude Stein.

Aloysius raised Hermann Göring on his right hand as Samuel played the melancholy music of *Liebesmelodie*, and on his left hand the demure puppet Gertrude Stein swayed to the steady beat of words and breathy sounds by Renata. We gathered near the entrance of the Jeu de Paume that cold afternoon as the sun grazed slowly between the winter clouds and created natural background scenes and elusive shadows in the Jardin des Tuileries.

Gertrude wore a signature cloche hat and wagged her huge wooden hands at the first people who gathered near the entrance to the museum. She jerked her head to the side, raised one huge hand, and firmly informed the audience that the last great performance as a hand puppet was seven years ago at the Panthéon. She wrangled at the time with blocky Adolf Hitler over art, Karl May, Winnetou the fake Apache, Natty Bumppo, Luther Standing Bear, and Ernest Hemingway, and gathered around the slow bonfire of torn pages from *Mein Kampf*, the decadent prison memoir that was read by millions of people around the world.

GÖRING: Hitler cursed the bonfire at the Panthéon.

GERTRUDE: *Mein Kampf* burns faster than *The Iron Heel*.

GÖRING: Hitler is the maestro of art and culture.

GERTRUDE: Adolf is a wimpy plagiarizer.

GÖRING: Nazis are connoisseurs of great art.

GERTRUDE: Adolf and your sort are nothing but thieves.

GÖRING: Jews are the thieves and decadent painters.

GERTRUDE: Adolf and you are jealous.

GÖRING: The Jews, they will be the death of me yet.

GERTRUDE: Worse to be envious than scared or dead.

GÖRING: Chagall and Soutine are decadent.

GERTRUDE: Soutine would paint you as a red bully.

GÖRING: Soutine distorts faces like yours, not mine.

GERTRUDE: Time to talk about sex and literature.

GÖRING: My wife loves the impressionists.

GERTRUDE: The Third Reich is a fascist blunder.

GÖRING: Great statesmen or the worst villains.

GERTRUDE: Third Reich has no culture or shame.

GÖRING: Jews must get out and stay out.

GERTRUDE: Third Reich is a degenerate delusion.

GÖRING: Come see my art show at Jeu de Paume.

GERTRUDE: Art isn't everything, it's just about everything.

GÖRING: Decadent cubists paint about nothing.

GERTRUDE: Picasso might paint your cubist mouth.

GÖRING: The Third Reich is our great vision.

GERTRUDE: Takes time to be an artist and genius.

GÖRING: Yes, so much easier with morphine.

GERTRUDE: True genius does not have to plunder art.

GÖRING: Plunder of decadent art saves the world.

GERTRUDE: Artists never die, plunderers never live.

GÖRING: Heil the great impressionists, burn the rest.

GERTRUDE: Heil to the soldiers of Jardin des Tuileries.

Gertrude raised two huge hands and then jerked her head to the side as several soldiers moved through the crowd around the puppet show. Göring shouted "Heil Montezuma, Heil Goethe, Heil Karl May, Heil Hitler," and raised both arms over his head. Samuel continued to play phrases from the melancholy *Liebesmelodie* by Hans Pfitzner, and Renata ended the breathy beat of poetic words.

Samuel was shied and silenced by a giant soldier who grabbed the violin, turned it over, and examined the origin and signature of the craftsman. Göring moved closer to the soldier and pretended to play the violin. The Nazi soldier shouted, *Französische Miracourt Violine, nicht Deutsch*, or the French Miracourt violin, not German, and handed the violin back to Samuel. Nathan had anticipated that very scene of cultural plunder when he decided to give the Miracourt to Samuel. The Nazi soldiers surely would have seized as cultural booty a German Cremona. The Nazis were not impressed with the French Miracourt.

Samuel wisely continued to play *Liebesmelodie* as the soldiers examined our identity papers. Two young soldiers interrogated me about reservations, native identity, and my alien passport, but not a word about my raucous voice as Hermann Göring. Nika saved me, and at the same time surprised the soldiers that she could speak German. The soldiers ordered her to translate the interrogations, but she outwitted them with stories. Nika explained that we were natives and lived on *Le Corbeau Bleu*, *Der Blaue Rabe*, a barge moored on the River Seine with no engine, and named me the chief international correspondent for *The Tomahawk*, the independent newspaper once published on the White Earth Nation.

Nika explained to the soldiers that the hand puppets were traditional in native culture, and declared that we were citizens of the White Earth Nation. The soldiers were crude and curious, of course, but our unique presence as native citizens seemed to ease the tension.

Nika related stories about her father, who was one of the few German fur traders, and convinced the soldiers that the puppet Hermann Göring had just warned Gertrude Stein about how decadent art aroused the spirit of the Third Reich, and how paintings were removed from private galleries and stored at the Jeu de Paume. The easy story of puppets and decadent art distracted the soldiers from the interrogations, and they revealed the obvious, that Reichsmarschall Göring had visited the museum earlier to examine the decadent art. Nika smiled and saluted the soldiers as they continued their occupation patrol on the Place de la Concorde.

Nazi soldiers were served generous meals to celebrate the season, and they decorated pagan trees with swastikas in place of angels or stars. The Nazis hailed the winter solstice, the heathen comeback of the sun, but not the birth of Jesus Christ the Jew. The Nazis sullied the saints and defiled the Eucharist and Torah. "Silent Night" became a godless carol, and was replaced with "Exalted Night of the Clear Sky."

"Chanukah in Berlin," shouted Heap of Words.

"Menorahs in Nuremberg," shouted Nathan.

German children were treated with chocolate soldiers and the precious toys of war, while the occupation children were malnourished and starving and the lucky ones were served *macedoine*, carrot and rutabaga mash, a tiny scrap of gristle, or a single thin slice of roasted domestic guinea pig for dinner on Christmas Day.

General Charles de Gaulle, the exiled leader of France Libre, Free France, broadcast messages to the citizens of France on the British Broadcasting Corporation radio station from London. He denounced the armistice as nothing more than capitulation to the Nazis, and encouraged the soldiers, citizen résistance leagues, and others not to be disheartened by the Nazi Occupation.

De Gaulle told the children of France in a radio message broadcast on Christmas Eve, 24 December 1941, to think about pride, glory, and hope. Nathan invited the crew of *Le Corbeau Bleu* to hear the broadcast and his translation at the Galerie Crémieux. Jews were forbidden to own radios, and any broadcasts were considered a criminal violation of the armistice and the occupation of Paris.

"Curse the Nazis," shouted Heap of Words.

"Chocolate violins," shouted Samuel.

"Sing 'La Marseillaise' in Berlin," said Nika.

Nathan and Nika translated the radio message by Charles de Gaulle from London. "My dear children of France, you are hungry because the enemy eats our bread and our meat. You are cold, because the enemy steals our wood and our coal; you suffer, because the enemy orders you to say that you are sons and daughters of the vanquished, nothing more. Well, my dear children of France, this is a Christmas promise, you will soon receive a visit, the visit of victory. How beautiful that will be, and you will see."

27

BLUE NIGHTS

Wednesday, 31 December 1941

Maréchal Philippe Pétain converted the principles and liberal watchwords, *liberté, égalité, fraternité*, of the French Third Republic to the fascist revisions, *travail, famille, partie*, of the Vichy Regime, otherwise the devious collaboration government of Nazi Germany.

The Vichy lackeys directed children to start the school day with a new Anthem about the Chief of State of Vichy France. *Maréchal, nous voila*, "Marshall, we are here," replaced "La Marseillaise" as the anthem in most of the public schools in France.

Renata handed out small posters that pictured two happy children skipping along in white shoes and socks, hair disheveled, puffy, rosy cheeks, and with bouquets of bright flowers under a cameo picture of Maréchal Pétain.

The poster proclaimed, *Grace a vous des Milliers d'Enfants Partiront en Vacances*, Thanks to You Thousands of Children Will Leave on Holiday.

"Cheeky not rosy," shouted Heap of Words.

"Cameo collaborators," said Aloysius.

Nathan was enraged over the poster, dismissed the homey message as sinister, and told us that Secours National was once a national help or relief organization for soldiers and their families who were victims of the First World War. The Vichy Regime continued the program in name only during the occupation, and with a "sinister source of money, the sale of property owned by Jews." The Secours National in Paris collaborated with the Nazis to set up the Entr'aide d'Hiver du Maréchal, Marshal Pétain's Winter Mutual Aid Society.

"Nazis gave millions of francs to the *Secours National* and most of the money was stolen from Jews in Paris," said Nathan. Kristallnacht and the vicious exclusion of Jews two years ago, and the Vichy *Statut des Juifs*, laws against Jews, enacted on 3 October 1940, endorsed the Nazi plunder of art and personal property owned by Jews. "That bloody money funded the Entr'aide d'Hiver du Maréchal, and the publication of the poster of cheery children on their way to a fantasy vacation."

"Pétain the Plunderer," said Aloysius.

"Time for us to leave," said Angelika.

"J'attendrai," shouted Heap of Words.

"Long live *Le Corbeau Bleu*," said Renata.

Pierre Dumont delivered a sack of carrots, potatoes, onions, and rutabaga, and By Now prepared a hot chunky vegetable stew over a fire of bundled twigs. Nathan had traded Columbian *Pielroja* cigarettes for three bottles of red wine to celebrate another week of native favors, the puppet show at the Jeu de Paume, the radio message to children by Charles de Gaulle, and the departure on the last day of the year of Angelika, Renata, and Samuel for New York by way of Marseilles, Spain, and Lisbon.

Aloysius surprised Renata with a gift of two puppets, Gertrude Stein and Hermann Göring. They were packed neatly together in a small blue shoulder pouch. Renata was teary as she raised bossy Gertrude on her right hand, Göring the mouthy Nazi on the other hand, and then rightly jerked their heads with wily wonder. The two hand puppets stared at my brother for a moment, then at me, and then cocked their heads close to Nathan.

"Last puppet stares," shouted Heap of Words.

Aloysius prepared a departure hand puppet show that cold night on *Le Corbeau Bleu*. By Now rehearsed the voice of Gertrude, and the big voice of Göring was delivered by Nathan. Samuel played *J'attendrai*, I Will Wait, on his violin as the hand puppets contended with racial conspiracies and the atrocities of the Third Reich. The barge mongrels, Pig Ears, The Vicar, Panzéra, Black Jack, and High Road, pranced and bumped Renata and Samuel, and bayed for a part in the puppet play and a place in the memory of Jews.

GÖRING: Where are you going tonight?

GERTRUDE: New York City to escape the Nazis.

GÖRING: Big Nazi Party in New York.

GERTRUDE: No Third Reich at Coney Island.

GÖRING: The Third Reich is everywhere.

GERTRUDE: Roller coasters scare the fascists.

GÖRING: Never under my command.

GERTRUDE: Third Reich converted to Judaism.

GÖRING: That would be the death of me.

GERTRUDE: Mongrels crap on your grave.

GÖRING: Double death for the mongrels.

GERTRUDE: Mongrels bay for liberty.

GÖRING: Then turn me into a hand puppet.

GERTRUDE: Last rites for the fascist toadies.

GÖRING: The Third Reich is always first.

GERTRUDE: Last Reich of misery.

Samuel played the tender melodies of Erik Satie at the end of the marvelous hand puppet show, and minutes later Michel Laroux arrived on the cold quay to escort Angelika, Renata, and Samuel by car overnight to Marseille.

The street lamps were painted blue, and we named the occupation, dispossession, antisemitic exclusions, and booty culture, *les nuits bleus*, the blue nights, a double irony, and the sound of the violin was moody and blue, and wavered with the dark, cold, blue shimmer of the River Seine.

28

STAR OF DAVID

Sunday, 14 June 1942

Eugène Delacroix painted *La Liberté Guidant le Peuple*, Liberty Leading the People, more than a century ago, and last week By Now Beaulieu posed as Marianne for the hand puppet parley between Henri Bergson and Joseph Goebbels outside the Maison de Molière, or Comédie Française. Our cousin carried a small tattered French *Tricolore* in her right hand, and in the other hand a shield decorated with a blue Star of David.

The Jews of occupied Paris were ordered last Sunday to wear a yellow badge with the Star of David and the single word *Juif* printed as an emblem of racial separatism. Jews were shunned in public, shunted in queues for food, and many children were scorned for the first time at school.

The romantic portrayal of Marianne with bare breasts and the Phrygian bonnet of *liberté* became a spectacle of the heart, the passion of résistance, motion, color, and courage. By Now raised a shield of peace rather than a weapon of the revolution, and the dramatic irony was carried out in a contentious parley between two hand puppets on a humid afternoon at the Comédie Française near the Musée du Louvre. She was dressed for the revolution, but refused to pose with bare breasts for *liberté* or any reason. Naturally we teased her to bare at least one breast in solemn memory of Eugène Delacroix.

"By Now on the ramparts," shouted Heap of Words.

The woodland heirs of the fur trade celebrated the past with a sense of natural motion in art, dream songs, stories about creation, totemic relations with animals and birds, but not with ancient representations of manly gods, missionaries of salvation, holy victims, conversions of empires, or a bare breasted goddess treading over bodies.

The native abstract drawings of dream songs on birch bark scrolls were related to the totemic scenes of cultural memory. Some songs were about courage, love, visions, and coup counts, and in some native cultures great

giveaway ceremonies were carried out, but they were not about mere conquest and empires.

Natives were natural markers and painters on stone, birch bark, leather,
sand, pottery, and canvas, and fashioned figures, pouches, shirts, blankets,
and jewelry with stones from other cultures on the continental trade routes.
The portrayals were abstract scenes of natural motion, and with the outcome of discovery, colonial wars, racial separatism, treaty reservations,
and massacres of the cavalry, native artists created marvelous scenes of
ceremonies, horses, hunters, and dancers with beads, cloth, colored pencils, and paint.

The Cheyenne Howling Wolf created a blue horse in the *Sand Creek
Massacre*, and Zotom the Kiowa portrayed ceremonial warriors on horseback with bright colors about forty years after Delacroix painted *La Liberté
Guidant le Peuple*. Zotom, Howling Wolf, and many other native ledger
artists, were political prisoners at Fort Marion, Florida. Ledger art was
created with colored pencils and measured in inches, eight by eleven,
and the great canvas portrayal of Marianne was measured in feet, nine
by twelve. The artistic celebrations of motion, color, and the birthright of
liberty created by the three artists forty years apart were honored in the
same visionary dimensions of character, spirit, and résistance.

Delacroix painted the romantic *Les Natchez* five years after *La Liberté
Guidant le Peuple*. Nathan viewed the painting for the first time thirteen
years ago at the Galerie Paul Rosenberg in Paris, and the for second time
about two years later in the *Centenaire du Romantisme: Exposition Eugène Delacroix* at the Musée du Louvre. Nathan described the portrayal
of the native Natchez in French Louisiana, *La Louisiane*, as shallow
sentimentality and derived from the novel *Atala*, by François René de
Chateaubriand.

Pierre Chaisson was critical of the French colonial soldiers and Choc-
taws for the massacre of the Natchez after four wars of résistance, and for
the sale of the survivors as slaves. French authors and artists converted the
history of that gruesome colonial war into a mawkish romance. The Natchez became eternal victims, first by massacre, cultural dissolution, and
slavery, and then betrayed by sentimental portrayals in art and literature.

Nathan described the somber scene of a native woman and a man
holding a miniature infant in *Les Natchez* as strange and fantastic. Dela-

croix never visited *La Louisiane*, and probably never met natives. Nathan related that the cheeks of the two natives were tapered, the native man had nicely coiffed hair with feathers, and the artist created aquiline noses, more French than Natchez. The natives somehow survived the massacre with a perfect romantic poise. The Natchez portrayed by Delacroix would have marched barefoot with Marianne in *La Liberté Guidant le Peuple*.

Nathan was convinced that because we were so moved when we viewed the monumental *Guernica* by Pablo Picasso, exhibited at the pavilion of the Spanish Republic during the International Exposition of Art and Technology, we would also be inspired by *La Liberté Guidant le Peuple* at the Musée du Louvre. We were indeed moved by the great scene of motion, and the romance of Marianne.

Guernica is a cubist portrayal of horror and savagery, and *La Liberté Guidant le Peuple* is the romance of *liberté*, as the dauntless Marianne, the grand character of denouement, walks barefoot and invincible over the grotesque bodies of citizens in the nostalgia of the revolution.

Aloysius carved two new hand puppets from heavy river wood, and polished and painted the heads for the show at the Comédie Française. Henri Bergson was distinctive with a huge smooth head, bushy eyebrows, and a long, curved nose, and the puppet was dressed in a high white collar. The great philosopher wore a huge yellow badge with the blue Star of David. Joseph Goebbels, the Third Reich Minister of Public Enlightenment and Propaganda, was a gray and sinister hand puppet with dark eyes and thin lips.

Nika was the smooth voice of Henri Bergson, and my brother persuaded me once again to imitate an antisemitic puppet character, because no one else would agree to even mock the fierce and scary voice of Joseph Goebbels.

Heap of Words told the audience gathered outside the Comédie Française that Henri Bergson the hand puppet would carry out an eternal résistance with the great Star of David against the vengeance of the Nazi Swastika. By Now raised the French *Tricolore* in one hand and the great shield of the Star of David in the other, and the audience cheered, and there was no doubt which hand puppet was more popular that afternoon.

Prometheus wore loose white gloves, moved around the audience, spread his fingers, and teased the two hand puppets with the silent gestures of a mime. Goebbels was short, a twitchy creature, and when he spoke the raconteur crouched with mistrust, turned his head from side to side, raised one white finger, then two, then three, and waved the puppet away with the same pathetic gestures as the propaganda minister.

Nika, Pierre, and Nathan selected the actual quotation of the two hand puppets from books and newspaper stories, and arranged the pithy thoughts as if the two puppets were in a real conversation. By Now refused to only follow the concise comments of Bergson and Goebbels, and the show was much richer for her spontaneous mockery of the hand puppets. Sometimes, and with perfect timing, she chanted these phrases, "Watch the shadows, not the sun," and "The tease of a hand puppet is better than an empire promise," and "The Star of David is an everlasting vision of *liberté*," and "The new swastika is antinazi, nothing more," and "The swastika was plundered by a bad painter."

Prometheus cocked his white fingers in the sign of the antinazi swastika, and the audience applauded, shouted the word antinazi several times, and then waited to hear the parley of the two hand puppets.

BERGSON: Think like a man of action, act like a man of thought.

GOEBBELS: The best propaganda is that which works invisibly, penetrates the whole of life without the public having any knowledge of the propagandistic initiative.

BERGSON: To exist is to change, to change is to mature, to mature is to go on creating oneself endlessly.

GOEBBELS: To attract people, to win over people to that which I have realized as being true, that is called propaganda.

BERGSON: Whenever anything lives, there is, open somewhere, a register in which time is being inscribed.

GOEBBELS: I do not care if I give wonderful, aesthetically elegant speeches, or speak so that women cry. The point of a political speech is to persuade people of what we think right. I speak differently in the provinces than I do in Berlin.

BERGSON: Sex appeal is the keynote of our civilization.

GOEBBELS: We do not want to be a movement of a few straw brains, but rather a movement that can conquer the broad masses. Propaganda should be popular, not intellectually pleasing. It is not the task of propaganda to discover intellectual truths.

BERGSON: The major task of the twentieth century will be to explore the unconscious, to investigate the subsoil of the mind.

GOEBBELS: The political bourgeoisie is about to leave the stage of history.

BERGSON: Life does not proceed by the association and addition of elements, but by dissociation and division.

GOEBBELS: We are not a charitable institution, but a party of revolutionary socialists.

BERGSON: A situation is always comic if it participates simultaneously in two series of events which are absolutely independent of each other, and if it can be interpreted in two quite different meanings.

GOEBBELS: The worker in a capitalist state—and that is his deepest misfortune—is no longer a living human being, a creator, a maker. He has become a machine. He is alienated from what he produces.

BERGSON: There is no greater joy than that of feeling oneself a creator. The triumph of life is expressed by creation.

GOEBBELS: We are against the political bourgeoisie, and for genuine nationalism. We are against Marxism, but for the true socialism. We are for the first German national state of a socialist nature. We are for the National Socialist German Workers Party.

BERGSON: In laughter we always find an unavowed intention to humiliate and, consequently, to correct our neighbor.

GOEBBELS: We have modernized and ennobled the concept of democracy. With us it means definitely the rule of the people, in accordance with its origin.

BERGSON: The present contains nothing more than the past, and what is found in the effect was already in the cause.

GOEBBELS: Capitalism is the immoral distribution of capital. Germany will become free at that moment when the thirty million on the left and thirty million in the right make common cause. Only one movement is capable of doing this: National Socialism, embodied in one Führer, Adolf Hitler.

BERGSON: I cannot escape the objection that there is no state of mind, however simple, that does not change every moment.

GOEBBELS: One class has fulfilled its historical mission and is about to yield to another. The bourgeoisie has to yield to the working class.

BERGSON: To perceive means to immobilize, and we seize, in the act
of perception, something which outruns perception itself.

GOEBBELS: How deeply the perverse Jewish spirit has penetrated
German cultural life is shown in the frightening and horrifying
forms of the Exhibition of Degenerate Art in München. This has
nothing at all to do with the suppression of artistic freedom and
modern progress. On the contrary, the botched artworks which
were exhibited there and their creators are of yesterday and before
yesterday.

BERGSON: Spirit borrows from matter the perceptions on which it
feeds and restores them to matter in the form of movements which
it has stamped with its own freedom.

GOEBBELS: I ask you, Do you want total war? If necessary, do you
want a war more total and radical than anything that we can even
yet imagine?

BERGSON: It seems that laughter needs an echo.

GOEBBELS: If German stays united and marches to the rhythm of its
revolutionary socialist outlook, it will be unbeatable. Our inde-
structible will to life, and the driving force of the personality of the
Führer guarantees this.

BERGSON: The motive power of democracy is love.

GOEBBELS: We can see the commencement of our own national and
socialist survival in an alliance with a truly national and socialist
Russia.

BERGSON: There is nothing in philosophy which could not be said in
everyday language.

By Now touched every person in the audience with the shield of the
Star of David during the parley between Henri Bergson and Joseph Goebbels that afternoon at the Comédie Française. At the end of the puppet
show, she presented the French *Tricolore* to a child who had moved closer
and closer to the hand puppets with each gesture, truly enchanted with
the motion of the puppets, despite the fast counterchitchat of propaganda
and moral philosophy.

29

Spring Wind

Saturday, 18 July 1942

Ravens are the clever guardians of native liberty, and they mock the stern missionaries and reservation agents with raucous teases, feathery bounces, flight tumbles, and grumbles. The ravens carry out the steady cut and derision of enemy soldiers with strident taunts on the quayside, at gardens, bridges, and boulevard cafés, and never hesitate to relay our rant and curses of the Third Reich.

The French heirs of the fur trade are weary, downcast and hungry, they depend on ration tickets to survive, and scarcely care about the distant connections with the animals and birds of native totems. Some of the heirs are only spectators at the great chorus of migrations, the weekend sightseers at state menageries, yet they must cry out in the night for a tease of liberty and a sense of totemic relations with animals and birds, and the ethos of an honorable government. Nazis and fascist outliers deride and menace the heirs and political exiles as expendables in the war of vengeance.

The heirs of the crown, cross, and revolution once wore the heavy furs of an empire, but the courtiers and minions were never directly related to the ancient trade and ruins of totemic animals in New France. Natives were once slaves of continental fashion, and with provincial lords, missionaries, charlatans, blacksmiths, apothecaries, farmers, teachers, and voyageurs were engaged in a colonial economy of peltry and the deadly tanneries. The royalists lost favor, their poses and poise of opulence were overturned, and some nobles lost their heads. The beaver hats and weasel wraps were cast aside as a dead couture with the rush of silken fashions, and today animal furs are collectibles at crowded street markets.

The Book of Genesis enabled the wicked trade of furry creatures as men were given dominion over animals, birds, and many creepy things. The native stories of associations with animals and birds were based on totemic visions, but never the covenants of godly conquest or supremacy.

Even so the ancient relations with animals were corrupted in the course of missionaries, greedy dealers of totemic peltry, and the deadly diseases of civilization.

The abuse and execution of animals were forbidden in some religions, but that ethos of creature sanctuaries has rarely protected humans in the chase of empires, turns of sovereignty, or in the past two days as occupation fascists conspired to malign, menace, capture, and remove stateless Jews from Paris.

Adolf Hitler created perverse doctrines and cockeyed aversions based only on the hearsay conspiracies about Jews in his wordy prison primer *Mein Kampf*. The wicked despot was eager to declare his love of animals, provided tender treats, and proposed protection laws, but never advanced the same rights or provisions for humans. The Führer was way outside the pale of weird and creepy on his rounds of catch, conquest, and racial booty. He was devious, vicious and insecure, mutinous and envious by nature, and his favors with animals were only domestic, conditional, but never with an ethos of totemic justice.

"Führer of the slugs," shouted Heap of Words.

"Clammy mosquito bait," said Nika.

The exhibition, *Le Juif et la France*, a crude antisemitic display of sculpture, photographs, detrimental documents, and nasty quotations opened in September last year at Palais Berlitz near the Opera House. Nathan paid three francs each for ten tickets and insisted that we stand in line on the first day of the exhibition, as part of the crowd, to avoid scrutiny. Our real purpose was to observe the responses of the curious spectators.

Nathan was amused that we moved so easily as agents of the résistance in every corner of the crowded exhibition. Nika, Pierre Chaisson, Heap of Words, Olivier Black Elk, By Now, Coyote Standing Bear, Prometheus, and Aloysius pretended to ponder over the crude antisemitic propaganda. The German Embassy and the Gestapo sponsored the show of antisemitism, and the ridiculous intention was more than obvious, to weaken any potential backlash to the capture and removal of Jews.

"Fascist *rafle* politics," said Pierre Chaisson.

"The spectators were mostly Jews," said Nika.

"Yes, to assess the spectators," said Nathan.

"Eerie Aryans," said Olivier Black Elk.

"Fascist cartoons," shouted Heap of Words.

The Jew depicted on an exhibition poster with a big beard, bulging eyes, monster nose, and clutching the globe with finger claws could have been "a crude caricature in the satire of republican politics, but for the menace of the fascists and racial assassins," said Aloysius.

"Deadly slapstick," shouted Heap of Words.

"Nazi decadence," said Standing Bear.

"The exhibition was lamentable, much too crude, and there was nothing truly original about antisemitism," said Nathan. "Similar caricatures and political broadsides were once posted about Prime Minister Léon Blum."

Nathan translated a few sentences of "Notre Combat" from the résistance bulletin *Liberté*, 30 June 1941, published when we were in Marseille. "After our defeat a year ago, we believe to have reached a paroxysm of patriotic pain and misfortune," he related from the first column of the rather oratorical editorial. "The civilization of France and spiritual values that give direction to men is in danger of dying in the world." *Liberté*, the résistance bulletin, distributed only in the Vichy Free Zone, merged last year with *Combat* for a wider circulation in the Free Zone and in Nazi Occupied Paris.

Two weeks earlier *Le Pilori*, an antisemitic newspaper, declared in an article translated by Nathan, "As all public dangers are pointed out to people in the street, why had not the Jewry worn any sign up until now? The filthy Jewish beast must be felled, and this victory should be the first revolutionary act of the new France."

Lucian Rebatet, the fascist journalist and collaborator, published an antisemitic editorial in the combative weekly journal *Je Suis Partout*, I Am Everywhere. Nathan translated a short selection from the 16 July 1942 edition, "I stated last winter in this paper my joy at having seen Jews in Germany marked with their yellow seal for the first time. It will be a much greater joy to see this star in our streets here in Paris, where not even three years ago this execrable race was walking all over us. Still, we have one deep regret: we regret that the yellow star has not been imposed by a French law."

Nathan learned from friends in the Le Comité Amelot, the underground committee that rescues stateless Jews in Paris, that the police had planned mass arrests of the exiles and removal to concentration camps in the next few weeks, and recently the clandestine newspaper *L'Université Libre* reported that Jews were no longer secure in Paris. The cagey Préfecture de Police had turned over resident address records of more than thirty thousand Jews to the Nazis.

"Last year synagogues were defiled and burned in Paris, an atrocious reminder of Kristallnacht, the Night of Broken Glass, four years ago in Germany, and a wicked notice of the future," said Pierre Chaisson.

"Paris is no longer celebrated as the city of the literary doyens Honoré Balzac, Molière, Marcel Proust," declared Nathan. "No, not even the journalists and literary masters interred at the Panthéon, Voltaire, Victor Hugo, Jean-Jacques Rousseau, Émile Zola, Jean-Paul Marat, and Jean Jaurés."

Michel Laroux, who was privy to confidential police plans and actions, arrived at *Le Corbeau Bleu* and revealed that the actual day of the arrests was scheduled early in the morning of 16 July 1942, two days after Bastille Day. Nathan rushed to inform his many friends about the fascist menace that would endanger the stateless Jews of Paris.

Michel continued with more details and the actual names of the four fascist antisemites who had organized the Opération Vent Printanier, Operation Spring Wind at the public bicycle stadium Vélodrome d'Hiver. He insisted that we never forget the names of the war criminals who devised the persecution of Jews, René Bousquet, secretary general of the Police Nationale; Louis Darquier de Pellepoix, Vichy general for Jewish Affairs in France; Nazi captain Theodor Dannecker, head of the *Judenreferat*, the Jewish Section in France; and Helmut Knochen, the Nazi senior commander of Security Police in Paris.

"Darquier de Pellepoix replaced the rabid fascist and antisemite Xavier Vallat as the Commissarait Général aux Questions Juives," said Nathan. "The Gestapo apparently thought Vallat was not vicious enough to persecute the Jews."

Hitler and his fascist cavalcade of greedy henchmen roused the hatred and deadly abuse of stateless Jews, and easily convinced the Préfecture de Police and René Bousquet to capture and remove thousands of Jews in *La Grand Rafle*, the great raid, two days ago in the early morning, and the police were unaided by enemy soldiers. More than four thousand police officers were mobilized before daybreak to apprehend and imprison more women and children than men, we were told, because many men had been warned about the raid a few days earlier and escaped with the false notion that the occupation soldiers and police would never arrest women and children.

"Unpardonable cruelty," said Pierre Chaisson.

The Jews were herded onto green and yellow buses with only small precious bundles of personal property, and detained on that hot and humid day with no food, water, or toilet facilities at the huge oval Vélodrome d'Hiver near the Eiffel Tower. More than thirteen thousand stateless men, women, and children were confined as prisoners with the free rein of the fascist Préfecture de Police, and in the name of the Third Reich. That hateful day was the absolute end of any pretense of justice or trace of *liberté* in Paris.

"Paris has been swamped with fascists and royalist traitors," shouted Heap of Words. "Nazis are the wicked cavalry, and the captives at the Vélodrome d'Hiver endured the same scares as Lakota women and children who were chased to death by the cavalry at Wounded Knee Creek in South Dakota."

"Cavalry war crimes," shouted Pierre Chaisson.

"Cavalry of fascists everywhere," said Nika.

"French police were the perpetrators, as you know," said Nathan. "The Wehrmacht prepared the details of persecution, and with no sense of justice or moral duty the Préfecture de Police obediently carried out the pitiful early morning purge as the merciless cavalry."

"Eternal shame," shouted Heap of Words.

Michel Laroux told me that last year more than three thousand stateless Jews had been arrested and imprisoned at Drancy. The fascist police carried out an early morning criminal scheme of vengeance to destroy families before breakfast, and then before dinner to debase the trust and tradition of justice and *liberté* in France.

"Drancy was once a prison camp for British soldiers," said Nathan, "but now the prisoners are related as Jews, nothing more, nothing criminal, nothing as serious as the fascist police, or the savagery of enemy soldiers."

The Drancy prison was located just northeast of Paris, and was managed by the Préfecture de Police, the very same police agency that dutifully carried out *La Grand Rafle*, the capture and removal of Jews to the Vélodrome d'Hiver. The Drancy windows were sealed and painted blue to block natural light and to deny the slightest glance of wives and relatives outside the prison. The police were cruel, methodical, and enforced the constant humiliation of public exposure, straw patches on the cold concrete overnight, extreme hunger, untreated diseases, overcrowded spaces, and there were no facilities for prisoners to bathe or stay clean.

Prometheus was devastated with the reports of so many purges and turned away in sorrow, and at that very moment a heavy military barge churned down the River Seine, and *Le Corbeau Bleu* leaned with the waves, unsteady on the quay. Pig Ears guarded the tiller, and with the other loyal mongrels always barked at the soldiers on the enemy barges, but not today. The Vicar responded to our moods, silent and despondent, and the other mongrels watched our moves. Black Jack was close to By Now, and Panzéra leaned closer to me, a familiar gesture, and with just the right touch of consolation.

Le Comité Amelot rescued children, provided daily meals, and at great risk forged necessary documents for stateless Jews to escape to Spain. The Amelot Committee was associated with La Colonie Scolaire, an agency dedicated to child welfare, and the Fédération des Sociétés Juives de France located at the same address, 36 Rue Amelot, a few blocks north of the Place de la Bastille.

Nathan has a good memory for names and events, and has actually teased me at times about my letters to the heirs of the fur trade, but in the past year he has insisted that the references to names, agencies, dates, and other information about antisemitism and the Nazi Occupation were specific and correct. He wanted my letters to become a personal history of our dangerous time together in Paris.

30

OPERATIC BAY

Thursday, 13 August 1942

Nathan Crémieux convinced me that the meaning of the word *liberté* was more poetic and resolute than freedom or liberty in English. "The word cannot be separated from *liberté, égalité, fraternité*, the grand promise of the revolution, and with great care *liberté* has been used in literature, music, names of ships at sea," he said, and then teased the analogies of the word in English. Freedom of religion, free speech, free will, free rein, free spirit, free votes, sovereignty, and the word liberty is associated with commercial products, soap, cars, cigarettes, and political slogans, but mercenaries have never "disgraced the Statue of Liberty, or *La Liberté Éclairant le Monde*, Liberty Enlightening the World, as a grand gift from the people of France in memory of the Declaration of Independence."

"Long live *liberté*," shouted Heap of Words.

"Long live the résistance," shouted Aloysius.

"Give me liberty, or give me death," said Nika.

Patrick Henry was a courageous orator, but he was "more secure than we are at the moment, and no doubt his words about liberty or death were more political, timely, and dramatic in stories," said Aloysius. Charles de Gaulle proclaimed *liberté*, but never death, and only a person with a death wish would dare to shout out *liberté ou mort* near the Hôtel Lutetia where the *Abwehr*, the enemy espionage service, is located, or brave the same stagy notion of liberty or death in cafés, or in the presence of fascist newspaper editors.

"Nazi expectations," shouted Heap of Words.

Jacques Bonsergent, Boris Vildé, and thousands of other citizens of résistance movements were executed as traitors, and the courageous display of *liberté ou mort* would not have mattered to the fascists and collaborators, or to the Gestapo.

Nathan turned away in silence, hesitated twice, and then calmly announced that the oath of the Armée Juive is *liberté* or death. Naturally we waited for an explanation, convinced that he was active in résistance movements, but he only repeated the complete oath in translation. "I swear allegiance to the Jewish Army and obedience to its leaders. Let my people live again. Let Eretz Israel, the land of Israel, be born again, *liberté* or death."

Michel told us later that the Armée Juive was a secret armed résistance movement that was organized in Toulouse earlier this year, and he said nothing more. Obviously, the active duties of the soldiery were secret. Nathan had been more hesitant and evasive since we returned from Sanary and Marseille, and that convinced us that the once generous owner the Galerie Crémieux was rightly involved in armed résistance.

"By Now is not Old Stand By Now," shouted By Now. She demanded some involvement in the résistance, "But not as some cozy matron of soup bowls, and teased for wearing heavy boots." A few days later she was in high spirits as a volunteer nurse at the American Hospital in Paris. Nathan had arranged the position at the hospital with Doctor Sumner Jackson, and that convinced us there were direct connections to résistance networks at the hospital.

Pierre Dumont gave By Now a rickety farm bicycle as transportation to the hospital, and for other reasons that became obvious at the end of the first week. The bicycle had a huge box on the front, and twice a week she was entrusted to meet the vegetable trains at various stations and discreetly deliver the produce to the hospital. The American volunteer ambulance drivers once met the growers and the trains, but that was before gasoline was rationed and commandeered by the Wehrmacht.

By Now stayed most nights at the hospital, and only once or twice a week at *Le Corbeau Bleu*. Pig Ears waited every day at the tiller and could sense when her favorite nurse was nearby. The other mongrels rushed to the quay, moaned and barked with anticipation, and then Panzéra the Basset Hound delivered a magnificent operatic bay. By Now carried the heavy bicycle on deck to avoid any chance of theft, and then declared, as she handed out a special treat of bones to the mongrels, that she would rather ride a horse than a bicycle.

"Black Jack bicycle," shouted Heap of Words.

By Now was surprised to learn that many patients in the hospital were

not soldiers, but workers from the state railroad company, Société Nationale des Chemins de Fer, who had been injured in accidents. The clever
strategy was to fully occupy at least fifty beds with *cheminots*, the railroad
workers, to avoid the admission of wounded enemy soldiers to the hospital.
Doctor Jackson treated the *cheminots*, and then revealed that they were
members of the first labor union to carry out résistance movements against
the Nazi Occupation.

"Maybe, but prisoners never walked to the prison camps," shouted
Heap of Words. "Jews and prisoners of war were crowded into cattle cars,
and the trains were no doubt run on union time to concentration camps."

"The *cheminots* delivered résistance newspapers across the country by
train, otherwise it would have been risky for anyone, even with a precious
permit to travel between the zones, to carry bundles of newspapers in a
suitcase," said Nathan.

Some Jews with money and those with personal and political connections have already moved away from the *Zone Occupée* and Paris, south
to the *Zone Libre*, a fantasy of the Vichy Free Zone. The stateless and
starving exiles were caught in empty moments of dread with no contacts,
no kith and kin nearby, and with no chance of *colis familiaux*, family food
packages from country relatives.

Jews were required to formally register names and addresses with the
Préfecture de Police, and to wear the yellow badge of the Star of David on
7 June 1942. The yellow badge of misery and degradation was proclaimed
only a month before *La Grand Rafle*.

Jew and exiles live with scarcely a trace of trust or security, and stateless
families had no chance of an escape, favors, or any choice of outside survival. The *Israélites*, or assimilated citizens, were favored more than the
Juifs, a derogatory name as in the Vichy *Statut des Juifs* of 3 October 1940.
The borders were closed, and the stateless *Juifs* could only pretend that
the police, fascists, and enemy soldiers of the occupation might shun their
mere presence and only spurn their poverty, but the rage of antisemitism
denies any sense of conscience, reason, mercy, or justice.

Paris has been rightly denounced for *La Grand Rafle*, shamed forever
in history. The Préfecture de Police brushed aside any sense of ethos,
justice, or democratic duty related to the French Third Republic. The

liberal promise of *liberté, égalité, fraternité* was deferred to the politics of nostalgia and the romantic culture deposed by the Third Reich.

"Paris is a deadly destination," said Aloysius.

"Shame of Sand Creek," shouted Heap of Words.

"Fascist masters of nostalgia," said Pierre.

Jews were blamed for the ruin of the economy, miseries of war and the occupation, the cause of lost children, and sometimes a sudden turn of the weather. Natives were abused in similar ways, wrongly cursed as savages with no husbandry, hunted down by state militias, denied the liberty of birthright citizens, and then drafted to serve in the First World War.

France was a promise of *liberté, égalité, fraternité*, and the heirs of the fur trade once shared that promise, covenant, and ethos with Jews. The stateless exiles waited for a chance, a steady pace to endure with their children, but the police and fascist collaborators provoked their misery. Jews were limited to late afternoon rations when the shelves were empty. Jews were denied the use of telephones and radios. Jews were confined to the back of trains, and only three Jews were allowed on a public bus at the same time. Jews were constrained to wear the yellow Star of David. No one can stand aside or turn away in the face of such fascist depravity, not natives, not nationalists. The Préfecture de Police and enemy soldiers have cursed everyone when they abuse the ethos of ancient cultures.

Nathan and Michel arrived last week with an urgent proposal to immediately change the name of *Le Corbeau Bleu* to avoid the suspicion of collaborators and the dreaded scrutiny of the police and Gestapo. Nathan had obviously rehearsed the reasons for the change of names, and mentioned the fear that some people have of ravens because they eat carrion, carry on with lost souls, the spirits of the dead, and were considered all the more fearsome since the occupation because the enemy stimulated suspicions, and surely someone would envy the natives living on a barge on the River Seine.

"Ravens of *liberté*," shouted Heap of Words.

"Escape with the blue ravens," said Aloysius.

Michel continued with stories about the thousands of secret *corbeaux* letters mailed to the Gestapo located on Avenue Foch. These were letters of betrayal, *la délation*, or denouncement letters, cruel, wicked letters about friends, relatives, and suspicious outsiders. "The hatred of those in the résistance was the subject of many letters written by informers and collaborators who would betray their own family, and for the paltry favors of the enemy," said Michel. Surprisingly more relatives, neighbors, and friends were betrayed in *la délation* letters than Jews, and women wrote most of the *corbeaux*, or poison pen letters, probably because there were fewer men around.

"Cockroach traitors," shouted Heap of Words.

"Jews betrayed by a concierge," said Aloysius.

Nathan persisted that natives could count on romantic favors before the occupation, and the enemy soldiers carried out a similar outlook, "But the suspicions, jealousy, and envy of any outsiders puts natives with their loyal mongrels on a barge named for a raven in the crosshairs of betrayal by insecure and hateful informers and collaborators."

Michel was convinced that we were probably already the subject of *la délation* letters, or even *la denunciation*, the denunciation missives of envious citizens who look down at the barge of natives and loyal mongrels from the parapets of the Pont de la Concorde.

The color blue had become the oppressive signature of the enemy and the occupation, the color of camouflage and military defense. The street lamps were painted blue, and the windows of the hospital were painted blue, unseen as bomber targets. The high ceiling windows of the ominous Vélodrome d'Hiver were painted blue, and the windows were blue at Drancy.

"Gestapo blue," shouted Heap of Words.

Nathan and Michel surely expected us to strongly resist any name change, but when the reasons were explained so dramatically, especially the blue windows and *corbeaux* hate letters we changed the name of the barge to *Liberté Indienne*, American Indian Liberty. We were aware that the accurate translation should have been *Liberté des Indiens d'Amérique*, but decided on the shorter ironic version derived from the mistake in navigation by Christopher Columbus. Nika the next day painted a necessary second name in much smaller letters, *Indianische Freiheit*, the translation in German.

Nathan praised the new name, and especially the use of the word *liberté*, and related a myth about the ravens that nested in the Tower of London. The Kingdom of England worried about the legend that ravens had lived in the tower for centuries, and if the ravens were removed to satisfy the singular demands of the Royal Astronomer it would be the death of the empire. The ravens stayed, and the Royal Observatory was moved to Greenwich Park near the River Thames. Today the government is worried because several families of ravens have moved away to avoid the Luftwaffe bombing raids near the Tower of London.

31

GESTAPO CAVALRY

Thursday, 8 October 1942

Prometheus scorned the conspiracies of the royalists and fascists in his résistance broadside posted two weeks ago when Gestapo agents and enemy
soldiers captured the entire crew of the *Liberté Indienne*. On that very
same day more than a thousand American men and hundreds of women
were rounded up and imprisoned as the enemy, including Sumner Jackson,
the surgeon, and many others at the American Hospital in Paris.

Gestapo agents were trained to observe manners, read gestures, hesitations, evasions, and treasons, the shame of rumors, and to carry out
brutal tortures. The hospital volunteers were separated for extensive interrogation, we learned later, including By Now Beaulieu and several
other women who were volunteer ambulance drivers. The agents wanted
information about résistance movements in the hospital, and they were
"focused directly on Doctor Jackson and Nathan Crémieux," said By Now.
Gestapo strategies were severe but easily sidetracked with details about
native history. By Now told the agents stories about the Truckers Strike in
Minneapolis, and her journey from the White Earth Reservation to Washington on a horse named Treaty to join the American Expeditionary Force.
She told the agents about dinner talks with farm families, the hard work
and poverty, and weather on every dusty rural road from the White Earth
Reservation to the National Mall.

"Natural motion," shouted Pierre.

"The agents seemed rather eager to hear more about the fear of communist agents in the Bonus Army," said By Now. "Naturally, they were not
disappointed with my stories, especially about John Pace, the communist
leader who tried to recruit veterans to serve Joseph Stalin."

"Soviet Alliance ended last year," said Pierre.

The Gestapo agents no doubt assumed that natives were born intuitive
and heroic, loyal but rather naïve, a common view of most Germans who

attended Wild West Shows and read the romance novels of Karl May. Natives fancy danced with horses for liberty and the money, and never strayed
far from that sovereign sense of guile and irony. By Now knew exactly how
to harness that notion of naiveté with totemic stories and dream songs
about the dance of sandhill cranes, the courage of bears, the deceptive
maneuvers of wolves, the pitch and cut of bald eagles.

"Stories about warrior coup counts were at hand, but not necessary,"
said By Now. "The agents were convinced that counter espionage and
résistance movements were way beyond my native reach of experience."

Sylvia Beach was captured on Rue de l'Odéon, and along with other
women interned at the Jardin d'Acclimatation, a menagerie in Bois de
Boulogne, a public park and garden near Neuilly-sur-Seine. Sylvia and
the other women were actually interned in monkey cages.

Aloysius heard about this much later, of course, and could not resist
teasing Heap of Words about his strange *zoologique* romance with a pale
and wirehaired bookseller interned as a small animal from New England,
and the entire crew turned to teases when he hired a bicycle taxi to the
menagerie in Bois de Boulogne.

"Monkey house duty," said Pierre.

"Monkey house love story," shouted Aloysius. One by one we delivered
steady teases as he packed a small bundle of food for Sylvia. Heap of Words
had bartered with friends at the hospital to obtain a small jar of honey. He
had never forgotten the story that Sylvia told about waiting in line for several hours for a ration of honey, but the rare honey ration was only a rumor.

Heap of Words arrived at the garden in the morning and paid the regular entrance fee, but he was not allowed to visit the monkey house, and
could only catch a glimpse of two or three older women in the distance.
Sylvia never knew that he tried to visit her with a precious jar of honey.
Sadly a few weeks later she and the other women were moved out of the
monkey house to the internment camp near the source of mineral waters
at Vittel.

"Nazis stole the honey," shouted Heap of Words.

Michel Laroux was privy to some police strategies, but not the secret
moves of the Gestapo, so we were not warned that Americans would be
captured on that balmy Thursday 24 September 1942. Admiral William
Leahy, the American ambassador, carried out diplomatic relations with

the Vichy Regime, the strange and virtual statecraft, until last month, for almost a year after the declaration of war with Japan and German.

The Gestapo Cavalry arrived in a glossy black Citroën Traction Avant, and two agents searched the seams of the cushions, and every corner and crevice of the ancient barge. They seized the ordinary maps and charts of the River Seine, and then ordered the nervous soldiers to march our crew to the military trucks parked nearby on the quay. Captain Pig Ears never moved from her secure position at the blue tiller, but when the other mongrels heard the trucks on the quay, they escaped to the Jardin des Tuileries.

Naturally we worried that the agents would discover my notebooks with comments and revisions of more than thirty letters. Ten notebooks were stowed in a secret panel below the tiller. Pig Ears always leaned on the tiller, and on that day the loyal mongrel guarded the handwritten notes and copies of the letters to the heirs of the fur trade.

The letters might have been confiscated, and if that had happened we would have been exposed as saboteurs and sponsors of résistance movements. Most of the letters were copied and then mailed to my mother for publication and distribution on the White Earth Reservation. The last few letters were never sent because the secure mail service had ended with the Nazi Occupation.

The Gestapo agents inquired about the second name printed on the barge, *Indianische Freiheit*. One agent inquired if the barge was actually for sale. The tone of his query was an enticement, and he could easily perceive the slightest evasiveness. Not for sale, "nicht für verkauf," shouted Nika. "*Indianische Freiheit*," she responded boldly and with no hesitation, "The barge is our native liberty in the language of the French and Germans."

"Captain Pig Ears," shouted Heap of Words as a rough soldier pointed his rifle at the cocked head and butterfly ears of the mongrel Papillon. The soldiers laughed, and that was the last of any ironic shouts for several days, or until we were released after the many examinations of our various documents that proved we were the actual owners of the *Liberté Indienne* and a native company of puppeteers with double passports of the United States of America and the White Earth Nation.

Aloysius raised several hand puppets to the agents and soldiers as evidence of our enterprise, but not with any play of voices. Herr Hitler was concealed in a water resistant pouch used as a barge bumper on the quay.

The agents were either not interested or did not recognize the distinct hand puppet Léon Blum.

The Galerie Liberté Indienne was created in the face of the enemy as a way to simulate our business activities in Paris. Pierre pretended to be at ease as he slowly explained that the traditional materials purchased for the gallery were detained on a cargo ship in the New York City Harbor, only because German submarines were attacking and sinking ships in the Atlantic.

"The *Indianische* objects of art come from great cultural traditions, and could never be replaced, so we must wait for the submarines to change course, and then we can open our gallery," said Pierre. The delay of the new gallery because of enemy submarines was a clever satire, and an easy one to remember. By Now was not aware of the new gallery, but she was perceptive and could easily carry on the tease and drift of any story.

The Gestapo agents were more interested in Nathan Crémieux than the delayed gallery story. The agents were casual at first, but then more direct and urgent about the whereabouts of Nathan. Again, we created similar stories, and without strategic rehearsals, that we had not seen him at any recent gallery events, but heard through rumors that he and his wife had moved to London.

The enemy soldiers revealed that our first destination was Gare du Nord. The truck was crowded after several stops on the cavalry roundup of Americans. Pierre was angry when he learned that some of the captives were the children of soldiers who had returned to America and England after the First World War. "Brutish," he said, "to hold a native born son accountable for the sex and liberty of an obscure soldier from America."

"Love, war, and prison," said Aloysius.

Doctor Jackson was the only person we recognized at Gare du Nord, and naturally he worried about his patients and others who had been arrested at the hospital. He had treated so many *cheminots*, railroad workers, that no one was surprised when he was saluted at the station.

The Gestapo interrogators were casual, deceptive, and scrupulous, starting at first with easy comments about our friends and acquaintances, Crémieux, Kahnweiler, Stein, Faÿ, Feuchtwanger, and Violette Morris. Some of the names were direct, familiar, but the names of Morris and Faÿ were presented as entrapments. We each revealed only the easy descriptive observations at barge parties and gallery events, nothing more. The agents continued to use two names as conversation bait, Violette Morris and Bernard Faÿ. Nathan had warned us to be cautious about Morris, she was likely a collaborator, and the agents were no doubt trying to assess her reputation as an informer and traitor.

Later the queries were tricky, more than entrapment, actual conversations about the great tradition of puppets in native cultures and in Austria and Germany. Obviously we were each prepared, but no native in our crew would ever declare that Germans borrowed the tradition of puppetry from the *Italian commedia dell'arte*, and with name changes of Kasperle and Grete.

Coyote Standing Bear and Olivier Black Elk were taken aside, and we naturally worried why they were singled out for intense interrogation, and likely persecution, but the reasons for the selection were only to ask them more personal questions about the warrior traditions of the great Oglala Lakota. Coyote and Olivier paid tribute to native relations, and then told several heroic stories about Sitting Bull and Crazy Horse.

American captives were moved to the Saint-Denis Internment Camp north of Paris. There we met prisoners from several countries, Canada, England, Australia, South Africa, Senegal, and other places. We had only minimal contact with other prisoners at the camp because we were interrogated for three days and then released at the same time.

We walked on the back streets for several hours to the *Liberté Indienne*, and saluted Coyote and Olivier for their cut and mastery of exotic warrior stories that must have inspired the interrogators. Aloysius was praised for his casual sense of memory and conversations about marionette puppetry in Germany. The agents were impressed when my brother described the distinctions and gestures of hand and string puppets, and then he celebrated Count Franz Pocci as the founder of the Munich Marionette Theatre.

"The Gestapo Cavalry never said a word about the book collection on the barge, and some of the books were listed as decadent," said Nika. "The agents were obviously looking for collaborators and wicked informers who might reveal the whereabouts of Nathan Crémieux."

"Long live the mystery of Nathan Crémieux," shouted Heap of Words.

We shouted long live the résistance, and the mongrels bayed that balmy afternoon on the deck of the *Liberté Indienne*.

"Long live our shouts," shouted Pierre.

The Gestapo Cavalry searched the barge a second time and said nothing about our collection of books, mostly by acceptable authors, *Moby-Dick*, by Hermann Melville, and the recent translation into French by Jean Giono; *Finnegans Wake*, by James Joyce; *Jean-Christophe*, by Romain Rolland; *L'Étranger*, by Albert Camus; *The Moon Is Down*, by John Steinbeck, and the speedy translation and publication of *Nuits Noires* by Les Éditions de Minuit; the novel *Le Ventre de Paris*, by Émile Zola; *Alcools*, by Guillaume Apollinaire; and Shakespeare plays, *Hamlet*, *King Lear*, *King John*, *The Merchant of Venice*, *Coriolanus*, and *The Tragedy of Macbeth*.

Ezra Pound and James Joyce were on various lists of decadent books, Marcel Proust was a Jew, Les Éditions de Miniut was a midnight résistance publishing house, but the agents seized nothing and discovered no evidence of critical notes or information about Nathan Crémieux.

32

EXISTENTIAL CUES

Sunday, 18 October 1942

The Frisian raconteur wrote his satirical broadsides at the Café Flore, or Les Deux Magots, aware that at least one collaborator was pretending to read newspapers at a nearby table. Prometheus destroyed the original notes and never returned with a single written word that might expose or incriminate the crew of *Liberté Indienne*.

The first broadside about the fascists was printed by hand on ordinary lined paper, and seven copies were posted near the Pont Neuf and Pont des Arts. Prometheus waited at a distance and observed the people who gathered to read his résistance diatribe. He was once a prominent raconteur, and now he must remain silent and anonymous with the ironic signature of Sigmund Freud.

Pierre Chaisson removed a copy of the first satirical broadside from a metal gate near the Pont Neuf, and read out loud the treatise about the royalists and fascists as we walked along the River Seine.

Prometheus wrote, "The royalists are at the end of reigns and reveries, court favors, banquet costumes, tedious cues, the romance of manners, and cannot last more than one or two generations, but the fascists are forever spawned in the muck of vengeance and depravity, and slowly evolve in every miserable slough, barn, town, and city in the world and carry out the wicked censure of distinction, gainsay the outsiders, envy the talents of exiles, and cut down the rights of others who fought to secure the liberty of a democracy. Nazi fascists forever lurked around the great circles of modern art, literature, and music, and waited for a cue to provoke the informers and depraved enemies of a liberal culture." The broadside was signed by Sigmund Freud.

Pierre was moved with the words and became rather oratorical as we walked back to the *Liberté Indienne*, but he decided not to read out loud the concise and lurid conditions at the end of the broadside for fear someone nearby on the quay would hear the curses of the Préfecture de Police and the bare descriptions of the severe venereal diseases transmitted by the Wehrmacht.

High Road, Black Jack, The Vicar, and Panzéra sensed that we were nearby and galloped out of the flower gardens, bounded, bounced, and bump each one of us on the quay. Captain Pig Ears had guarded the tiller the entire time we were in captivity, and she almost leaped in the river with excitement when we saluted and boarded our marvelous native sanctuary moored on the River Seine.

Nathan could not have forewarned or prevented our internment, but no doubt he would have contacted his close friends to intervene, and at great risk. He always thought about us, and a few months ago contributed three novels to the barge library. The books had been published this year, *L'Étranger* in French, *The Moon Is Down*, or *Nuits Noires*, and the first translation of *Moby-Dick* in French. No doubt the novels were related in some way, natural motion, *l'absurde*, surreal occupation, or the likeness of the Führer and Ahab, but no particular theme was obvious. That was the last time we saw Nathan, and since then we were told that he had secretly moved to serve with the Armée Juive near Limoges, but then we heard that he had returned to Marseille.

Michel warned him last summer that the Nazis were about to extend the occupation to the south, or the Vichy Free Zone, and the entire country would be under the same extreme fascist rules of the Third Reich.

Jews were put to death every day at concentration camps, and at the same time thousands more were cast out of the great culture of revolution and *liberté*, unwanted laborers, artists, poets, musicians, and philosophers, at the gruesome close of democratic ethos, and their stories were in the clouds with the last gasps of the enlightenment.

Jews were envied, cursed, and murdered for centuries, and millions of natives were put to shame as savages and massacred in the course of discovery and democracy. Was that yesterday, or was that dread in the distant past? No, the pretense of that question does not deserve a position or reference to the horrors perpetrated today and yesterday by the Third Reich.

Albert Camus, the novelist, created existential cues of the absurd in literary motion and a wanton first person storier in *L'Étranger* who has no natural connections with natives or the depravity of the occupation. Meursault was convicted of murder, but not of stateless children. The absence of ethos, the senseless moods of an outlier, free rein of existential experience, and the tenor of atheism cannot be compared to the sentiments of chance in native stories or dream songs, because totemic unions were never chased to the existential extremes of mere existence in trickster stories or in the tease of creation.

The mercenary entitlements of the fur trade and the deadly diseases of discovery were only two of the many serious plights of natives, and even then the totemic stories hardly strayed from a sense of chance, natural motion, and lively mockery of the cavalry, treaty reservations, federal agents, and the ancient traces of continental liberty.

L'Étranger, the stranger, or outsider, a novel by Albert Camus, was published last June, only a few weeks before the deadly crusade of the Préfecture de Police and internment of the *Juifs* or stateless Jews in the Vélodrome d'Hiver. The novel was one of three delivered to the barge with the favor and praise of Nathan Crémieux. Serious readers would never consider the menace of the occupation as a shroud revealed on the pages of a novel, the moods of a stranger, or the absence of mode and custom in the course of a vacuous culture. *L'Étranger* was probably close to completion two years ago at the start of the Nazi Occupation in Paris.

The French Algerian narrator named Meursault, the outsider, presents an absurd unease about the actual day that his mother died, today, or "perhaps it was yesterday."

L'Étranger starts with a moment of personal doubt and cultural uncertainty. *Aujourd'hui, maman est morte. Ou peut-être hier, je ne sais pas. J'ai reçu un télégramme de l'asile: "Mère décédée. Enterrement demain. Sentiments distingués." Cela ne veut rien dire. C'était peut-être hier.*

Today, mother died, perhaps it was yesterday. I do not know. I received a telegram from the asylum, "Mother deceased, burial service tomorrow. Sentiments of respect." There is nothing more to say. Perhaps, it was yesterday.

The pose and pretense of an isolated and dispassionate character, the stranger, and the casual doubt about the death of his mother was never an escape story, and must be read today, or yesterday, with the consciousness of the capture and abuse of thousands of Jews packed in railroad cars and slowly moving east to concentration camps and death. The existential literary style of doubt and aesthetic estrangement, or the slights of nihilism, were favored over creative turns of ethos and the rush of *liberté*, and with that in mind we were cut and run readers with the absolute awareness of the savage strategies that interned and murder stateless Jews in the Nazi Occupation of France.

"*L'auteur étrange*," shouted Heap of Words.

Nathan delivered *Nuits Noires, The Moon Is Down*, by John Steinbeck, but with no explanation. The novel was published earlier this year in New York, and then translated straightaway by Les Éditions de Minuit, or Midnight Press, the courageous literary résistance publisher founded last year. Steinbeck was aware of the Nazi Occupation of Paris, and yet he created wintery scenes of the enemy occupation of a coastal town, and for some obscure reason, the story is staged in an unnamed country. That Sunday morning in the fanciful novel of an enemy occupation the postman and policeman had gone to fish in the sea, and the old doctor was named Winter.

"Piece of cake fiction," shouted Heap of Words.

"Fake occupation is a daft idea," said Aloysius.

Camus created hot and humid scenes of a stranger in Algeria, and the fierce glance of sunlight becomes a silent character on the stony beach of the Mediterranean Sea, but *The Moon Is Down* slowly crawls through the cold winter of war and a feigned occupation with crisscross conversations that creates only a bare sense of an enemy conquest by an omniscient author.

The characters in *L'Étranger* were concise and evasive, and the absurdities of cultural covenants were more emotive than the pathetic metaphors of the ridiculous occupation of a fictitious coastal town that never comes close to the absolute miseries of the Nazi Occupation of Paris.

"Occupation apology," shouted Heap of Words.

Pierre Chaisson stood near the tiller that night and read out loud the first three short sentence of *The Moon Is Down*, "By ten forty-five it was all over. The town was occupied, the defenders defeated, and the war finished. The invader had prepared for this campaign as carefully as he had for larger ones." Pierre closed the novel, looked around the barge in silence, and declared, "Steinbeck has presented a suitable closure of the novel in the first three concise sentences, and he revealed that the occu-

pation was outright, the war was over, citizens were worried, but clearly
with unintended irony the actual start of the story was the conclusion of
the novel and the war."

Nathan has initiated discussions about *Moby-Dick* by Herman Melville
many times in the past few years, and with the other two novels, *L'Étranger*
and *The Moon Is Down*; he also delivered the first reliable translation of
Moby-Dick in French, *Je m'appelle Ishmael*, by Jean Giono, Joan Smith,
and Lucien Jacques. "Call me Ishmael," those first three words were the
start of a marvelous adventure of natural motion and whalers in "the watery parts of the world." Ishmael created incredible scenes of motion, the
character of waves and whales, and readily goes to sea when he begins to
"grow hazy about the eyes."

Pierre Chaisson speculated that Nathan was drawing the native barge
crew into that elusive literary corner of reality and fiction with the presen-
tation of three new novels, existential sway, a farcical occupation, and the
visionary adventures of whales and the mighty Moby Dick.

Nathan might have intended to tease our romance of the résistance and
direct our rage about enemy soldiers and the occupation with the literary
analogy of the moody Captain Ahab of the *Pequod*, and, of course, the
demon of war, the Führer Adolf Hitler.

"Ahab the fascist," shouted Heap of Words.

"Whalers of the résistance," said Aloysius.

Pierre opened *Moby-Dick* and read out loud a short description of Captain Ahab, "He looked like a man cut away from the stake, when the fire
has overrunningly wasted all the limbs without consuming them, or taking
away one particle from their compacted aged robustness. His whole high,
broad form, seemed made of solid bronze, and shaped in an unalterable
mould."

"Nazi throwback," shouted Heap of Words.

"Adolf Hitler was never solid anything, and certainly not bronze," said
Nika. "Maybe fool's gold, aluminum, or tin hammered into the caricature
of a diseased weasel with dead blue eyes, and in uniform."

Today, or was it yesterday, the stateless Jews in the Vichy Zone were
ordered to show their personal documents, identity cards, and ration tickets marked with the word *Juif*, or *Juive*, Jewish? That single abusive word
marked stateless exiles as outcasts, the strangers.

Today, or was it yesterday, the *Juifs* were denounced as personae non gratae, and wrongly shamed as bankers, black marketeers, or worldly arms dealers, and with no obvious traces of irony? The *Juifs* were stateless because of envy and vengeance, and considered dangerous to the war, not peace. Jews were condemned by the occupation and adrift with no chance of place or presence, the strangers.

Today, or was it yesterday that Jews were forbidden to travel, use telephones, or carry on a conversation in a café? Jews were shamed in public and banned from concerts, museums, markets, gardens, cultural events, and yet the fascists were worried about the résistance and ordered every Jew, six years or older, to wear the badge of a yellow star, the strangers.

Today, or was it yesterday that natives were removed to reservations, and cavalry soldiers on horseback chased down and murdered hundreds of women and children at Wounded Knee Creek in South Dakota? The stories of envy, vengeance, and mass murder are in clouds, and these scenes come to mind with the yellow star and every exiled Jew in Paris.

33

HEARSAY MAESTRO

Thursday, 12 November 1942

The River Seine shivers on the easy waves, an eternal course almost silent on this cold night, only the rumble of military trucks in the distance and the hourly menace of enemy soldiers on the Pont de la Concorde.

The Vicar, Pig Ears, and Black Jack are at my side near the tiller of the *Liberté Indienne*. These moments of solitude are transient in another winter of war and distant memories of totemic animals and birds. The fugitive ghosts of our breath are heirs of the fur trade, and move slowly in the faint blue light of the Quai des Tuileries.

The Wehrmacht extended the occupation yesterday to include the southern zone, and the entire country. France is now completely occupied by the enemy from La Manche to the Bay of Biscay and the Mediterranean Sea. The fantasy of the free zone has ended, and at the same time thousands of enraged citizens and exiles have volunteered to serve in the résistance.

Jews once meandered on the boulevards and quays, and paused at the cafés, Les Deux Magots, Le Dôme Café, and Café de Flore. Jews once mocked the names of Adolf Hitler and Benito Moussolini, and at the same time celebrated with commentary the perceptions of Henri Bergson and Émile Durkheim. Jews once revered and teased the visionary literature of Marcel Proust and Paul Celan and the enchantment of artists Camille Pissarro, Moïse Kisling, Chaïm Soutine, and Marc Chagall. Jews were secure as citizens, and as exiles, to praise or demur the celebration of the literary socialist Léon Blum, once the Prime Minister of France.

"Natives created continental trade routes, mapped the rivers and mountains, and exchanged stories and precious stones, and then were restrained on fascist reservations," said Aloysius.

"Praise and demur in the clouds," said Nika.

"Natives served and saluted in the Civil War," said Pierre. "But the civil rights of reconstruction were never intended for natives on federal reservations."

Solomon Heap of Words would tease me now and ridicule my romantic memory of furriers and junk dealers with college degrees who were denied professional positions because they were Jews. Rightly, since the conventions of antisemitism in Minnesota are not easily compared to the Nazi Occupation, mostly because the exiles are stateless and the city police, nationalist executives, select leagues, and the bankers and breeders of the Citizens Alliance in Minneapolis were severe fascists but not the Gestapo.

The enemies of *liberté* are poised at every quay and corner now, perched on wicker chairs at the same cafés where artists and authors once gathered, and no doubt the wicked collaborators are composing hateful *corbeau* letters as they pretended to read the censored newspapers and instead calmly carry out the deceit and proxy terror of the Third Reich.

Stateless Jews and natives must tease memories on lonesome nights, and create fantastic stories for their children about merciful animals and generous birds in magical flight. The stories continue over dead bread, the scent of bone, and totemic unions. Ghost Dancers and the righteous people of the world recover creased photographs, trade ration tickets, patches of yellow cloth, bright buttons, dream songs, and pages from a book of poems packed in bundles for an easy escape should federal agents or the police beat on the door in the early morning light.

Thousands of stateless exiles were captured at home and on the avenues of Le Marais, one of the most spirited communities of Jews. The singular district is located in sections of the third and fourth *arrondissements* on the Rive Droite, or Right Bank, of the River Seine. The lively culture of old commerce, narrow avenues, and crowded apartments, extends from Rue de Renard and Rue du Temple to the east between the Place de la Bastille and Place de la République, and including Place des Vosges, once the rich and feathery parade route of the aristocracy, and the famous Goldenberg Delicatessen on Rue des Rosiers.

Le Marais was one of the most persistent and hearty districts of culture, turns of tradition, and *liberté* of the mind and heart in Paris. Much richer in stories, music, irony, and tasty fare than the learned salutes and clever café teases of the Sorbonne and Latin Quarter on the Rive Gauche, or Left Bank, of the River Seine.

Nothing was ever the same after the Préfecture de Police staged the early morning raids to accuse and capture the stateless Jews. The fascist police removed the worried hearts of a great people and a spirited culture of the book with an agonistic tradition and common ethos that served the very core of charitable communities for centuries around the world, and in the Third French Republic.

Natives created totemic and visionary stories about clever animals and birds, bears at the early spring cascades, eagles in the red pine, ravens in the birch, and the fancy dance of sandhill cranes as associations and testaments to the natural world, and the lonesome heirs of the fur trade were doubly inspired with the culture of the book.

Jews and natives were accused, summoned to account for rituals and aesthetic mysteries, and then captured and removed from cities, states, and continents, but never from totemic stories or the creative power of the book.

Michel revealed that Françoise Crémieux and daughter Hélène had escaped early last year when seven friends and colleagues at the Musée de l'Homme, Georges Ithier, Boris Vildé, René Sénéchal, Anatole Lewitsky, Jules Andrieu, Leon Nordmann, and Pierre Walter were convicted of espionage for their actions in the résistance, and executed by the Nazis on 23 February 1942. Boris Vildé, ethnographer and linguist, and Paul Rivet, anthropologist and one of the founders of the Musée de l'Homme, created with others the Réseau du Musée de l'Homme, the first résistance movement, a few months after the Nazi Occupation of Paris. Later they united with other résistance groups to rescue downed airmen, relay intelligence to the United States Embassy, and publish the *Résistance*, a clandestine newspaper that circulated only five issues. The collaborators of envy betrayed the entire résistance network. Paul Rivet escaped to the Vichy Free Zone.

"Dead hearts of betrayal," said Aloysius.

"Betrayal is never forgiven," said Nika.

Françoise surely would have been directly involved in the *mouvement de résistance*, but she had wisely set aside her independent research on stone inscriptions, and first became a teacher and later a director at Radio Paris about six years ago, when the Musée d'Ethnographie du Trocadéro closed and became part of the new Musée de l'Homme.

Radio Paris was taken over with the whiny drone of fascists who delivered collaboration news reports and other broadcasts that were daily digests of breathy rants against the United Kingdom.

Françoise and Hélène were secure in London. Nathan said at the time that she reviews the strategic information of many résistance movements and assesses the potential of war rumors for France Libre, Free France, and reports directly to General Charles de Gaulle.

Daniel-Henry Kahnweiler, the famous gallery owner, was on several enemy persecution lists, and would not have survived if he and his wife, Lucie Godon, had not moved south to Le Repaire-l'Abbaye, a mansion in the woods near Saint-Léonard de Noblat, east of Limoges. Raymond Queneau, Elie Lascaux, the painter, and many other artists and authors lived nearby.

Gertrude Stein, the hearsay maestro of modern art and literary cubism, moved with her dour lover Alice Toklas and Basket, a rangy white poodle, to a country house at Bilignin in the mountains east of Lyon.

Gertrude survived as a Jew, and maybe the collection of art in her apartment was spared because she had friends in the Vichy Regime. Surely the soldiers and art thieves of the occupation were not confused that she moved with Alice and Basket from their apartment at 27 Rue de Fleurus five years ago to a new salon closer to the River Seine at 5 Rue Christine, around the corner from the studio of Pablo Picasso on Rue des Grands Augustins.

"Picasso was a warrior and diplomat with a great heart, and he sidestepped the thieves and soldiers with strategic silence and artistic pluck in the enemy camp," said Nika.

Nathan once revealed that Bernard Faÿ, the royalist and antisemitic professor at the Collège de France, replaced a Jew as the new director of the Bibliothèque Nationale. Gertrude was a close friend of Faÿ, and they shared similar ideas about art, music, and literature, so he must have found ways to protect her during the Nazi Occupation.

Gertrude told me several years ago at a gallery event that she would never support the election of Franklin Delano Roosevelt because "Republicans are the only natural rulers." She must have meant, of course, the unnamed rulers of the United States.

Gertrude worried more about the communists than about the fascists or royalists, and raised a literary banner for antisemites and royalists, truly a surprise, and at the same time she never overlooked an invitation or hesitated to eat the liberal food and drink the good wine at the Galerie Crémieux and *Le Corbeau Bleu*, and at the many galleries owned by Jews in Paris.

"Basket is a royalist," shouted Heap of Words.

"White Russian," said Pierre Chaisson.

Nathan told me later that Gertrude had actually used that same notion of natural rulers in a speech that she had delivered a year earlier for Bernard Faÿ, as a personal favor, at a dinner party in Paris. Nathan related the responses of two friends who attended the "Democracy and President Roosevelt" lecture. Gertrude responded to a woman who was critical of modern art and literature that she "was crazy for thinking that modern art was nothing more than a sensation."

"Gertrude was strong, steady, and always defended modern art," said Nathan. She agreed with the woman that the political positions of Democrats were only seductive, and President Roosevelt was half as seductive as other elected presidents, and intellectuals were not suited for governing because they "have a mental obliquity."

Gertrude once surprised an international reporter for the *New York Times Magazine* when she said, apparently with intended irony, that Adolf Hitler should be given the Nobel Peace Prize. Jews and democratic governments were obstacles, she reasoned, and "removing all elements of contest and struggle from Germany," driving them out, "means peace," she told the reporter. Yet, she was critical of strict immigration laws in the United States. There were only "two wholly sincere democracies," she declared, the "American and French."

"Gertrude is warped," said Aloysius.

"Basket is a spy," shouted Heap of Words.

"Paris is the absence of culture, nothing is secure, no tease or irony, no dare or trace of satire, only caution and sly résistance, or the *refus absurde* at the noisy cafés that host the enemy," said Pierre. "Jews and most of the artists, authors, and gallery owners moved south to escape the fascist police and Gestapo."

"Paris on the run," shouted Heap of Words.

"Now the south is occupied," said Pierre.

"Safer here than on the enemy road," said Nika.

Nika, Pierre, and Prometheus decided to participate in résistance movements. Michel warned them many times about the risk of betrayal, arrest, torture, and execution, but that was never a distraction. Nathan was more cautious and introduced them to the transient editor of the résistance newspapers *L'Université Libre* and *Combat* that were founded last year.

Prometheus was determined to work directly for the résistance and undertake duties without favors, but not the local delivery of newspapers. He was a raconteur, and set out to write critical and satirical broadsides about fascists, pathetic royalists, and the corruption of street soldiers, and to report on the strategic theft of art and furniture from the galleries and homes of Jews. Family heirlooms, chairs, chests, china, and antique cut glass were stolen by senior officers, stored and sorted in commandeered warehouses, and delivered to loyal military families in Germany.

His satirical broadsides were printed on single pages, placed in cafés and ration stations, and posted around the city with the signature of Sigmund Freud. "Nazi soldiers wriggle like bloated worms under the blocky wooden shoes of partisan women," and "Fascist newspaper codes reveal the venereal diseases that undermine the Third Reich," and "Les Zazous seize the German Embassy," and "The Gestapo green fedoras were stolen and sold to the American German Bund," and "French soldiers capture the Führer in a silky evening gown," were five of more than twenty stories that had been posted.

"Göring in a negligee," shouted Heap of Words.

"Goebbels in a corset," said Nika.

Michel surprised Prometheus with an expertly forged passport as a native born citizen of the United States of America. Feikes Feikema was his name on the new passport. The name was Frisian, and once used as the actual birth name of Frederick Manfred. Feikes Feikema was an absolutely perfect disguise, because Prometheus could easily pose with the actual name and declare his own experience as a third generation Frisian. Manfred was born in Iowa, and his ancestors migrated from Tzum in the province of Friesland. He was close to seven feet tall, and worked for a few years in the late thirties as a sports writer for the *Minneapolis Journal.*

Prometheus Feikema could easily be convincing about his name, origins, and migration of his ancestors to the United States. Aloysius likewise prepared a new passport as a citizen of the White Earth Nation. Prometheus was now a double Frisian with two passports.

34

WHITE ROSE

Wednesday, 24 February 1943

Prometheus composed a memorial broadside to honor the memory of three courageous students at the University of Munich who started the White Rose and denounced the war, fascist deceptions, and the atrocities of the Third Reich.

Sophie Scholl, her older brother Hans, and Christoph Probst were executed two day ago by guillotine at the Stadelheim Prison near Munich, because they had produced and distributed six learned antiwar leaflets that condemned passive résistance and urged citizens to sabotage the fascist armament industries. They berated subservient newspapers, and declared that anarchy was a generative power.

"Three students beheaded for maybe only a total of six thousand words of résistance in six leaflets that praised the past glories of a great country, and then valiantly challenged the warmongers with erudite indictments," said Nika.

"Words of glory and chance," said Pierre.

"Leaflets of execution," shouted Heap of Words.

Nika translated every leaflet received through the résistance movements. Sophie and many other students were convinced the Wehrmacht lost the war in Stalingrad, and there was no cause or reason to continue the evil crusade and slaughter.

The White Rose published only six single Leaflets of the Résistance in the past year, and thousands of copies of each leaflet were placed in public areas, stands, and depots, inserted in public telephone books, and distributed at the University of Munich. The sixth and last antiwar leaflet was circulated at universities in several other cities in Austria and Germany.

Prometheus read the last leaflet and then composed a memorial broadside that was covertly distributed at public places in Paris. The literary manner of the leaflets was academic, direct, and righteous about the rise of fascism and the submissive state of citizens, but the wild broadside of the résistance raconteur was a more ironic condemnation of the Third Reich.

"Clever renunciations," shouted Heap of Words.

The memorial broadside was printed with the banner headline, *Liberté de la Rose Blanche*, White Rose Liberty. Prometheus calculated the sly manners of informers and collaborators and placed broadsides signed by Sigmund Freud in newspapers at the Café de Flore. He waited for the fascist collaborators to fold and pocket the broadside and then casually search the faces in the crowd.

Liberté de la Rose Blanche

Civilized nations would never consent to the sinister thugs of the occupation that steal food and starve citizens, but a ritzy meal of black market meat and champagne might turn a hungry grass eater into a furtive collaborator.

Dare not doze on a park bench in the afternoon sun at the Jardin du Luxembourg, or catch the cold gray eyes of an enemy soldier on guard duty at the French Senate, because Hermann Göring, the dopey plunderer of art, has occupied the Palais du Luxembourg with other thick and deadly bandits of the notorious Luftwaffe in France.

The Gestapo torture of résistance warriors is heard around the world, and yet the agony of hunger, the slow starvation of children, and the steady hatred of the enemy is seldom heard outside of France. The men and women of the occupation count the hours of misery, and are much too weak to turn a dream of feasts into ironic stories.

Hunger overcomes the danger of grass harvests at the Jardin du Luxembourg and the Jardin des Tuileries, but the graze of tough and tender garden turf is not pocketed for a feast of watery soup. The grass is fed to rabbits caged in cupboards and bathtubs for a final feast of boiled bunny, or rabbit soup with green grass.

Thousands of tiny testicular ticks have invaded the favored brothels, *les maisons closes*, of the occupation, and the nasty ticks are trained and ready to bite only officers of the Wehrmacht. Thousands of the résistance ticks have been released at the One Two Two, Le Sphynx, Le Chabanais, and other haute bourgeoisie brothels in Paris. The tiny tick bite poison slowly shrinks the penis and inflates the testicles, *testicules gonflés*, at the same time. Early medical reports of the severe poison have indicated testicles the size of melons, and a penis shriveled to the size of a minnow. There are no effective cures for this unbearable disease, and advanced cases of *testicules gonflés* have transformed the officers into brothel sycophants.

Hermann Göring can hardly view the size of his penis over his big belly, and according to reports of the madam of the Chez Marguerite, the proportions of his testicles have been inflated, but with no noticeable lack of pleasure.

Chaïm Soutine painted a bloody image of a side of beef and other fleshy creatures, and inspired poseurs would make haste to portray the greasy gray and stringy vegetarian carcass of the creepy Führer Adolf Hitler.

Signature of *Sigmund Freud*

Prometheus conducted a singular tour of selected brothels as a fantastic testicular tick crusade of *liberté*, only to imagine the sweaty sauerkraut sex scenes of black market fascists and criminal officers of the Wehrmacht. Naturally we were eager to carry out the brothel tour, and for security reasons we circled only one tick site a day in the late afternoon.

Sunday was the perfect day for our first campaign of the tick crusade. The One Two Two at 122 Rue de Provence, located between Rue du Havre and Rue de Rome was one of the most popular brothels. We circled the brothel two at a time that gray cold afternoon, and the blinds were always closed. Several black Citroëns were parked nearby, and a cart of food and wine had just been delivered. Nothing was ever rationed at the favored brothels, of course, because the fascists and occupation officers were active in the black market.

The Gestapo had mustered Pierre Bonny, a corrupt former policeman, and two criminal thugs, Henri Lafont, and Pierre Loutrel, or Crazy Pete, as agents of the Carlingue, a paramilitary gang that ruled the black market, captured and tortured members of résistance movements, and favored the best brothels.

The next day we circled the erotic dance bar, pedicure, and hair salon rightly named Le Sphynx at 31 Boulevard Edgar Quinet. The brothel was located near the cemetery, Cimetière du Montparnasse, and was reserved

for officers of the Wehrmacht. Adolf Hitler, we were told, paused to have
a meal at Le Sphynx, and the gossip grows with stories about his speedy
sex scene during the three hours of his only tour of Paris on 23 June 1940.

"Legionnaire ticks of *liberté*," shouted Pierre.

"Big ticks for the tiny führers," said Aloysius.

"Tick totems," shouted Heap of Words.

Nika heard stories that Humphrey Bogart, Cary Grant, and the Prince
of Wales were habitués of *Le Chabanais*, the third reserved brothel on
the tick crusade of *liberté*, the most opulent of *les maisons closes*, at 12
Rue Chabanais near the Jardin du Palais Royal and the Musée du Louvre.
The brothel easily rivaled Le Sphynx and One Two Two for the pleasure
of officers of the Wehrmacht. The last on our tick tour was the favorite
brothel of Hermann Göring, the Chez Marguerite at 50 Rue Saint George,
a long walk directly north of the Musée du Louvre near Rue Montmartre.

35

KING JOHN

Monday, 10 May 1943

Nika arrived at the *Liberté Indienne* yesterday afternoon with a handsome, rather hesitant enemy medical officer who wore casual clothes. We never expected anyone to invite the enemy to visit the barge. The crew was very anxious, almost ready to escape with the five mongrels and camp overnight in the Jardin des Tuileries.

Nika agreed at the start of the war that we would never court the enemy, and yet she believed we would appreciate a medical doctor who celebrates art, literature, theatre, and who could easily procure food and wine.

Hermann Göring, the military monster who loved art, came to mind, of course, and the grand puppet show about two years ago near the Jeu de Paume. Maybe medical school was a more humane introduction to art and literature than opium addiction, obesity, thievery, and the atrocities carried out by the German Luftwaffe.

Heap of Words was silent, but the hesitation of ironic teases of enemy medicine men was obvious. We avoided eye contact, and waited for an introduction at an escape distance. Even the mongrels were shy around the enemy. Pierre was the first to reach out and shake hands with the medicine man, and at that very moment a military barge churned down the River Seine. The officer moved slowly with the heavy waves as the moored barge bumped against the quay.

Nika introduced Captain Johannes Hoffmann to the crew and mongrels of the *Liberté Indienne*. Herr Hoffmann shook hands with everyone but me that afternoon. I turned away and sat near the blue tiller with Pig Ears on my lap, and waved her ears at the officer. The Nazi officer smiled and related in perfect English that he was never raised with dogs, and held out his gentle white hand close to the nose of Pig Ears. She dutifully snuffled his fingers with approval, and then sneezed twice.

Nika had attended last week the first production of *King John* by William Shakespeare at the Théâtre de l'Odéon near the Sénat and the Jardin du Luxembourg. "The rumor spread quickly that someone had thrown a grenade at an enemy soldier just outside the theatre," she calmly related, "but the play had opened earlier in the week and was so popular that hearsay of mayhem would not distract the audience from the regal chaos of King John."

Nika and Herr Hoffmann, who finally insisted that we address him as Johannes, met in the commotion caused by the rumor, and they decided then and there to sit next to each other for the performance. Naturally, Johannes was curious about her German father, an exile in the fur trade, and was obviously fascinated with her experiences as a native of portages and promises, and as a student at the Sorbonne.

The crew resisted every natural moment to tease the princess of the fur trade, and the besotted medical officer would not likely survive our mockery to the end of the war. We waited until she returned later than night to start our tease and stories about the enemy and the deadly truism of the occupation.

"How many bitty bruises did the good doctor heal during the play and on the slow way to the quay," said Aloysius

"More than you can count," shouted Nika.

"Doctor play," shouted Heap of Words.

Nika easily predicted our unease, and would never mistake our cagey responses to the enemy doctor. So, she wisely encouraged Johannes to bring treats for the crew and loyal mongrels on his first visit to *Liberté Indienne* on the River Seine.

Johannes delivered pâté de foie gras, heavy bread, two regional cheeses, and three bottles of a Château Sauterne from two favorite restaurants, he revealed, Lucas Catron on the Place de la Madeleine, and Lapérouse on Quai des Grands Augustins. These two restaurants, and many others favored the Gestapo and Nazi officers, were either excused from the severe ration regulations, or were active in black market eatables. We refused to be shamed over the sources of pâté and fine wine that spring afternoon. Johannes bought the favor of the mongrels with five small chunks of horse bone, and the ecstatic gnawing lasted for most of the night.

Johannes was actually winsome that afternoon, and we assumed it was the sway of the barge and his adoration of Nika. The good doctor was born

2 January 1900 at the German Embassy in Washington, where his father
was an envoy, and attended private schools until the First World War.
Later he studied medicine at the Friedrich Wilhelm University in Berlin,
and he told the crew between salutes of wine to James Joyce, Ezra Pound,
and Walter Benjamin that he was a Doktor at the Charité Universitäts-
medizin Berlin until the start of the Second World War.

Pierre leaned closer to listen, and we were tempted to confront the
Doktor with antisemitism, the absolute cruelty of the occupation, and
inquire about his service to violence, but we were distracted by his absolute
infatuation with the princess of the fur trade, Nika Montezuma.

Nika lingered near the blue tiller and spoke quietly with Johannes in
German. We were devoted listeners, of course, and our comments were
seasonal and nonsense about the lovely bloom of leaves in the Jardin des
Tuileries, and we never once hesitated to eat the cheese, pour the wine,
and praise the generosity of the enemy medicine man.

"The enemy way with pâté," whispered Pierre.

"I walk alone in the early morning," said Johannes, "and several times
a week cross over the River Seine on the Pont de la Concorde, and could
not help but notice the moored barge, and sometimes pause to watch the
dogs and wonder about who lived on the Quai des Tuileries."

"Native navy," shouted Heap of Words.

"I should have waved," said Johannes.

"Next time, even in bad weather," said Pierre.

Shakespeare never could have imagined the popularity of *King John*
during the Nazi Occupation of Paris. The court chronicle was first published more than three centuries ago and seldom produced in any country.
The audiences at the Théâtre de l'Odéon were captivated with the play,
and at the same time were worried and wary about the presence of enemy
officers in the best seats.

Johannes listened closely, but remained silent when we talked about
King John. He was always attentive, of course, especially when Nika talked
about the play, or talked about anything, and frequently he indicated
agreement with slight gestures, mostly toothy smiles. "No sense of ethos,
no tease of unity, no natural course of dramatic action in *Roi Jean*," said
Nika. "Nothing heroic, tragic, or even ironic, but rather a strange play
about royal fortunes, and the desperate vindication of a kingdom."

"Paris is the same, an overnight play of destiny, but without the bloody royal heads," said Prometheus. He was very cautious the entire afternoon, and worried, of course, that he might enter the conversation with similar words or phrases from his most recent broadsides.

"Shakespeare wrote about liberty, the eternal rush of liberty, and the royal crush of birthrights and sovereignty," shouted Heap of Words.

"Royal manners," said Pierre.

France was represented as the enemy of England in the contentious historical play, and every citizen that night in the theatre must have heard the characters deliver the poetic actualities of the enemy occupation, the nihilistic schemes of an execution, castle suicide, and poison. Familiar allegories of the kingly chronicles of empire wars were played on stage that spring in Paris.

Clara Longworth de Chambrun, or by cachet marriage to Count Alde-bert de Chambrun, Contesse de Chambrun was named the occupation director of the American Library in Paris. The Contesse could have been one of the characters in the very play she had translated, *The Life and Death of King John*, as her son, Count René de Chambrun, married Josée Laval, daughter of Pierre Laval, the fascist and antisemite politician who served the deadly collaboration of the Vichy Regime. René de Cham-brun was an aristocrat and lawyer and related to the Marquis de Lafay-ette through his father and to President Theodore Roosevelt through his mother, and the precious godson of Philippe Pétain.

"Pretense of royalty," said Pierre.

"Fascist comedy," shouted Heap of Words.

"Résistance intrigue," said Aloysius.

Clara had studied Shakespeare at Sorbonne University and was per-suaded by René Rocher, director of the Théâtre de l'Odéon, to translate the tangled chronicle *La Vie et la Mort du Roi Jean* for the complete production in French. The historic play in five acts opened on 6 May 1943 with the permission of the enemy. At least five positive reviews were pub-lished in the censored newspapers of Paris. The first favorable review was by Alain Laubreaux in the once distinguished *Le Petit Parisien*, and four other reviews followed in the collaborationist newspapers *Le Matin* and *L'Appel*, the widely circulated *Paris Soir*, and the antisemitic propaganda rag *Aujourd'hui*, and more, more, more in the name of royal intrigue.

Nika and Prometheus had prepared selected passages from *King John* for a short play of voices, similar to a puppet show, and with designated readers from the native crew of the *Liberté Indienne*, and, at the last minute it was necessary to included Doktor Johannes. The quotations were selected from a copy of the play in the barge library a few days before Nika attended the Théâtre de l'Odéon, and obviously before she met Johannes. The characters of *King John* were heard late last night on the River Seine. The mongrels were at our side, and at the blue tiller, Pig Ears.

COYOTE AS CHÂTILLON:

The proud control of fierce and bloody war,
To enforce these rights so forcibly withheld.

PROMETHEUS AS KING JOHN:

Here have we war, and blood for blood,
Controlment for controlment: so answer France.

COYOTE AS CHÂTILLON:

Then take my king's defiance from my mouth,
The farthest limit of my embassy.

PROMETHEUS AS KING JOHN:

Bear mine to him, and so depart in peace:
Be thou as lightning in the eyes of France;
For ere thou canst report I will be there,
The thunder of my cannon shall be heard:
So hence! Be thou the trumpet of our wrath
And sullen presage of your own decay.

NIKA AS QUEEN ELEANOR:

What now, my son! Have I not ever said
How that ambitious Constance would not cease
Till she had kindled France and all the world,
Upon the right and party of her son?
This might have been prevented and made whole
With very easy argument of love,

Which now the manage of two kingdoms must
With fearful bloody issue arbitrate.

PROMETHEUS AS KING JOHN:
Is that the elder, and art thou the heir?
You came not of one mother then, it seems.

ALOYSIUS AS BASTARD:
Most certain of one mother, mighty king;
That is well known; and, as I think, one father:
But for the certain knowledge of that truth
I put you o'er to heaven and to my mother:
Of that I doubt, as all men's children may.

NIKA AS QUEEN ELEANOR:
Out on thee, rude man! Thou dost shame thy mother
And wound her honor with this diffidence.

SOLOMON AS KING PHILIP:
Well then, to work! Our cannon shall be bent
Against the brows of this resisting town.
Call for our chiefest men of discipline,
To cull the plots of best advantages.
We'll lay before this town our royal bones,
Wade to the marketplace in Frenchmen's blood,
But we will make it subject to this boy.

PROMETHEUS AS KING JOHN:
Peace be to France, if France in peace permit
Our just and lineal entrance to our own.
If not, bleed France, and peace ascend to heaven,
Whiles we, God's wrathful agent, do correct
Their proud contempt that beats His peace to heaven.

SOLOMON AS KING PHILIP:

Peace be to England, if that war return
From France to England, there to live in peace.
England we love; and for that England's sake
With burden of our armour here we sweat.

PROMETHEUS AS KING JOHN:

Doth not the crown of England prove the king?
And if not that, I bring you witnesses:
Twice fifteen thousand hearts of England's breed.

ALOYSIUS AS BASTARD:

Bastards and else.

PROMETHEUS AS KING JOHN:

To verify our title with their lives.

SOLOMON AS KING PHILIP:

As many and as wellborn bloods as those.

ALOYSIUS AS BASTARD:

Some bastards too.

PROMETHEUS AS KING JOHN:

Then God forgive the sin of all those souls
That to their everlasting residence,
Before the dew of evening fall, shall fleet
In dreadful trial of our kingdom's king.

SOLOMON AS KING PHILIP:

Amen, amen! Mount, chevaliers to arms!

PROMETHEUS AS KING JOHN:

France, hast thou yet more blood to cast away?
Say, shall the current of our right run on?
Whose passage, vexed with thy impediment,

Shall leave his native channel and o'erswell
With course disturbed even thy confining shores,
Unless thou let his silver water keep
A peaceful progress to the ocean?

SOLOMON AS KING PHILIP:
England, thou hast not saved one drop of blood,
In this hot trial, more than we of France;
Rather, lost more. And by this hand I swear,
That sways the earth this climate overlooks,
Before we will lay down our just-borne arms,
We'll put thee down, 'gainst whom these arms we bear,
Or add a royal number to the dead,
Gracing the scroll that tells of this war's loss
With slaughter coupled to the name of kings.

ALOYSIUS AS BASTARD:
Ha, majesty! How high thy glory towers
When the rich blood of kings is set on fire!
O, now doth Death line his dead chaps with steel;
The swords of soldiers are his teeth, his fangs;
And now he feasts, mousing the flesh of men,
In undetermined differences of kings.

PROMETHEUS AS KING JOHN:
France, I am burned up with inflaming wrath,
A rage whose heat hath this condition:
That nothing can allay, nothing but blood,
The blood, and dearest-valued blood, of France.

SOLOMON AS KING PHILIP:
Thy rage sham burn thee up, and thou shalt turn
To ashes, ere our blood shall quench that fire.
Look to thyself, thou art in jeopardy.

PROMETHEUS AS KING JOHN:

It is the curse of kings to be attended
By slaves that take their humours for a warrant
To break within the bloody house of life,
And on the winking of authority
To understand a law, to know the meaning
Of dangerous majesty, when perchance it frowns
More upon humour than advised respect.

ALOYSIUS AS BASTARD:

O, let us pay the time but needful woe,
Since it hath been beforehand with our griefs.
This England never did, nor never shall,
Lie at the proud foot of a conqueror
But when it first did help to wound itself.
Now these her princes are come home again,
Come the three corners of the world in arms
And we shall shock them. Naught shall make us rue
If England to itself do rest but true.

JOHANNES THE MESSANGER:

From France to England. Never such a power
For any foreign preparation
Was levied in the body of a land.
The copy of your speed is learned by them,
For when you should be told they do prepare,
The tidings come that they are all arrived.

"The audience shouted and applauded," said Nika, when the Messenger in *King John* declared that never a power for "any foreign preparation was levied in the body of the land." The word "preparation" meant a military expedition, and crowned the coincidence between France and England in the historical play with the Nazi Occupation, and, of course, the anticipated liberation of France.

Coyote Standing Bear declared that native students at the Carlisle Indian School had staged more serious drama, *Julius Caesar, Merchant of*

Venice, *King Lear*, and many other original plays by William Shakespeare than were produced in the revolutionary history of the French Republic.

Maybe the *Ancien Régime*, French Revolution, *Révolution Française*, Reign of Terror, *La Terreur*, and the steady, bloody guillotine execution of thousands, including Queen Marie Antoinette, Maximilien Robespierre, Charlotte Corday, and Georges Danton at the Place de la Révolution, now the busy Place de la Concorde, created more than enough subversion, savagery, royal mayhem, decapitations, political graveyards, and gallows humor than any playwrights, actors, or theatres could ever produce. The *Révolution Française* was one of the most complicated and deadly theatre productions, and the encores of the revolution have continued almost as long as the royal chaos, schemes, tragedies, and comedies of William Shakespeare.

36

LITERARY REVENGE

Thursday, 16 September 1943

Pig Ears ruled the blue tiller of the *Liberté Indienne*, but she could not steady the waves from military barges on the River Seine. The enemy wakes were a constant reminder of the heave and surge of savagery in the occupation, night and day the rush of water on the quay, and mercy was at bay.

So far the crew of the moored barge had never been teased, coaxed, invited, or ordered to serve the cause of résistance movements. We created our own missions of literary résistance, the *refus absurde* of hand puppets and broadsides. Other émigrés and exiles volunteered to wage overnight sorties against enemy soldiers and decadent envoys of the Vichy Regime.

The bay of loyal mongrels and the casual sense of balance on the barge became a daily fantasy of whalers at sea, and our stories were enhanced with the heavy wake of the *Île de France* on the Atlantic Ocean. Native stories were necessary because every day the occupation and deadly war was the absence of natural motion. Memory and chance were overcome with empire fury and the fascist devastation of the Nazi Occupation.

The promises of armaments for the partisans were almost forgotten when British Royal Air Force bombers destroyed the Renault Factory in Île Seguin and Boulongne Billancourt near Port de Saint Cloud. Nathan said the plant had been converted with slave labor to manufacture tanks for the Wehrmacht. The thick smoke from huge explosions two weeks ago wafted slowly over the River Seine.

American exiles and mainly women were sometimes selected to provide safe houses, deliver secret messages, drive ambulances, translate directions and documents for downed airmen, or serve as scouts and spies, but rarely ever considered as assassins or combatants.

Natives were born with a sense of totemic cues, the airs and graces of

motion, the secrecy and deception of animals and birds, the chance turns
of the seasons. Later natives learned sly strategies, witching hour stealth,
mockery, ironic political moves, and crafty maneuvers from enemy agents
on federal reservations. Even that elusive native portrayal was overlooked
by résistance movements, along with combat experience as soldiers during
the First World War.

"Natives were more than standard coup counters or tricky sidewinders,"
shouted Heap of Words. "Maybe the résistance leaders sidelined the old
warriors of the last war, and never heard the stories about the courage of
native soldiers in combat."

"Natives everywhere were cut for anthropology, and not considered
ready for résistance," said Aloysius. "The French forgot about the fur trade
and our loyal support during the colonial French and Indian War."

"French conceit," said Coyote Standing Bear.

Prometheus created his own literary résistance with occasional broadsides that were outrageous satires and mockery of enemy soldiers, the
brothel tick diseases, and savagery of the Gestapo, creepy vegetarian talk
downs with Adolf Hitler, and the corruption of double agents.

The duty and engagement of a literary denunciator never seemed as
dangerous as the sabotage of enemy tanks, supply lines, or the assassination of military officers, but satirical vilification of the Wehrmacht and
Gestapo by a covert author and the agents of the résistance movement
that printed and posted the broadsides ran with the same risks of capture,
torture, and execution.

"Fight, outwit, or write," said Pierre.

"Nathan serves in the Armée Juive," said Nika.

By Now volunteered as a nurse to care for wounded airmen at secure
apartments around the city, and she secretly treated soldiers at the American Hospital of Paris. Doctor Sumner Jackson was her covert supervisor,
but our cousin never mentioned his name, not once, and avoided any discussion of the airmen or wounded soldiers.

By Now told me that the vegetable delivery was only part of her duties,
and an easy disguise. The bicycle basket loaded with cabbages, potatoes,
and bundles of carrots was partly an undercover operation to visit the various secure residences in Paris.

Nika was convinced that the broadsides and puppet shows were crucial expressions of our résistance to the cruelty of occupation soldiers, the suppression of art and literature, and the persecution of Jews. She protested that no one should ever apologize for aesthetic aversions and literary revenge, or for the public denunciation and assassination of the enemy.

Prometheus turned back yesterday when the contact for the résistance newspaper was not the same person. He met the contact every Wednesday in a market queue on Rue de Buci near Rue de Seine with a handwritten manuscript for the next single page broadside. Yesterday he walked near the market at an escape distance and assumed, at first, that the regular contact had been exposed and replaced by a collaborator.

Prometheus was always uneasy when he waited in a queue to deliver the handwritten satirical messages for the broadsides, and he was even more nervous on the day the regular contact was absent. He was always ready to eat the words if necessary, but instead he decided to read the message out loud to Aloysius, Nika, Heap of Words, Pierre, and the loyal mongrels on the *Liberté Indienne*, after he made sure no one was on the quay that afternoon.

Vengeance of the Third Reich

The Wehrmacht subverts ethos, plunders art, burns books, casts aside *liberté, égalité, fraternité, humanité*, and entrusts the ruins to double agents and collaborators. We are nothing in the face of the enemy, dead, dead, dead, only a silent queue of vengeance. Change the thoughts of envy and we are gone, nothing, not even a shadow, and stateless with no trace or sound.

Enemy soldiers were nothing at the start, nothing was their start, and they arrived dead at the occupation in gray uniforms. The assassination of enemy soldiers was never a crime because they were already delivered dead, dead, dead in Paris.

Yet, with every sidestep of the dead gray soldiers, there are just moments day and night to carry out the new spirit of revenge and retribution in the ruins of a great democracy, with cutthroats and executioners on nightly hunts for the enemy. Make good the executions with guns, cudgels, a pencil stab in the eye, and deadly bacterial poisons in meat, vegetables, wine, and champagne served at homey enemy cafés, occupation *Soldatenheim*, and sideline the soldiers dead, dead, dead, wounded, blinded, and with the deadly shits.

There are no persuasive reasons to outlive atrocities, only to rename survival another war, or to remember terror every night. No reason to open the gate, reach inside to find the voice of a scared child, because the child died a thousand times a stateless Jew. We are dead, dead, dead, and there are no songs of liberty or justice to sing at dawn, no trace of dream songs in the clouds.

Nothing, not even nothing, has a cause, and nothing has become a renunciation of that pathetic sway of double agents and dead fugitives of chance.

Nothing becomes an obligation, a dead duty, another dead cause, and the very reason to blot our bloody gums once more, treat sores with muck, and terminate the third fascist empire of führers, one meal and lure at a time with dinner party poisons, deadly enticements of river woman, explosives at every *Soldatenheim*, and without fear because we are already dead, dead, dead and nothing, and nothing is our duty as the dead.

Murder the enemy soldiers for nothing, the nothing of vengeance, and tag their ears, scar their empire bodies with the great Star of David, and paint cubist swastikas on their dead gray cheeks.

Signature of *Sigmund Freud*

"The Frisian raconteur runs with the avengers of the dead," shouted Heap of Words. "Native warriors honor the dead, taunt the enemy, and cavalry soldiers once heard overnight shouts about their tiny migrant pricks, but the countdown of the revenge broadside, poisons, pencils, and explosives are much better river stories."

"Dead for cause, dead for nothing," said Nika.

Martin, the code name of the regular résistance contact, returned the following week and explained that names and contacts were frequently changed for security, and no one has been secure since the Réseau Gloria group was betrayed last year by a treasonous priest, and the rumor has circulated for the past two months that Jean Moulin, the foremost organizer of résistance movements, was betrayed at a secret gathering, arrested by Klaus Barbie, tortured, and slowly murdered on a train to Germany.

The Gloria SMH was a large network of résistance in Paris and other sections of northern France that gathered and prepared covert information about enemy positions and maneuvers for the British Special Operations Executive in London. The name of the network was the reverse initials for His Majesty's Service,

Jeanine Picabia founded the Réseau Gloria in January 1941 in Paris. At the time of the betrayal by a double agent, hundreds of agents had gathered secret information about enemy positions, and the crucial reports were translated with concision by Samuel Beckett and sent to London. Jeanine was the daughter of Francis Picabia, the innovative cubist painter and poet, and the art critic Gabrièle Buffet Picabia.

The Réseau Gloria enlisted various specialists to print, engrave, and forge documents, and the translated chronicles were microfilmed and delivered to *boîtes aux lettres*, a mail or letter box in a public office, to avoid notice. Gabrièle Picabia, a small woman in her sixties, was hardly noticed with a shopping bag as she delivered documents to secure sites around Paris. She also looked after exiles and provided a safe house in her apartment at 11 Rue Chateaubriand.

Nika Montezuma had met Francis Picabia, the surrealist and cubist artist, and attended his *Relâche* ballet, a tease of André Breton, almost twenty years ago in Paris. "I was a new student at Sorbonne University at the time of the ballet production, and Jeanine Picabia was about eight years old," said Nika. "Now she leads a critical network of partisans, including the secretive Samuel Beckett, the author who worked closely with James Joyce."

Nika first met Beckett at Shakespeare and Company, and praised his brilliant aesthetic study on Marcel Proust, and dared to mention *More Pricks Than Kicks*, a collection of stories about a character named Belacqua Shuah. Belacqua was a shiftless character in *Purgatorio*, the second part of the *Divine Comedy* by Dante. "Beckett was pensive, very concise, almost silent, and at other times the bookstore was too busy with literary events to carry on a conversation."

Beckett lived with Suzanne Déchevaux-Dumesnil, a piano teacher, and his lover, at 6 Rue des Favorites near Rue de Vaugirard. Alfred Péron, a close friend from Trinity College Dublin, was a teacher at the Lycée Buffon and recruited Beckett to become active in the Réseau Gloria, but last year the network was exposed, and the Gestapo arrested Péron. Luckily

Beckett and Suzanne were warned and escaped in the nick of time from their apartment.

The Lycée Buffon was a center of résistance, and many students were inspired with the radical lessons and protests of Raymond Burgard, a literature professor who was active in trade union politics and the Jeune République, a socialist league that protested against the enemy occupation. The league declared on a poster, *Vive la République, Quand Même*, Long Live the Republic, All the Same, Whatever Happens, Anyway.

Burgard continued his support of the résistance, and joined a public celebration of Joan of Arc, the saint, and sang "La Marseillaise" with others to protest the Nazi Occupation. The gathering was held at about the same time as the last performance of a new play, *Jeanne Avec Nous* by Claude Vermorel. There were earlier productions of *Saint Jeanne* by George Bernard Shaw and *Jeanne d'Arc* by Charles Péguy that were also very popular.

The Germans and Vichy Regime sponsored theatre productions in the past few years, a fascist objective, no doubt, to distract the public from the extreme shortage of food during the occupation.

Joan of Arc represented a suitable story and saint for almost every fascist faction, churchy nostalgia, nationalist cabal, and political adventure. The Germans favored the cause of an ancient empire and the portrayal of cruelty by the English. The Vichy Regime toadies absurdly compared *Jeanne d'Arc* to the military and ministerial meanders of Maréchal Pétain, and the résistance movements honored the mission of *La Pucelle d'Orléans*, the Maid of Orléans, for her courage in the face of foreign invaders.

The German *Abwehr*, military intelligence service, in the Hôtel Lutetia, obviously read the poster, *Vive la République*, maintained surveillance of the résistance, and six months ago arrested Raymond Burgard at his home and sent him to prison.

Lycée Buffon students protested his arrest, printed and distributed leaflets that denounced the occupation, and later turned to armed attacks. Five students were arrested at a demonstration on Rue de Buci, and were falsely accused in court of theft, conspiracy, and sabotage. The Préfecture de Police turned the five students over to the Wehrmacht, and on 8 February 1943 they were executed at a shooting range in Paris.

Nika recently learned that Robert Alesch, a priest and double agent for the *Abwehr* intelligence service, betrayed the Réseau Gloria agents. Abbé Alesch was a trusted priest in La Varenne-Saint-Hilaire, a village near Paris. He was a mole and traitor paid to hand over names of the résistance members, and photographs, covert military documents, and maritime information to the secret *Abwehr* and Wehrmacht.

"Dismember Alesch," shouted Heap of Words.

"He deserves the guillotine," said Nika.

"Betrayal of the sacred," shouted Pierre.

Michel Laroux decided to meet with me two or three times a month on Sunday afternoons in the Jardin des Tuileries near the Grand Bassin Rond. Our conversations were less likely to be overheard in a casual crowd, and it was necessary to avoid scrutiny since the *Liberté Indienne* was raided and the crew arrested last year by the Gestapo.

Michel was convinced that we were under surveillance by collaborators and agents of the *Abwehr*. The activities on the *Liberté Indienne* were easily observed from the quay and the Pont de la Concorde, and for that reason any visits to the barge were chancy.

Nathan Crémieux was always in our stories, and last week Michel assured me that our loyal friend had not been exposed in any of the recent betrayals and arrests of agents in the résistance movements. Nathan was active in the Armée Juive, and naturally we were worried about enemy soldiers on the move because the occupation had been expanded to include the *Zone Libre* in southern France.

Michel was familiar with the betrayal of Réseau Gloria, and presented other interesting details of the story about Samuel Beckett and Suzanne. They stayed at small hotels to escape the attention of collaborators, and were invited later to stay with Nathalie Sarraute, the author of *Tropisms*, and her husband and family for a short time at a rustic garden house just outside of Paris.

Beckett and Suzanne waited for the delivery of forged documents, and then crossed the *Zone Occupée* border near Chalon-sur-Saône with the assistance of a *passeur*, a frontier résistance courier. "Beckett and Suzanne rented a country house in Roussillon, east of Avignon and Gordes," said Michel. "Actually, about three years ago we crossed at the same place on the Saône River into the *Zone Libre* on our way to Sanary-sur-Mer."

Roussillon is very close to the village where Marc and Bella Chagall lived in a stone house, and where Chagall painted *The Madonna of the Village*. Varian Fry and Harry Bingham persuaded them to escape two years ago from Marseille to Lisbon, and then by ship to freedom in New York City.

37

TRAITOR OF LYON

Monday, 20 September 1943

Maréchal Philippe Pétain, Chief of the French State, announced early this year the overnight creation of a new national fascist militia, La Milice Française, directed by two political extremists and antisemites, Pierre Laval, and Joseph Darnand.

Laval was the Minister of Foreign Affairs in the Vichy Regime at the time. Darnand, a lieutenant at the start of the war, founded the Service d'Ordre Légionnaire, an early militia that supported Philippe Pétain, and the Legionary Order of Service became La Milice Française. Darnand was named a *Sturmführer*, a paramilitary lieutenant in the Nazi Party, and was an eager collaborator for the Wehrmacht.

The Milice mustered hateful fascists and nationalists to fight against the résistance and to prepare for the wicked new Europe of the Third Reich. The Milicians were mostly volunteers, some fascists who wore wide blue berets, and the regular members of the Franc-Garde were armed and active with enemy soldiers.

Jean Moulin met with Charles de Gaulle, the exiled leader of France Libre, about two years ago in London. De Gaulle trusted Moulin, and encouraged him to unite the various factions of résistance networks and movements and initiate the Conseil National de la Résistance, the first National Council of Résistance. The secret premier conference of résistance networks was held three months ago in Paris.

The specific objectives of the résistance were never actually defined, and concise definitions were impossible because the origins of movements and leaders were diverse, and one account would never resolve the actions of various networks that carried out covert sabotage, assassinations, public denunciations of the occupation, rescued downed airmen, and published résistance network newspapers.

The movements were dedicated to the defeat of the enemy occupation, that was certain, but the actual methods of espionage, the sabotage of railroads and armed assaults, were not easily reduced to comprehensive definitions or strategies. The objectives were liberation, of course, but the actual means of résistance were elusive, literary, political, and military.

Charles de Gaulle advocated a military defeat of the Wehrmacht and Vichy Regime, and he secretly ordered the résistance movements to carry out sabotage, and counted on the loyalty of French military officers to beat the Americans to establish a provisional national government in Paris and, at the same time, sidestep a communist, socialist, fascist, or nationalist revolution, and, most crucial, restore the French Third Republic. The Communist Party was always ready to seize the spoils of war, stage an uprising, and then await the tricky political instructions from Joseph Stalin.

Michel Laroux learned that an occupation currency had been printed, *fausse monnaie*, or counterfeit money, and he was convinced that President Roosevelt, Winston Churchill, and American military officers were preparing to liberate, occupy, and establish with phoney money a dependent and limited democracy in France. The occupation strategy was similar to the phoney native sovereignty of treaties and federal reservations. The résistance movements throughout the country would never consent to a second occupation of the French Third Republic.

Michel was silent as we circled the Grand Bassin Rond in the Jardin des Tuileries yesterday afternoon, and then in a sullen mood he declared that Jean Moulin had been betrayed by a double agent, along with many other members of the résistance movement in Lyon.

"Soon after the unity conference that established the Conseil National de la Résistance in Paris, Jean Moulin, Colonel Émile Schwarzfeld, Raymond Aubrac Henri Aubry, Bruno Larat, André Lassagne, Colonel Albert Lacaze, and René Hardy gathered at the home of Doctor Fréderic Dugoujon in Caluire-et-Cuire, a commune near Lyon," said Michel. "The Gestapo seized the house on 21 June 1943, and arrested the résistance leaders."

Michel directed me to a bench, and we sat together to honor and mourn in silence the courage and miserable death by torture of Jean Moulin.

"René Hardy betrayed Moulin and the others," said Michel. He provided more details about the movement that had been betrayed, the rescue of airmen, but nothing related to other résistance movements or Nathan Crémieux. Later we crossed the River Seine on the Pont de la Concorde to the almost deserted Gare d'Orsay.

"The first intense rumors are sometimes conclusive, and in this case even more so because René Hardy was the only agent not secured, and somehow he managed to escape the armed Gestapo," said Michel. "René had a lover who was a double agent, and she reported the secret meetings of the résistance to the notorious Klaus Barbie, otherwise known as the Butcher of Lyon."

I recounted the story of the arrest of Jean Moulin later that night on the *Liberté Indienne*, with the two mongrels at my side, High Road and The Vicar. Pig Ears steadied the blue tiller and raised her nose to detect any scent of enemy soldiers. The crew cursed the name of René Hardy, cursed him for emotional weakness and the betrayal of honorable citizens of the résistance who were always ready to serve and to restore the French Third Republic.

"Hardy does not deserve to enjoy the *liberté* that the résistance fought to restore and protect," shouted Pierre. "Sticks, stones, cudgels, ropes, fire, and poison were not enough to torture and execute the Traitor of Lyon."

"Castration," shouted Heap of Words.

Nika gestured for a moment of silence, time to honor those who were betrayed, and to remember the dreadful death of Jean Moulin. We would have toasted the spirit of the résistance organizer, but there was nothing at hand to trade for wine, so we perched on the barge gunwales and told overplayed stories of château wine at a ritzy restaurant in Paris.

"Salute Moby Dick," shouted Heap of Words.

"Ishmael on the *Liberté Indienne*," said Pierre.

Nika raised a dirty empty glass and shouted out the four literary names of James Joyce, Henri Bergson, Herman Melville, and Samuel Beckett. "Joyce, Bergson, Melville, Beckett, *salut avec du vin*, tiptoptippy canoodle, duration means invention, watery parts of the world, and the rage of empty scenes in *More Pricks Than Dicks* at Shakespeare and Company."

Prometheus teased Nika about Johannes Hoffman, the enemy medicine man. "Time to chant his name, warn him the mongrels mourn his absence, and attend another play so he might deliver a few more bottles of wine."

Nika sidestepped the teases and continued with the diversion story about Samuel Beckett. On the day after Christmas about six years ago

James Joyce, Nora Joyce, Peggy Guggenheim, Samuel Beckett, Giorgio and Helen Fleischmann, were seated for dinner near the window under the red canopies at Le Fouquet's, the world famous restaurant on Avenue des Champs-Élysées in Paris.

"Peggy Guggenheim would remember that dinner, no doubt, because she probably had sex more than once with everyone at the table, and maybe with the *maître d'hôtel* and *serveur* at Le Fouquet's, and rightly so because the wealthy bohemian art collector promoted and rescued some of the most magnificent art in the world, and did so in the face of the enemy," said Pierre.

"The Führer and decadent Third Reich cannot endure without the plunder of cubist and surrealist art," said Nika. "And certainly not without the tiptoptippy canoodle of modern literature."

By Now arrived by bicycle from the hospital with a stash of root vegetables bundled with issues of *Le Matin*, and a heavy loaf of stale bread. The stew was tasty that night, and nutritious, but the crew of the *Liberté Indienne* each lost more than fifteen pounds in the past year, and the barge of liberty became much lighter on the constant waves.

The once popular nationalist and now collaborationist, *Le Matin* became a source of teases and stories as we slowly ate dinner, without wine. The ink print and pictures of the newspaper were poison in every sense of the word, the headlines were toxic collusions with the enemy, and the actual chemical stew of the printed page was part of the meal because we never peeled vegetables.

Nathan was gone, and the ironic pleasure of mocking the fascist and traitorous stories in the daily newspaper was no longer easy, because he was always ready to translate the idiomatic and unintended ironic headlines and cartoons of censored newspapers.

38

EMPTY PLINTHS

Friday, 3 December 1943

Justice and egalitarianism were brushed aside during the Nazi Occupation, and the Vichy Regime established the menace of the Milice Française. The last traces of ethos and moral governance were reversed when thousands of citizens and stateless exiles were persecuted and murdered in the past three years.

The Milice assassinated Maurice Sarraut yesterday at his home in Toulouse. Sarraut was the executive editor of *La Dépêche de Toulouse*, a newspaper with wide circulation in France. Philippe Pétain was favored in the newspaper at first, but later Sarraut was openly critical of the fascists and the treacherous directors of the Milice Française, Pierre Laval, and Joseph Darnand.

Jean Jaurès, the antimilitarist who was assassinated more than thirty years earlier, published his first socialist editorials in *La Dépêche de Toulouse*, but that was hardly the reason to murder the current editor. The Milice pitched the blame for the assassination on the résistance, but the dopey diversion failed, and police arrested the actual killers and the person who provided the weapons. The Nazis, Laval, and Darnand intervened, and the obvious assassins were released from police custody.

The Milice threatens, and sometimes assassinates the enemies of the Nazi Occupation and Vichy Regime, and the fascists carry out executions with impunity. The liberal sentiments of newspaper editors were perilous, and active members of the résistance were betrayed, tortured, and assassinated, and at the same time cultural monuments and statues were removed from plinths. The statues were smelted for enemy munitions in Germany.

"Betrayal of culture," shouted Heap of Words

More than a thousand bronze statues of prominent philosophers, scientists, literary masters, and many other torchbearers were removed, and the empty plinths became an absence of cultural history. The statues and memorials of the French Third Republic were carried away as nothing more than scrap metal.

The Vichy Regime promised that some bronze statues would be replaced with stone sculptures, but that contract was deceptive, and meant only to distract the angry citizens who would gather almost every day near familiar statues in village squares. The statues were part of the community history and cultural memory, and many citizens refused to comply with the *impôt métal*, or metal tax. Bronze sculptures and village bells were smelted for the copper to manufacture munitions for the Third Reich, not for the vineyards or agriculture as the fascist collaborators had broadcast.

The Vichy Regime posted broadsides to promote the metal tax for the defense of the country and agriculture, but copper, lead, nickel, and tin were collected only for enemy munitions.

SANS CUIVRE
Sans Plomb, Sans Nickel, Sans Étain
NOTRE INDUSTRIE
Est Privée de Matières Premières Irremplacables
NOTRE AGRICULTURE
Est Sans Défense Contre les Maladies

The résistance movements strongly rejected the metal tax and removal of national monuments and statues, and declared in a counterbroadside, the "Boches have stolen everything, copper, bronze, tin, nickel, lead. They remove the statues from our squares and gardens, the stairs of the subway, our coins. Should we give them our cookware, our doorknobs and our jewelry? No! They will not have a gram of metal anymore!"

The bronze statues of Voltaire, Jean-Paul Marat, Émile Zola, and many others were smelted down for copper to manufacture bullet casings and other munitions. Surely the ammunition would malfunction in the chamber of cannons and rifles used to carry out the war and executions by the Third Reich.

"Breech backfire," shouted Heap of Words.

Shakespeare; Victor Hugo, the poet and novelist; Étienne Dolet, the glorious heretic burned alive with his books in the inquisition; Jean-Jacques Rousseau, political philosopher; Voltaire, philosopher, historian, and satirist; Émile Zola, novelist of naturalism; Alphonse de Lamartine, poet and politician of the French *Tricolore* and the Second Republic; Marquis de Condorcet, mathematician and political philosopher; the great bronze crocodile fountain at Place de la Nation; The Bear the Eagle, and the Vulture bronze sculpture of the Fontaine du Square Montholon; and many other statues were removed and hauled away with other metals to scrap yards, cut, crushed, and loaded onto railroad cars bound for enemy smelters.

"Barren plinths," shouted Heap of Words.

By Now was told by railroad workers at the hospital that the French National Railway had transported more than fifty shipments of bronze scrap metal to Germany. The railroad workers would not dare to protest or derail the shipments, but coal miners shut down an operation three months ago to rescue the bronze statue of a famous trade union organizer, Michel Rondet.

Pierre remembered an article in *Université Libre*, the occasional résistance newspaper, about public resentment over the removal and destruction of bronze statues. The plinths were "new monuments" to remind people of "the crimes we must avenge."

Adolf Hitler ordered soldiers in the first week of the occupation to remove the marble bas-relief monument that honored the memory of Edith Cavell, the English nurse who rescued and treated British and French soldiers in Belgium at the start of the First World War. Cavell, one of only a few women honored with a memorial sculpture, was portrayed in bright marble as a dead nurse, and the executioners were German.

"Bas-relief fury," shouted Heap of Words.

"She would heal the enemy," said Nika.

"That courageous nurse was accused of treason and executed on 4 August 1915 by firing squad," said By Now. "Death was never enough for the monster of bad breath, so he destroyed the monument."

The Führer toured central Paris for only a few hours early in the morning on 23 July 1940, about a week after the Nazi Occupation, and never actually saw the marble ruins of Edith Cavell at the Jeu de Paume. Hitler praised selected architectural monuments on the speedy conquest day trip, and no doubt he was anxious to return to the fascist culture of his secure bunker.

Nika denounced the thousands of bronze statues that had been smelted for enemy munitions, and then whispered that scraps of copper wire or other precious metals could be traded for liters of wine. After a rigorous ironic search of the entire *Liberté Indienne*, we located only one source of copper, a solid brass mount around the blue tiller, dutifully guarded by the mongrel Pig Ears.

39

MORAL DUTY

Sunday, 26 December 1943

Aloysius collected scraps from street markets, gardens, and quays, buttons, remnants of bright cloth, and rusty tins that could be bent into the famous faces of hand puppets to perform around the empty plinths in Paris. He envisioned native visionaries, leaders, poets, artists, and warriors, each united with an eminent name on an absent statue, and then fashioned the faces, clothes, hands, and gestures of the hand puppets.

The entire crew of the *Liberté Indienne* was haunted by the empty plinths, the absence of memorial statues, and resolved to dedicate the blank plinths with the names of natives, new monuments of a native presence in the very culture of the ancient fur trade. The chance of native names on memorial plinths was ironic, of course, and possible only because of the military want of copper, the metal tax, and deceptive broadsides of the Vichy Regime.

Nika, Pierre, and Coyote created a new world of native names and a sense of literary and historical presence in the ruins of bronze statues. Seven native names were painted in blue block letters on the same number of blank plinths, a native league with great scientists, literary artists, inventors, and philosophers, and to remember the moral duty of native nations that lived in peace more than two centuries ago with La Grande Paix de Montréal, the Great Peace of Montreal in New France.

Sitting Bull, the Hunkpapa Lakota visionary leader of native resistance movements on the Great Plains, united with the literary artist Victor Hugo on the empty plinth at Place Victor Hugo.

Chief Joseph, the humanitarian résistance leader and philosopher of the Nez Perce, united with Voltaire, Francois-Marie Arouet, on the empty plinth at the Institut de France on Quai de Conti near the Pont des Arts.

Carlos Montezuma, or Wassaja, the brilliant Yavapai Apache and second native to earn a medical degree and practice medicine, founder and

activist of the Society of American Indians, united with Émile Zola, novelist and author of *J'accuse*, on the empty plinth at the Avenue Émile Zola
near the Pont Mirabeau.

Bugonaygeshig, Hole in the Day, elusive and eminent Anishinaabe résistance leader at the Battle of Sugar Point on the Leech Lake Reservation,
united with the philosopher and mathematician Marquis de Condorcet
on the empty plinth at Quai Malaquais near the River Seine between the
Pont du Carrousel and the Pont des Arts.

Crazy Horse, warrior leader of the Oglala Lakota, who resisted the
enemy settlers on the Great Plains and fought against the cavalry, replaced
Claude Chappe, who invented the semaphore method of communications, on the empty plinth located at the busy intersection of Rue de Bac,
Boulevard Saint Germain, and the Boulevard Raspail.

Popé, the Tewa native of *Ohkay Owingeh*, the visionary healer and résistance leader who inspired the Pueblo Revolt of 1680 against the brutal
colonial occupation of the Spanish near *Posoge*, the Big River in Tewa,
or Rio Grande River, was united with Jean-Paul Marat, the court doctor,
scientist, and fierce journalist, on the empty plinth in the Parc des Buttes
Chaumont between Rue Manin and Rue Botzaris northeast of Paris.
Marat wrote editorials for *L'Ami du Peuple*, Friend of the People, during
the French Revolution.

Ellanora Beaulieu, Anishinaabe nurse from the White Earth Reservation who served in the First World War and died of influenza at an
occupation hospital in Germany, united with Edith Cavell, the English
nurse who also served English and Belgian soldiers at the start of the First
World War. She was accused of treason and executed by the Germans. By
Now painted with uneven letters the name Ellanora Beaulieu in the ruins
of the marble sculpture on the eastern wall of the Jeu de Paume.

Doktor Hoffmann was doubly enchanted with Nika Montezuma, and
he became an ironic character in an Enemy Way ceremony of tease and
play, a new situational résistance strategy to obtain precious treats and
wine.

Nathan always provided the food and wine at earlier ceremonies of the
Enemy Way, and in the past seven months since the first encounter with
the good enemy doctor at the Théâtre de l'Odéon production of *King John*,
the tasty cheese, pâté de foie gras, boiled eggs, chocolate desserts, white

wine, and bones for the mongrels were delivered at least once a week by Johannes to secure the romance of Nika.

"Doktor Gunflint," shouted Heap of Words.

"Star of David progeny," said Prometheus.

Aloysius asked the enemy doctor last month for horse bones, and then explained that the proximal phalanx, or cannon bone, and the middle phalanx or short pastern of a horse were necessary to make several new hand puppets for a gossip show on Christmas Day. Johannes delivered horse bones once a week for the mongrels, and a few days later he dutifully secured the specific puppet bones for Aloysius.

Johannes actually appreciated the creative use of the bones because he had met Paul Klee, the surrealist and expressionist artist when he had been a professor at Kunstakademie Düsseldorf, the Düsseldorf Arts Academy, more than ten years ago. Johannes described a few hand puppets that the artist had made with plaster, debris, electrical parts, scraps of metal, and cloth.

"Klee created an incredible Devil, a hand puppet partly made with a discarded glove," said Johannes. "He made the puppets for his son, and the hand puppet in the name of the artist was made with a beef bone, and with two enormous eyes painted on the bone."

Aloysius carved the horse bones into seven puppets with long hollow necks for gossip shows with Edith Cavell and Adolf Hitler at the Jeu de Paume, Sitting Bull and Victor Hugo at the Panthéon, Carlos Montezuma and Émile Zola at the Panthéon, and Chief Joseph and Voltaire near the plinth at the Institut de France. The four puppet shows were held at three different locations on Christmas Day.

The Victor Hugo and Émile Zola hand puppet shows were held at the Panthéon because the plinths were located in places where people could not easily gather. Hugo and Zola were buried with honors at the secular mausoleum with Voltaire, Jean-Jacques Rousseau, Jean-Paul Marat, Jean Jaurès, and many other prominent citizens of France.

The Führer was the only hand puppet that was not carved out of horse bone, and not because the fascist was a vegetarian. Adolf Hitler was a new puppet head created with a wide rusty tin box of *Pastilles Vichy État*. The original polished birch head of Herr Hitler the hand puppet was held back for more ceremonial scenes, and because soldiers might seize the hand puppets.

The native hand puppets were darker than the polished pale faces and
necks of the nurse, philosopher, and novelists, and the various remnants
of tattered cloth became abstract fashions of the puppet shows, more char-
acteristic of the enemy occupation and poverty than literary traditions or
political familiarity.

Victor Hugo, Émile Zola, Edith Cavell, and Voltaire were carved as
heads with similar polished horse bones, but in every other way the features of the hand puppets, and the attire made with fragments, debris,
remnants, ribbons, and tatters from the street markets, were distinctive.
Nika and Pierre selected the actual quotations for the hand puppet shows
at the Jeu de Paume, Institut de France, and twice at the Panthéon.

Edith Cavell the hand puppet was carved with a long face and neck
with enormous dark oval eyes, rouge lips, a slight pout, and a white hat
made of thin cuts of canvas. She wore a bright red neck scarf, and a gray
cape from neck to foot, with a bright red cross on the chest and armholes
cut on each side.

Aloysius carved huge wooden hands, almost grotesque, for each hand
puppet and manipulated the hands with his thumb and ring finger. Edith
Cavell slowly reached out with her long fingers, and touched her head
on both sides.

The hands for Victor Hugo were heavy and blunt, and Émile Zola gestured with thick hands and fingers. Voltaire reached out of the armholes
of a tattered brocade cape with long, thin, graceful hands. Carlos Montezuma was the only puppet with gentle, elegant wooden hands.

Adolf Hitler, the manifest monster who protected dogs, only the pedi-
grees, but never humans, jiggled his wide rusty head made from a dented
tin box of *Pastilles*. The political confection was invented more than a
hundred years ago in the same spa town as the Vichy Regime. The sugary
pastille was brand marketed during the war as *Pastilles Vichy État*, the
Vichy State.

The Führer deserved a pastille container as a puppet head, and the grotesque eyes were painted with wavy black lines on the rusty tin, with tiny
swastikas as pupils. He wore a thick black cape with a tiny bell attached
at the shoulder. His wooden hands were huge, and the giant thumbs were
curved downward. Swastika emblems were painted on each hand. The

rusty pastille container and four swastikas were necessary clichés in a severe winter of scarce rations and the near starvation of children.

Prometheus wore big white gloves and moved slowly with the silent gestures of a mime yesterday morning in the Jardin des Tuileries. He carried a decorative broadside that announced the first hand puppet gossip show with Edith Cavell and Adolf Hitler to be staged near the ruins of the marble sculpture at the Jeu de Paume.

Aloysius raised the tin head of Adolf Hitler, waved the huge hands with swastikas, and the audience laughed and waved back, and at that very moment a woman raised a new white tin of *Pastilles Vichy État*, shook the box three times, and the audience laughed louder. The Führer became a double feature of sugary, satirical swastikas, and would forever be remembered as a rusty tin of pastilles.

"Hitler feeds his dogs pastilles," said Coyote.

By Now was the spiritual voice of the puppet Edith Cavell, and no one on the crew of the *Liberté Indienne* would volunteer, as usual, to play the whiny voice and incredible neigh of Adolf Hitler; so my brother drafted me once again to play the wicked puppet voice of the Führer. Prometheus gestured in silence with his hands, mouth, and bright eyes the emotions of the gossip show at the Jeu de Paume.

ADOLF: Cold Christmas morning in Paris.

CAVELL: Much colder since the occupation.

ADOLF: You were executed by a firing squad as a traitor and collaborator almost thirty years ago for helping wounded enemy soldiers.

CAVELL: My death was material not spiritual.

ADOLF: My dogs are more spiritual than humans.

CAVELL: Standing as I do in the view of God and eternity, I realize that patriotism is not enough. I must have no hatred or bitterness for anyone.

ADOLF: Soldiers destroyed your marble sculpture.

CAVELL: Every shard of marble is my spirit.

ADOLF: You lost the war twice in blood and stone.

CAVELL: Patriotism alone is not enough.

ADOLF: Jews, cripples, communists are the enemies of perfect people
and the Third Reich.

CAVELL: No hatred or bitterness towards anyone.

ADOLF: Treat the enemy twice the traitor.

CAVELL: Someday, somehow, I am going to do something useful,
something for people. They are, most of them, so helpless, so hurt
and so unhappy.

Herr Hitler raised both hands, giant thumbs curved down, and waved at
three enemy soldiers. The gesture alerted me to lower the tone of my voice
and convert the satirical gossip show to a promotion of *Pastilles Vichy État*.
The woman with the fresh pastilles perceived the cue and shook the tin
three times. The audience smiled in silence, and then slowly moved away
from the Jeu de Paume. The soldiers closely examined the hand puppet,
pointed at the tiny red swastikas in the eyes, and without a word removed
the tin head of Adolf Hitler. Only the huge hands remained of the headless
monster of the Third Reich.

Aloysius created the horse bone puppets for gossip shows at empty
plinths and at the Panthéon. My brother was prepared for the confiscation of the tin head fascist, a minor death of a puppet, and wisely had not
presented the carved and polished birch puppet head of Adolf Hitler. The
shows were original literary satires with hand puppets, and not mere slapstick, dingbats, or smacks and staggers feigned in vaudeville. The puppets
honored the league of prominent names that were related to the absent
bronze statues and seven celebrated native visionaries and résistance leaders in the new ironic history of the fur trade.

Sitting Bull was a warrior of the résistance with dark eyes, a poignant
stare, the posture of great cultural burdens, and a sense of presence and
association a world apart from Victor Hugo. Aloysius etched wrinkles on
the angular face, chin, cheeks, and between the eyebrows of the horse
bone hand puppet. The eminent chief wore a gray felt hat over his braids,
and a ceremonial sash over one shoulder.

"Solitary eyes of eternity," said Pierre.

Victor Hugo was a romance novelist with lighter eyes, a poignant stare,
a similar pose of literary and cultural burdens, and a sense of presence
and association a world apart from Sitting Bull. Aloysius etched a beard,

moustache, and four rows of wrinkles across the forehead of the horse
bone puppet that curved downward at the temples. The etched beard was
painted white. The poet wore a rumpled bow tie, painted waistcoat, and a
patchwork morning coat with wide wrinkled lapels.

The Sitting Bull and Victor Hugo hand puppet show was staged at the
entrance to the Panthéon at Place du Panthéon near Sorbonne University.
Olivier Black Elk was the puppet voice of Sitting Bull, and Victor Hugo
was heard in the voice of Prometheus.

HUGO: Let us fear ourselves, prejudices are the real robbers, vices are
the real murderers. The great dangers lie within ourselves.

SITTING BULL: Inside of me there are two dogs, one is mean and evil
and the other is good, and they fight each other all the time. When
asked which one wins, I answer, the one I feed the most.

HUGO: Nature is pitiless, she never withdraws her flowers, her music,
her fragrance and her sunlight, from before human cruelty or
suffering. She overwhelms man by the contrasts between divine
beauty and social hideousness.

SITTING BULL: The warrior is not someone who fights, because no
one has the right to take another life. The warrior for us is one who
sacrifices himself for the good of others.

HUGO: It is nothing to die, it is frightful not to live.

SITTING BULL: The life my people want is a life of freedom. I have
seen nothing that a white man has, houses or railways or clothing
or food, that is as good as the right to move in the open country
and live in our fashion.

HUGO: The greatest happiness of life is the conviction that we are
loved, loved for ourselves, or rather, loved in spite of ourselves.

SITTING BULL: It is not necessary for eagles to be crows.

Aloysius created Carlos Montezuma from a perfectly rounded cannon horse bone. Nika would rather have seen the head of her visionary
namesake carved from a block of white pine, perfect birch, or oak, but
she understood the situation and materials, and contributed visual stories
about his face, touch, and gentle smile. The scene of the carver and the
devoted romancer might have revived the spirit of the native doctor, as

every mark and detail on the polished bone was precise, the creases on the brow were exact, the puckers near the eyes were singular and related to a story, and the shy smile was the most precious curve on the entire face of the hand puppet.

Nika insisted that Carlos Montezuma wear a white bow tie made of remnants from a shirt, and a tailored morning coat. The gentle polished hands of the puppet were carved from weathered wood, and the pointer finger on the right hand was raised for necessary gestures.

Émile Zola was carved from a larger horse bone, and a beard and heavy eyebrows were etched on the face of the puppet and then darkened with grease from the quay. Zola wore a wide beret, white shirt, thick necktie, and a tattered morning coat without sleeves. The pince-nez eyeglasses with a black cord were made from wire, and attached to the head of the great literary puppet.

Nika was the emotive voice of Carlos Montezuma, and Pierre was very pleased to be the voice of Émile Zola at the gossip show of two brilliant hand puppets at the Panthéon on Christmas Day.

ÉMILE: I have but one passion, to enlighten those who have been kept in the dark, in the name of humanity, which has suffered so much and is entitled to happiness. My fiery protest is simply the cry of my very soul.

CARLOS: The Indian Bureau system is wrong. The only way to adjust wrong is to abolish it, and the only reform is to let my people go.

ÉMILE: And then there are always clever people about to promise you that everything will be all right if only you put yourself out a bit, and you get carried away, you suffer so much from the things that exist that you ask for what can't ever exist.

CARLOS: American Indians are not free. We are not free! We are hoodwinked, duped more and more every year, we are made to feel that we are free when we are not.

ÉMILE: Civilization will not attain to its perfection until the last stone from the last church falls on the last priest.

CARLOS: If the world be against us, let us die on the pathways that lead to the emancipation of our race, keeping in our hearts that our children will pass over our graves to victory.

ÉMILE: I would rather die of passion than of boredom.

CARLOS: It is the same with Indians as with all other people. There is only one way to achieve, do things for yourself. This rule is not abridged for the Indian because his skin is brown or red.

ÉMILE: Sin ought to be something exquisite, my dear boy.

CARLOS: The guiding policy seemed to be that the Indian must be cared for like a child. The feeling was general that if he was allowed to look out for himself, he would be cheated out of his property and would starve.

Chief Joseph and Voltaire were the last puppets in the gossip shows yesterday afternoon at the Institut de France. Prometheus played the giant mime with white gloves and raised a broadside on the Pont des Arts that announced the gossip show by great men of the ancient fur trade in two worlds of travail and great principles.

Voltaire, the handsome hand puppet, wore a gray curly wig made with mongrel hair from The Vicar and Black Jack on the *Liberté Indienne*. Aloysius painted bright round eyes, and etched curved lines on his brow and around his wide mouth. Voltaire wore a brocade cape with a wide collar, a ruffled cravat, and a lacy flounce fastened at the wrists of the wooden hands.

Voltaire held an open book in one hand with the title of a French periodical, *L'Année Littéraire*, printed on the open page. The miniature book was carved from a thin wooden box. Pierre revealed that the periodical was published more than two centuries ago, and that the "actual essay recorded in *L'Année Littéraire* was a satirical critique of selected letters written by Voltaire." The image of the book was based on an engraving made by an unknown artist in Germany.

Aloysius created Chief Joseph as weary and downcast, based on photographs of the great philosopher of peace and résistance leader of the Wallowa Nez Perce at the time of his surrender to the cavalry and removal to a reservation. My brother painted the puppet with heavy eyes, and etched the horse bone with curved creases from his nose to the sides of his mouth; and the chief wore large shell earrings, and seven polished shell chain necklaces.

Chief Joseph and Voltaire lived in separate material and political worlds, more than a century apart in cultural experiences, and yet they come together as hand puppet in a league of empty plinths, and with eternal principles of philosophy. Coyote Standing Bear was the voice of Chief Joseph, and Solomon Heap of Words shouted out the words of Voltaire yesterday afternoon at the Institut de France on Christmas Day.

> VOLTAIRE: Animals have these advantages over man: they never hear the clock strike, they die without any idea of death, they have no theologians to instruct them, their last moments are not disturbed by unwelcome and unpleasant ceremonies, their funerals cost them nothing, and no one starts lawsuits over their wills.

> CHIEF JOSEPH: All men were made brothers. The earth is the mother of all people, and all people should have equal rights upon it. You might as well expect the rivers to run backward as that any man who was born free should be content when penned up and denied liberty to go where he pleases.

> VOLTAIRE: Those who can make you believe absurdities, can make you commit atrocities.

> CHIEF JOSEPH: It does not require many words to speak the truth.

> VOLTAIRE: So long as the people do not care to exercise their freedom, those who wish to tyrannize will do so, for tyrants are active and ardent, and will devote themselves in the name of any number of gods, religious and otherwise, to put shackles upon sleeping men.

> CHIEF JOSEPH: Let me be a free man, free to travel, free to stop, free to work, free to trade where I choose, free to choose my own teachers, free to follow the religion of my fathers, free to think and talk and act for myself, and I will obey every law, or submit to the penalty.

> VOLTAIRE: It is dangerous to be right in matters on which the established authorities are wrong.

> CHIEF JOSEPH: We gave up some of our country to the white man, thinking that then we could have peace. We were mistaken. The white man would not let us alone.

> VOLTAIRE: Doubt is an uncomfortable condition, but certainty is a ridiculous one.

CHIEF JOSEPH: We live, we die, and like the grass and trees, renew ourselves from the soft earth of the grave. Stones crumble and decay, faiths grow old and they are forgotten, but new beliefs are born. The faith of the villages is dust now, but it will grow again, like the trees.

VOLTAIRE: Life is a shipwreck, but we must not forget to sing in the lifeboats.

CHIEF JOSEPH: I am tired of talk that comes to nothing. It makes my heart sick when I remember all the good words and all the broken promises. There has been too much talking by men who had no right to talk.

VOLTAIRE: Let us read, and let us dance, these two amusements will never do any harm to the world.

CHIEF JOSEPH: The earth and myself are of one mind. The measure of the land and the measure of our bodies are the same.

VOLTAIRE: Common sense is not common.

Voltaire revealed the elusive similes of godly and cultural dominance over animals derived from creation stories in his pithy comments about animals, an ironic presence compared to the "advantages over man," and he delivered these principles without the slightest conception of totemic associations or native visions of animals and birds, and with no mention of the deadly consequences of the fur trade and fashions in France.

Chief Joseph would never reveal or declare a totemic advantage in the league of memorial plinths, but surely he would have teased Voltaire that the absence of a bronze statue near the Institut de France was never the same as a totemic vision in a native dream song, a poem, letters to the heirs of the fur trade, or the marvelous hand puppet show during the enemy occupation of Paris.

40

FADED PRESENCE

Sunday, 20 February 1944

Charles Anderson, a veteran of the French Foreign Legion, and his devoted wife, Eugénie Delmar, were walking in the Jardin des Tuilieries that cold and sunny afternoon about three years ago on Christmas Day. They hesitated for a moment near the Jeu de Paume, and were captivated by a fantastic world of jerky gestures, marvelous adventures, and the tough talk back of two hand puppets, Gertrude Stein and Hermann Göring.

Prometheus, the clever raconteur, roused the audience with lively gestures. He wore loose white gloves, mimed the show of the hand puppets, feigned laughter, teased the art thievery of Göring, sneered at the haut manners of Gertrude, and then turned toward the old veteran and his wife and mocked their expressions, a raised eyebrow, hand over the mouth, finger on the cheek, and with an uneasy turn away. Eugénie was worried about enemy surveillance, and turned away several times. Charles smiled, saluted the mime, and then returned the same hand and facial gestures.

Prometheus encountered Charles and Eugénie a second time last year on Christmas Day at the popular Chief Joseph and Voltaire hand puppet show in the cobbled courtyard of the Institut de France near the Pont des Arts. Charles raised one hand that cold and cloudy afternoon, and then repeated a single sentence from Chief Joseph, "Yes, let me be a free man."

"Native *liberté*," shouted Heap of Words.

Eugénie could not believe that a crew of natives had staged puppet shows and lived on a barge on the River Seine. "Crowded with the loyal mongrels and almost free on the *Liberté Indienne*," said Aloysius. Chief Joseph turned and invited the couple to visit the barge after the last puppet show at the empty plinth.

Charles was bumped and nosed by the mongrels as he boarded the *Liberté Indienne*, and sat near the blue tiller with Pig Ears. The Vicar leaned against Eugénie on one side, and on the other side was the wooly Black Jack. Everyone was at ease that cold evening, and at first we traded cautious stories about people, places, and friends as the barge moved with the waves on the River Seine.

Prometheus posed on deck and read three stanzas of a long poem by Paul Éluard, a surrealist poet of résistance and a veteran who was ordered to write poetic letters to parents of the dead and wounded in the First World War.

The British Royal Air Force dropped thousands of copies of the poem "Liberté" over France. Nika read out loud three stanzas of the poem by Paul Éluard in French. Prometheus read the translation with great emotion from the tattered copy of the poem that someone caught last year in midair over Paris.

Sur mes cahiers d'écolier
Sur mon pupitre et les arbres
Sur le sable sur la neige
J'écris ton nom

On my school notebooks
On my desk and the trees
On the sand on the snow
I write your name

Sur l'absence sans désir
Sur la solitude nue
Sur les marches de la mort
J'écris ton nom

On absence without desire
On the bare loneliness
On the steps of death
I write your name

Et par le pouvoir d'un mot
Je recommence ma vie
Je suis né pour te connaître
Pour te nommer

And by the power of a word
I start my life again
I was born to know you
To name you

Coyote Standing Bear told stories about Shakespeare, the Carlisle Indian School, and his service in the First World War. Nika recited a shorter account of her studies with the philosopher Henri Bergson. Pierre compared the French résistance movements to native dissent and protests on reservations. Solomon Heap of Words shouted out the name of Sylvia Beach, and mourned the end of romantic book talks at Shakespeare and Company. Aloysius praised the name *Écharpe Bleue*, the woman in the blue scarf who played the piano music of Erik Satie on the River Seine.

Charles was born in Lebanon, Illinois, the same year the Civil War started in 1861, and fifteen years later he traveled to several cities with the P. T. Barnum circus, the Greatest Show on Earth. Then, after a few years with the circus, he enlisted in the Army and served in the American West.

"Chasing Indians?" shouted Heap of Words.

Charles smiled and explained that the Nez Perce War and the Battle of Little Big Horn were over, and that he was never ordered to fire his Springfield rifle at anyone. Chief Joseph, he declared, was a man of peace and smarter than any rank of cavalry soldiers. Pig Ears raised her ears, and seemed to agree with the old soldier.

Aloysius changed the subject with stories about our parents, Dummy Trout, hand puppets and mongrels on the White Earth Reservation, and our combat service in the First World War. "Here we are on this very barge because of the generosity of a great friend, otherwise we might never have stayed in Paris." My brother never mentioned the name of Nathan or the Galerie Crémieux.

Charles labored on a merchant ship, enlisted in the French Foreign Legion, and served in North Africa during the First World War. He married

Eugénie at the end of the war, and has worked as an interpreter since then for Maurice de Brosse, who owns the International Transport Company in Paris.

De Brosse tried to persuade Charles and Eugénie to move with him to the south, away from the occupation, and warned them about the racial hatred of blacks by the Nazis. Charles was almost eighty and told his boss that he was too old to move. "No, I'll stay, no need to run."

Eugénie said her loyal husband arrives on time every morning at an empty office of the International Transport Company, and his boss sends a weekly salary check by mail. Charles and Eugénie continue to live in the same apartment in Montmartre, and have never been menaced by the enemy soldiers who live on the same street.

Charles was true to his words about the enemy, and was not surprised when Doktor Johannes Hoffmann arrived with the usual gifts of fine food, wine, horse bones for the mongrels, and, of course, romance time with Nika. The good doctor delivered enough food to share with our new friends.

Johannes saluted the Hot Club de France and the great jazz concerts and cabarets in the past few years in Paris. He was obviously nostalgic, but the sudden mention of jazz was a non sequitur that could only be related to the only black face on the barge. Charles smiled, turned away, and waited in silence with Pig Ears. Eugénie was not at ease, and patted the heads of Black Jack and The Vicar.

Prometheus moved closer to Johannes, and in silence mimed his salon manner, waved white gloves near his face, and mocked the swing, wags, high struts, and dance moves of the *zazous*, the rage and feral prance of young rebels who wore bizarre clothes, clunky shoes, carried umbrellas, and resisted the fascist occupation, royalists, and collaborators of the Vichy Regime.

The good doctor was entertained by the description of swing mutiny, but apparently was not aware of the actual résistance of the wild dance and eccentric wear, or the racial cues and connections of cultural irony.

"Nazi jazz, none," shouted Heap of Words.

"Black jazz, black hot jazz" said Johannes, and with no obvious sense of the ironic diversions. "The Harlem of Montmartre, Louis Armstrong, Duke Ellington, and gypsy jazz *manouche* by Django Reinhardt."

"Decadent jazz," shouted Heap of Words.

Johannes turned away in silence, and at last he seemed to grasp the moment of his separatist and racial rave about jazz. He raised his glass of wine, saluted everyone on the deck of the *Liberté Indienne*, including the five mongrels, and announced his regrets to the only black person on the barge, Charles Anderson.

"Jazz is the creation, not decadence, and nothing bests the liberty of jazz, the Quintette de Hot Club with the strings of Django Reinhardt and Stéphane Grappelly," said Pierre. "The big heart of blues, swing and sway, totemic shouts, hollers, ballads, and the tender moods of creation."

Pierre asked the doctor how many times he had visited Le Grand Duc, the jazz club on Rue Pigalle. The popular club was first managed and then owned by Eugene Bullard, the brilliant son of a former slave from Columbus, Georgia. His parents were black and native, crossbloods of futurity, the outcome of two great cultures under duress in a nation of racial supremacists.

"Bloody futurity," shouted Heap of Words.

"Only twice before the war," said Johannes. "Le Grand Duc and L'Escadrille were devoted to my kind of jazz, and by the time of my return both of his clubs were closed."

"Eugene Jacques Bullard was right to worry about the racial hatred of the Nazis and returned about three years ago to New York City, when the United States declared war against Japan and Germany," said Pierre.

"Shameful the way Jesse Owens was treated at the Summer Olympics," said Johannes. "I was there at the time, a doctor in Berlin, and learned to avoid politics."

"Betrayal is fascism, loyalty is totemic, and nothing is ever primitive," said Nika. She tried to turn back the risky race talk to the tease of politics, manners, and stories about food, wine, and the honor of the mongrels, but the choice of words during the occupation was no longer the easy play of irony.

Pierre was annoyed with the evasive responses of the doctor, and resumed the lecture and adventure stories about the black pilot. Eugene had escaped the race baiters, fascists, and assassins of the Deep South stowed away on a merchant ship, traveled as a black boxer and dancer around Europe, enlisted in the French Foreign Legion, volunteered with other Americans to train as a biplane pilot for the Escadrille de La Fayette, French Air Force, early in the First World War, and was awarded the Croix de Guerre and Médaille Militaire for his bravery at the Battle of Verdun.

"Eugene Bullard was the only pilot who was denied a transfer by Doctor Gros at the American Hospital of Paris to serve in the Army Air Force when the Americans entered the war," said Charles. "Bullard was honored by the French, and shunned by most Americans, and for no other reason than the color of his skin."

Johannes never knew that Eugene spoke German and was a jazz club spy that first year of the occupation before he returned to New York. Eugene overheard conversations at L'Escadrille, and reported the critical enemy chitchat to the police. Obviously the résistance movements were never mentioned that night, and yet behind every word and story there were traces of obstruction, subversion, silent salutes and tributes to partisans, and testaments of sabotage against the Nazi Occupation.

Charles Delaunay, a founder of the Hot Club de France and the publisher of *Le Jazz Hot*, the magazine, was active in the résistance movements, and delivered critical documents because he was permitted to travel with jazz concerts and festivals around the country.

Johannes must have known that Delaunay, code name Benny, had been arrested and interrogated about three months ago by the Gestapo. He was released a month later, but his secretary and other members of the Hot Club de France and résistance movement were sent to concentration camps.

Nika returned later that night and declared that the good doctor was evasive and cagey, much too generous to trust in any conversation, and would never be invited back to the *Liberté Indienne*. Pig Ears and the other mongrels had already shunned the good doctor.

"Faded presence," shouted Heap of Words.

"Nazis never had a presence," said Pierre.

"Henri Bergson never fades," said Nika.

"Nathan never fades," was my comment.

Michel Laroux told me late last week on a walk in the Jardin des Tuileries that Nathan was secure and active in the Armée Juive in an unnamed place, but Benjamin Crémieux, the brilliant literary scholar who suggested critical categories of native literature, had assumed the code name of Lamy, and with his son Francis joined Combat, the résistance movement active in Marseille.

Benjamin and others in the same résistance movement were betrayed by an envious fascist and traitor, and were arrested by the Gestapo. They were sent to Fresnes, a prison located near Paris. Michel knew nothing more about his betrayal and imprisonment except that he had been involved in the résistance movement named Noyautage des Administrations Publiques, the infiltration of the public administration of the Vichy Regime.

Jean Moulin had suggested the infiltration of the command of the government and Vichy Regime, and Benjamin was active in that covert operation with Claude Bourdet, the journalist, and Henri Frenay, the founders of *Combat*, the résistance newspaper. Michel reminded me once again that *Combat* the newspaper was related but not the same as Combat the résistance movement.

Michel told me another incredible story as we crossed the Pont de la Concorde on our way to Gare d'Orsay. Nazi moral corruption was expected at the highest level of the Nazi Occupation, but this was a new scheme of depravity. The Gestapo recently established two secret labor camps to process the massive organized theft of Jewish property from apartments in Paris. The Nazi code name was *Möbel Aktion*, the Furniture Operation.

Last summer more than a hundred Jews were moved from Drancy to work in secret at Lévitan on Rue Faubourg Saint Martin, a former furniture company owned by Wolff Lévitan who escaped the Nazi Occupation. The prisoners sorted, cleaned, and processed pots, pans, dishes, clothes, clocks, stolen furniture, and other personal property from apartments of Jews who had either escaped the occupation, or who were arrested and sent to concentration camps. The most valuable furniture was boxed and shipped to the families of loyal officers in the Wehrmacht.

Michel warned me to be wary of strangers, and doubly wary of casual friends, because of the Milice Française and the Bonny Lafont Gang. "They are everywhere now, wild and vicious, and always ready for betrayal, capture, torture, and assassinate." Once more he reminded the crew never to invite anyone to the *Liberté Indienne.* "The danger is much greater with new friends, and especially with Doktor Hoffmann." Johannes has probably reported our conversations on the barge to the Gestapo. They might enjoy the jazz talk, but that was not enough to feel secure with any conversations, and certainly not with the enemy.

Michel suggested that we read *Le silence de la mer*, the *Silence of the Sea* by Vercors, code name for Jean Bruller, and released about two years ago by Éditions de Minuit, the résistance publisher. The novel is about an old man and his niece who are forced to live with a good Nazi officer, but remain silent, never utter a word as the officer blathers on about the fraternity of France and Germany, unaware of the cruelties of the Nazi Occupation of Paris. The novel could have been reversed, and a barge of natives talked too much with the good doctor who delivered pâté favors and surely knew every sordid detail of the occupation. Nika was uneasy about the entire pâté episode and barge jazz word play with the good enemy doctor.

Michel saved a newspaper article for me about the assassination of Victor Basch and his wife Ilona near Lyon last month. The Milice was responsible. The *New York Times* reported on 14 January 1944, that Victor Basch and his wife were assassinated, "and their bodies were found on the highway." Basch had been a "Professor of Esthetics and History of Art at the Sorbonne." He was "best known as leader of the French peace move-ment." Basch was also involved in the Zionist Movement, and president of the Ligue des Droits de l'Homme, League for the Rights of Man. The Milice murdered an amicable professor, but never the ethos of peace or the rights of Jews.

The Milice was allowed last month to carry out fascist acts of terror for the first time in Paris, and at the same time President Franklin Roosevelt established the War Refugee Board, apparently to safely rescue persecuted refugees by official memoranda, five years too late to secure the rights and lives of millions of Jews. The War Refugee Board was a signature in the wind, not the heart, another evasive promise, and the president has never earned the trust of the crew on the *Liberté Indienne*.

"The fascists of the torture trains and death terminals never listen to po-litical promises or executive orders of salvation, nothing new, and nothing lost," said Aloysius. The only truth is the torment and silence of persecu-tion as elite politicians favor paper promises over the actual rescue and liberty of Jews.

The Milice was more persuasive than presidents, more dedicated to

torture and death than the executive promises of rescue and a vague existence in memoranda. Varian Fry and dedicated volunteers rescued more
refugees and Jews in hotel rooms and crowded offices in Marseille, and
arranged more escorts over the mountains to liberty, than the War Refugee
Board manifesto with high society secretaries.

President Roosevelt should have resolved the cruel duplicity of antisemitic politics and the aversion to rescue Jewish refugees in the past
six years, or since the evasive international Évian Conference in France.
Breckinridge Long was the cutthroat of exit visas and policies to rescue
Jews, and the refugee board was one more betrayal common in presidential
politics.

Adolf Hitler declared in 1938 that the world should convert sympathy to
practical assistance, but only delegates of the Dominican Republic agreed
at the time to accept a small number of refugee Jews.

I wrote to the heirs of the fur trade eight years ago that Nazi antisemitism had driven more than a hundred thousand Jews out of Germany, and
at the very same time the Führer promised to pay the break out fare of the
others, an evil kickback after the plunder of personal property owned by
Jews.

The United States, United Kingdom, France, Australia, Canada, Ireland, New Zealand, Argentina, Brazil, Chile, and twenty more countries
turned their backs on the persecution of Jews in the Third Reich. That was
many years ago, and not much has changed since the Reich Citizenship
Law.

"Nazi double talkers," shouted Heap of Words.

"Party promises and pogroms," said Nika.

Yes, the dread of nationalism and fascist terror hidden in the fakery
of conscience at international conferences over the past ten years was
measured only in booty and body counts in a decade of thievery and the
massacre of Jews.

Olivier Black Elk and Coyote Standing Bear proposed a rescue program
at the time of the Évian Conference, and since then no nation, council, or
association in the world has put forward a more cogent and enlightened
relocation plan that involved native enclaves and reservations based on
the public projects and reforms of the New Deal.

President Roosevelt promised the New Deal for the country to assist the men and women who were "forgotten in the political philosophy of the government." The federal "new deal" for the "forgotten man" could have become a Native New Deal for abandoned and persecuted Jews.

The New Deal of the White Earth Trace, so named six years ago, proposed that at least a hundred to three hundred refugees, individuals and families, would relocate to each of the three hundred reservations in the country, a native and national moral duty that would provide, as long as the grass grows and the rivers flow, a secure chance of liberty for more than thirty thousand to ninety thousand Jews.

41

Escape Distance

Saturday, 8 July 1944

Allied forces landed early last month on the beaches of Normandy, and the invasion was rightly named Operation Overlord. The memory of light, color, and the easy shimmer of sailboats in *Le Port de Trouville* by Claude Monet turned into a mirage of mercy on the deadly beaches between Le Havre and Sainte-Mère-Église.

Thousands of American, British, and Canadian soldiers died on the beaches codenamed Utah, Omaha, Gold, Juno, and Sword. The hazy light of the amphibious invasion, and the bodies that washed ashore changed forever the romantic impressions of crashing waves, the pastel hues of sand, and the serenity of Normandy.

The *Liberté Indienne* is our sanctuary of natural motion on the River Seine. Every night for the past month since the invasion we imagine the courage of the soldiers with every wave and bump of the barge on the Quai des Tuileries.

Natives, farmers, and city boys rushed the beaches to liberate the heirs of the fur trade, and at the same time children were weakened with hunger in the worst year of food shortages, near starvation at every plinth, place, and garden in Paris. The beauty of the summer flowers never lasted in the glance of a weary mother with gray children, and only the bright miniature sailboats seem to tack and mask one more afternoon of starvation at the Grand Bassin Rond in the Jardin des Tuileries.

"Rutabaga patties," shouted Heap of Words.

"Starvation has weakened a generation of children, but they continue to play," said Pierre. "The Montmartre boys play marbles in the shadow of the Basilique du Sacré Coeur, and the boys of the Jardin de Luxembourg sail miniature boats on the Grand Bassin."

The Nazi brothels are favored with more food than the fleshy officers, dressed in war dance ribbons, riding crops, and tight shiny boots, could eat in an entire season of erotic decadence, and fascist criminals continue to dominate the trade of scarce edibles on the black market.

The Milice Française and La Carlingue, or the French Gestapo, are the most notorious gangs of fascists and collaboration criminals in Paris. Michel Laroux told me the Bonny Lafont Gang was named the Active Group Hesse by the Gestapo, and the criminals carried out assassinations, the torture of résistance prisoners, and other dreadful activities at 93 Rue Lauriston near the Arc de Triomphe.

Pierre Bonny was a former police inspector who was convicted of corruption and sentenced to prison before he became an agent for the Gestapo. He actually recruited new members of the gang from prison. Henri Lafont, an extreme antisemite, and criminal collaborator stole the property of Jews. The gang directly served the enemy by capturing members of the résistance.

Michel warned the crew of the *Liberté Indienne* that we were probably under surveillance by the *Abwehr* and at least three gangs of criminal perpetrators, the Gestapo, the Bonny Lafont Gang, and most recently the Milice in Paris. He worried because we were much too visible, and suggested that we move to avoid easy surveillance on the Quai des Tuileries and the Pont de La Concorde.

Michel invited Olivier Black Elk and Coyote Standing Bear to stay at the apartment that Nathan Crémieux owned on Avenue Émile Zola near the Pont Mirabeau. The title had been transferred only for security reasons. Michel provided a letter of introduction for Olivier and Coyote to present as renters to the concierge, and advised them never to mention or respond to the name Nathan Crémieux.

The rest of the barge crew would return to stay at the shuttered Galerie Crémieux on Rue de la Bûcherie near the Cathédrale Notre Dame. We once erased the past of the gallery, and now we must reverse the course and erase our presence on the barge. The next day we painted out the two names on the barge, and carried our clothes, bundles of books, revered hand puppets, and with five loyal mongrels in tow moved back to the gallery. Pig Ears refused at first to leave the blue tiller, but finally she leaped into my arms and we marched to the familiar Galerie Crémieux.

My only real concern about the move was carrying on the street the notebooks of my stories and letters to the heirs of the fur trade, so we walked close to the River Seine. The notebooks were stowed in the false ceiling of the toilet at the gallery.

"Ishmael ashore," shouted Heap of Words.

The first few nights at the gallery were unbearable, we heard nothing, only timber creaks and rodents, not even a soft chime of cathedral bells. There was no constant motion of the waves and familiar barge bump on the dock or the sounds on the quay and Pont de la Concorde.

Nika told her best stories that first night about canoe portages on Gunflint Lake in Minnesota. Aloysius told fantastic stories about hand puppets at Normandy and the diva mongrels that saved the last dance for Dummy Trout. Pierre read selections of watery scenes every night for more than a week from *Moby-Dick* by Herman Melville.

"But not only is the sea such a foe to man who is an alien to it, but it is also a fiend to its own offspring; worse than the Parisian host who murdered his own guests; sparing not the creatures which itself hath spawned," read Pierre. "Like a savage tigress that tossing in the jungle overlays her own cubs, so the sea dashes even the mightiest whales against the rocks, and leaves them there side by side with the split wrecks of ships. No mercy, no power but its own controls it. Panting and snorting like a mad battle steed that has lost its rider, the masterless ocean overruns the globe."

Late one night of the second week at the gallery we heard the swish and murmur of native dancers, the rush of water, scent of cedar, tease of breathy traders, and the slight sound of bells. The natural motions of that ceremony of the night were the native spirits of the masks and blankets and pottery that returned to the Galerie Crémieux.

Pierre was given six precious tickets to *Huis Clos*, an original play by Jean-Paul Sartre, the philosopher, at the Théâtre du Vieux Colombier two months ago in May. The enemy censors had approved the play for production, and that became the subject of our discussion about the limited literary knowledge of the enemy, along with the curious culture of the play. Pierre revealed later that the occupation censor Sonderführer Gerhard Heller was the representative of propaganda service at the German Embassy. He actually approved the production of the play and provided the tickets because they had become friends after a chance encounter one night near Sorbonne University.

"Good German," mocked Nika.

"Literary Nazi," shouted Heap of Words.

Pierre never convinced my brother or me that it was possible to meet a good enemy officer, because the misery of the occupation and the removal and murder of Jews denied any sense of personal liberty or pleasure of irony. The best of the enemy was about as believable as a good federal agent on the reservation, but the rest of the crew was persuaded that Sonderführer Heller, an occupation literary specialist who reviewed and considered what books would be published and what plays would be produced and poetic favors secured, was a good German.

Pierre walks late at night several times a week, and with care and caution he twice encountered Gerhard Heller, who was not in uniform, once on Rue Valette and later on Rue Clotaire, near the Panthéon. Pierre did not know that he was an enemy officer, and said he was not concerned when they continued to walk and talk until dawn.

The good enemy officer studied literature at Berlin and Toulouse, and was fluent in several languages. Many walks and three weeks later they decided to continue their literary conversation at Les Deux Magots. Heller was very generous and introduced Pierre to several authors, and later revealed that he had approved the publication of the play *Huis Clos*, translated as private, or closed doors, and the extraordinary novel *L'Étranger* by Albert Camus. Pierre realized only then that Gerhard Heller was an officer and censor for the Nazi Occupation.

Heller had many friends, poets, novelists, playwrights, artists, publishers, occupation flâneurs, and favor courtiers, and on one occasion he introduced Pierre to Jean-Paul Sartre and Ernst Jünger, the nationalist, enemy officer, and author of *Stahlgewittern*, *The Storm of Steel*, a memoir of his service in the First World War.

"Jünger was undeniably steely," said Pierre.

"Obviously risky," shouted Heap of Words.

Nika met a good enemy doctor who delivered black market food and horse bones for the mongrels and carried on with exotic jazz talk. Pierre walks and talks at night with an enemy censor who promotes literature, cuts favors, and secures theatre tickets. The fear and starvation continue, and the enemy literary censors are never reliable because they are the undeniable agents who deliver the momentary diversions of the fascist deception, vengeance, and summary executions carried out by the Nazi Occupation.

"Sorbonne relations," shouted Heap of Words.

Jean-Paul Sartre, the literary philosopher with puffy lips and an eye that wanders, was seated on a cane chair at Les Deux Magots, mostly at the cozy side of the author Simone de Beauvoir. Sartre was the author of the social torments in a room named hell in *Huis Clos*, the existential play that now comes to mind almost every day.

The eager theatre audience was crowded in narrow rows of seats, and there was no escape distance from the miseries of social burdens in the tidy scenes, counterwords, and wordy denials of three characters on stage. The end of natural motion and the descent of the dead to hell were not delivered in measures of rage, damnation, or purgatory, but rather through the eternal torment of the human gaze in an ordinary room with no mirrors, and with no escape from memory.

The play was the taunt of hell, caught in a hot theatre during the occupation with sweaty collaborators in the best seats, and with no *sortie* or exit door to liberty. The stage could have been a federal treaty reservation, and the only punishment after death was the nightmare of exposure and social reflection of the past in a deadend room with no exit, and three miserable people.

Nika responded to my occasional nudges about the meaning of a word, and whispered in my ear the necessary translations of the three characters, and there were no final ironic words or shout backs from the audience. Outside the theatre we were captives of an unbearable occupation of terror, betrayal, and death, and the hell fire of fascism was always nearby.

Mercifully *Huis Clos* was only one act, and the dead talk of the characters was concise, and reactive. No last lectures in the room of the dead, no tease, no intended irony, and no memorable touch, only the cues of dead memories and the steady gaze of others. The three characters were forced to face each other forever with no sense of time, day or night, and with no fire, redemption, or godly salvation ready in the wings.

Sartre created the scenes of the play at a small round table surrounded by occupation collaborators ready for the demonic duty of betrayal, and not one bell sounded on the statues of Les Deux Magots.

"The *Huis Clos* of Paris," shouted Heap of Words as we walked back to the shrouded gallery past Les Deux Magots on Boulevard Saint Germain. Sartre was not there, not in session at any back tables, and the doors were closed on time every night at the curfew hour ordered by demons of the Nazi Occupation.

The actual terror of the underworld was the constant betrayal of informers and torture by the Gestapo and Bonny Lafont Gang. The gruesome torture was staged across the River Seine, through the liberty trees to the chambers of the Gestapo at 74 Avenue Foch. The Bonny Lafont Gang torture rooms were located nearby at 93 Rue Lauriston.

Pierre Brossolette was a brilliant student, an astute political journalist for *Le Populaire* and other socialist newspapers, and owned with his wife, Gilberte, a literary bookstore, Librairie Universelle, located east of the Place du Trocadero at 89 Rue de la Pompe.

Nathan Crémieux once told me that Pierre Brossolette had worked closely with Léon Blum and was active in the Front Populaire, but we never met him at any public events or at the Galerie Crémieux. Françoise Crémieux was a research scholar and knew Brossolette from the résistance network of intellectuals at Musée de l'Homme. Nathan told me that Françoise had already left the museum by the time the network was betrayed, and because so many friends and associates were executed or imprisoned by the enemy, she escaped with her daughter Hélène to London and worked for France Libre and General Charles de Gaulle.

Agnès Humbert, an art historian, and Jean Cassou, an art conservator, persuaded Pierre Brossolette to serve in the Réseau du Musée de l'Homme, Museum of Man Network, one of the first résistance networks of scholars, art historians, curators, and scientists in Paris. Pierre was eager to unite the diverse résistance movements, along with Jean Moulin, in support of France Libre, and was on his way a few months ago to meet once again with Charles de Gaulle in London.

The Westland Lysander liaison flight was cancelled because of the winter weather, and then the boat was wrecked in the same storm. Pierre was rescued by the local résistance network near Pointe du Raz in Brittany, and then betrayed by an older woman in the community.

Pierre Brossolette was detained for several weeks at Rennes, and later when his code name *Brumaire* was recognized, he was moved to the *Si-*

cherheitsdienst, Counter Intelligence Security Services, located at 84 Avenue Foch, and tortured for three days by the Gestapo. Michel told me that during a short break in torture sessions he managed to leap from the window on the fifth floor, and died later in the hospital on 22 March 1944.

Seven résistance members out of twenty-eight in the Réseau du Musée de l'Homme, Boris Vildé, ethnographer and linguist; René Sénéchal, an accountant; Pierre Walter, photographer; Léon Maurice Nordmann, a lawyer; Anatole Lewitsky, anthropologist; Jules Andrieu, school director; and Georges Ithier-Lavergneau, interpreter, were executed by a Nazi firing squad on 23 February 1942 at Fort Mont Valérien in western Paris. Yvonne Oddon, Head Librarian of the Musée de l'Homme, Alice Simmonet, and Sylvette Leleu, automobile garage manager, were sent to concentration camps. Raymond Burgard, the literature professor, was beheaded at a prison in Germany. Pierre Brossolette was tortured and then committed suicide. Agnés Humbert, Jean Cassou, and Émile Muller were sentenced to prison.

The Milice carried out a revenge murder of Georges Mandel, a close associate of Léon Blum, and Paul Reynaud, who served as the last Prime Minister of the French Third Republic. Mandel, Blum, and Reynaud strongly opposed the armistice with the Germans. They were sent to a prison camp with other liberals and socialists, and yesterday, 7 July 1944, the Milice assassinated Georges Mandel near Forét de Fontainebleau during a strategic transfer to a prison near the Vichy Regime.

Violette Morris, the lesbian and athlete who dressed as a man and managed an automobile parts store, was a fascist collaborator and informer for the Gestapo. She lived on a houseboat on the River Seine, downriver and around the curve near Neuilly-sur-Seine. She had attended one of our celebrations several years ago on *Le Corbeau Bleu*, and we were warned at the time that she had betrayed old friends and enemies. The résistance assassinated Violette Morris on 26 April 1944 as she drove her Citroën Traction Avant on a narrow road in Normandy.

"Justice in motion," shouted Heap of Words.

The American Hospital of Paris was a casualty of war once again, and in spite of every setback, the medical care continued with distinction. Four years ago the nurses and loyal staff were devastated over the suicide of a brilliant surgeon, Doctor Thierry de Martel, on the first morning of the

Nazi Occupation of Paris. He was a medical officer in the First World War, and never recovered from the death of his son in combat. Friday, 14 June 1940. Doctor de Martel was found dead at his apartment on 18 Rue Weber with a syringe of strychnine. He decided not to continue living for even one day in the Nazi Occupation of Paris.

Earlier that year Doctor Charles Bove returned to the United States, and the senior surgeon and surly veteran of the First World War, Doctor Edmund Gros, was mentally handicapped and unable to practice medicine. Then early on Thursday, 25 May 1944, two Milice agents invaded the hospital wards and arrested Doctor Sumner Jackson as he carried out his medical rounds and treatment of patients.

By Now saw the notorious Milice, dressed in black shirts and berets, park a black Citroën at the entrance of the hospital, and she immediately rushed to the wards to warn the doctor, but not in time, he had already been removed.

She watched the Milice agents force Doctor Jackson into the car and speed away through the arch. By Now warned the members of the Goélette Frégate, the résistance network with a schooner and warship as a code name, at the hospital, and then quickly removed her white uniform, gathered her belongings, and rushed to several secure apartments to alert the downed airmen and others waiting for travel documents and contacts to escape to the south and over the mountains to Spain.

By Now related scenes from a perfect visual memory. She always provided the essential details of an event that others could only generalize, and sometimes she was teased, of course, at the point of detail boredom. This time we demanded more details than she could provide, partly because she was worried about betrayal and had hurried to leave the hospital. We worried too about betrayal as she related the hesitant responses of other members of the résistance group in the hospital and at secure apartments.

Doctor Jackson, his wife, Toquette, and son, Phillip, deserved every detail she could imagine. Yet, even with more precise information there was no reasonable way for the crew to intervene, short of a gangster movie shoot out with the Milice and Gestapo.

Pierre was ready to ride past the rented apartment of Doctor Jackson on the bicycle with Pig Ears and Panzéra in the box as a disguise. He wore a beret and pedaled to the apartment at 11 Avenue Foch, one of the most dangerous avenues in the city, in the early afternoon. He saw nothing at the front of the house, and avoided gestures and eye contact with anyone near the houses commandeered by the Gestapo, especially the *Sicherheitsdienst* at 84 Avenue Foch.

Pierre stopped at the corner and noticed that there was a side entrance to the apartment at Rue de Traktir. Slowly he pedaled down the side street toward Avenue Victor Hugo. Pig Ears raised an ear when she saw Doctor Jackson in the back garden of the apartment with three Milice agents, but not Toquette or Phillip. Pierre circled back once more and noticed that the four men were smoking cigars.

Michel Laroux arranged to meet me early that Sunday at the nearby Cathédrale Notre Dame. We sat on a bench at the back, and the voice of the priest echoed between the pillars. I leaned closer and whispered my first concern about the scene of cigar smokers. Michel smiled, and explained that the Milice pretend to be friendly, and later the torture starts.

Michel had obtained more information about Doctor Jackson, mostly because many of his colleagues had been treated at the American Hospital of Paris. Doctor Jackson and his family were taken directly to Vichy. Phillip was separated from his parents and held at the headquarters of the Milice, the Petit Casino de Vichy. Sumner and Toquette were taken for interrogation at the Château des Brosses, a prison camp of the Vichy Regime. The Milice tactic was to interrogate the prisoners separately.

Michel leaned closer, and whispered that it was very urgent for By Now and Prometheus to leave as soon as they obtained identity papers and contacts to travel around the checkpoints and enemy soldiers. They did not hesitate, and prepared for a speedy late night departure.

Michel arrived two days later at the gallery, and we were introduced to Madame Promesse, the résistance contact agent with a code name. She was older and seasoned, and seemed rather bored, but in minutes she firmly described the rules of travel, fast, determined, silent, and there would be no chitchat or hand holding on the way to Sanary-sur-Mer.

"Promesse is my kind of agent," said By Now.

They were gone at midnight, and we were informed later that they had arrived safely at Villa Penina. Nathan Crémieux must have contacted a local résistance network to deliver food to the exiles. By Now and Prometheus were told to stay close to the house, not visit any markets, or walk near the harbor at night because some eager informer might report them as enemy spies. The nurse and genial raconteur were too obvious in public places. Madame Promesse must have wagged her fingers and warned them never to linger anywhere, especially on the beaches, or to walk together near the Baie de Bandol.

42

JARDIN DE GUERRE

Saturday, 19 August 1944

The French Forces of the Interior, Forces Françaises de l'Intérieur, and the great coalition of discrete résistance networks started the insurrection today with barricades on strategic boulevards, and strategic armed attacks to liberate Paris. Nazi soldiers at the same time established defensive positions in Jardin de Luxembourg, Porte Maillot, Jardin des Tuileries, Arc de Triomphe, École Militaire, Hôtel Majestic, Place de la République, Place de la Nation, Place de la Concorde, and Gare de Lyon.

"Jardin de Guerre," shouted Heap of Words.

"The liberty trees are not secure," said Pierre.

"The barge is in a battle zone," said Nika.

General Charles de Gaulle was ready to march down the Avenue des Champs-Élysées, and honor the memory of loyal soldiers at the Tomb of the Unknown Soldier and the Arc de Triomphe. Maréchal Philippe Pétain was disgraced and never ready to revise the course of his complicity with the enemy occupation, or concede any responsibility for the betrayal of cultural ethos and democratic governance of the French Third Republic.

Pierre Chaisson heard the first radio broadcast by Charles de Gaulle from London on 18 June 1940, and was reassured by his sincere words that France was not alone and that the great flame of national résistance would never be extinguished, no matter what happens.

Maréchal Pétain had broadcast his first message on radio one day earlier, an unsure collusion with the enemy and pathetic praise of honor and homely traditions. The past gallantry of an old soldier from an earlier war does not lessen the treason of capitulation. His words were scanty, never memorable, not then, not ever, and his comments were more evasive last April when he visited Paris for the first time since the Nazi Occupation.

Maréchal Pétain, the weary military officer with rows of brag ribbons, including the Légion d'Honneur, leaned forward to launch his whiny voice

from the balcony of the Hôtel de Ville, the City Hall of Paris. Pétain might
have raised his voice to honor the cause of national unity and the French
Third Republic. Surely he was aware that the Third Reich would never
last to rule Europe. The old warrior could have easily reversed his pious
revisions, *travail, famille, partie*, the fascist conversions of *liberté, égalité,
fraternité*, but instead he wallowed in the cheers of thousands of hungry
citizens who later sang "La Marseillaise" for the first time at a huge public
event.

Porte de la Chapelle in northern Paris was heavily bombed on 21 April
1944. The next day *Le Matin* reported with a banner headline, "Nouveau
bombardement de Paris par les terroristes anglo-américains," New Bombing of Paris by the Anglo-American Terrorists. The targets were railroad
yards, and the censored newspapers reported that the destruction caused
the death of more than six hundred citizens, and that more than four hundred were wounded.

The tragic news reports of the civilian casualties caused by more than a
hundred aircraft, mostly bombers, prompted Maréchal Pétain to attend a
memorial service for the victims at the Cathédrale Notre Dame de Paris.

Pig Ears raised her head and pranced in circles, and the other mongrels
moaned in the gallery when they heard the bombs explode in the distance
that night, and obviously we were worried about casualties; but we could
not believe that American and British bombers would deliberately attack
civilians in Paris.

Five days later crowds of people gathered outside the Cathédrale on the
Parvis Notre Dame, and we learned that Maréchal Pétain had arrived at
the service for the dead and wounded. Later, at the end of the memorial,
his admirers praised the old warrior and shouted out, *Vive le Maréchal*. We
were part of the slow sway of the crowd, thousands of citizens that moved
slowly across the Pont d'Arcole to the Courtyard of the Hôtel de Ville.
The whine and waver of the old political warrior was barely audible, but
together we managed to mock his short homily later at the gallery.

Nika translated several phrases, and Heap of Words mocked the tone
and tedious waver of the maréchal of collusions, "Today, this is my first
visit with you, meeting with you."

Maréchal Pétain teased the eager audience with a salute, and never
mentioned the obvious burdens and starvation under the Nazi Occupa-

tion. Rather, his patter from the balcony was to collaborate, and of course, "maintain a correct and loyal attitude toward the occupying troops." Once again, he was obtuse with vanity.

One by one our crew repeated the faint nasal waver of mundane words several times to enhance the pleasure of mockery. "Hope I will be able to return to Paris, and with no reason to oblige or warn my jailers, I will come without them, and we would be at ease together." The audience did not hesitate to favor the moment with "La Marseillaise," *Allons enfants de la Patrie*, Arise, Children of the Fatherland, *Le jour de gloire est arrivé*, The day of glory has arrived.

The newspapers were censored and published banner headlines with propaganda stories about Anglo-American soldiers defeated on the beaches of Normandy, enemy air force terrorists, the great defense of the Wehrmacht, and the false victory of the Japanese in the Mariana Islands, but not a single word was published in *Le Matin* about the massacre of more than six hundred citizens of Oradour-sur-Glane near Limoges on 10 June 1944 by the Waffen SS Panzer Division *Das Reich* four days after the invasion of Normandy.

Many of the citizens were herded into the church and burned alive. Only résistance newspapers published stories about the enemy atrocities, and the previous day the same savage *Das Reich* band of soldiers carried out a massacre of more citizens, and hanged more than ninety men in Tulle, about seventy miles southeast of Oradour-sur-Glane.

One of the first reports on the torture and massacre carried out by young soldiers of *Das Reich* was published in a special edition of *Les Lettres Françaises*, French Letters, with the title, "Sur les ruines de la morale, Oradour-sur-Glane," On the Ruins of Morality. *Les Lettres Françaises* was a literary journal of the résistance founded three years ago by Jacques Decour, a novelist and teacher, and Jean Paulhan, publisher of *Nouvelle Revue Française*. The literary journal named and denounced the traitors of the mass murders of the ordinary and unarmed citizens at Oradour-sur-Glane.

Nika read out loud in translation the entire gruesome story of mass murder, the separation of men, women, and children, tortured, wounded, and mutilated, and every home and business burned to the ground. Women and children were burned alive in the church. Nothing remained at the end of the day but heaps of human ashes, the black burned bricks and stone foundations, automobile and truck frames, and the curved tram tracks through the ruins of the market town.

"Butcher the savages," shouted Heap of Words.

"Slowly sliced to death," said Pierre

"Much too easy," shouted Coyote.

"Poison, rash, suffocation," said Nika.

Aloysius had hidden several blocks of perfect birch at the gallery and started to carve two new hand puppets the moment he returned that afternoon from the Hôtel de Ville. At the end of the spectacle he walked ahead in silence, and as usual we heard nothing from my brother until he had completed the polished heads of the two puppets.

"Hallelujah," shouted Heap of Words.

Aloysius unveiled the marvelous two hand puppets named General Charles de Gaulle and Maréchal Philippe Pétain. The puppets stared at each other, moved back, jerked their heads from side to side, and then the two hand puppets turned away in silence.

Charles de Gaulle had a long face, thick, narrow nose, dark eyes and brows, a perfect moustache, and he wore a light brown coat with gold tabs on the shoulders, and a képi with two stars and a single braid of gold leaves. His hands were sculpted with wire.

"Hands of steel," shouted Heap of Words.

Maréchal Pétain had a sharp, pinched nose, and weary, beady blue eyes, a bushy white moustache, and he wore a gray coat with a high collar and brass buttons, and a képi with a red top and three bands of gold leaves. The crooked spectacles were made from rusty wire. On his chest he wore a huge simulated Légion d'Honneur with five double pointed stars. His hands were carved from a shrub.

The puppet talk between Charles de Gaulle and Maréchal Pétain was selected mostly from the transcriptions of radio speeches and newspaper stories. Pierre Chaisson was the translator of the bold voice of résistance and liberté in French and English. Nika translated the sly and whiny voice of the premier capitulator. The puppet show was staged on Friday, Bastille Day, 14 July 1944, and captured a very eager audience in the Courtyard of the Hôtel de Ville, City Hall of Paris.

Aloysius raised Charles de Gaulle on his left hand, and the puppet bowed and waved to the audience, and then on his right hand he slowly raised the head of Maréchal Pétain and gestured with two twiggy hands. The two puppets faced the audience, and avoided the sight of each other.

DE GAULLE: Whatever happens, the flame of the French résistance must not be extinguished and will not be extinguished.

PÉTAIN: I have grave things to tell you.

DE GAULLE: France is not lost. The very factors that brought about our defeat may one day lead us to victory.

PÉTAIN: An ill wind is rising in many regions of France.

DE GAULLE: The destiny of the world is at stake.

PÉTAIN: Disquiet is overtaking your minds.

DE GAULLE: The French refuse to accept either capitulation or slavery, for reasons of honor, common sense, and the higher interests of the country.

PÉTAIN: I have received the heritage of a wounded France. It is my duty to defend that heritage by maintaining your aspirations and your rights.

DE GAULLE: Soldiers of France, wherever you may be, arise!

PÉTAIN: In 1917 I put an end to mutiny. In 1940 I put an end to rout. Today I wish to save you from yourselves.

DE GAULLE: It is the duty of all Frenchmen who still bear arms to continue the struggle.

PÉTAIN: Cruel hours are always followed by difficult times.

DE GAULLE: We lost the battle of France through a faulty military system, mistakes in the conduct of operations, and the defeatist spirit shown by the government during recent battles.

PÉTAIN: Some feel themselves betrayed.

DE GAULLE: This war is not limited to our unfortunate country.

PÉTAIN: Some feel they are abandoned.

DE GAULLE: France does not stand alone. She is not isolated. Behind her is a vast empire, and she can make common cause with the British Empire, which commands the seas and is continuing the struggle.

PÉTAIN: We must be able to overcome a heavy heritage of distrust handed down by centuries of dissensions and quarrels.

DE GAULLE: Honor, common sense, and the interests of our country require that all free French, wherever they be, should continue to fight as best they may.

PÉTAIN: A long wait will be needed to overcome the résistance of all these opponents of the new order.

DE GAULLE: At the root of our civilization, there is the freedom of each person of thought, of belief, of opinion, of work, of leisure.

PÉTAIN: A nation like ours, forged in the crucible of races and passions, proud and courageous, as ready for sacrifice as for violence.

DE GAULLE: France has lost a battle, but France has not lost the war.

PÉTAIN: I will double the means of police action, whose discipline and loyalty should guarantee public order.

DE GAULLE: Let us be firm, pure, and faithful, at the end of our sorrow there is the greatest glory of the world, that of the men who did not give in.

PÉTAIN: The answers are in the confines of your conscience.

Charles de Gaulle turned toward the audience and boldly declared a second time two sentences in French and English that moved the crowd, *La France a perdu une bataille, mais la France n'a pas perdu la guerre,* France has lost a battle, but France has not lost the war. *A la base de notre civilisation, il y a la liberté de chacun dans sa pensée, ses croyances, ses opinions, son travail, ses loisirs,* At the root of our civilization, there is the freedom of each person of thought, of belief, of opinion, of work, of leisure.

"Great cause of liberty," shouted Heap of Words.

Maréchal Pétain ducked from the words, turned away from the audience, and was silent. The turns and ducks of fascists were familiar traits, and the custom of his command. A day later the sounds of armed résistance might have scared away the puppets and audience.

The French Forces of the Interior, an armed union of résistance movements came together under Charles de Gaulle to liberate France. The résistance posted broadsides that encouraged citizens to "struggle against the invader," and other posters declared that "victory is near," and revenge for the collaborators and traitors.

Charles de Gaulle called for the unity of hundreds of résistance networks around the country, and the courage of loyal units to establish a new government of liberation in Paris. The Free French Forces represented the government and scrupulously avoided riots and civil war between the communists and others, and astutely sidestepped the military liberation and peacetime occupation designed by General Dwight Eisenhower, Supreme Commander of Allied Forces in Western Europe.

43

Solemn Repose

Sunday, 27 August 1944

French soldiers arrived at the Hôtel de Ville close to midnight three days ago, the advanced guard of liberation, and the last summer of occupation misery, heartbreak, and dread ended with the marvelous deep sound of Le Bourdon Emmanuel, the great bell in the south tower of Cathédrale Notre Dame de Paris.

The steady thunder of the bell swayed in our bodies, and the gallery windows trembled. Pig Ears whined and leaped into my arms, ready to return to the barge and the easy waves of the River Seine. The other mongrels were on guard, sniffed the air, and raised their heads to celebrate the liberation with harmonic bays.

The enemy was almost chased out of the city, but the aftermath of the surrender was dangerous. No one dared to wait for the absolution of the fascists, collaborators, or the retreat of the Milice Française. The résistance casualties were high in the last few days of the insurrection and liberation. Nazi soldiers were entrenched in the Palais du Luxembourg, Palais Bourbon, and the École Militaire, and enemy tanks surrounded the Préfecture de Police ready to defend the Nazi Occupation.

The Milice marauders, fascist weasels, and traitors were disguised as loyal citizens, and prepared for a civil war. The cowards lingered in high windows, on rooftops, and in cracks and crevices on the boulevards, and fired at the crowds of elated civilians near the Place de la Concorde, Hôtel de Ville, and the Cathédrale Notre Dame.

The natural response was to run for cover, of course, but some citizens had enough of the fascist menace and ignored the gunfire at the Place de la Concorde. An older man who wore a tailored suit, bowler hat, and carried a fashionable cane, walked calmly and with dignity through the last rage of gunfire.

"The poise of certainty," said Pierre.

"Pretense of liberty," shouted Heap of Words.

Aloysius rescued two shabby Guignol hand puppets last month at a street market. He freshened their faces and decorated the chest of each puppet with huge, red, white, and blue rosettes. The Guignols pointed and we followed over the Pont de l'Archevêché with hundreds of citizens to the Parvis Notre Dame.

"Vive la France," shouted the first Guignol.

"Vive Charles de Gaulle," said Coyote.

"Vive Général Leclerc," said Pierre.

"Vive la liberté," shouted the other Guignol.

The French Nation Radio, Radiodiffusion de la Nation Française, was taken over by the résistance and started to broadcast early in the evening, 18 August 1944, for the first time after four years of wretched collaboration propaganda from 37 Rue de l'Université. Pierre Chaisson learned that the fascists and enemy soldiers had abandoned the national radio station. We heard the announcements of liberation on the radio console in the gallery.

Pierre Crénesse, a radio journalist, made the first very brief broadcast, "Broadcasting of the French Nation," and then played mostly recorded music. News reports of the insurrection were broadcast on Tuesday, 22 August 1944, and every word emboldened the résistance and weary citizens of Paris. The station announced, "The time has come to definitively drive the enemy out of the capital, and the whole population must rise up, set up barricades, boldly taking action, and finish the invader." Later that night the same message was repeated several times an hour.

Pierre Schaeffer, composer and producer, announced two days later and the night before the formal surrender of Dietrich von Choltitz and the end of the Nazi Occupation, "May the priests ring the bells of the churches." Le Bourdon Emmanuel bell at the Cathédrale Notre Dame started just before midnight, and for several hours there was a great liberation concert of church bells throughout Paris.

"The resurrection," shouted Heap of Words.

Nazi soldiers were insecure since the union strikes and recent declaration of insurrection, and hidden snipers were ready to shoot citizens on the street. Nazi tanks fired at the Préfecture de Police, and we heard explosions and the sharp sounds of gunshots every night.

Pierre Chaisson, who braved the walk to and from the Sorbonne, told a story about a young woman in a bright red dress who rode her bicycle on Rue de Vaugirard near the Théâtre de l'Odéon, and with a small pistol shot at the tires of an enemy armored car, an ecstatic moment of résistance, and then vanished from the scene. The soldiers overreacted with vengeance, as always, and with automatic weapons randomly fired at the apartment building near the Jardin du Luxembourg.

Countess Clara de Chambrun survived the heavy machine gun fire in her apartment, but the bullets shattered the windows, pierced books in a library, and destroyed art in the futile counterattack. Enemy soldiers were betrayed, abandoned, frightened by the insurrection and the force of the résistance, and ready to carry out the random murder of citizens and then escape to Germany.

General Philippe Leclerc arrived with the Deuxième Division Blindée on Friday, 25 August 1944, and later that day Dietrich von Choltitz, the pudgy military governor of Paris, a newcomer to the occupation, saved Paris. The Führer ordered him to totally destroy the city, but instead he surrendered to Free French Forces at the hotel Le Meurice. Von Choltitz signed the formal documents of surrender, and ended the depraved Nazi Occupation of Paris.

General Charles de Gaulle arrived in Paris late that afternoon at the Hôtel de Ville, and secured the nation as President of the Provisional Government of the French Republic, and immediately appointed loyal ministers, a strategic maneuver to prevent a communist takeover and threat of civil war. Later he gave a heartfelt speech to the citizens who had gathered around the Hôtel de Ville. Nika and Pierre translated a few sections of the speech, and we learned later that the entire speech was broadcast live on Radiodiffusion de la Nation Française.

No, we will never hide our emotions, because these are the moments that reach beyond our lives. Paris is outraged, Paris is broken, Paris is martyred, and Paris is liberated with the French, as the real France, and the eternal France.

France returns to her home in Paris. She returns bloodied but resolute, and she returns enlightened with a great lesson, but more certain that ever of the national rights and duties.

The war demands national unity, and we live in the greatest

hour of our history. We have nothing more to show the world than
ourselves, and the worth of France. Vive la France.

Yesterday, 26 August 1944, Charles de Gaulle placed two floral wreaths
on the Tomb of the Unknown Soldier, one circular, and the second in the
shape of the Croix de Lorraine, the emblem of the Free French Forces.

ICI

REPOSE

UN SOLDAT

FRANÇAIS

MORT

POUR LA PATRIE

1914–1918

De Gaulle and Leclerc saluted the memorial of solemn repose, and
thousands of free citizens surrounded the Place de l'Étoile that hot and
humid day to honor the memory of the loyal soldiers who had served in the
military and died for France. The huge flags of France, the United States,
Britain, Soviet Union, and the Republic of China waved under the great
arch of the Arc de Triomphe.

The Republican Guard, Garde Républicaine, was present for the first
time in four years, two columns on each side of the Tomb of the Unknown
Soldier. The ceremonial cavalry uniforms were spectacular, high black
boots with spurs, silver helmets decorated with red rooster plumes, and
the guards were ordered to *present saber*. Later that afternoon the Horse
Guards trooped across the Pont de la Concorde from the Palais Bourbon,
a spectacular cavalry procession.

De Gaulle, Leclerc, and other senior officers marched abreast down
Avenue des Champs-Élysées, and thousands of people gathered to salute
the great general for the first time. Most citizens had only seen pictures
of the general, and never forgot his steady radio voice with messages of
courage and resolve from London. He towered over the other officers, and
saluted the crowds on both sides of the avenue. A woman rushed forward
with a posy of flowers, and a man raised a baby overhead to honor the

trust of liberation and the promise of the earnest general to secure and reinstated the French Third Republic.

Nika wore an enormous rosette, and was nominated our escort for the day. She calculated the time, motion, and distance of the military delegation, and we marched at the left side and slightly behind the gang of generals from the Arc de Triomphe to the Place de la Concorde. The liberation parade moved much slower than a casual walk and lasted for more than an hour.

Nika was one the few women in the liberation parade, and yet thousands of women served in various résistance movements as nurses, couriers, organizers, and fighters who carried out armed assaults against enemy soldiers during the liberation of Paris.

Most of the marchers were in uniform, white and manly, except for Georges Dukson, who was the only black face in the parade. He marched just ahead of us and close to General de Gaulle and two men who were dressed in suits and neckties, Alexandre Parodi, a member of the Council of State, and Georges Bidault, leader of the Conseil National de la Résistance, the National Council of the Résistance.

The parade was fully underway and a short distance from the Arc de Triomphe, when soldiers pushed George Dukson aside and ordered him out of the parade. Dukson marched with his arm in a sling, and refused to leave. We heard later that he was recovering from a gunshot wounded in a battle with enemy soldiers a few days earlier. He moved ahead of the white soldiers, and continued his pace in the parade to Place de la Concorde.

Heap of Words noticed Charles Anderson and his wife, Eugénie, standing in the crowd between the Embassy of the United States and the Hôtel de Crillon, once headquarters of the Wehrmacht. Charles wore a dark blue coat with military ribbons, red trousers, and a képi, the uniform of the French Foreign Legion. Naturally we saluted our friend and shared stories of the liberation as the columns of French, American, and British soldiers marched past the Place de la Concorde.

Charles revealed the obvious, that only white soldiers were mustered to march in the liberation parade. The black soldiers were removed from the Deuxième Division Blindée, and the Free French Forces.

The Nazis had surrendered, the antisemites and fascists were over-

thrown, but the racists and separatists had already revised the great promise of *liberté, égalité, fraternité,* and removed the presence of black combat
soldiers. The rumors of the partition and racial disunion were cruel, heartless, and unbearably true on that glorious day of the liberation of Paris.

Magazine and newspaper photographers captured the scenes of the
parade from every angle, and the cameramen for the military were perched
on jeeps. Thousands of citizens carried cameras to record forever a concocted racial history of the Deuxième Division Blindée and Free French
Forces. The history of the war and liberation was made white, always
white, and in the same way natives were removed to reservations and the
courage and cultures of natives were reduced to curious traditions and an
absence in history.

General Charles de Gaulle insisted that Free French Forces would lead
the liberation celebration and parade down the Champs-Élysées to the
Place de la Concorde. The Supreme Allied Commander General Dwight
Eisenhower agreed that French soldiers could lead the liberation march,
but only if the soldiers were white, not black, as the rumors of exclusion
avowed, and racial hearsay at any celebration moves much faster than a
column of white soldiers.

General Eisenhower turned back the black soldiers, the most loyal and
valorous in military service, and denied black colonial soldiers the right
to be seen in the liberation parade. Georges Dukson, a wounded black
warrior of the résistance in Paris, was scorned and pushed aside during
the liberation parade.

"Whitey Dwighty," shouted Heap of Words.

"The race war never ends," shouted Aloysius.

"The Free French Forces were mostly the courageous soldiers from
colonial Senegal," said Pierre. "How could any officer disrespect the Tirailleurs Sénégalais who served with courage in the infantry, fought against
the Nazis in Italy, and liberated southern France, and now the presence
of these brave soldiers has been removed by racist generals, and denied a
rightful place in the military history of the liberation of Paris."

The First World War came to mind that afternoon as we pretended to
count the great white faces that marched in wide columns past the gates
of the Embassy of the United States. The constant face of a white liberation could only be celebrated in ironic stories, and we started with the

Harlem Hellfighters, or Black Rattlers, the black infantry regiment from New York City that served in the First World War. The black soldiers were segregated and denied combat duty in the American Expeditionary Forces, but they were accepted as honorable combat soldiers in the French Army. The Black Rattlers defeated the enemy with great valor in the Argonne and earned the French Croix de Guerre.

Major Dwight Eisenhower wore tight boots as the aide to General Douglas MacArthur twelve years ago, and never hesitated to carry out the cruel order to roust with tanks, tear gas, and infantry soldiers with fixed bayonets the thousands of war veterans from around the country who had served in the First World War. The Bonus Expeditionary Force was integrated, black, white, and native, and the honorable veterans gathered to demand a bonus for their service, but racial unity and the decent demand for a bonus bothered the military commanders, especially the heartless President Herbert Hoover.

Colonel James Forsyth ordered soldiers in the Seventh Cavalry Regiment to massacre hundreds of native women, children, and unarmed men at an encampment at Wounded Knee, South Dakota, on 26 December 1890. Forever a day of disgrace and national shame, but not in the minds of many politicians and military leaders who awarded the Medal of Honor to more than twenty cavalry soldiers who had murdered unarmed natives.

Eight years later the United States Third Infantry, a regiment composed mostly of immigrant soldiers, and with no desire to shoot at natives, lost the Battle of Sugar Point on Leech Lake in Minnesota. Racial and cultural dominance and military arrogance were the only plausible reasons for the crude and backward assault on natives that cold and rainy October in 1898. Seven soldiers were killed in action, and sixteen were wounded, but there were no native casualties. That tragic defeat has been deleted from the military archives, but the story of racial separatism remains forever in the memory of native families. Natives were rarely honored as strategic warriors in military histories, unless, of course, the natives were portrayed as ruthless savages who were defeated by the courageous cavalry.

The last ironic story we told to overcome the clumsy racial maneuvers of a white liberation was very familiar to Charles Anderson. Eugene Bullard was the son of a slave from Columbus, Georgia. He had served honorably in the Foreign Legion, and then became the first black aviator in the Escadrille de La Fayette, the French Air Service. Bullard earned the French Croix de Guerre and Légion d'Honneur, but when the United States decided to enter the First World War, Doctor Edmund Gros, the supreme racial separatist at the American Hospital of Paris, concocted a false medical report to deny the right of a decorated black pilot to serve in the Army Air Force.

General Charles de Gaulle boarded a fancy Hotchkiss convertible for the remainder of the liberation cavalcade to the Cathédrale Notre Dame. He saluted with both hands, and escaped another menace when a sniper started shooting at citizens on the Place de la Concorde. We waited out of the line of fire near the Hôtel de Crillon, and recounted a similar situation about ten years ago when we escaped from police gunfire near the entrance of the hotel during the attempted coup d'état by the fascists and royalists.

Nika continued as our escort of liberation with the natural security of a parade and the honor of our totemic associations. Shoulder to shoulder we moved together with the crowd down Rue de Rivoli toward the Cathédrale Notre Dame. The massive crowds of citizens blocked the roads and bridges, so the short service and ceremony had ended by the time we reached the courtyard and heard about another sniper that menaced the general and citizens on the Parvis Notre Dame.

This morning the Marché aux Oiseaux, the bird market, returned to Île de la Cité after several years, and for many citizens the return of the birds was the most reliable display of the liberation of Paris. The Sunday market of caged birds, doves, budgies, spirited lovebirds, canaries, perky finches, and rare cockatiels chirped, cheeped, warbled, and twittered the avian songs of liberty in a cage.

Most of the pigeons had been hunted and eaten during the occupation, and the wild birds were poisoned by the heavy smoke from petroleum fires that were intended to eliminate the supply of gasoline to the enemy soldiers.

Panzéra bayed a few bars of a lovely aria from the opera *Lucrezia* by Ottonino Respighi when we returned to the gallery. The other mongrels waited in a circle, and they created an original harmonic moan that was clearly critical of our absence the entire day, but the main aria was about the hunger of the mongrels. Pig Ears could not resist my gestures, and she leaped into my arms and licked my face.

The liberated crew moved back to the barge last night, and for the first time in four years my notebooks were free, carried in the open with no fear of censure or confiscation by enemy soldiers. We quickly packed the books, art, puppets, and meager food, and slowly and freely walked down Rue de la Bûcherie to Boulevard Saint Michel, turned with other light-hearted people onto Quai des Grands Augustins, and crossed the River Seine on the Pont Neuf. We chatted with children and joyous citizens gathered in the parapets, and then we walked along the Quai des Tuileries to our barge, renamed *La Péniche Léon Blum*, in honor of the great liberal scholar and socialist leader who had been sent last year to a Nazi concentration camp at Buchenwald near Weimar, Germany.

Nika painted the name *La Péniche Léon Blum* in large letters on the bow of the barge early this morning, and then we heard the glorious and moody piano music of Erik Satie. Together we gathered on the Pont de la Concorde near the piano barge, and shouted *Brava, Brava, Brava, Vive la France, Vive la Satie, Vive la Paris*, and *Vive l'Écharpe Bleue*.

The young woman in the blue scarf smiled, but never looked away from the piano keys. Obviously she survived the enemy occupation, and yesterday she returned to tune the piano; and this morning after four years of fear, torment, silence, and seclusion she played the poignant *Gymnopédies*, the elusive and poetic chords composed by Erik Satie. The grand concerts resumed today on the first Sunday morning of the liberation of Paris.

44

STANDBY SOLACE

Sunday, 3 September 1944

Native dream songs are visual memories of natural motion, the sway of totemic associations, and reveals of creation in the seasons, the tumble of summer clouds, the pitch of leaves on the plane trees, the tease of certainties and form in modern art, and this morning we heard the poetic come back of *liberté*, *égalité*, *fraternité* on the boulevards and quays, and a glorious liberation piano concert of Erik Satie on the Pont de la Concorde and the River Seine.

The enemy occupation ended last week, and citizens paraded with the colors of liberation, red, white, and blue, the flags of France, Britain, and the United States. The sense of triumph, elation, and standby solace turned overnight into crusades of vengeance, the execution of traitors, and communal humiliation, *épuration sauvage*, or the savage degradation of *collaboration horizontale*, sexual collaboration. Many women accused of sex and survival with the enemy were shaved on the street, and other women were paraded in public with swastikas painted on their bodies, branded as occupation scapegoats of rage and resentment.

The résistance leaders posted broadsides that warned citizens of reprisals for persecutions and executions, but the notice never turned back the fury against public scapegoats. The Provisional Government outlined two general forms of punishment, *épuration légale*, the legal purge, and judgment of unworthy citizens, *indignité nationale*, those who had acted against the democratic unity of France. The most serious penalty, or retributive justice, was *dégradation nationale*, the removal of status and civil rights.

The Vichy Regime traitors and fascist toadies were guilty of far more than indignity, disunity, and deception. The Milice Française and other criminals and collaborators were certain targets, and rightly so, but those connivers with means and connections had already escaped with the favors of enemy officers to Germany.

The heirs of the fur trade have counted seasons and wars for more than two centuries, and have endured the steady tease of time, menace, silence, truce, and peace. Now the heirs pause once more to honor the courage of warriors and to remember the thousands of loyal citizens who were tortured and executed for the courage of résistance against the Nazi Occupation and Vichy Regime.

"Jean Moulin," shouted Heap of Words.

"Benjamin Crémieux," said Pierre Chaisson.

"Pierre Brossolette," shouted Aloysius.

"Jacques Bonsergeant," said Nika.

"Raymond Burgard," shouted Coyote.

"Marcel Rayman," shouted Heap of Words.

"Lycée Buffon boys," said Nika.

"Groupe du Musée de l'Homme," said Pierre.

"Maurice Sarraut," shouted Olivier.

"Missak Manouchian," said Aloysius.

"Olga Bancic," shouted Heap of Words.

Missak Manouchian was a poet and communist who had survived the Ottoman Empire massacre of Armenians almost thirty years ago and moved to Paris. He founded the Manouchian Résistance Group with other refugees, part of the Francs Tireurs et Partisans Français, the armed movement of partisans who were members of the Communist Party. The résistance group carried out assassinations of enemy soldiers, derailed trains, destroyed enemy factories, and published covert newspapers in Romanian, Armenian, Spanish, Italian, and Yiddish.

Manouchian, Olga Bancic, Marcel Rayman, and twenty other résistance fighters were betrayed by a collaborator, arrested by the Milice, tortured, convicted of assassinations and sabotage at a show trial, and the men were executed at Fort Mont Valérien near Paris. Olga Bancic, the only woman in the group, was beheaded at a prison in Germany. Eleven of the refugee résistance fighters were Jews.

The children dream of dead fathers and sail miniature boats on the Grand Bassin Rond, and the migratory booted eagles circle the monuments in the Jardin des Tuileries. The flights of peace might last for a day, a decade, a century, but the native dream songs of liberty were heard forever in the stories of the heirs of the fur trade.

General Dietrich von Choltitz, the military governor of Paris, ended the misery and treachery of the occupation last Friday, 25 August 1944. He was captured by the Free Forces of France at the hotel Le Meurice, and signed the documents of surrender at the Préfecture de Police on Île de la Cité. Later that day Henri Rol-Tanguy, communist leader of the Forces Françaises de l'Intérieur, signed the same surrender of the Nazi Occupation of Paris. These signatures were essential to show that the enemy commander had surrendered to the French Free Forces and the French Forces of the Interior. Americans were not signatories of the surrender, and would have no authority to carry out a second allied occupation of France. The French *Tricolore* was raised for the first time in four years at the Hôtel de Ville and the Eiffel Tower.

The Nazi Occupation had ended, and the nasty flap, flap, flap of swastika banners and flags was removed from schools, public buildings, hotels, and boulevards. Enemy flags were trampled and burned, and the street signs of conquest were trashed along with other directions and public reminders of the enemy, but the actual bloody war continued against the Wehrmacht in Germany.

The communist newspaper *L'Humanité* published a banner headline, "La Bataille de France et de Paris Continue," The Battle for France and Paris Continues, on 21 August 1944, and with exclamations printed in a box on the right hand corner of the front page, "Vivent nos vaillants allies anglo-soviéto-américains!" Long Live Our Brave Allies, British, Soviets, and Americans! "Vive la république!" Long Live the Republic! "Vive notre grand Paris!" Long Live the Great City of Paris! "Vive la france libre, indépendante et démocratique!" Long Live the Liberty, Independence and Democracy of France!

The first German newspaper of the Nazi Occupation, *Pariser Zeitung*, published the last edition on 16 August 1944, the same day the dreaded Gestapo was ordered to withdraw from Paris. Newspapers were censored, of course, and most editors had collaborated with the enemy. The nasty *Le Pilori* expired overnight, and the fascist *Je Suis Partout*, mostly edited by antisemitic members of the Parti Populaire Français, stopped the presses when the Forces Françaises de l'Intérieur declared the insurrection, and the police and unions staged a general strike in Paris.

The editors of *L'Humanité* were apparently secure enough during the insurrection and before the actual surrender to calculate the absolute demise of the Nazi Occupation of Paris and the Vichy Regime.

Paris was liberated on 25 August 1944 and *L'Humanité* published two banner headlines, "L'armée française du général Leclerc fait son entrée dans Paris achevant de briser ses chaînes," The French Army of General Leclerc Made His Entrance to Paris and Finally Breaking the Shackles. The box in the right hand corner of the front page declared the obvious, "Seuls les traitres ont peur du peuple," Only the Traitors Fear the People.

Clearly the message was directed at the *collabos horizontales*, horizontal collaborators, and every other position, envious informers, savage gangs, the vicious Milice Française, La Carlingue, or the French Gestapo, and the overthrown traitors and toadies of the Vichy Regime. Maréchal Pétain, Pierre Laval, René Bousquet, Joseph Darnand, and many other deposed leaders of the fascist conspiracy would never outmaneuver the liberation of France. The notion of a civil war had ended when General Charles de Gaulle established the Provisional Government of the French Republic.

"The fascist thieves ran away," said Pierre. "But the communists stayed around with the résistance movements and continued to publish a free daily newspaper on a single page during the insurrection and liberation of Paris."

L'Humanité cost two francs, a franc a page on the day of liberation, 25 August 1944, but copies were free on the two days before and seven days after the surrender of the enemy and liberation of Paris.

The editors of *L'Humanité* were dedicated communists, and the editorial intrusions were mostly in the strange and evasive autocratic aura of Joseph Stalin. At the same time the name Jean Jaurès, the *fondateur*, was listed as the founder on the masthead of the newspaper, and that revealed a vital socialist dedication to the workers and labor unions that had confronted the editors of nationalist, fascist, and royalist newspapers published decades before the Nazi Occupation of Paris.

The Normandy invasion only three months ago was the great promise of liberation and sovereignty, the survival of blood, bones, poetry, and the return of democracy. The soldiers advanced slowly, and the casualties were much higher than the commanders had anticipated. Charles de Gaulle and the spirit of the résistance could not wait another day for the magisterial directives from the Supreme Allied Commander General Dwight Eisenhower to liberate Paris.

Jean Moulin was ordered by General Charles de Gaulle to unite the many résistance networks to be more effective as a force against the enemy occupation and corruption of the Vichy Regime. Moulin was arrested, brutally tortured for his silence, and then murdered last year by the notorious Klaus Barbie. No one believed that Moulin died on a slow train to a concentration camp.

Moulin was persuasive and participated in the first union, Mouvements Unis de la Résistance, and despite the intense singularity of some résistance networks, a coalition of political parties, communists, socialists, and others, trade unions, newspapers, and desperate veterans established the Conseil National de la Résistance, the National Council of the Resistance. Finally the council of résistance movements was recognized as the Forces Françaises de l'Intérieur, the French Forces of the Interior, and the leader of the united forces of résistance movements was the steadfast communist Henri Rol-Tanguy.

Albert Camus, the author of *L'Étranger*, the existential novel published two years ago, was the principal editor and writer for *Combat*, the résistance newspaper. We saw him a few times with his friends at the Café de Flore, but there was no casual way to interrupt his conversation only to ask him about existentialism. Camus might have shared a few critical thoughts about the play *Huis Clos* by Jean Paul Sartre. Nika translated selections from the editorial he published on the day of the liberation.

"As the bullets of *liberté* continue to whistle on the streets," wrote Camus on 25 August 1944 in *Combat*, "the cannons of liberation pass through the gates of Paris.

"This is the night of truth, the truth in arms, the truth in battle, the truth in power, after so many years with a bared chest. Truth is everywhere tonight.

"What gives our hearts peace, and gave peace to our comrades who died, is the forthcoming victory, and with no rebuke or reproach, or claim of our own."

Pig Ears steadied the blue tiller, and we moved with the natural motion of the River Seine. We were at home and secure on *La Péniche Léon Blum* for the first time in several years.

» 45 «

SHADOWS OF SHAME

Sunday, 8 October 1944

Generals, priests, ministers, deputies, and contenders honor the sacrifice
of loyal citizens, and distant politicians feign the tributes of the résistance
and liberation. The constant torments of fascism and the consequences
of collaboration, betrayal, and executions are never put right with political
maneuvers, literary promises, or churchy absolutions. The heirs of the fur
trade continue to heal the heart wounds of treachery with ironic stories of
the savage occupation.

The occupation predators of misery and murder left behind blood
stained mansions, a uniform stench in hotel rooms, bullet marks on statues,
antisemitic newspapers, black market restaurateurs, publishers and authors
who conspired with the enemy, vacant plinths, streetlamps and windows
painted blue, and hungry children with pockets packed with grass.

"The stains of silence," shouted Heap of Words.

"Shame in every mirror," said Nika.

This letter to the heirs of the fur trade is dedicated to the memory of a
distant relative, Jean-Baptiste Beaulieu, the village *forgeron*, or blacksmith
at Oradour-sur-Glane near Limoges. He was murdered with more than six
hundred residents and visitors on 10 June 1944, four days after the landing
of allied soldiers at Normandy.

"Jean-Baptiste Beaulieu was born on 22 December 1884 in Oradour,"
said Nathan. He was a respected citizen of the village, and held a grand
wedding when his son Camille married Solange Dupic.

Michel Laroux visited *La Péniche Léon Blum* for the first time since the
liberation. He celebrated the new name of the barge, and delivered the
great news that Nathan Crémieux survived his service in the Armée Juive
near Toulouse. His wife, Françoise, who had escaped to London and was
active in the exiled France Libre with General Charles de Gaulle, plans
to return next month with daughter, Hélène, to Paris.

Nathan was in Limoges and suggested that the barge crew gather at Oradour-sur-Glane, and then continue the journey to Sanary-sur-Mer. Michel said he would borrow the same Citroën van that we had traveled in four years ago, first on the road as a moving company, and later as a traveling puppet show. Olivier and Coyote realized that they must move out of the apartment, and decided to stay behind as guardians of *La Péniche Léon Blum* with the five mongrels.

Michel arrived very early last Tuesday and drove south through Orléans, Vierzon, Chateauroux, and through several small villages near Limoges. Nathan told us to park and wait at the south end of the village near the bridge over the River Glane. The river was somber that afternoon, and the once radiant trees were in mourning. The ghastly stench of burned bodies remained in the air near the ruins of the village.

"Dream songs of the dead," said Pierre.

"Children in the clouds," said Nika.

The national railway system had not yet returned to regular service, and there were other serious reasons that Nathan wanted to meet the crew at Oradour-sur-Glane and continue to Sanary-sur-Mer. He wanted me to write letters to the heirs of the fur trade that were emotive, descriptive, and particular, especially about the massacre of the village. Nathan announced at the same time that the old Galerie Crémieux would open later this month with a new name, Galerie de la Danse des Esprits, the Galerie Ghost Dance.

Nathan had been active in the Armée Juive for more than two years, and we assumed that he would reveal something at last about the résistance maneuvers. He sidestepped every question that involved the Maquis or any other networks around Limoges, and avoided references to his duties or experiences with the Armée Juive and other armed partisans of the résistance.

Nathan suddenly changed the subject and declared, "Your collection of letters will be the first book published by the gallery after the occupation." My first response was silence, and then surprise that he would choose the village of a massacre to announce the publication of my letters to the heirs of the fur trade.

"Salutes and solace," said Aloysius.

"Totemic miseries," shouted Heap of Words.

Nathan was anxious and easily distracted as we walked toward the village, and then he revealed that enemy soldiers had arrived at the very same time of day, early afternoon, and from the same direction on Saturday, 10 June 1944, a market day. Silence was necessary as we slowly entered the shadows of shame, the scenes of a massacre.

Nathan was our leader and wanted us to witness the ruins of the mass murder of unarmed citizens by Der Führer regiment of the Waffen SS *Das Reich* Panzer Division. He emphasized several times that afternoon that résistance movements were in the general area, but never actually present or active in Oradour. The Maquis and Maquisards were armed fighters who carried out the sabotage of enemy soldiers, installations, railroads, and communication in the Limousin region, but never carried out sorties in or near the village of Oradour-sur-Glane.

Slowly we followed the steel tracks of the tram from Limoges to Oradour and Saint Junien. Line three once ran five times a day through the village, and we walked in the shadows of eternal agony and shame as witnesses only four months after the massacre.

Even the shadows were dead, buried in the charred ruins, and every structure in the village, restaurants, hotels, schools, businesses, and the church, were destroyed by the gruesome fury of enemy soldiers, and with no cause but evil and savagery.

The burned frames of automobiles and trucks were parked forever around the village. Only the row of concrete and steel poles, the overhead electrical wires of the tram, and the mission cross at the church were intact, an eerie scene of silence, the misery of absence, and not a single bird flew near the village. The stench of burned bodies was carried on the wind for several miles.

The ruins of the stone church were on the left as we walked into the village, and on the right there were two schools, École Enfantine and École des Réfugiés, for children and refugees. Around the turn on the left was another school, and on the right the Boulangerie, and further down the street the Beaulieu forge and garage, and behind the building, a large fairgrounds. Nearby the Oak Tree of Liberty, *Le Chêne de la Liberté*, planted about a century ago, had survived the enemy fury.

Most of the buildings had collapsed from explosions and the intense heat of the fire, but some of the stone walls were standing; a doorway on the street revealed the charred ruins of personal property, a fork, an iron pan, the frame of a bicycle, and a Singer sewing machine. In another red brick and stone house there was a black metal bed frame, and outside charred pumps and machines, the frame of a wagon wheel, decorative gates, and a crushed miniature car.

Near the pathway to the Champ de Foire, the village fairgrounds or market place, and the Beaulieu forge and garage on the corner, there was a brass plate on a petrol pump that read, *Société Générale des Huiles de Pétrole* 3071. The men who had once used that pump were herded into the nearby garage, shot in the legs, and then burned alive by the soldiers.

"Puppets are dead here," said Aloysius.

"Dead memories," shouted Heap of Words.

"Absolute death of irony," said Nika.

Jean-Baptiste Beaulieu, the *forgeron*, was at work at his forge on Rue Émile Desourteaux, the main street, and his wife, Elise Mauveroux Beaulieu, was at home when enemy soldiers arrived shortly after *déjeuner* in the early afternoon. Camille Beaulieu, their son, the handsome policeman, and Solange Dupic were married last year and had moved away from Oradour. The soldiers murdered Jean Dupic and Marie Couty, the parents of Solange, and several other members of her family. Odette Couty was a school teacher who lived in Limoges and was murdered when she visited her parents that day in Oradour.

Pierre Poularaud and Gabrielle Faure were married twelve years ago, and their seven children, six girls, Andrée, Suzanne, Yvette, Simone, Odette, Danielle, and Pierre, there only son, were murdered by enemy soldiers. Gabrielle and the children were herded into the village church and burned to death.

French Jewish citizens, Loyalists in the Spanish Civil War, Alsatians, and other refugees were invited to live in Oradour-sur-Glane. Robert Pinède and his wife, Carmen Espinosa-Juanos, and his mother, Gabrielle Delvaille, lived in the Hôtel Avril, and were murdered in separate places by enemy soldiers. Jacqueline, Francine, and André Pinède, their three children, survived the massacre. They remained hidden under the stairs until the soldiers set fire to the hotel, and then escaped to a nearby chateau north of Oradour.

Robert Pinède once owned a tannery in Bayonne near Biarritz and the border with Spain. He moved to Oradour when he was forced to sell his company because he was a Jew. His identity card was stamped with the red word *Juive*, and the family always worried that the enemy soldiers might come for them because they were Jews. Not this time, the fascist and antisemitic soldiers were there that afternoon to massacre everyone, not only the Jews.

Roger Godfrin escaped from the school and survived the massacre. He heard the shouts of the soldiers and ran out the back door of the École des Réfugiés. His father, Arthur, mother, Georgette, sisters Marie-Jeanne, Pierrette, Josette, and younger brother Claude Godfrin were executed that afternoon as he hid until dark near the River Glane. The soldiers shot at the scared boy with red hair, but missed and instead killed a village dog. André Pinède was the only other school age child who escaped the massacre.

The men were separated from women and children, and executed by the soldiers. The bodies were burned at several locations in the village. The women and children were locked in the church, and the soldiers detonated an explosive. When the women rushed to the exit doors they were shot with machine guns, and the bodies of the women and children were burned. The roof of the church collapsed a few days later, and the church bell melted from the heat of the fire, but the altar was only charred. Two women and an infant escaped through a back window of the church, and they were shot, but one woman, badly wounded, hid in the garden and was rescued the next day. Elise Beaulieu, who was fifty years old, died in the church fire.

Jean-Baptiste Beaulieu was shot in the legs and burned alive with about thirty other men in his own garage. He was fifty-nine years old at the time of the massacre. The other men of the village and visitors were shot and burned in the Laudy garage, the Desourteaux garage, and in the Milord garage. The *lieux de supplices*, places of torment, were at the church and at several garages in the village, and became the *charniers*, or mass graves.

Aloysius was the first to weep, and then Nika and Heap of Words, and everyone wept as we moved closer to the altar and bowed in silence at the *lieu de supplice* in the ruins of the church, and later at the Beaulieu garage and forge, and at the other garages of the massacre.

Nathan was very perceptive to start our walk through the village at the same time that the enemy soldiers had arrived, about two in the afternoon, and then we paused at the *charniers*, mass graves, at the same time that enemy soldiers started shooting more than six hundred citizens.

At that grievous hour of agony and death in the church we became the solemn witnesses with the moral duty and rights of conscience to create heart stories in memory of the citizens who were tortured and murdered.

Nathan had obtained an official document about the massacre from a contact in the résistance movement near Limoges. The report was based on an investigation and prepared on 23 June 1944 by Félix Dufour, a policeman from the commune of Lapalisse, about twenty miles northeast of Vichy. Nika translated several sections from the report of the massacre.

Félix Dufour estimated that two hundred people were at the market village only for the day to shop and "visit their parents. There were several circumstances that increased the temporary population on 10 June 1944: First communion for children, vaccination, and distribution of tobacco. The first communion brought in numerous families and parents from far away.

"We were told that the inhabitants were gathered in the barns and machine gunned while sentries posted on the outskirts of the village shot at and pursued those fleeing. Nearly all the children of Oradour were in the church, those from the holiday camp and some women who had sought asylum.

"It was the Germans who conducted the collection of the bodies that had not been burned. The bodies were thrown into wells or gathered in piles and covered with quick lime. The Red Cross and especially the seminarians from Limoges took care to collect the charred remains, and an awful stench arose from the mass graves and filled the air throughout the countryside for many kilometers around.

"Generally speaking, the identification of the bodies was impossible. Only occasionally there was jewelry, or in the case of the Mayor of Oradour, his wallet was spared from the fire, that allowed identification of a few victims.

"Elsewhere the human remains were mixed with the other debris, and created the heaps of remains that were removed with a shovel. In the church the charred remains formed a layer twenty centimeters high. These remains of bones, carried in filled washtubs, were put in graves and a priest said prayers over them. One gets an idea of the condition of the collected remains when, after calculations, each washtub could hold the remains of fifty people."

"Traces of sorrow are forever in the clouds," said Pierre. "Never here in the black ruins, not in the names alone, or the *lieux de supplices*, or in the ghastly heaps of ashes and mass graves."

"Reason to never speak again," said Aloysius.

"Silence and shame," shouted Heap of Words.

Nathan revealed that Jews had not been separated, and were executed with the other citizens in the village church and garages. "Nothing mattered to the savage soldiers, nothing, and the mass murders included twelve Jews," said Nathan. Somehow he had obtained the names of every Jew murdered in Oradour.

We mourned in silence, and later that afternoon as we return to the truck, Nathan recited several times the twelve names of the dead Jews, a solemn chant as we crossed the River Glane. Joseph, Marla, and Serge Bergmann, Raymond Engiel, Gabrielle Delvaille, Sarah Jakobowicz, Joseph, Marla, Dora, and Simone Kanzler, and Robert and Carmen Pinède. Joseph Bergmann, the local hairdresser for the good citizens of Oradour-sur-Glane, was born in Budapest.

This letter to the heirs of the fur trade is a solemn chant that honors the dead at Oradour-sur-Glane, and the memory of millions of Jews and millions of Native Americans who were massacred in the name of racial dominion, fascism, and nationalism.

46

CLOWN OF SANARY

Thursday, 12 October 1944

Michel drove the Citroën van from Oradour-sur-Glane through Limoges, and south to Toulouse. Memory of the massacre and the massive shadows of shame could not be turned away. The stench of the deadly ruins lingered on our clothes and in the air that night.

Nathan reminded me that the Galerie Ghost Dance would publish my letters to the heirs of the fur trade. He insisted once again on the actual names and details of scenes in the letters, and then turned the conversation back to the massacre and misery of the Jews. "Jews were actually the founders of the Musée de l'Homme, and they created one of the first résistance networks at the very start of the Nazi Occupation of Paris."

Michel drove in silence for several hours that night, and the gentle air turned sweeter with the scent of moist autumn leaves. Nathan had scheduled a secret meeting in Toulouse, so we stayed in a shabby hotel, walked together on the dark streets, and before dawn the next day continued the drive east through Carcassone, Narbonne, and Montpellier, and at last the familiar road from Aix-en-Provence to Bandol and Sanary-sur-Mer.

General Charles de Gaulle, the provisional president, restored the confidence of the French Third Republic. Henri and André and other *mutilés de guerre* returned as fishers on the Quai des Tuileries. The soldiers of the liberation were honored, and casual citizens praised the turn of seasons, teased the Place de la Concorde pigeons, visited museums, and meandered without caution along the River Seine, the Arc de Triomphe, the Jardin des Tuileries, the bird market, and the Jardin du Luxembourg. Yet the deadly war was not over.

The Battle of Aachen was underway a few hundred miles to the east, a critical military advance on the western border of Germany. After two weeks of heavy combat on the Siegfried Line, the United States Army entered the ancient city of Aachen. The Wehrmacht lost more than five thousand dead and wounded in their own country, according to the radio reports, and the same count of enemy soldiers were captured.

"Germans dead at home," said Nathan.

Operation Overlord was the amphibious invasion on the beaches of Normandy, and about two months later, on Tuesday, 15 August 1944, Operation Dragoon was underway with a curious cavalry code name for the strategic military landing on the beaches of the Côte d'Azur at Saint Raphaël, Saint Tropez, and Cavalaire-sur-Mer.

United States aircraft had bombed enemy installations along the coast several times in the past few months, from the Côte d'Azur to Toulon and Marseille, and destroyed enemy munitions, storage facilities, and artillery batteries at La Cride and Portissol in Sanary. Some bombs were not accurate and destroyed several residential buildings on the Quai Marie Esménard in Sanary. At least five citizens were killed in the bomb raids, and the explosions shredded the majestic plane trees and shattered every window in the Hôtel de la Tour.

The Baie de Bandol was brilliant that afternoon, and the blue shimmer healed our mood and restored our humor as we drove slowly into Sanary-sur-Mer. The memories of the *lieux de supplices* in Oradour-sur-Glane almost retreated in the balmy breeze along the bay. The heart stories of the massacre were related later that night in the good company of Prometheus and By Now Beaulieu.

Michel turned into the driveway of Villa Penina, and our cousin and the raconteur of natural motion rushed out of the house with hands raised and wanted to know about the barge, the mongrels, and everyone in Paris. They departed in a hurry more than a year ago to avoid the suspicion and curse of collaborators, and the possibility of arrest when the fearsome Milice removed Doctor Sumner Jackson from the American Hospital of Paris.

By Now and Prometheus were cautious at first, and stayed away from public places in Sanary. They carried out every precaution to avoid the scrutiny of collaborators, but that manner lasted only about three weeks. Nathan was not surprised when he learned from contacts in the résistance that our cousin served as a covert nurse, and the raconteur collected and translated secret documents for the résistance movements. Their subversive duties were dangerous, of course, and they strategically avoided the more than three hundred enemy soldiers on duty in Sanary.

"The résistance needed a nurse," said By Now. "So my arrival was considered a double favor because every man wanted nursey care, and all the better with a heavy tease and native stories."

"At first the résistance men shouted, *infirmière indienne*, only for attention," said Prometheus. "By Now teased the older men with stories about the risky and erotic reservation Ice Woman."

"The younger résistance men were always ready to hear new versions of the Niinag Trickster stories," said By Now. "My stories were never as bold as the shaman stories about wild priests and nasty pricks, but mostly about how the trickster never seemed to get his parts to work, especially versions of the trickster whose *niinag* was so huge that he toppled over when it was on the rise."

Prometheus was never surprised when people pointed and commented on his height, and most children, and even some adults, were shied by his mere presence. Sometimes a boy would move closer and expand his chest. The raconteur was a gentle giant with no fear of fire, and judiciously used his altitude to create a contradiction of his obvious presence. He learned as a young raconteur to use his huge hands to gesture in small ways, a finger story, or tiny pretend pinches with white gloves, a slow walk with knees bent, and in that way mocked his own stature.

"Prometheus dressed as a clown in purple pantaloons, an orange vest with huge red buttons, and white gloves to entertain children and the *pêcheurs*, the fishermen, on the Place de la Tour with magical stories about heroic animals, fairies, butterflies, and a plump prince named Aubergine Violette," said By Now. "He did this once or twice a week for a few months, long enough for enemy soldiers to appreciate the comic play, and then moved closer to the Hôtel de la Tour and started a mime routine with fine finger movements as he danced in clown shoes."

"White glove spy," shouted Heap of Words.

"Once he mimed his comic way right into the salon of the hotel, and gestured to the soldiers long enough to report on the stored munitions," said By Now.

Prometheus was named the Clown of Sanary, an astute raconteur who entertained people in the cafés and on the quay near the dock. His presence as a peculiar entertainer was always expected, never a surprise, and in this way he performed as usual and gathered critical information about the enemy at the same time.

The Hôtel de la Tour on the Port of Sanary was used as a coastal rampart occupied by enemy soldiers, a cannon was mounted on the terrace, and munitions were stored in the salon of the hotel. Prometheus said the résistance networks transmitted the information that he collected about enemy positions and equipment to the Allied Forces.

Général Jean de Lattre de Tassigny commanded the Free French Forces, and together with the French Forces of the Interior, Forces Françaises de l'Intérieur, liberated Toulon, Sanary, and Marseille. The enemy was overcome in a few days and surrendered artillery emplacements at La Cride on the Bay of Portissol, and at the Hôtel de la Tour. Général Tassigny was given the nickname, *Le Roi Jean*, King John by the loyal combat soldiers in his command.

Prometheus told several stories about the deliverance of Sanary by the Régiment de Tirailleurs Sénégalais, the combat soldiers in the Free French Forces, the French Forces of the Interior, and résistance warriors who marched together in a liberation parade down the Quai Victor Hugo at the Port of Sanary on Sunday, 27 August 1944. The Sénégalais soldiers were honored for their gallantry that afternoon at a formal ceremony.

Michel Laroux reminded everyone that night about a combat unit of colonial Sénégalais soldiers that served with honor and courage in the Deuxième Division Blindée, Second Armored Division of the Free French Forces, commanded by Général Philippe Leclerc. The black soldiers were sidelined a few months before the liberation of Paris on 25 August 1944. The Sénégalais were denied the right to march abreast with white soldiers from the Arc de Triomphe to the Place de la Concorde. General Dwight Eisenhower, Supreme Commander of the Allied Expeditionary Forces made the racist decision and altered the actual history of the liberation of France.

"The Sénégalais were honored," said Nika.

"No Whitey Dwighty," shouted Heap of Words.

"Yes, and the city should have changed the name of the Quai Victor Hugo to the Quai Tirailleurs Sénégalais, or at least change the Place de la Tour to Place Sénégalais," said Prometheus.

"The Sénégalais soldiers were engaged as equals in the liberation," said Nathan. "That duty of engagement, an alliance in combat, counts more than parades, no matter the command and color of the soldiers."

"White soldiers, white statues," said Nika.

"Whitety Dwighty," shouted Heap of Words.

"Present in the memories and stories of soldiers, but forever absent in photographs and history," said Pierre. "Black soldiers from the colonies share the same absence as natives in the counterfeit histories of war and culture."

Romain Rolland eased my need for "reliable accounts and explanations for gruesome events when he wrote about alliances and illusions," said Prometheus. "He played out illusions, doubt, and despair with the pessimistic court of intelligence, the critical reveal of the delusions of history, and advanced the idea of optimism, or the spirit and will of desire that saved me as a raconteur."

"Rolland wrote that a good thinker is pessimistic of intelligence, and optimistic about the will or spirit," said Nathan.

"The mind creates stories, and at the same time cuts through the mirage of empires and the fantasy of fascism," said Prometheus. "My best stories create an engagement with the delusions of reality, the apparitions of the trompe l'oeil, and the spirit of imagination."

Nathan mentioned a review that Rolland wrote more than twenty years ago about pessimism, intelligence, and the confidence of the spirit in *La Sacrifice d'Abraham* by Raymond Lefebvre. Rolland considered the First World War novel, published a year after *Le feu, Under Fire*, by Henri Barbusse, an "intimate alliance" that "penetrates every illusion." The literary style and scenes of irony in the novel were more heartfelt to me than the stagey strains of torment and horror in war novels, such as *Three Soldiers* by John Dos Passos. Nathan told me later that Lefebvre was a communist and vanished in the Barents Sea on his way back from the Second World Congress of the Comintern in Moscow.

"Rolland honors résistance fighters with positive ideas of engagement," said Nathan. "For me, creative stories of the spirit, and vital communal memories of the names, places, and documents, changed the burden of trying to understand the cause of fascism, betrayal, and the massacre at Oradour-sur-Glane."

"Native heart stories," said Nika.

Rolland was a pacifist with a great spirit who evaded ideologies and carried out his résistance against the fascists and clerical nationalists of the Vichy Regime with creative literature.

"Rolland created a literary sense of pessimism or doubt that revealed courage, and at the same time, he wrote in a review that skepticism of intelligence penetrates every illusion, or perception," said Nathan.

Maréchal Pétain and his vicious gang of antisemites and conspirators had more than manners and the fascist turns of *travail, famille, partie,* labor, family, and homeland to worry about since the liberation of France.

47

SLEEVE STORIES

Sunday, 15 October 1944

By Now charmed the fishermen, and she was invited many times to sail on the *pointus*, the wooden fishing boats rounded on both ends. The fishermen set sail early in the morning, and returned to the Port of Sanary five or six hours later with the catch of the day, and sometimes netted the tasty sardines from the Mediterranean Sea.

By Now prepared *dorade royale*, gilthead bream for dinner, fresh from the *grand marché*, and the fish was served with aubergine, tomatoes, olive oil, mushrooms, turnips, butter glazed carrots, fresh baguette, and goat cheese from Provence.

Prometheus wore white gloves to serve the rosé wine, *Domaine de l'Olivette* from Bandol. The first salutes, as usual, were to native chance and natural motion. Yes, chance and the marvelous coincidence of our presence and survival with stories of favor, and the courage of résistance movements over the past four years of enemy cruelty, brutality, fascist betrayal, and executions by the Milice and Gestapo.

"Never silenced," shouted Prometheus.

"Never teased with nostalgia," said By Now.

"Jews served with honor," shouted Nathan. He raised a glass and continued with a celebration of the thousands of Jews who were active in résistance movements, and saluted the "Jews who were betrayed by collaborators, executed by the enemy, or removed to concentration camps, and the men, women, and children who were massacred on what should have been a community religious festival and market day at Oradour-sur-Glane."

"Benjamin Crémieux," was my shout of honorable names to remember that night. Salute the great literary scholar and editor who served in the résistance and was arrested, tortured, and sent to a concentration camp for no other crime than his love of literature and his confidence and courage as a Jew.

"Jews of the book," shouted Heap of Words.

"Natives forever of the book," shouted Pierre.

"Olga Bancic," shouted By Now. "She served in the armed Missak Manouchian Résistance group in Paris and was executed by the Nazis."

By Now drank several glasses of wine at dinner and then counted out the memories of four lovers. This was her night of liberty, gratitude, reveals, and tributes. "Only four, no more," she shouted, and then named each lover. "Pierre Légume Dumont, that wounded romancer scared away with stories of the Ice Woman, returned to his dear mother, a farm horse, and the vegetables of war."

"Smitten by a nurse," said Pierre Chaisson.

"Scary snow stories," shouted Heap of Words.

"William Hushka, an honorable veteran of the First World War, and my lover at the Bonus March was shot for no reason by the police, and died alone in the debris near the United States Capitol," said By Now. "I salute his gentle spirit, love, and great heart stories."

"Hushka lives forever in our memories, a generous veteran who shared his meager meal with my brother and me when we arrived that summer twelve years ago at the Bonus March in Washington," said Aloysius.

"Bugle calls," shouted Heap of Words.

"Doctor Sumner Jackson was my erotic sleeve lover, we never touched in any sexual way, but as a nurse on rounds with the doctor at the American Hospital of Paris, our coat sleeves grazed and elbows bumped over wounded soldiers, a touch of love that was not comparable."

"Long live Doctor Jackson," said Nathan.

"Sleeve stories," shouted Heap of Words.

"Prometheus is my greatest lover, and the marvelous raconteur in my dream songs," said By Now. She raised her glass, moved closer, and saluted her lover. He removed his white gloves, leaned over, and kissed our sublime cousin at least four times.

"By Now, my only nurse," said Prometheus.

"Long live By Nurse," shouted Heap of Words.

"Long live the pale rosé," said Pierre.

"Long live the loyal raconteur," said Nika.

Nathan raised his wine glass and saluted the memory of Romain Rolland, "For his spirit of buoyant stories and natural bravery."

Aloysius, the puppet master, was surprised when two new hand puppets were raised at the table after dinner and gestured for recognition.
Everyone burst into laughter, and my brother almost burst into tears. He
was downcast with the racial turns of the liberation, and sullen after our
visit to the ruins of Oradour-sur-Glane, but his spirit was healed when the
brilliant hand puppets wagged, shivered, preached, and teased at the end
of the dinner table.

The Aubergine Violette and the Rabbin Royale were hurriedly created
along with the dinner to tease Aloysius with tricky puppets. The head of
the trickster puppet was a hollow purple aubergine with tiny slits cut for
a mouth, and oval holes for eyes. The trickster wore a tea towel cape with
armholes. Under the cape was a stout carrot that rose as a *niinag*, or giant
penis.

The Rabbin Royale hand puppet was created with a threadbare black
sock packed with shredded newspaper, and the eyes, ears, and mouth of
the puppet were butter stains, a rushed construction of anything at hand
during the preparation of dinner. The rabbi trickster wore the torn sleeve
of a shirt, and with holes cut for a thumb and middle finger to gesture as
hands and arms.

Prometheus raised Rabbin Royale on his right hand, and the rabbi
bowed to everyone at the table, and bowed twice to Nathan. By Now
raised the Aubergine Violette, and the puppet pitched his head to the
sides, and then the two dinner characters embraced, a purple aubergine
with a curved stem for a cocked hat, and a discarded black sock, and
started the first hand puppet tease and talk show since the liberation of
Sanary-sur-Mer.

Nathan pointed at Rabbin Royale, threw back his hands, and laughed
no doubt over something familiar in the gestures of a sock as a hand puppet rabbi. Nika pushed her chair back for a full view of the play. Heap of
Words leaned forward and was ready to mock the hand puppets with his
own hand gestures.

By Now and Prometheus practiced only a few ideas, teases, and lines of
the hand puppets during the preparation of the dinner, back and forth in
the kitchen, and the rest of the puppet talk was creative and spontaneous.
Prometheus, of course, was a great raconteur and could easily create a
memorable story. The hand puppet head jerks, gestures, and quick re-

sponses of Rabbin Royale, and the ironic talk back were encouraged by the Aubergine Violette in the voice of By Now Rose Beaulieu.

AUBERGINE: Rabbis must be natural raconteurs.
RABBIN: More than ever tonight in Sanary.
AUBERGINE: Do your stories last overnight?
RABBIN: My stories are better than daydreams.
AUBERGINE: What was your first tease of sex?
RABBIN: Naturally and with two words.
AUBERGINE: Two words for sex with a hand puppet?
RABBIN: Night and day and up and down.
AUBERGINE: The rise of a *niinag* is always a surprise.
RABBIN: My stories are always ready to surprise.

The Aubergine Violette raised his giant *niinag* from under the tea towel and wagged the carrot erection in front of Rabbin Royale. Everybody raised a finger, two fingers, and more fingers to mock the jerky motions of the unstable penis as the trickster hand puppet touched the head and shoulders of everyone at the dinner table.

AUBERGINE: Sometimes my *niinag* and me topple over.
RABBIN: Sometimes big talkers topple over.
AUBERGINE: Adolf Hitler toppled over his salute.
RABBIN: Führers never survived the tease of puppets.
AUBERGINE: Göring was a decadent hand puppet.
RABBIN: Much too fat to ever see his *niinag* rise.
AUBERGINE: Basile creates puppets on the page.
RABBIN: Better in the book than on the cross.
AUBERGINE: Nathan frowns about the cross.
RABBIN: New fashions and Stations of the Cross.
AUBERGINE: Nathan hides natives in wooden crates.
RABBIN: Must be why natives tease the light of day.
AUBERGINE: Jews live forever in the book.
RABBIN: Jews and natives mingle in the book.
AUBERGINE: Natives are in the crates tonight because they might lose their way back to the Galerie Ghost Dance.

RABBIN: Nathan and Michel are masters of the crates.

AUBERGINE: Good reasons to be hand puppets tonight.

That night our humor was revived by two clumsy hand puppets. The tricky gestures and talk back honored the creative solidarity of raconteurs. When the sock head rabbi raised his head and mentioned two wise men, and when the trickster puppet in a tea towel closed with the declaration that there were good reasons to be puppets tonight, everyone laughed, and then we turned to silence. The moment of silence was the solace of close friends, and yet the war continued, but no longer in our stories.

Prometheus Postma was born on the North Sea and set his name in wet sand to tease the waves, an outsider in a world of treacherous empires, and as a raconteur he delivered the promise of creative stories to endure with irony the dead letters of fascism and conspirators.

Michel, Nathan, and the native crew could not resist his generous manner, ethereal gestures in white gloves, sense of irony at a time of the counts and furies of antisemitism, and his lofty pose four years ago on Rue de la République in Bandol. The raconteur leaned on a lamppost that early morning, and waited for a ride to liberty in California. He carried a metal suitcase with the curious catchwords printed on the side, *Célébrité de Rien*, Celebrity of Nothing. Prometheus was actually waiting that early morning to discover a native crew of hand puppet masters, a generous gallery owner, and a loyal friend and retired policeman on their way to Marseille.

48

MORNING STAR

Wednesday, 25 October 1944

The heirs of the fur trade endure with shame and remorse the colonial wars over beaver, marten, and mink. New France voyageurs and native perpetrators of peltry have waited centuries to hear the legion of honors for the sacrifice of totemic animals, or at least the sway of human and animal rights, but peace and liberty are declared in constitutional democracies.

"Silence of totemic tributes," said Aloysius.

New France secured a union of natives in the great cause and commerce of peltry, and missions of peace and continental liberty, but no colonial treaty could ever restore the natural motion and totemic associations with animals and birds that natives and our relations culled and ravaged in the centuries of the fur trade.

"Silk totems," shouted Heap of Words.

"Only a shaman could imagine the beaver saved by a silkworm, not by notables in the godly colonies, not nations, treaties, or totemic conscience of the native fur trade," said Aloysius. "The great peace was the ruin of totemic animals, and the tease and patois of beaver and bear only disguised the chance to escape the greedy voyageurs and the colonial irony of peace."

The Great Peace of Montréal and Treaty of Versailles were conventions of peace, and comparable now only as the covenants and détentes of nations to end the empire wars of supremacy. The Montréal peace treaty was endorsed by forty nations and sustained with native respect for more than sixty years in North America.

The Versailles treaty, first an armistice, and then the concessions and reparations composed by five colonial empires, Germany, France, the United States, Japan, and the British Empire, ended twenty years later with the Second World War, massacre of Jews and the Nazi Occupation of France.

"Treaty endgames," shouted Heap of Words.

"The Treaty of Paris was the end of the Great Peace of Montréal," said Pierre. "French Louisiana was handed over to the Kingdom of Great Britain, but the French had already given the territory to the Spanish, so the native Houma were divided by the Mississippi River, English manners and tea time on one side of the river, Spanish grandees, priests, and the merchants of gold on the other, and tricky catechism on both sides."

"Ten years later the Boston Tea Party and the Sons of Liberty were on the road to revolution," said Aloysius. "So, since the American Revolution natives have been tormented by wayward pioneers, puritans, and timber barons, served in six wars, and here we are with the heirs of the fur trade after the liberation of Paris."

"The Treaty of Versailles was terminated with deadly fascism, antisemitism, and vengeance," said Nathan. "The Nazis invaded Poland, and Britain and France declared war against Germany, and here we are with the native spirit of the Ghost Dance, the poignant memories of wounded and dead Jews, and the massacre at Oradour-sur-Glane."

"Generations of solace," said Nika.

"Mockery of good cheer," said Pierre.

More than a thousand natives were summoned by the Governor of New France Louis Hector de Callière to parley about peace night and day on the Saint Lawrence River near Montréal in August 1701, and after the courageous oratory of native leaders, La Grande Paix de Montréal was ratified by forty nations, Nouvelle France, Lac Supérieur Anishinaabe, Ojibwé, or Saulteurs, Abenaki, Potawatomi, Sauk, Kickapoo, Menominee, Ho Chunk, Cree, Meskwaki, and thirty other native nations delayed the colonial empire wars over the fur trade for more than sixty years in North America.

"Three generations of peace," said Nika.

"Totemic ruins," shouted Heap of Words.

The native dream songs and solace of totemic animals were never considered in the parleys of peace, and yet most of the native leaders used the totem marks of animals and birds as signatures on the peace treaty documents, and "every totemic animal was forsaken, an absence of native conscience, and sentenced to death by signatories of the Great Peace of Montréal," shouted Aloysius.

"Breach of totemic bonds," said Nika.

"Native deceit," shouted Heap of Words.

Chief Oubangué was the Anishinaabe, Saulteurs, or Ojibwé orator and leader who made the totemic mark of a Sandhill Crane on the actual treaty document. The word *waaban* in Anishinaabe means dawn or daybreak, and the word *gué* in French means a ford, or a place of crossing, and the native name can only be transcribed as *Waaban Gué*, a name of the Saulteurs, or the natives of the rapids. The Ojibwé orator wore a red feather crown, a costume with no sense of totemic shame, and the beaver, fox, and marten were sacrificed for another sixty years.

Chief Waaban Gué and La Grande Paix de Montréal were just two of the native stories we related last week on the drive back to Paris. Complicated stories of native virtues and totemic custody were necessary on the long journey because the truck was packed with eight huge crates of native art, and nine passengers crowded in two rows and between the crates. Nathan deserved the front seat, but he generously gave the space to Prometheus to extend his long legs and giant feet.

Nathan reminded the crew of the ironic Enemy Way ceremonies eleven years ago at the Galerie Crémieux. That last union of harmony was staged at the gallery to ridicule the birthday of Adolf Hitler, on 20 April 1933. The taunt of despots and fascist newspapers had overturned any cultural or political sense of balance, ethos, or natural motion in the world. Führer stories and mockery of the barbaric enemy that afternoon became a parody that simulated the memory of cultural balance and the natural motion of the Enemy Way.

"Salutes of mockery," shouted Heap of Words.

"Enemy Way satires," said Pierre.

By Now and Prometheus related that they heard the murmurs of native spirits coming from the crates that were stored at Villa Penina in Sanary, and for that reason alone each crate was opened with care in the gallery, and nothing was removed for two days. At dawn on the third day the display cabinets had been cleaned and restored, and native pottery, carvings, and art objects were mounted in the cases and on the shelves of the new Galerie Ghost Dance.

Nathan envisioned a new gallery display of native art, as the objects were placed in relation to others in the cases, rather than separated as cultural or commercial products. The Horse Dance Sticks, ledger art, clay figures, pueblo pottery, stone and turquoise jewelry, natural dyed blankets, and other native objects were presented as interrelated in the cases. The native art was not set apart to face only the viewer or spectator. The Horse Dance Sticks faced ceremonial clay pueblo figures, and a scene from the Sand Creek Massacre by Howling Wolf, the Southern Cheyenne ledger artist, was surrounded with turquoise and folded blankets.

"Native similitude," shouted Heap of Words.

Most of the people who visited the gallery in the past few days were naturally cautious about money because of the unsteady currency. Very few people could afford to buy native art without the sacrifice of food, fuel, and winter clothes. Poor people, the quiet people with raggedy coats and tattered shoes, returned several times to float in the muted light of a silent and secure place with five sacred shirts of the Ghost Dance. The natural motion of the ghost shirts was a spiritual dance that touched on memories of the dead and healed the heart.

The Ghost Dance shirts were evocative and the public responses melancholy. The display room walls and ceiling were painted black. The five shirts were mounted on wire mesh forms, and suspended from the ceiling on single strands of thin wire. The special area at the back of the gallery was enclosed and darkened, and the five shirts floated in space and turned slowly in the muted light with the natural motion of native spirits.

"First Ghost Dance in Paris," said Aloysius.

"Return of the dead," shouted Heap of Words.

"The return of spirit stories," said Nathan.

The creative display of native art was very popular, and reviewers praised the Galerie de la Danse des Esprits, Galerie Ghost Dance, and the new native exhibition and extraordinary display of native shirts of the Ghost Dance. Nathan Crémieux was rightly honored in every review for his service in the Armée Juive, and his secure return to a new gallery in Paris.

Nathan convinced us that the shirts had been rescued from a dubious native art dealer in Germany. The five shirts were not marked with bullet holes, and we were certain the shirts would never be traded or sold. Four of the shirts were deer or antelope hides. The Lakota ghost shirt was cut from thick muslin, and the dancer had painted ravens and stars on the cloth, and decorated the front with two golden eagle feathers. The Cheyenne ghost shirt was made of antelope hide and decorated with a crescent,

the morning star, and crosses for protection. The three Arapaho ghost
shirts were decorated with a row of beads, painted ravens, crescents, and
a leather fringe on the sleeves. One Arapaho ghost shirt was marked with
handprints of ancient ghosts.

Nathan had acquired a Ghost Dance figure and two painted hand
drums at a desperation auction several years ago. The ceremonial doll was
decorated with bright blue beads and feathers and displayed with other
sacred objects in a glass case. The art objects faced each other, not the
viewer or spectator.

"New gaze of native art," said Nika.

Pig Ears was always on duty at the blue tiller, and she waited to leap
into my arms once the other loyal mongrels bumped and bayed over our
return to *La Péniche Léon Blum* last week. The deck was damp and cold
that autumn morning, but Coyote and Olivier had obtained enough coal
to heat the cabin, and that alone was a great celebration of the liberation.

Nathan named Coyote and Olivier the managers of the Galerie Ghost
Dance, and invited them to live in the back room under the *giiwedin
anang*, or the polestar painted on the ceiling. They were doubly grateful,
of course, and the native crew agreed they were the most worthy natives
to represent the gallery.

By Now and Prometheus renewed their associations with the résistance
networks in Paris, mourned the absence of Doctor Sumner Jackson and
those who were tortured and executed, and so many good friends who
were sent to concentration camps.

By Now and Prometheus moved into an apartment that had been used
as a secure space for downed airmen during the occupation, because *La
Péniche Léon Blum* was much too crowded and there was no sense of
privacy.

By Now volunteered to serve as a nurse at a free clinic near the Galerie
Ghost Dance. Prometheus established his public reputation as a brilliant
raconteur with fantastic and ironic stories about totemic animals, the résistance of hand puppets, and demons as the enemies of liberty. He told
stories two or three times a week at the Grand Bassin Rond in the Jardin
des Tuileries.

49

TOTEMIC CUSTODY

Thursday, 26 October 1944

The Galerie Ghost Dance was one of the first galleries and art salons to schedule exhibitions since the liberation two months ago, and the art connoisseurs were ready to appreciate and critique the work of painters in the past four years of the Nazi Occupation of Paris.

The Salon d'Automne opened on 6 October 1944 with more than sixty new paintings by Pablo Picasso, and on that occasion was named the Salon de la Liberation. The Salon had held the first exhibition of modernist art thirty years ago to confront the favors of conservative salons, and in the first few years held popular exhibitions of sculpture by Auguste Rodin, and paintings by Paul Cézanne, Henri Matisse, Paul Gauguin, Marcel Duchamp, and other innovative artists. Fauvist, modernist, expressionist, cubist, and surrealist painters became known at the singular salon. The recent exhibition of paintings and sculpture of Pablo Picasso was presented for the first time at the Salon d'Automne.

"Kahnweiler did not want to expose his cubist painters, Picasso, Georges Braque, and others to public ridicule at the eccentric Salon d'Automne," said Nathan. "So, the artists and paintings he represented were exhibited only at the Galerie Kahnweiler, and later at the Galerie Simon."

Picasso declared that he was a member of the French Communist Party, and *L'Humanité* celebrated the decision of the artist to join the party with a photograph on the top left corner of the communist newspaper on 5 October 1944, and with a three column wide headline:

PICASSO
A APPORTÉ SON ADHÉSION
Au Parti de la Renaissance Française

Nathan translated, "Picasso Gave His Support to the French Renaissance Party." The artist was sixty-three years old at the time, and was pictured that cold afternoon in a leather chair wearing a suit, overcoat, and holding a dark fedora between his knees.

"Hat in hand communist," shouted Pierre.

Picasso always seemed ready to leave the scene in photographs, especially in staged pictures with editors and politicians. The newspaper photograph included Marcel Cachin, editor of L'Humanité, and Jacques Duclos, former deputy of the Assemblée Nationale, a staunch Stalinist and dedicated leader of the French Communist Party.

"Heavy company," shouted Head of Words.

"Picasso always breached the obvious, and turned away from tedious outlines of familiarity, but this time he posed with his fedora in hand for the strange favors of the vicious totalitarianism of Joseph Stalin," said Nathan.

Daniel-Henry Kahnweiler and his wife, Lucie, moved back a few days after the liberation, and rented an apartment on Quai des Grands Augustins, not far from Rue des Grands Augustins where Picasso had a studio during most of the occupation. Kahnweiler visited his artist friend almost daily, and for some reason he did not return to the Galerie Louise Leiris. Most gallery owners escaped the enemy occupation, moved to London or the United States, and the Nazis thieves systematically plundered their valuable art collections.

Pablo Picasso was enchanted with Françoise Gilot, a young art student, and forgot to attend the grand opening of the new gallery and the exhibition of native art and Ghost Dance shirts last Sunday. Kahnweiler was moved by the exhibition, and was certain that Picasso would have been excited about the native images and natural motion of the Ghost Dance shirts.

Picasso was inspired by African carved masks at the Musée d'Ethnographie du Trocadéro, and simulated two masks in Les Demoiselles d'Avignon, The Young Ladies of Avignon, and at the time, almost forty years ago, he painted in a shabby studio at Le Bateau Lavoir in Montmartre. Later he attended an exhibition of Inuit masks at the Galerie Charles Ratton on Rue de Marignan, and viewed a collection of native carved ivory from the Pacific Northwest in the United States. Picasso would have seen the masks in the nineteen thirties, and surely he would have related the ghostly presence of the masks, carved from driftwood and decorated with paint, bones, and feathers. He might have been inspired by the evocative motion of the Ghost Dance shirts. Traces of natural motion and native spirits were always present in masks, shirts, face paint, and stories of totemic animals.

"Picasso would have become the exhibition, a celebrity with hat in hand walking through the Ghost Dance shirts," said Aloysius. "The spirit of the dance and motion of the shirts would have mocked his breezy tour."

"Maybe, yet some abstract guise of a Ghost Shirt would surely appear in a one of his painting," said Heap of Words. "Feathers, Venus, handprints, and the morning star on a prostitute."

Nathan had attended the *Exposition Surréaliste d'Objèts* at the Galerie Charles Ratton in May 1936, and viewed the magical display of surreal objects, found, captured, and created for the original exhibition that was organized by André Breton. The catalogue listed surreal and natural objects by Man Ray, the visual artist, Marcel Duchamp, the painter and sculptor, Alexander Calder, the abstract sculptor, Salvador Dalí, the surrealist painter, Pablo Picasso, and many other surrealist artists were represented at the exhibition.

Nathan realized the obvious at the exposition, that the surreal scenes and objects created by prominent artists were customary spiritual encounters, events, and episodes that arise in native visionary stories, shamanic ecstasy, dream songs, and ceremonial masks and shirts. Native visionary scenes were necessary in trickster stories of animals, birds, and the creation of the earth, but were not simulations, surreal, strange, weird, or unearthly. The stories of native creation and dream songs were in the clouds, not in a sculpted stump, erotic shoe, chocolate gloves, or an unusual fold of paper in the march of time.

Aloysius created fractured images of the totemic ruins of animals and birds in black and white with slight bruises of blue and rouge in his most recent paintings. The abstract portrayals of bones, claws, paws, wing feathers, and the distorted faces of beaver, bear, marten, wolf, river otter, fox, muskrat, crane, golden eagle, raven and more totemic animals and birds of the fur trade lakes and woodland were created for the gallery exhibition, *Totemic Custody and Casualty*, and opened with the solemn display of the Ghost Dance shirts last Sunday, 22 October 1944, on our forty ninth birthday.

Nathan bartered the last case of his cache of *Pielroja* Columbian cigarettes for wine, cheese, and baguette for the exhibition audience, and extended invitations to his old friends, gallery owners and painters, authors,
poets, and musicians who were loyal to the gallery long before the Nazi
Occupation of Paris.

The Gestapo and Milice Française tortured and executed thousands
of artists, writers, and museum scholars, teachers, laborers, students, and
gallery flâneurs during the four years of the occupation, and we honored
their spirit in our stories at the Galerie Ghost Dance.

Benjamin Crémieux was honored, and many other names were mentioned, of course, and it would have taken the entire afternoon just to call
out the names of courageous members of the résistance movements who
had been executed.

Sylvia Beach decided not to reopen Shakespeare and Company after
the liberation, and Heap of Words was worried about her health, so he
walked to Rue de l'Odeon and personally invited Sylvia and Adrienne
Monnier, the owner of the bookstore La Maison des Amis des Livres, to
visit the exhibition of new abstract totemic animals by Aloysius, and the
display of Ghost Dance shirts.

Michel Laroux carried his honored Lakota Horse Stick around the gallery and delivered a short history of sacred sticks to gallery visitors. Later
he told several stories about his experiences as a young man with Lakota
warriors on the Great Plains.

Henri and André, the *mutilés de guerre*, painted blue morning stars
of the Ghost Dance on the metal masks that covered their face wounds.
They saluted everyone who entered the gallery, and in silence directed
the visitors to the *Exposition de la Danse des Esprits*, and then pointed
at the display of the *Totemic Custody and Casualty* paintings by Aloysius.

Coyote Standing Bear created the solemn spirit of the exhibition with
the steady beat of a hand drum as Olivier Black Elk created a song that
proclaimed the sentiments of the return of the dead in the Ghost Dance
of Wovoka:

> *the father says we will see our grandfathers*
> *our families will return*

now we are floating with the spirits
the world turns blue
the cavalry vanished with our dance
dead relatives and honored friends
return with the morning star as natives and Jews

Coyote and Olivier recited from memory eighteen honored names out of several hundred natives who were massacred at Wounded Knee by soldiers of the Seventh Cavalry Regiment on 29 December 1890, and related to the same number of names of résistance members who were executed by the Milice Française and Gestapo. The coupled names of the dead were chanted with reverence as the gallery visitors entered the darkened exhibition of Ghost Dance shirts.

Benjamin Crémieux and Sitting Bull, Chief Big Foot and Jean Moulin, Horned Cloud and Boris Vildé, Pretty Enemy and Léon Maurice Nordmann, Shedding Bear and Victor Basch, Bear Woman and Olga Bancic, Crazy Bear and Missak Manouchian, Old Good Bear and Georges Mandel, Black Coyote and Anatole Lewitsky, Has a Dog and Pierre Walter, Pretty Woman and René Sénéchal, One Feather and Jacques Bonsergeant, White Wolf and Robert Pinède, Last Talking and Jules Andrieu, Wounded Hand and Marcel Rayman, Comes Out Rattling and Jean Baptiste Beaulieu, She Bear and Bertie Albrecht, Bird Wings and Élie Wallach, Yellow Robe and Maurice Sarraut.

The Nazis executed most of the résistance members at Fort Mont Valérien, Forteresse du Mont Valérien, in Suresnes, a commune near Paris. The Milice murdered Georges Mandel and Maurice Sarraut, and Bertie Albrecht hanged herself after several days of torture by the Gestapo. Robert Pinède and Jean Baptiste Beaulieu, and more than six hundred other unarmed citizens were massacred on 10 June 1944 by enemy soldiers at Oradour-sur-Glane. Sitting Bull, the Hunkpapa Lakota spiritual leader, was murdered on 15 December 1890 by a federal agency native policeman on the Standing Rock Reservation in South Dakota.

50

ROLLAND OF ETHOS

Wednesday, 3 January 1945

Romain Rolland, the pacifist, novelist, philosopher, playwright, and historian of music composers and opera died last Saturday, 30 December 1944, at his home in Vézelay, a commune in Parc Naturel Régional du Morvan. He was buried in Cimetière de Brèves near Vézelay.

The 1915 Nobel Prize winner in literature earned the respect of scholars around the world, mainly for his novel *Jean-Christophe*, a roman fleuve, or grand sequence of ten narratives grouped into three novels and translated by the British novelist Gilbert Cannon. Rolland was read more widely than André Gide or Paul Valéry, and some younger readers at the time celebrated his ethos, idealism, tolerance, and *littérature engagée* of the human spirit.

"Disorder is order," is the first evocative sentence of *Jean-Christophe*. "Untidy officials were offhanded in manner. Travelers protesting the rules and regulations, to which they submitted all the same. Christophe was in France."

"French scenes of irony," said Pierre.

"Poet of the untidy," shouted Heap of Words.

"Rolland was a moral artist," said Nathan.

The obituary was published with a photograph on the front page of *L'Humanité* four days after his death, and with three headlines: "Samedi est mort Romain Rolland," Romain Rolland Died Saturday, "Écrivain d'un rayonnement universel," Writer of Universal Influence, "Valeureux champion de la liberté," Brave Champion of Liberty.

"France has lost a great writer who has lived with danger, barbarism, fascism, and the menace of the world," declared the reporter in the first sentence of the obituary. Rolland wrote about peace, justice, and "duties of the spirit" at a time of unbelievable destruction in the First World War. He told an editor at *L'Humanité* more than twenty years ago that he would support the "proletariat whenever it respects truth and humanity," and was against the "proletariat whenever it violates truth and humanity."

Rolland engaged in literary résistance, and was more than a mere passive author. He denounced the collusion of the Vichy Regime as the "weary, dark, somber years of moral oppression and disease," said Nathan.

Thirty years ago Romain Rolland was awarded the Grand Prix de Littérature by the Académie Française, and his celebration of rights, justice, and liberty in literature has never surrendered to politics or fame. He boldly opposed state violence, and yet his crucial moral declarations were hardly noticed during the Nazi Occupation of Paris and the Second World War.

Rolland never compromised the ethos of pacifism with the sentiments of nationalism, or with the diversions and delusions of patriotic violence. The honor and celebration of his moral literature deserved more comments than the two column wide obituary in the bottom corner of *L'Humanité* yesterday. Obviously the obituary would have been given more space on the front page if he had not refused to become a member of the Communist Party.

"Communists are always more newsy in *L'Humanité* than a brilliant literary artist who refused to tow the heavy socialist realism of Joseph Stalin," said Nathan.

"Stalin rules the news," said Pierre.

"The Führer Stalin," shouted Heap of Words.

Gabriel Péri was pictured on the top left corner, and Lucien Sampaix on the top right corner on the front page of *L'Humanité* two weeks earlier on 14 December 1944. They were members of the résistance and Communist Party, and were executed three years ago on 15 December 1941. Enemy soldiers executed more than two hundred other résistance members that same year in Paris.

The photographs were two columns wide, and more than half of the entire front page of *L'Humanité* was devoted to stories about Gabriel Péri and Lucien Sampaix. Péri was an intellectual journalist who was active in the résistance, a former deputy in the Assemblée Nationale, and manager of foreign policy at *L'Humanité*.

Lucian Sampaix, the radical labor leader who became a communist journalist, was executed with thirteen others at the Beaulieu Prison, a former leprosarium, near Caen on 15 December 1941. He served as an editor at *L'Humanité,* and denounced the fascist leagues and Otto Abetz, the German ambassador to the Vichy Regime.

Yvonne Sampaix, his wife, and daughter Simone, continued to serve as communist partisans. Simone was arrested several months after the death of her father and deported with a convoy of more than two hundred women who were active in the résistance.

By Now met Charlotte Delbo, who was active in the résistance with Louis Aragon and other communists, and heard stories about Simone and the execution of her father, Lucien Sampaix. "Charlotte was betrayed and arrested for working on the résistance journal *Les Lettres Françaises,* and she was deported with other women to a concentration camp." *Les Lettres Françaises* was the first journal to report on the massacre at Oradour-sur-Glane.

Delbo, Simone Sampaix, Hélène Solomon, Maï Politzer, Danielle Casanova, and hundreds of other partisans were either executed or deported to a concentration camp based on the new decree by Adolf Hitler, *Nacht und Nebel,* Night and Fog.

Maurice Thorez, the former coal miner, union member, and principal leader of the Communist Party was the author of the article about Lucien Sampaix. The headline declared that Maurice Thorez would pay homage to Sampaix and Péri the next day at the Vélodrome d'Hiver.

"How could anyone dare to pretend ignorance about the atrocity at the Vel d'Hiv Roundup of more than thirteen thousand Jews," said Nathan. "The police provided the names and address of Jews, and then carried out the vicious Rafle du Véledrome d'Hiver that was diabolically referred to as the Opération Vent Printanier, or the Operation Spring Wind."

Maurice Thorez and his communist speech about two honorable party members might have been informative, and was surely favored by the Stalinists, but his words were contemptible in the actual place of police savagery toward the Jews of Paris. The misery and horrible memories of occupation cruelty never ended with the liberation, and the torment continued with the notice of a lecture and the moral expediency of the Communist Party.

"Thorez was a communist opportunist, and his savior was Joseph Stalin," said Nathan. "He was sentenced to death *in absentia* for desertion at the start of the war, but he had already escaped to the Soviet Union."

The number of favorable stories about the Communist Party, Red Army, and Joseph Stalin increased in *L'Humanité* since the Soviet Union and France signed and adopted the Treaty of Alliance and Mutual Assistance on 10 December 1944. The Treaty provided that the parties would not participate in "separate negotiations with Germany," and "to undertake mutually all necessary measures for the removal of any new threat on the part of Germany." The Soviet Union strategically signed similar treaties with other nations in Europe.

Romain Rolland was in his seventies and weakened with heart disease and other maladies during the war, and yet he carried out the moral literary résistance of heart and spirit as a champion of *littérature engagée*, the literature of engagement and liberty.

Rolland wrote letters to Élie Wallach, a member of the Mouvement Jeunes Communistes de France, the first communist résistance youth movement, mostly emigrants, that engaged in critical propaganda and strategic protests against the Nazi Occupation of Paris. Élie was a Jew from Poland and one of the early résistance communist activists not connected to the French Communist Party.

Rolland was inspired with the antifascist sentiments and spontaneity of the youth movement compared to the bombastic communist ideology and the deadly delusions of Stalinism. Clearly he recognized the perils of the youth résistance movement, yet the engagement with fascism and the enemy of liberty was moral and political, and celebrated the start of a new intellectual culture of youth résistance that portrayed the courage, sacrifice, and diversity of ancestry and religious origins.

Élie Wallach and many other communist members of the résistance staged a protest at the Strasbourg Saint-Denis Paris Métro on 13 August 1941. The French *Tricolore* was displayed at the entrance to the station, and the young partisans sang "La Marseillaise." Later they shouted, "Down with Hitler," and *Vive la France* until the police and soldiers arrived at the station. Samuel Tyszelman, an active communist and Jew from Poland, was arrested with others, including Henri Gautherot.

The French Communist Party was banned the next day, and the protesters were tried and convicted of sabotage and the crime of aiding the enemy. Nazi soldiers executed Tyszelman and Gautherot on 19 August 1941.

Élie Wallach, George Ghertman, and Charles Wolmarck started their opposition with broadsides and propaganda, and then turned to armed attacks against enemy soldiers. They had stolen explosives from a nearby quarry and were prepared to carry out deadly assaults. Élie was arrested, tortured, and executed on 29 June 1942. He was twenty years old and barely remembered in the chronicle of moral engagement with the enemy in the Second World War.

Romain Rolland was never swayed by political cues or delusions, the pretense of *liberté*, feigns of *egalité*, rescripts of *fraternité*, or the favors of fascism. His résistance was the ethos of literary engagement, and his stories inspire the spirit. He restated the obvious, that résistance movements were the unity of necessity in the face of a "common enemy," and the outcome was violence, not reason or peace. He was worried that the great thoughts of religion and intellectual history of the past century had been disregarded in the second rush to war in a generation.

Pessimism of the mind and perceptions, and optimism of the spirit, truth, and resolve were his principle concepts and critical ideas about the natural bravery of good people. Rolland was not a spectator, but engaged in the moral cause of literature, and he never trusted the politics of violence, or the mutual measures of collusion for supremacy. He rightly despised the doctrines of political power and celebrated courage and the natural motion of the spirit.

Rolland would have surely engaged the fascist federal agents on the Standing Rock Reservations in South Dakota, and united with Sitting Bull in the moral politics of natural motion, liberty of the spirit and the stories and music of the Ghost Dance Religion.

"Rolland is a Ghost Dancer," chanted Nathan.

"Says the father," shouted Heap of Words.

"Says the mother," shouted By Now.

"You shall grow to be a nation," said Pierre.

The mongrels surrounded my brother for several days on the deck of *La Péniche Léon Blum* as he carefully carved a new hand puppet, polished the head, and when the face emerged from the birch block the Vicar bounced, Panzéra the Basset Hound bayed, and High Road the Spaniel nosed the sweet scent of the wood, Black Jack the wooly Barbet barked three times, and Pig Ears leaned on the blue tiller and steadied the barge of totemic companions.

Rolland of Ethos, the new hand puppet, wore a black morning coat and high white collar, and his forehead and dome were touched with rouge. Aloysius created an almost perfect simulation of the novelist and philosopher, including a narrow nose, bushy moustache, and bright blue eyes. His hands were carved from fallen branches with the knots and checks of age, and he was ready for the literary engagement with the hand puppet Adolf Hitler. Aloysius sentenced the Führer hand puppet to four years of absolute isolation, only to avoid the betrayal of collaborators and the misconception of fascists who might liberate and destroy the puppet.

Adolf Hitler last appeared with the high and mighty hand puppet Gertrude Stein eleven years ago at the Place du Panthéon. My brother was determined to save the demon of death for one more public performance, and this time with Romain Rolland. Adolf of Shame was ready, after so many years in the dark, for the last route of his métier of violence at the miserable end of the Third Reich.

The Rolland of Ethos and Adolf of Shame hand puppet show was presented last Sunday, 31 December 1944, on a sunny and cold afternoon at the Place du Panthéon. We did not know at the time that Romain Rolland had died the day before his performance as a revered hand puppet.

Nathan had read the actual obituary of his death in L'Humanité. My brother surely would not have carried out the puppet show had he learned of his death, and no one in the audience was aware, or they chose not to burden the performance that afternoon with a solemn report of the death of Romain Rolland in Vézelay.

Aloysius searched for a second copy of Mein Kampf by Adolf Hitler published in any format or language, but he could not find a bookstore that carried the most despised manual of racial hatred and fascism. He searched for two days and at last found a tattered and stained copy for sale by a bouquiniste near the Pont Neuf. The bookseller was astounded that anyone wanted to buy Mein Kampf for any reason, and he was delighted to part with the copy four months after the liberation of Paris.

The first copy of Mein Kampf my brother had bought eleven years ago was slowly burned, page by fascist page in a mock bonfire of books at Place du Panthéon during the marvelous hand puppet show of Adolf Hitler and Gertrude Stein. Now with the end of the war in sight, my brother was determined to burn page by page one more copy of *Mein Kampf* at the same place, but with a hand puppet show of Adolf of Shame and Rolland of Ethos.

Pierre agreed to be the voice of Adolf of Shame, and my brother decided the voice of the pacifist and novelist must be bold and resolute, so he named Heap of Words as the voice of Rolland of Ethos. Nika, Pierre, and Nathan selected and translated the actual published quotations for the two hand puppets.

My duties at the puppet show were more pleasurable than imitating the whiny voice of Adolf of Shame. Aloysius told me to start a small fire with newspaper and twigs, and then slowly tear out pages of *Mein Kampf* and create a mock bonfire as the hand puppets debated and reproved each other about fascism, résistance, *liberté, égalité, fraternité*, and peace.

A crowd gathered at Place de Panthéon, mostly college students from nearby Sorbonne University, and the news spread widely that the great moral philosopher Romain Rolland and the notorious mass murderer Adolf Hitler were hand puppets in a public debate about justice, carried out over pages from *Mein Kampf* in a bonfire.

ADOLF: You tore apart my *Mein Kampf*.

ROLLAND: Deadly delusions of the Third Reich.

ADOLF: Reich envy torments the pacifists.

ROLLAND: Fascists envy moral literature.

ADOLF: To conquer a nation, first disarm its citizens.

ROLLAND: I find war detestable but those who praise it without participating in it even more so.

ADOLF: Those who want to live, let them fight, and those who do not want to fight in this world of eternal struggle do not deserve to live.

ROLLAND: You are a vain fellow, and you want to be a hero, that is why you do such silly things.

ADOLF: Success is the sole judge of right and wrong.

ROLLAND: A limited number of types, good and bad, serve for the ages.

ADOLF: It is not truth that matters, but victory.

ROLLAND: Discussion is impossible with someone who claims not to seek the truth, but already possesses it.

ADOLF: The great masses of the people will more easily fall victim to a big lie than to a small one.

ROLLAND: A great nation assailed by war has not only its frontiers to protect, it must also protect its good sense, it must protect itself from the hallucinations, injustices, and follies which the plague let loose.

ADOLF: It is always more difficult to fight against faith than against knowledge.

ROLLAND: For a year I have been rich in enemies, let me say this to them, they can hate me, but they cannot teach me to hate.

ADOLF: Humanitarianism is the expression of cowardice.

ROLLAND: To understand everything is to hate nothing.

ADOLF: I use emotion for the many and reserve reason for the few.

ROLLAND: There are some dead who are more alive than the living.

ADOLF: The victor will never be asked if he told the truth.

ROLLAND: Skepticism, riddling the faith of yesterday, prepared the way for the faith of tomorrow.

ADOLF: Mankind has grown stronger in eternal struggles, and it will only perish through eternal peace.

ROLLAND: Artists create sunshine when the sun fails.

ADOLF: The leader of genius must have the ability to make different opponents appear as if they belonged to one category.

ROLLAND: Each man must learn his own ideal and try to accomplish it, and that is a surer way of progress than to take the ideas of another.

ADOLF: The very first essential for success is a perpetually constant and regular employment of violence.

ROLLAND: Stones are hard everywhere.

ADOLF: As in everything, nature is the best instructor.

ROLLAND: You have never been a companion of liberty.

Rolland of Ethos earned the closing line of contention that afternoon, as the last pages of *Mein Kampf* were tossed into the bonfire. The two puppets slowly bowed in turn to the audience. Hitler of Shame clapped his clunky hands, raised one long arm to salute, and then backed away when he was cursed and shouted down by the audience. Rolland of Ethos was honored with cheers, and my brother raised the great hand puppet over his head, and they both bowed several times.

Nathan marched into the circle near the bonfire and surprised everyone as he read from a scroll, "Adolf Hitler, Führer of the Last Reich, you have been formally charged with every crime in the history of the world, what is your plea this cold afternoon at Place du Panthéon?"

"You make big lies," shouted Hitler of Shame.

"Rolland of Ethos, Jean Jaurès, Voltaire, Victor Hugo, Albert Camus, and many others opposed the death penalty, but today at this puppet trial they might have agreed to carry out a summary execution of the demon and mass murderer Adolf Hitler," shouted Nathan.

Hitler of Shame jerked his head from side to side, stared at the audience with defiance, and then shouted, "The one who owns the youth gains the future."

The Sorbonne University students shouted that the demon puppet was "guilty, guilty, guilty of massacres, and he deserves to be executed by guillotine."

"War is not a crime," shouted Hitler of Shame.

"The world court of eternal memory and moral liberty has sentenced you to death by guillotine, *condamné à mort par la guillotine*," shouted Nathan. "And may your heavy head and the last pages of your fascist book of feigned struggles crackle in the bonfire."

Nathan raised and then quickly lowered his arm to simulate the blade of a guillotine. Aloysius understood the gesture, and released the head of Hitler of Shame. The bloated cheeks bounced on the street, and several good citizens kicked the puppet head toward the bonfire. Hitler of Shame the headless monster wagged his arms in space as his head rolled into the fire, slowly browned, and then burst into flames.

Hitler of Shame raised his one long arm to salute, and a student in the audience rushed forward and tore the arm out of the cape and threw it into the fire. Aloysius waited for the arm to catch fire, and then he tossed the remains of the black cape with the red swastika on the bonfire.

"Führer done," shouted Heap of Words.

Rolland of Ethos is my last letter to the heirs of the fur trade. My first letter revealed the autumn scene of the liberty trees on that dewy morning thirteen years ago, and the moody piano music of Erik Satie on the River

Seine. A year later, in my fourth letter, the hand puppets Gertrude Stein and Adolf Hitler engaged in literary combat over a bonfire of *Mein Kampf* at the Place du Panthéon. Gertrude wore a cloche hat, and with huge wooden hands told Herr Hitler that *Mein Kampf* was a "wet dream" with too many prepositions and "shouts out for an editor."

Nathan Crémieux, Nika Montezuma, and Pierre Chaisson translated *Satie on the Seine: Letters to the Heirs of the Fur Trade* into French for publication by the Galerie Ghost Dance. Nathan confirmed the historical sources, institutions, Vélodrome d'Hiver, place names, Sanary-sur-Mer, Varian Fry, Oradour-sur-Glane, museum exhibitions, music, and quotations of Romain Rolland. Nika considered the translation of natural motion, native dream songs, poetry, art, and confirmed stories of Amedeo Modigliani, Francis Picabia, scenes of the hand puppets, and the quotations of Henri Bergson, James Joyce, Sigmund Freud. Pierre Chaisson secured the titles of books, plays, and other literary sources, including the quotations of Victor Hugo and Sitting Bull, Voltaire and Chief Joseph, Émile Zola and Carlos Montezuma, and Charles de Gaulle and Maréchal Pétain.

The covers of the six volume chronicle or *roman fleuve* of *Satie sur la Seine: Des Lettres aux Légataires de la Commerce de la Fourrure* are various hazy black and white photographs of *Le Corbeau Bleu, Liberté Indienne,* and *La Péniche Léon Blum* moored near the Pont de la Concorde on the River Seine.